The Listeners

There were no chairs available. Ned sat on the floor across from the bunk bed bolted into the wall, a toilet and sink on his right. Frances leaned upright against the far wall. In combination with the sober red light, her straightjacket and bald head made her look like a mummy dug from a burning tomb. Her mouth was twisted in a voracious maw, her nostrils peeled back like mucus dripping snouts. Her long pointed tongue raked the air in search of invisible flies. The hiss of her breath was the death rattle of a cobra pit.

"Frances," he began. "My name is Ned Calendar. I'm an FBI agent in charge of finding out the truth about what happened to you and your sister in Africa."

The thing suddenly sucked in a deep hissing breath. Ned heard a mighty ripping sound, but it took him a second to understand what was happening. By the time he did, it was too late.

Jesus help me!

00858

About the Author

Christopher Pike was born in New York but grew up in Los Angeles, where he lives to this day. Before becoming a writer, he worked in a factory, painted houses and programmed computers. His hobbies included astronomy, meditating, running and making sure his books are prominently displayed in his local bookshop. He is the author of many internationally bestselling novels of horror.

The Listeners

Christopher Pike

NEW ENGLISH LIBRARY
Hodder and Stoughton

Copyright © 1994 by Christopher Pike

First published in Great Britain in 1994
by Hodder and Stoughton
A division of Hodder Headline PLC

A New English Library paperback

The right of Christopher Pike to be identified as the author
of this work has been asserted by him in accordance with the
Copyright, Designs and Patents Act 1988.

10 9 8 7 6 5 4 3 2 1

A CIP catalogue record for this title is available from the
British Library

ISBN 0 340 62571 6

Typeset by Hewer Text Composition Services, Edinburgh
Printed and bound in Great Britain by
Cox & Wyman Ltd, Reading, Berks.

Hodder and Stoughton Ltd,
A division of Hodder Headline PLC
338 Euston Road
London NW1 3BH

THE LISTENERS

CHAPTER ONE

David Conner had shot three people in his life, blown up three, and burned another guy to death. Within the walls of the FBI field office in Los Angeles he had the nickname 'Dirty Dave,' and maybe the appellation would have been harsher if the seven people had not been guilty as sin and deserved to die. Most FBI agents were fans of Clint Eastwood, and the nickname had stuck and was considered a compliment among David's partners. But it was not a title he appreciated because he had always considered himself as one of the good guys.

Now he had to wonder. Now that he was quitting.

David Conner was thirty-nine years old, a fifteen year veteran of the Federal Bureau of Investigation. His experience as an agent was varied. He had sent organized crime figures to prison, caught bank robbers, and rescued victims of kidnapping. He was the stuff of legend, as the old cliché went, and he was handsome, too, and because his office was located in the same time zone as Hollywood, that almost made him a star as well. Professionally, however, he considered himself a failure, and not because long ago he had blown the big one and not saved the day, but because, in his own opinion, he was a cynic. Nevertheless, there were two failed cases in his past, one a month old, one seven years gone, that made him feel old. But he blamed the outcome of those cases more on God than on his own incompetence. God must not have been a fan of Dirty Harry, David thought, or else he would have known that in the end the good guy was supposed to win. That

1

was one of the reasons that David was quitting the FBI. He didn't believe in God any more, or, for that matter, truth, justice and the American way. He just wanted to get out.

He had read in the paper, though, the other day, that one of the major studios had purchased the rights to the Angela Moore case. He wondered who would play himself. Clint Eastwood was too old. He had a hard time imagining why Angela's parents, after all they had gone through, had agreed to the film project.

The Los Angeles office was one of the fifty-six field offices directed by the FBI's ten headquarter divisions. The divisions set policy and became involved in cases at important junctures. For example, the laboratory division might help a field office by doing an autopsy of a murder victim. The field office did the actual job of investigating crimes. With 570 agents, Los Angeles was the third largest field office in the country after New York and Washington DC. David had spent his first ten years in the FBI in the LA office, and his last month also there, trying to rescue Angela. Each field office was headed by a special agent in charge (SAC), except the New York office, which was headed by an assistant FBI director, and which, David thought, was a crazy place to work anyway. Ned Calendar was the LA SAC, and by coincidence, he was also about to retire, but for far different reasons than David. Ned had been in charge of Los Angeles for the last twenty-two years, and was unofficially seventy years old, although he was still on the job. He was a master of organization and inspiration and his official ID miraculously had him listed at a mere sixty-five. Ned still believed in truth, justice and the American way, but despite that, Ned and David were good friends.

It was Ned who had called for David to come down to headquarters. He said he had an important case that only David could handle. David couldn't imagine how important it could be when they were both due to be unemployed in two weeks. Ned's office was on the seventeenth floor, a corner suite that overlooked Westwood Village. Ned's secretary waved David in as he came out of the elevator. David found Ned at the window staring at the nearby UCLA campus.

'I remember when I was in school,' Ned said without turning. 'I used to pray for summer vacation. Now I dread retirement. Why is that, David? Retirement is supposed to be like one long vacation.'

'It's because now you're too old to get laid,' David said.

Ned turned with a frown on his face. He was a tall man, gangly, with thinning sandy hair that chased a cluster of faint liver spots up the northern hemisphere of his skull. He had intense blue eyes; they changed shade with the burdens of his position, which, make no mistake, were great. He was fit; he had run 10 Ks up until six months ago, when he had broken a bone in his foot kicking a mob informant who had James Bond fantasies of being a double agent. The injury still caused him to walk with a slight limp. Ned was a pleasant enough gentleman in social situations, but at work he liked to be in complete control – not a problem since he had, for the last two decades, run the LA office with a rare mixture of tyranny and compassion. Many agents, when they first started to work for Ned, made the mistake of thinking him laid back, what with his California tan, his years, his casual dress. But he had been known to transfer agents who screwed up to difficult to pronounce places that even the CIA did not count as under their jurisdiction. David had known Ned from the day he had walked into the LA office, fifteen years ago. They had solved many tough cases together, working hours that would have killed most men. For those reasons, and a few others, David was the only person in the LA office who could speak his mind to Ned and get away with it.

'Am I too old?' Ned asked. 'Who told you that?'

'Your wife.'

Ned waved the remark away. 'She would be the last person to know.' He nodded to the chair in front of his mahogany desk. Ned's office was relatively austere, compared to the days before personal computer terminals. In the good old days he used to have files stacked everywhere. Now there was only an abstract art work on one wall, pictures of family on the other, and a couple of files on his desk. David's own office was equally sparse, and had only two pictures: one of Angela Moore, the other of Sandy Quin, another casualty of FBI involvement. David took the offered chair as Ned sat down across from him.

'You'll have fun,' David said. 'You can take up fishing.'

'I don't like fish.'

'You can always throw them back.'

'Like the justice system does with all our hard work?'

'I suppose.' David put his hands to his head and rubbed his temples. 'Why did you want me in so early? You know I don't get up before ten these days.'

'Hangover?'

David dropped his hands and shrugged. 'My head hurts, what can I say? Maybe it was the alcohol. Maybe it was the loud music at the club.'

'Which club was that?'

'I can't remember.'

Ned nodded. 'What are you going to do in a couple of weeks when you have nowhere to go?'

'I only drink when it gets dark. I don't have a problem, and even if I did, I don't want to talk about it. Why am I here?'

'I have a case for you.'

'I don't want it.'

Ned lifted a folder on his desk. 'This is an unusual case. It's perfect for you. I think you can complete your investigation and file a report before we both walk. I might even help you out in the field with it.'

'Is Sanders climbing into your chair already?' Chip Sanders was in line to be LA's next SAC. Headquarters had recently brought him in from New York. A splendid choice, David thought. Sanders took taxis into work; he had still to buy a car.

'He sits in my chair after I leave in the evenings,' Ned said, opening the file in his hands. 'But my secretary likes him. That's all that matters. I want to do some field work before I take up fishing.' He paused. 'You have to take this case. We're paying your salary for the next two weeks and you're going to earn it. But you'll like it. I guarantee you, no can get hurt. Are you listening?'

David had returned to massaging his head. He did indeed have a nasty hangover, although, Ned's suspicions aside, he had yet to make a habit of them. It was as if his blood were being fed through a two horse power motor before it was rammed into his swollen brain. He'd chewed four dry Tylenol on the drive in and was wondering if they needed a gulp of whiskey to start working. What club had he been at? He remembered a middle-aged woman, vaguely, with blonde hair that curled with the gentle grandeur of straw and lipstick the colour of strawberry chewing gum who had bought him a couple of drinks and who had asked, after catching sight of the gun in his coat, if he was an assassin for hire. Sounded like she disliked her husband. He had declined her offer to accompany her back home.

'Yes,' David said. 'I'm listening. A fish guaranteed you no one would get hurt.'

Ned frowned. 'One day you're going to have to drop it. It wasn't your fault.'

'I never said it was my fault. It was your fault.'

'It was nobody's fault. We did everything we could for Angela. It's a hard world. People die. Sometimes they're young and pretty.' He paused. 'You know, you look like shit.'

'Thank you.'

Ned shook his head. 'What am I going to do with you?'

'Let me go home and go to bed.'

'No. You're going to study all day and this evening you're going to take a plane to Boise, Idaho.'

David sat up and winced at the sunlight pouring through the window behind Ned. 'Who's in Boise? Don Corleone?'

'Professor Stephen Spear and his channelling group.'

'Come again?'

'Do you know what channelling is?'

'Yes. It's a New Age term. Channellers go into a trance and a spirit speaks through them. Clearly an activity the Federal Bureau of Investigation should be deeply concerned about.'

'Shut up and listen. Professor Spear is a fascinating character, as is his group. I've been going over the information we have on them for the last two days. There's something here besides crystal healing and tarot cards. Sharp's group channels an entity called the "Big Mind". A number of transcripts from their sessions have been collected into book form and published under the same name. It isn't a book you can find at Waldens, but it's available at New Age bookstores like Hollywood's Boddhi Tree. The majority of information in the book resembles similar New Age texts. There's talk of a new era of peace dawning for mankind, global disasters, reincarnation, higher states of consciousness. But there's a section of the book where the Big Mind talks about what's going on inside the government. It says how we've already developed the process of cold fusion. How we have supersonic jets capable of attaining shallow earth orbit. How we have the technology to transform the waste from nuclear reactors into harmless isotopes.'

'So?' David said.

Ned set down his folder and stared at David. 'So my most brilliant field agent, the Big Mind, is right. Every time it mentions something specific that we are able to check out, it does check out.'

'We already have cold fusion?'

'Yes. It's still in the experimental stages, but it has been secretly developed.'

David shook his head. 'I must read that book. Do we have colonies on the moon too?'

'Don't be ridiculous.'

'*I'm* being ridiculous? Surely you don't want me to fly to Idaho to investigate a channelling group?'

'That's exactly what I want you to do.'

David chuckled. 'Is this what happens to burnt out agents before they're put out to pasture?'

'I know it sounds like a waste of your time. But that's only because you don't know all the facts. When you do, I think you'll be anxious to meet Professor Spear.'

'Is he anxious to meet me?' David asked.

'No. You'll be going in undercover as a magazine reporter.'

David laughed. 'A magazine reporter is undercover? Don't these intuitive giants know that *normal* people read magazines?'

'The channelling group is not opposed to outside interest, obviously, or they would not have published their book. But to be approached by a curious reporter with credentials is a lot different than being questioned by a government agent. You must first gain their trust to learn anything of value. That's why I've chosen you, David. You're handsome and, when it suits you, you can be charming. Besides, you could use some fresh air.'

'I don't want to go. I can't go.'

'Why not?'

'The Big Mind will be able to pierce through my aura and see that I'm a fake.'

Ned stood. 'On the contrary. The Big Mind has already approved of your visit. Come, one of our agents in Boise stole a video of one their group sessions. I want you to see it. I think you'll find it interesting.'

David sat in a dark conference room with Ned, waiting for the video on the wall monitor to start. Often in the past Ned had referred to David's good looks as one of the reasons he was the man for the job. Since a primary function of an FBI agent was to elicit information from people who didn't want to give it, half of whom were female, the point was valid. However, David believed Ned saw him as a Casanova largely because most of the agents in the office looked like lawyers and accountants, which a high percentage of them had been before joining the bureau. Certainly David was not being chased by the producers of the *Angela Moore Story*.

David was six foot tall. He had been a champion swimmer in college and had come within two tenths of a second of qualifying for the hundred metre butterfly for the Olympic swimming team. He still had a swimmer's tapered body, but these days got his exercise practising martial arts. He was fit, quick, strong – he could kill with his hands if he needed to, but he carried a 10-millimetre semiautomatic pistol for such messy work. His father had been Irish, his mother Italian. As a result his cheeks reddened when he drank, and his hands grew animated. His hair and eyes were dark. He had inherited his mother's wide, sensual mouth, her olive skin. His stamina occasionally surprised even him. Ned had once invited him for a workout on the track. Without regular running, he had worn his boss to the ground over twenty laps.

Yet the same could not be said for the endurance of his liver. Even with the Scotch whiskey and red wine in his genes, if he spent the night at the bar, he woke up beside the toilet. He was not an alcoholic yet, but he knew he would be soon if he didn't get his act together. The trouble was, he had no inspiration to do so. The autopsy had been performed on Sandy Quin, and Angela Moore would not be invited to her prom. Then there was Rudy Failla, a close cousin of the mythical Don Corleone, and every bit as dead, a 10-millimetre slug in his burned forehead, buried in a sandy grave outside Las Vegas, where the real losers played the slots. Dirty Dave.

'How did our man manage to steal this tape?' David asked Ned, who sat to his right.

'He picked the lock on Spear's office cabinet. Why?'

'Just wondering. Why doesn't this lock picker pose as the magazine reporter? Why send in an agent from out of state?'

'The Boise office is not interested in the case.'

'Does that tell us something about the case?'

'Sh . . . Watch the tape. It starts here.'

A school classroom appeared on the screen, complete with green chalkboard and uncomfortable chairs. Five people, three males and two females, sat gathered in a small circle, facing each other, their eyes closed. At the edge of the circle, standing against the wall, hovered a middle-aged gentleman with a bushy grey moustache and a wild Einstein haircut. He had not shaved that morning; his face was cold, his eyes dark.

'That's Professor Spear,' Ned said.

'What's he a professor of?'

'He holds twin doctorates, one in anthropology, the other in psychology. Both were awarded by Stanford University.'

'What are they doing?' David asked. The camera was angled from the corner of the room, stationary. The image quality was fair to poor. The group appeared to be taking long slow deep breaths, nothing else.

'Regressing,' Ned said.

'Is that healthy?'

'Watch. Listen.'

'So we come to a point of simplicity,' one of the men said. He appeared to be from India, in his early thirties, his face thin and aesthetic. His voice was soothing. 'We breathe in and we breathe out. We do so with awareness and as a result our awareness comes into the present moment. It is only in the present that we know the past. The past is an illusion, of course, it no longer exists. But if we desire we can step through this illusion and enjoy the sights. We breathe in and we breathe out. We close our eyes and see what is behind us.'

'Are they hyperventilating?' David asked.

'No,' Ned muttered.

'We close our eyes and see what is,' another man said. He was approximately forty-five, big and burly – looked like a truck driver. He wore a red and white Pendleton and could have just downed a few beers with Paul Bunyon. His voice was as calm as his partner's. 'Between every inhalation and exhalation is a point of simplicity, a moment when creation's pendulum halts. A moment when the fluctuations of the mind cease. We breathe in and we breathe out. We are happy.'

'Are they . . .' David began.

'Don't say it,' Ned interrupted.

'We are joy itself,' the third man said. He was obviously a body builder, tanned and handsome in an innocent, perhaps foolish fashion. He had a faint Swedish accent. The camera moved to focus on him. There was a seventh person in the room, David noted. 'We breathe in and we breathe out. The inward breath raises us up. The outward breath calms. The present moment is huge. But we choose the illusion. We choose the past.'

David shifted in his seat.

'Yes?' Ned said, getting annoyed.

'Nothing. My ass was going to sleep,' David said.

'We choose to go back,' one of the two women said. She was young, perhaps twenty-five, with long curly red hair, freckles, the face of a modern angel. David sat up and leaned forward. She held the hand of the woman who sat close beside her and who must have been her identical twin. The other woman's face quivered as her sister spoke; a tense line appeared in her forehead. Yet she remained silent as her sister continued, 'We move without changing position. We see without vision. There is no personality. There is no emotion. There is no distortion. We breathe in and we breathe out. The ego is tied to the breath. We let the breath go. The process of inhalation and exhalation begins to slow. The breath begins to stop. The ego begins to dissolve. The Big Mind dawns.'

The group fell silent. Their eyes remained shut. A minute went by. Professor Spear stirred from his place against the wall. He held a yellow notepad in his right hand and studied it as if to refresh his memory. He took a step towards the group.

'Follow the Nordic chain,' he instructed. 'What do you see? What do you feel?'

Another silent minute went by.

'The wind,' the fellow from India said finally. 'The salty air. We are on a boat, on a mission. Our women have been taken, our children killed. We must have revenge. We are strong. We are not afraid. The gods hear our prayers.'

'Where do you live?' the Professor asked. 'What is your destination?'

'We live in our green land,' the beautiful girl replied. 'We go to the enemy's land of stone. They steal our women. We will cut their throats and hack off their heads. Our swords are sharp, our hearts hot.'

'What kind of swords do you carry?' the Professor asked. 'Describe them. Are they iron? Are they made of steel? How are they shaped?'

11

'They are black like the iron of the earth,' the truck driver said. 'They are thick and curved like the crescent moon.'

'Describe your vessel,' the Professor said. 'The shape of the sails, their colour.'

'Our ship is wooden,' the Indian fellow said. 'It rocks in the cold waves. Our sails are the colour of blood. A black hammer waves atop our mast.'

Professor Spear was interested. 'What's the name of your main god?'

'Thor,' they all said in unison.

The tape suddenly stopped. Ned stood and turned on the lights.

'Is that it?' David asked, disappointed.

'You're not impressed?'

'Well,' David said diplomatically. 'Are you?'

Ned leaned against the nearby conference table. He had the folder he had studied in his office with him. He picked it up and opened it in response to David's question.

'I find the tape interesting,' Ned said. 'The coherence of the group. That last line, when they spoke the word Thor simultaneously, caught me by surprise. It lends credence to one of Professor Spear's central theories.'

'Which is what?' David asked.

'Before I answer that question let me give you some background on the man.' Ned consulted his notes. 'Up until twelve years ago, Professor Stephen Spear was a moderately known anthropologist. His primary field of study was the culture of the ancient Australian Aborigines, which until the Europeans arrived hadn't changed much in the last thirty thousand years. He wrote well received papers on the subject, and even published a small volume on Dreamtime, the Aborigines' mystical tradition. He lived in Australia with his wife for five years. They had no children. After a brief return to the United States, he

12

developed an interest in the Dogon people of Mali Africa. Have you heard of them?'

'No. But Mali – that's between Algeria and the Ivory Coast?'

'Correct. Sub-Sahara land – the former French Sudan. The Dogon are an ancient tribe that has preserved predynastic Egyptian religious mysteries more accurately than the Egyptians themselves. The Dogon are descended culturally as well as physically from the Egyptians. They go way back, before 3200 BC.' Ned paused. 'I have to tell you what drew Spear's attention to the Dogon. Listen with an open mind.'

'Of course,' David said.

Ned consulted his notes again. 'Between the years 1946 and 1950 two French anthropologists, Marcel Griaule and Germaine Dieterlen, managed to gain the trust of two priests, one priestess, and a patriarch of the Dogon people. That was not an easy task. First, they had to learn the languages Sanga and Wazouba. Also, for thousand of years the Dogon have guarded the inner secrets of their religious tradition with great fervour. Even among the tribe, only high initiates were given the type of information Griaule and Dieterlen obtained. The two French anthropologists eventually published the information in a paper entitled "A Sudanese Sirus System". I have a translation of this article and want you to study it. Professor Spear read it and it was this article that led him to bring his wife and a number of associates to Mali.' Ned paused again. 'Are you familiar with the star Sirius?'

David shrugged. 'I know it's the brightest star in the sky.'

'Then you can understand why it would be of particular importance to an ancient culture. Particularly one as inquisitive as the Egyptians.'

'I thought we were talking about the Dogon here?'

'We are talking about what the Dogon know of the

ancient Egyptians'. Facts that are not found by studying the pyramids. The main deity of the ancient Egyptians was the Goddess Isis, who is usually associated with the star Sirus. I won't go into all the details of how frequently the Egyptians' traditions are connected to the star. Suffice to say it was important to them, and to the Dogon.'

'Just because it was bright?' David asked.

'No. There's more to it than that. Let me cut to the chase. The Dogon people have a tradition that states that their culture, and that of the Egyptians, was formed by a race of heavenly beings that came from the Sirian star system thousands of years ago. Of course any anthropologist could show you dozens of isolated tribes throughout the world that believe almost the same thing. The difference is that the Dogon people know things about the Sirus star system that modern astronomers are only beginning to find out. The most significant of these facts is that Sirus has a white dwarf for a companion. Do you know what that is?'

'Yes. A star that has collapsed back in upon itself. They're usually planet size, rather than as big as an ordinary star.'

'You're right. The white dwarf, Sirus B, was not discovered until the advent of large telescopes. That's because it's extremely faint, only magnitude eight, invisible to the naked eye under the best of circumstances, even if it wasn't completely obliterated by the light of nearby Sirus. It circles Sirus every fifty years. Now you must be thinking, so what?'

'I am,' David agreed. 'I am also thinking that I don't believe in little green men.'

Ned straightened himself. 'The Dogon people have known for thousands of years that Sirus had an invisible companion circling it. They knew its period of rotation around the central sun. They also knew that it was, and I quote, "The smallest and the heaviest of all stars".

14

Wipe that smile off your face, David. They knew about condensed states of matter even before modern physicists dreamed of them.'

David was smiling. 'I just can't believe all this is worth a trip to Idaho. And that this discussion is taking place inside an office of the FBI.'

'There is more. But before I go on let me impress upon you that the Dogons' knowledge of Sirus is irrefutable according to anthropologists who have studied them. For they also have drawings of exactly how Sirus B orbits Sirus, which is in an ellipse.'

'All planets revolve in an ellipse. The Earth traces an ellipse around the Sun.'

'Yes. Kepler explained that over three centuries ago. But the Dogon people had no access to Kepler and his laws of planetary motion. How do you explain that?'

'I don't have to. I'm retiring in two weeks.'

'You are playing the smart ass. I expected that. But I have piqued your interest. I know you, David, you love a mystery. That's another reason I'm choosing you for this case. Let me go on, because the tale leads in an unexpected direction. Professor Spear read these things about the Dogon and quickly decided he had to study them first-hand. Like I said, he brought his wife and several associates with him to Mali. His sister-in-law came as well. They stayed six months. From all accounts, they managed to probe even deeper into the Dogon's inner circle than had the two French anthropologists. Spear learned to speak Sanga and Wazouba fluently, no small feat. Then there was a tragedy. Spear's wife died and the sister-in-law went insane. The group returned to the States.'

'How did the wife die?' David asked.

'A wild animal killed her.'

'What kind of wild animal?'

'We don't know,' Ned said. 'We are talking about a

small group that was studying an isolated tribe. The details are sketchy. What information we do have on the death of Mrs Spear comes from the LAPD, who interviewed the group when they reentered the country'.

'Why did the LAPD investigate a crime that took place in Africa?'

'Penny was initially from Los Angeles. I believe Spear re-entered the US through Los Angeles, without Penny. You can't just lose your wife in a foreign country without somebody asking questions. But it was a cursory investigation. No criminal charges were brought against anyone.'

'Has the sister-in-law recovered from her insanity?'

'No. At present she is locked away in a sanatorium in South Carolina.'

'Did the death of her sister bring about the insanity?'

'We don't know. But the two events did coincide. All we know for sure is that Spear was devastated when he returned to America, and spent the next year in solitude, before embarking on his current field of interest.' Ned paused. 'Have you heard of past life regressions?'

'Yes. It's another New Age term. Under hypnosis people regress their memory past their birth and into the memories of other lives.' David added, 'I give the process as much validity as I do the theory of little green men.'

Ned nodded. 'You might be surprised to hear that Professor Spear doesn't believe in past lives either. The man appears to be an atheist. However, he's investigating a concept that runs parallel to reincarnation. He believes – and I might add that he is not alone in the belief – that each of us carries within us the memories of our ancestors. That when we were conceived in the womb, our genes were embedded with the pasts of our mother and father, and in turn their mothers and fathers, and so on, back through time. The video tape you just saw was an example of how his group tries to probe the memories of a particular genetic line. You might have noticed Spear gave the instruction, "Follow the Nordic chain."

'When you say others support his theory, do you mean other scientists?'

'A few, not many. But Spear has published his research into genetic memories in a number of prestigious journals. The topic, at least, is being debated in scientific circles.'

'But these things his group knows about that are going on inside the government – that seems to me a separate topic?' David said.

'Yes and no. It's the same group that you saw that probes genetic memories and that also speaks for the Big Mind about current events. Supposedly, what we saw was the Big Mind talking, not individual people.'

'I'm confused,' David said. 'What does Spear's experience with the Dogons have to do with his research into genetic memories? For that matter, what about the aliens?'

'I didn't say anything about aliens.'

'Yes, you did. I heard you. I wish I was wearing a wire.'

Ned gave an exaggerated sigh. 'I simply pointed out that the Dogon people possess extraordinary knowledge of our local universe. As for your other question – we're not sure. That's one of the things we want you to find out. Why he shifted from anthropology to parapsychological research. But we do know that Spear uses some type of group hypnosis to bring his five subjects to a deep state. The Dogon may have taught him the technique.'

'Who were in turn taught by the aliens from Sirus?'

Ned shook his head wearily. 'That must be it.'

'What's the deal with the identical twins?'

'You noticed them?'

'They're hard not to notice.'

Ned nodded. 'Beautiful women. Their names are Lucy and Vera Temple. Lucy was the one who spoke. She's older by two minutes. They're both twenty-eight, graduate students of Professor Spear's.'

'What university is he affiliated with?' David asked.

'Stanford.'

'What subject are the girls getting their degrees in?'

'Psychology. Remember, Spear holds a doctorate in that field as well.'

'Does Stanford approve of his research?'

'They have an open mind,' Ned said.

'What's he doing up in Idaho?'

'He has taken his group there on a retreat. They're at some kind of camp for the next few days. He grew up in Idaho and apparently feels the isolation is conducive to his research.'

'If he wants isolation, why will he want me there?'

'He wants acceptance as well as isolation. You're a writer. You can make him famous.'

'David considered. Then he burst out laughing. 'This is the craziest thing I've ever heard of. I keep waiting for the punch line. Tell me the truth, why are you sending me to spy on a group of trance channellers?'

Ned smiled with him. 'If the Big Mind knows all the things it appears to know, maybe it can tell us what next month's lottery numbers are going to be. Seriously, David, have you anything better to do for the next few days? Go up there and see what they're all about. If nothing else you might hit it off with either Lucy or Vera.'

'I have your official permission? Becoming entangled with an informant is grounds for dismissal.'

Ned shrugged. 'They are hardly informants. Who are they informing on? The Big Mind? Besides, like you said, I don't get laid anymore. You have my permission as long as you tell me all about it. While you're there, I'll pay a visit to Professor Spear's old partner – Professor Buckley.

He's down in Florida. Talk is he hasn't spoken to Spear since they were both in Mali. They had some kind of falling out.'

'You're really going back out in the field? Sanders must be driving you nuts.'

Ned snorted. 'He's biting on my nuts. I wish the Dogon were cannibals. I'd convince Sanders that Jimmy Hoffa was still alive and underground in Mali and that he had to personally check out the situation.'

David chuckled. 'What a way for two agents to end their glorious careers. Spying on psychics who worship Thor and Isis. Hey, do you have photographs of everyone in Spear's group?'

'Yes.' Ned opened his folder again. 'I know you just want Lucy's and Vera's.'

'No. Let me see them all.' David accepted Ned's stack of four by five black and whites. He did not bother asking where Ned had obtained them, nor the sources of his information on Professor Spear. There were few activities in the United States that Ned Calendar could not find out about if he wished.

David studied the pictures. The young women were every bit as attractive without colour. Lucy's smile could have burned through the negative, David thought. She looked too wholesome to be sailing the cold sea in vengeance. Vera, on the other hand, appeared serious, as she had on the tape, even with her eyes open. He had trouble telling the two of them apart; their hair and dress were similar.

At the bottom of the stack were another two women who also looked similar.

'Spear's wife and his sister-in-law,' Ned said as David separated the pictures out. 'Those are copies of their passport photos, before they went to Africa.'

A wave of disquiet settled over David. 'What were their names?'

'Spear's wife was named Penny. The sister-in-law is called Frances Cumberly. Remember, she's still alive.'

'That's no life, being locked in a mental institution.' David did not understand the source of his uneasiness, except that it had hit him the moment he saw the women. Surely, he thought, it couldn't be because of the cruel fates they had each suffered. His career had been an extended exercise in the madness of mankind. He had seen the photographs of hundreds of victims over the last fifteen years, many of whom had been ripped and torn by bullets and knives, and by bare hands. Yet there was something about these two women that he was missing. Yes, strange as it felt to him, it was a warning of some kind. Ned noticed his concern.

'What is it?' he asked.

'See if you can visit the sister-in-law while you're checking out Spear's ex-partner,' David said softly. 'I want to know what drove her mad.'

CHAPTER TWO

Why did he become an FBI agent? He thought it would be fun. He believed, when he graduated from the University of Iowa with a degree in chemistry and no desire to go on to medical school – as he had initially planned – that he would enjoy rescuing stolen children and putting serial murderers in prison. He had watched Efrem Zimbalist Jr in the reruns of *The FBI*. He thought he knew what he was getting into.

He studied the requirements. A candidate had to be between the ages of twenty-three and thirty-seven, hold a degree from a four year college, and pass a background check and receive a top-secret clearance. There were tests, too, IQ and moral fibre exams, plus two lengthy interviews. The FBI accepted fewer than one out of twenty applicants, but he must have answered their question well because they took him. Then he was off to the famed Quantico, the FBI Academy, which was located forty miles south of Washington. The training was sixteen intensive weeks.

There was a 'town' located in Quantico named Hogan's Alley. It had the highest crime rate in the United States. They had kidnappings and murders every day. It was where the trainees practised the skills they learned in the classroom. One day a guy tried to rob their bank and David and his four partners swooped in to save the day. Only this robbery was towards the end of their four month training and it had a twist in it. While they surrounded the bank and shouted for the guy to give himself up, the trash man down the street started his truck and began to drive off.

Much to the surprise of his partners, and to himself, David chased after him. That was his first experience of a 'gut feeling' that the best law enforcement officers often spoke of. He just *knew* the garbage truck was the getaway car. He arrested the driver over the protestations of his group, but it turned out the trash man had a fully automatic Uzi under his front seat. David received a special commendation for his quick thinking. Yet in reality he had acted without thinking. It was a lesson he was to remember. Logic could only serve him so far.

He was assigned to the Los Angeles office. Ned Calendar was his SAC even back then. Besides being the bank robbery capital of the world, Los Angeles had problems such as 'star harassment' and ferocious gang violence that were unique to the city. But the banks were the big thing and David was happy to be assigned to a squad specializing in robberies. The action was fast and there was a lot of it. Compared to working on white collar cases or organized crime, there was little paperwork. No two days were ever alike. The year he arrived over two thousand banks were hit in LA. But the FBI solved over eighty per cent of the cases, demonstrating that it was the most foolish crime one could commit. The literary quality of many of the hold-up notes further demonstrated the level of intelligence of the average thief. David collected them on a board beside his desk. *'Give me your money or I will shoot it.'* *'Don't worry I not kill you. I just want kill money.'* *'This is a stickup. Put your hands in the air and keep them there. Put your money in my bag.'* *'Don't be afraid. I have a gun.'* *'Excuse me. This is a hold up. Sorry to wreck your great hair day.'*

He loved the funny money as well. To make it easier to catch robbers, bank tellers carried marked bills that contained dye packs that exploded. Often, the packs exploded while the bad guys were trying to escape in their car. More than a few times he spotted the getaway car as it drove away by all the red dye pouring out of it. Once a guy robbed a bank and stopped in the 7-Eleven around the block for a pack of beer. David apprehended him in the convenience store parking lot when he just happened to stop there for a Coke, after going over the scene of the crime. The guy was red from head to toe, sitting calmly in his car getting drunk, twenty thousand in messed up bills on the seat beside him.

Then there was the day of big life event number one. It was a Friday afternoon, three years into his stint as FBI agent. David had the day off and had stopped in his own bank to cash his cheque. He was flirting with the teller when a young man in a business suit to his right let out a cry. Sure enough, a guy who looked and smelled like he had spent the last forty years in a grocery dumpster had a gun to the young man's head. The bank had a bandit barrier installed, a bulletproof sheet of Plexiglas that separated the customers from the tellers. Bandit barrier banks were seldom robbed; they were that much harder to crack. When David looked over, the robber's teller had already dropped down behind the counter – as she had undoubtedly been instructed to do in the event of a hold-up – and put the robber in a foul mood.

'Give me your goddam money or I waste this fucker!' the guy screamed.

Of course, the teller was safe behind the counter and didn't want to put her head back up, bulletproof sheet of Plexiglas notwithstanding. David could understand. He suspected she had already pressed a silent alarm, but he could see this guy was not going to wait around for the swat team. There was a wild fury in his eyes, no doubt drug assisted. Methedrine soaked in Valvoline. PCP spelled backwards – something toxic bubbled in the guy's bloodstream. It was one of those few times when David was not carrying his gun. The bank had a security guard, however. Unfortunately the gentleman was in his seventies, and loved nothing more exciting than playing

Clue with his grandchildren. He carried a gun but David wasn't even sure if it was loaded. The guard knew David was an FBI agent and his eyes immediately went to him for help. David shook his head minutely. He wished the teller, or somebody, would stand back up and give the robber what he wanted. He knew a short fuse dipped in gasoline when he saw one.

'Motherfuckers!' the robber yelled. He pulled the trigger. The young man in the nice suit suddenly had a red hole in each eardrum. He went down in a messy puddle. The customers in the bank turned to frozen Jello. The robber grabbed a nearby middle-aged woman. 'I'm not waiting!' he shouted.

Everyone else was, including the bank president, cowering behind his desk in the corner. There was terror in the woman's eyes. She struggled feebly with her captor. The robber smacked her on the back of the head with his gun to let her know he didn't like that, but not hard enough to knock her out. David felt he had no choice. He took a step towards the robber, his outstretched hands saying everything was cool.

'I work here, sir,' David said, even though he had on blue jeans and a teeshirt. 'I can get you all the money you want. Just relax and give me a minute. No one else has to get hurt.'

The robber drilled the muzzle in the woman's ear. He snorted. 'You don't work here.'

'I sure do,' David said. 'I'm senior vice president of this branch. Today just happens to be my day off. Just relax and let me get you your money. Would you like large bills or small?'

The guy thought a moment, then yelled, 'I want all your bills!'

David nodded. 'You shall have them. Did you happen by chance to bring a bag with you?' He could see the guy had not thought of that. Before the guy's frustration could peak again, David hastily added, 'It doesn't matter. I can get you a bag. You can have your money and be on your way in one minute.' He paused to allow his calming words to sink in. 'Would that be all right?'

The guy flashed a wide toothy grin. 'No funny shit.'

David nodded. 'No funny shit.' He glanced at the teller he had been flirting with before all the excitement started. At least she had kept her composure and not lowered her head. He said, 'Mary, do we have any of those sacks we take our deliveries in?'

'Yes,' she said. 'In the back.'

'Could you please get our guest two of those big bags and stuff them full of cash from the teller drawers. Give him everything we have.'

Mary was a resourceful woman. Quickly, she fetched the bags and while everyone stood and stared as the puddle of blood around the dead man spread to the tips of David's shoes, she emptied the front drawers. She was wise enough to appear calm as she worked, which helped relax the robber. When she had finished she passed the bags through an electronically controlled door to David. He handed them to the robber, his shoes actually splashing in the dead man's blood. The robber tossed the middle-aged woman aside and levelled his black Colt .38 revolver at David, his expression a mixture of money bag high and bad acid blues.

'You still don't look to me like you work in a bank,' he said.

'But I do,' David said calmly, knowing the guy was half an inch away from putting a round in his belly, where it would hurt worse than almost anything. 'I can prove it to you.'

'How?'

'I know the combination of the vault in the back.'

The guy was interested. 'What is it?'

'Left six. Right five. Right five. Left two. Right nine.'

The guy grinned. 'No shit? I'll remember that. Hey, I'll be back here next year and take your whole fucking stash!'

David chuckled. 'Repeat business is the heart of any successful bank.' He nodded to the clock. 'You'd better get out of here before the cops come.'

The guy blinked as if he had just heard the earth was round, then nodded. 'You're right. Thanks.' He lowered his weapon. 'You have a nice day, you hear.'

'You too,' David said.

The guy left. David dashed to the guard. Ed was already pulling out his gun to give him. 'It's loaded,' he said quickly, as if reading David's mind.

'Keep everyone here,' David barked. 'Call for backup.'

Mild mannered Ed had handed him a .44 Magnum. David was out on the street in a second, scanning the four quarters of the globe. The robber, despite his dilated chrome pupils, had good leg speed. He was already a hundred yards down the road, climbing into the driver's side of a rusty blue Mustang that looked as if it had been parked on Venus the last year. He glanced back at the bank as he tossed his loot in the passenger seat, and saw David and Magnum. He switched into high gear. David was less than halfway to the car when it lay down twin trails of sizzling rubber. David raised Ed's gun and, taking aim with both hands, fired three rounds at the back tyre on the right. The kick on the gun was like a fastbreak basketball tossed by Magic Johnson; he was lucky to land a round in the rubber. But it was enough – a .44 Magnum in a Michelin four wall. The tyre exploded like a Tanya Harding alibi. The front of the car careened into a yellow fire hydrant. Had it been TV, water would have gushed on to the sidewalk. But it didn't. David sprinted towards the *passenger's* side of the Mustang. Mr Money Bags slowly climbed out of the car, weapon in hand.

'Halt!' David shouted. 'Slowly, drop your gun and put your hands in the air.'

Dazed, the guy raised his hands but did not drop his gun.

'Drop your gun,' David repeated firmly.

Blood the colour of Koolaid poured from a gash on his forehead. 'You said you worked for the bank,' he complained.

'I work for the FBI. Drop your weapon this instant or I will blow off your fucking head.'

The guy was annoyed. 'You lied to me, motherfucker. That wasn't the combination of the vault.'

'I will count to three. If you do not drop your gun by the number three, your head will explode. It's that simple. One . . .'

The guy stared at him. 'Shit.'

'Two.'

Since David had lied to the guy about being a bank VP, he could understand why the robber didn't believe his statement that he was an FBI agent. Still, he did have an awfully big gun pointed at the asshole. The guy should have listened.

'Three.'

The guy whipped down his gun and tried to get off a round. His personal poison had to be in the higher frequencies bands; he was fast. But he was also just another low life with the IQ of a lousy blackjack hand. David shot him in the chest. The force of the round sent the guy flying backwards. His arms flung out like he was preparing for crucifixion. Vital organs exploded out the rear of his spine. He landed like something dropped from a condemned skyscraper. David stopped to take a breath. He thought of the young man lying dead on the floor of the bank. Of the two big bags of money sitting in the driver's seat of the Mustang. Of how his right wrist hurt from the recoil of Ed's howitzer. He realized that he had just killed someone, for the first time in his life, and that he should feel either disgust or elation or at least some powerful emotion. But all he felt was a great weariness. He heard sirens in the distance. He had walked the mile to the bank. He wondered if a policeman would give him a ride home so he could rest.

Later, though, there was elation when the office heard what he had done. The secretaries looked at him in a new light. His partners often volunteered to buy him lunch. The nickname went around. A .44 Magnum. Just wasted the bastard out in the middle of the street. That's Dirty Dave for you.

Then Ned came to him and asked him to go after kidnappers. The action was a lot slower, he said. The success rate was a lot lower. But the reward could be great, to return a son or a daughter to their parents. Ned made a persuasive argument. David always liked to try something new. He said OK.

His first case, which he handled with three other agents, concerned a sixteen-year-old boy, Harold Murray, who had apparently been kidnapped while he was all alone in his house. The parents had been contacted and a ransom of one million dollars in cash was the asking price to see their son alive again. The family was wealthy. Harold had left no signs of struggle behind, but by the glasses on the kitchen table, it did look as if he had offered one or more people a drink. On top of that, when David questioned the parents, he learned that Harold was home alone once in a blue moon. David's brain hummed. The kidnappers not only knew Harold, they knew him well. That probably meant they were young, Harold was being held in the neighbourhood, and the kidnappers could not possibly let Harold live once they collected their money. David told his partners his deduction but they thought he was moving too fast with too little information. They felt the voice that had called for the ransom sounded older. David thought the detail unimportant. He *knew* he was right. That gut feeling was back.

David instructed the parents to stall for time, tell the kidnappers a million was not gathered overnight, and went to Harold's school and spoke to every single teacher. Did they have any troublemakers who had hassled Harold in the past, he asked? Were any of them absent lately, nervous, talking together in the corners of campus at lunch? David made up a list of a dozen possible candidates and that same day visited each of their homes. At the third house a long-haired droopy-eyed boy answered the door. He had a twitch in his left cheek and bloodshot eyes. As soon as David identified himself as an FBI agent, he knew he had hit the jackpot. The kid practically fell over.

'Are you a friend of Harold Murray?' David asked.

The kid held his head so low he might have been trying to snort coke from the floor. 'No. I mean, yeah, I know him. Why?'

'Do you know where he is?'

Shuffling, foot to foot. 'No.'

'Are you sure?'

'No.'

'You're not sure?'

'I don't know where he is, officer. I swear it.'

David smiled. 'I'm not a cop. You don't have to call me officer. You can just call me Dirty Dave. What's your name?'

'Ralph.'

'Ralph, do you know how I earned my nickname?'

'No.'

'I blew away a kidnapper with a .44 Magnum. Blew off his balls. He bled to death in the middle of the street. That's the honest truth. He died screaming.' David reached into his coat. 'Are you sure you don't know where Harold is?'

The kid jumped back. 'I don't know. I heard he was kidnapped.'

David took a step in the house. 'Are your parents home, Ralph?'

No.' The kid sweated. 'Can you just come in my house like that? Don't you need a warrant?'

'No. Only cops need warrants. I'm an FBI agent, remember? You got any drugs here?'

'No. I swear it.'

'Your eyes are red, Ralph. You're lying. You've been smoking it, I can tell.'

David pulled out his gun and pointed it at the boy. 'Tell me where Harold is.'

The kid was in tears. 'I don't know!'

David aimed at the guy's balls. 'One of your partners has already tipped us off. We know you've got Harold. But if you don't want to talk now, that's all right. You'll be talking with a squeaky voice the rest of your life. That is if you don't bleed to death right now in front of me.'

'You can't shoot me!'

David cocked the hammer. 'Why not? I like shooting people. I won't get in trouble. You'll probably be dead – you won't be able to identify me.'

The boy shook. 'Who told you about Harold?'

David chuckled. 'Ah. That's a secret. I'm good at keeping secrets. If you tell me where Harold is now, I won't tell any of the other guys you told me. It'll be our secret.'

The boy buried his face in his hands. 'I didn't want to do it. They made me do it. They talked me into it.'

David put away his gun. He walked over and put his hand on the boy's shoulder. 'Ralph,' he said. 'That's the last thing in the world you want to tell the jury.'

The kid took him around the block to a classmate's house. The parents were home. The father demanded that David show a warrant. David pushed him out of the way. It was permissible under the law; he had verification a hostage was being held in the house and that the said hostage was in danger. He found Harold tied up in the guest house. The parents didn't even know he had been there, and Harold had been missing four weeks. David ended up arresting five youths. He went to their trial, of course, he had to testify against them. He didn't give Ralph any brownie points for his assistance. Ralph tried to convince the jury that David had almost killed him but David testified that at all times he had treated the boy gently. The jury believed him.

God, if only the rest of them were so easy. It was not to be. He had far more successes than failures, but each of the latter stayed with him ten times as long. He lost wives and husbands, sons and daughters. But he kept going, he had to keep going. He knew he was too good at his job to quit. He felt he had a responsibility to society.

Then, in the middle of David's ninth year at the Bureau, Ned again came to him with something different. Ned was always pushing him to his limits. This time Ned said he would be overseeing the case, which meant those limits would be blown away like Mr . . . Money Bags' heart. Ned was not just a workaholic; hundred hour weeks were standard with him, especially as of late. Ned wanted David with him on an OC case – organized crime. Despite all he had heard about how slow OC work could be, as he listened to the facts, David found himself getting excited.

Rudy Failla was the target. The head of the most powerful Mafia family on the west coast, Failla's tentacles reached into a dozen mob-friendly businesses: construction, loan sharking, drugs, prostitution, topless bars, gambling. It was this last area where Ned planned to strike. While the majority of the public blissfully believed that Las Vegas had been swept clean of the mob with the construction of the family-orientated high rises on the Strip, the FBI knew better. Failla did not own any of the major hotels on the Strip but he did control several of the larger downtown casinos, and his influence was felt throughout the city. Yet he was based in Los Angeles and that gave Ned the right to kick his ass if he could locate the right boot. Ned believed he might have found it.

Ned had turned one of Failla's men into an informant. The guy was not a low level wiseguy, but a ruthless henchman who regularly travelled with the Don. He had already provided Ned with a list of people Failla had ordered hit. The problem was the henchman – Ned called him Gary Garrott – had never received a direct order to murder from Failla, who had an almost invisible *consigliere*, and two underbosses to take care of such details. The other problem, Ned told David, was that none of them had heard from Gary Garrott in a month.

'He's probably dead,' David said.

Ned shook his head impatiently. 'We did think of that, you know. But we still have the list he gave us. All we have to do is tie Failla to it and we can lock him up.'

'Is that all?'

'It's not as bad as it sounds. We have the RICO, electronic surveillance, the new toys the tech boys whipped up for us. We can bug the roaches in his hotels. Gary Garrott led us to six of the bodies he dumped. We connect Failla to two or three of those and he'll be presumed guilty. Most people on a jury will tell you they loved *The Godfather*. But Failla's a fat fuck, looks like Marlon Brando before the diet. No jury's going to like him. Place those bugs for me, David. Put one in his lover's snatch.'

'Is that within the jurisdiction of the RICO?' David asked, surprised at the crude remarks. Ned was unusually conservative when it came to matters of sex. David could see that going after Failla had affected Ned's psyche. He had a dart board hung in his office, a map of Las Vegas hotels behind it to catch the bite of his misses. Ned did not like to miss, David knew. But when he did, he did not let the opposition walk away smiling.

The RICO, or the Racketeer-Influenced and Corrupt

Organizations Act, was the Bureau's main weapon against organized crime, although it had been in existence for over a decade with few in the agency really knowing how to use it. The RICO allowed them to build a case against entire families instead of taking out just a few soldiers. The key to it was that it allowed them to attack the structural essence of the Cosa Nostra. In court, a Mob 'family' could be shown to be an ongoing criminal organization, rather than just a collection of hot-tempered relatives.

Ned had smiled in response to his question. 'It will be, after your bug sticks its ear out.'

So David moved to Las Vegas. He became Blake Nichols, half owner in a well established and highly successful pool construction company. The cover was excellent. It gave him a past and money to gamble with. He also got to work on his tan, even though he did most of his real work at night. He began to haunt Failla's casinos, playing blackjack mostly. Because he used the Bureau's money, and was a conscientious employee, he learned to count cards so that he usually left a winner. But he did not win so much that he drew suspicion, and at Failla's pride and joy, the Silver Shamrock, he always left a few hundred at the tables. It was at the Shamrock, five weeks after moving to Vegas, that he met and fell in love with Sandy Quin. She worked for the casino, for Failla. At first it had seemed a fortunate coincidence. But he should have known how quick fortune could change to despair in the city of sin.

He was sitting at the counter in the casino coffee shop after playing against a dealer who busted as often as meteors landed in the desert, counting his losses and thinking he hadn't even said hello to Failla's lover, much less asked her if she had a condom. A slim dark blonde with lips the colour of Christmas stocking candy and a smile as sweet as vanilla ice cream, chased her ice cream around her pie plate two seats to his right. Thirtyish, with a tan that said she was local, she wore a smart orange dress and a white ribbon in her hair. Had it been a black ribbon he supposed she would have reminded him of Halloween. Trick or treat. Hello, I love you. Two different ways to say hello late at night. He didn't know which was better, which was worse. But he did believe he loved her the moment he saw her, although he normally didn't indulge in ridiculous sentiments. When had he last let himself care for a woman? In college? For the last nine years his career had been all-consuming, a vampire of romance. Had Ned asked him right then if he would have used the woman to go after Failla, he would have told him he was crazy.

'Hi,' he said. 'You might want to grab that scoop of ice cream with your hand. It doesn't like your fork.'

Blushing, she put down her fork. 'I shouldn't be eating this late at night anyway.'

'This is Vegas. It's never late here. There's no clocks.'

She smiled and picked up a folder of papers on her right. 'It's going to be late for me if I don't have this work on my boss's desk by tomorrow morning at nine.'

'What are you working on?'

'An ad for this hotel.'

'Are you trying to sell it?'

She chuckled. 'I'm afraid I don't own it. I'm just a poor working girl.'

David had a sinking feeling, even then. 'You work for the Silver Shamrock?'

'Yes. I'd tell you my title if I knew it. Four years ago I started as a secretary but when Mr Failla, that's my boss, learned I could write he put me in charge of hotel publicity. Since then I've picked up the jobs of payroll and menu maker and overall errand runner. Occasionally, I still take shorthand and type.' She paused, studying him. 'What do you do Mr . . .'

'Nichols. Blake Nichols.' The first thing he told her was a lie. It would be the same with the last thing, when he said everything would be all right. He offered his hand. 'Pleased to meet you Ms . . .'

She took his offer, and although he did not mean it so, she took the bait.

'Ms Quin. Sandy Quin,' she said.

They started to date. She liked hiking, water skiing, kite flying, baking, him, most of all him. Why did he use her? Because she was there? His love was as true as hers. It was only a desire for truth that led him to tell her who he really was. At first she did not believe him. Not that he was an FBI agent, but that her wonderful boss was a cold-blooded murderer. David didn't want to tell her the stories. He didn't want to place the horrific images in her kind heart. But she made him talk, show her the pictures, the secret files. Ned would have nailed him to Shamrock's crap table to know that he gave away so much of their case. But David trusted her, with his life, literally.

They covered the dirty details early in the morning before the sun came up. See, he said, here is what happens when your boss gets angry. The chainsaw that cut up this guy started at the toes, with the guys legs still kicking, and took forever to get to the head. The testicles in this guy's mouth belonged to his baby brother. This woman used to go out with Mr Failla. I recognize her, Sandy cried. That's amazing, David said. The woman was missing her eyeballs. She should never have slept with Failla's poker partner. The partner should never have slept with her. But Sandy did not want to see that man's body, what was left of it. She ran into the bathroom then, locked the door behind her, and threw up. He could hear her vomiting. She didn't come out for a long time. But when she did, her clear blue eyes were as colourless as dusty windshields. Her voice, however, was filled with resolve.

'I want to help you get him,' she said.

He said no, of course, he would not risk her for the world, although the fact that she was dating an FBI agent put her in peril. What he wanted her to do was leave her job and move to Los Angeles with him. But he couldn't go back home yet, Ned said, not until he got his man.

David never realized how strong Sandy was until too late. Maybe she, too, had watched *The FBI* reruns while growing up. She shocked him when she went over his head to Ned. She actually called the FBI office in LA and said she wanted to speak to the boss. Ned listened to her offer. She could tell Failla that they desperately needed to upgrade their phone equipment. His agents could take the place of the phone crew. They could install all the bugs they wanted in both Failla's offices and private quarters, with her personally supervising their work. No one would question the work order. Sandy thought the plan up all by herself. Ned was interested, of course he was. He later told David he had visions of Failla framed by metal bars while Sandy talked.

David, when he heard about the private talk, flipped. Absolutely not, he said. Then he backed down slightly, and that was a mistake, to open the door even a little bit. He agreed that Sandy could help them get the bugs in, but then she had to get out. Ned vetoed the idea. He said her sudden departure might alert Failla. With the bugs in place, business had to go forward as usual and that meant Sandy had to stay. Ned also feared any changes in Sandy's routine might cause Failla to have a closer look at whom she was dating.

'The phone company will cooperate a hundred per cent,' Ned tried to reassure David. 'Failla can call them himself and they'll tell him they had their people out. There's no reason to think he will go looking for bugs, and if he does get suspicious then we'll hear about it from his own lips. This is our big break. We can have Failla and his top men in jail by the end of the year. Think about that, David. How much it will mean to have these bastards out of society.'

He did think about it and it seemed, on the surface, that

the possible gain out-weighed the risk, which reasonably appeared very small. Yet his gut feeling said they were making a huge mistake. Yet Ned asked him for his permission. Ned understood his relationship with Sandy. Ned didn't force him. And in the end David did say fine, all right, we'll use her if she wants to be used. He was never to forgive himself for that.

Sandy set up the visit from the phone company. That night, excited, Sandy said Failla only grunted his approval when she asked him about the installation. He trusted her judgement on such matters completely. She was Efrem Zimbalist Jr's girlfriend playing in the big leagues. Dancing around her apartment, she playfully mocked David for his lack of daring. But David saw even then that Sandy had yet to connect the man she worked for with the photographs he had shown her. She couldn't picture Failla wielding the chainsaw himself. But David could, and he hardly slept that night.

The private mob conversations started to come in loud and clear. Failla was only in Vegas on the weekends, preferring his mansion in Malibu to his penthouse on the top floor of the Shamrock. But it appeared he did most of his business in Vegas. On the first weekend alone they listened as Failla blatantly discussed how he had personally blown off the back of Gary Garrott's skull, and even where he had dumped the body – in Lake Mead beside the Hoover Dam. David lost all enthusiasm for the tap water after that. With that tape in the can, David wanted to blow the lid on Failla. He felt they had enough to prosecute. But Ned wanted to tear up the foundation of the family, put the underbosses and the *consigliere* in jail. He was ready to listen for the next year if that's what it took.

A month after the bugs were planted, Failla discussed with his *consigliere* a local businessman he wanted hit. David listened to the tape several times. He knew the man who was to be killed, James Holt, the largest movie theatre owner in Las Vegas. Blake Nichols' company had just put in a pool for Mr Holt. David had even had lunch with the guy. The tape came to them courtesy of a bug behind the painting behind Failla's office desk.

> Failla: 'Holt licks my girls and then spits in my face. I gave him his start. I handed it to him on a silver platter. He thinks he doesn't owe me on his other projects, he's full of shit. Do him this week. Put a rocket in his chest. Make it burn.'
> Consigliere: 'Should we give the job to Frankie?'
> Failla: 'Fuck. Frankie's too old. He can't even get it up for his hand. Give it to George. He's a fucking lunatic. He'll enjoy torturing the guy.'
> Consigliere: 'Do you want it to look like a professional hit?'
> Failla: 'No. We don't need the shit. Not after Gary. Holt has to disappear. Put him in a hole somewhere that no one will ever dig up.'

So the fates conspired to wreck David's life. He wouldn't have said anything to Ned about trying to save Mr Holt if he hadn't met him personally. Holt would have just been another statistic of Failla's reign of terror. But Holt had spent half the lunch talking to David about how much his three kids were going to enjoy their new swimming pool. David told Ned they had to get Holt and Sandy out of town, obtain arrest warrants with what they had and take their chances in court. Ned was more daring.

'Let's put a watch on Holt,' Ned said. 'Let's be there when they pick him up. Then, after we save the guy, we can put him on the stand. His testimony together with this tape will make it impossible for Failla to walk.'

'But we have enough already,' David said. 'Too many things can go wrong. I know the George that Failla's talking about. He is a fucking lunatic. He gets a whiff of our presence and people will die.'

'You can handle him, David. I know you can.'

But David had to wonder about that one line on the tape. '*Not after Gary.*'

In the Bureau's enthusiasm to get Failla, no one was talking about the remark. But to David it spoke volumes. Failla knew Gary Garrott had ratted to the FBI. He had his antenna up. Soon it would sense the tiny electronic device behind his head, and he would remember Sandy's request for a new phone system.

'If we're doing this, we're getting Sandy out of town now,' David said. 'I don't give a damn if it makes waves.'

Ned hesitated. 'Maybe you should. Get her out now, then. Tonight.'

'Thanks,' David said.

David called Sandy after he hung up. But she was at work, where he definitely did not want to call her. Failla had spoken of hitting Holt sometime during the week, but to David such a timetable included the present moment. Calling a partner and grabbing his gun, he decided to spend the night watching Holt's home. Failla's people were not above dragging someone from their own bed.

Lunatic George was already there when David cruised by. David cursed the speed with which the henchman had moved. David didn't know the status of Holt's family, but George was dragging Holt down the front steps of Holt's mansion with a gun to his head. It was a Friday, close to midnight. David's backup had yet to appear, but he would have betted a stack of black honeybees that George had his people nearby. David felt he had no choice. He knew if George got Holt in his car, the man would die. David did what any other agent raised on TV reruns would have done in a similar situation. He rammed George's car with his own car just as George opened the back door to throw his victim inside.

The door whacked Holt and sent the man flying free, probably unconscious, to the ground. Lunatic George took one look at David trying to climb out of his car and quickly raised his gun. David ducked in time to hear a bullet pierce his windshield and the top half of his front seat. When he peeked up, George was running down the block. David jumped out, his 10-millimetre semiautomatic pistol in hand. He stood rock still and took aim. Only on TV could people shoot accurately while running at full speed.

'Stop or I'll shoot!' he shouted, intentionally failing to identify himself as an FBI agent. He didn't want every wiseguy on the block to know who was around. George didn't stop. David shot him in the back. The guy fell like a fleeing bull. Further down the street, perhaps a hundred yards, car headlights went on as a car pivoted in the middle of the street and roared away. David ran to where George lay crumpled. The man was dead. God bless his hairy soul, David thought. He ran back to Holt. The businessman was alive but groggy, a nasty bump on his forehead. David got on his car phone and called for an ambulance.

Then he thought of Sandy. Failla's quick mind.

He could practically hear the Don shouting at his people.

'How the fuck did anyone know we were going to hit Holt? There must be a mole here. Or else this hotel is bugged.'

Failla would pause and look behind the picture.

It didn't matter what Ned said. Failla would know.

David drove towards the Silver Shamrock at high speed.

He arrived just in time to catch the midnight special into the land of nightmares.

There was a crowd gathered out front beside the silver fountain. Police lights flashed in dizzy circles. An ambulance shaped like a busy hearse stood nearby. David tried to push himself through the crowd but a civilian stopped him, a hand on his arm, a teenage boy

who looked like Harold Murray the day he was rescued.

'Man, you don't want to see it,' the boy said. 'She
jumped from the top floor.'

David croaked. 'Is it a young blonde woman?'

'I don't know. Her hair's red now.'

'What is she wearing?'

'An orange dress.' The pale kid squinted at him. 'Did
you know her?'

David hung his head. 'No. I didn't know her at all.'

Even in that moment, in that black well of despair, the
red light of revenge shimmered before him like an ancient
star guiding him towards a forsaken paradise where the
innocent gnawed on the bones of their tormentors. David
took a couple of deep breaths, composed his expression,
and strode into the casino. He was a robot, his program
clear. His gun set off an alarm. Security was on him in an
instant. No problem. He flashed his badge and said he
wanted to speak to Mr Failla. They said fine, no problem.
But they took his gun, something they had no right to do.
It was still no problem, not to David. He would not kill
Failla tonight. He had time, he thought. He would kill him
tomorrow.

They led him to Mr Failla's private office. Failla sat
behind a desk as wide as his belly, his stiff hair the colour
of dirty silver dollars. He was one of those disgusting men
who had a hippo leg for a throat. He wore a fine grey suit,
however, and his hands were remarkably fine. He cracked
and chewed on peanuts as David entered. He snacked
while Sandy's blood still drained from her head. The rage
David experienced right then was a thing beyond emotion.
It lifted him up and deposited him in a place where he
honestly believed he was capable of anything. Still, the
robot was all he showed. He flashed a grin as he was led
forward to meet the great man. Failla's two underbosses
stood behind their leader like grotesque stumps grown out

41

of a volcanic hillside, their hands in their fat pockets, fingering guns they wished weren't so much bigger than their dicks.

'Who the fuck are you?' Failla asked.

David's grin widened. 'May I sit down?' he asked.

Failla hesitated. Then he snapped a finger. A chair was brought out. David sat down and crossed his legs. 'So you caught her,' he said smoothly. 'I knew you would. I knew it was only a matter of time.'

Failla's eyes narrowed. 'I don't know what you're talking about.'

David gestured around the room. 'I'm sure you've swept this place clean. We can talk freely. My name's Blake Nichols. I work for the FBI. I've been spying on you for the last two months. I recruited Sandy. She was my stooge.' David shrugged. 'I let her fall in love with me. She did what I told her.'

Failla considered. 'You don't sound too shook up about her unfortunate fall.'

'I told her not to look down, that she'd get dizzy. What can I say? To me, it's just business. That's why I'm here. I want to do business with you.'

Failla was cautious. 'What do you have to offer?'

'The details of the FBI's case against you. Also, the name of a high-placed mole in your organization.'

'There is no mole in my organization,' Failla said flatly.

'What about Gary?'

'He's not with us anymore.'

'Too bad. You should have talked to him before you laid him off. He could have told you about his partner.' David paused. 'I have the records. I can prove everything I say.'

Failla thought for a full minute. 'How strong is the FBI case?'

'A bitch if you don't know what's coming. Bullshit if you've got alibis ready.'

'What do you want in return for these records?'

'One million in cash.'

Failla snorted. 'You have balls asking for that. What if I say you're still working for the FBI? What if I say my boys take you for a ride right now? Dump you where they dumped Gary?'

'You can say what you want. Without my help you'll be in jail in less than six months. And you won't be getting out. By the way, that was pretty sloppy work tonight. Dumping the girl beside your own fountain.'

Here David spoke the truth. Failla was so shrewd, so calculating, to build and maintain such a large empire. At the same time, he was just another hot-headed thug.

Failla shook his head. 'So I have a temper? What can I say? She just pissed me off. She seemed like such a nice girl.'

'She was a cunt,' David said.

Failla slowly smiled. 'I'm beginning to like you, Mr Nichols. But I'm still not convinced that what you've got is worth a million in cash. Tell me the name of the mole now as a sign of good faith and then maybe we can do business.'

David stood and removed a card from his back pocket. He threw it on the Don's desk. 'I'd like to but my answer would not be appropriate, given the situation. That's my number. Let's meet again tomorrow evening, out in the desert somewhere. You pick the location. Leave me a message giving directions. No one in the FBI knows that number. I have to return to LA to get everything you need. Don't have me followed, it will only cause complications for you. Bring unmarked bills, hundreds. By the way, I'll give you most of what I have tomorrow, but not all. Just in case you don't want to pay for my services.' David paused and stared Failla in the eye, and saw a dead man. 'I hope we understand each other, Mr Failla?'

Failla stood and nodded. He offered his hand across the

wide desk. 'You come alone, unarmed. You understand, Mr Nichols?'

David smiled and shook his hand. 'Yes. Clearly.'

David called Charles Gordon when he got back to his Vegas apartment. Mr Gordon owned a large construction company in Los Angeles. Three years ago, his wife had been kidnapped and the FBI had been called in. David had been put in charge of the case. It turned out to be one of the easier kidnappings David ever worked on, largely because the kidnappers were as shrewd as Harold Murray's. The kidnappers asked that the half million in ransom money be placed in a specific trash can and when they arrived to pick it up David arrested them. David had Gordon's wife back to him inside two days. The man had told him if he ever needed a favour, no matter what it was, to call him. So David called him. Gordon answered, was happy to hear from him. David didn't waste time on pleasantries.

'Charles,' David said. 'I need a big favour.'

'Anything. What is it?'

'I need two hundred pounds of dynamite, detonators, wiring, and a timer. I need it in the next twelve hours, preferably sooner. Can you get it for me?'

Gordon took a moment. 'Can't the Bureau get it for you?'

'This isn't a Bureau job.'

'What is it?'

'It's personal.'

'Where are you?'

'Las Vegas. I can leave now to drive to your place.'

Gordon paused. 'That's not necessary. It sounds like you've got your hands full there. Let me bring it to you.'

'You can get the two hundred pounds?'

'Yes. But I have to warn you. That many sticks will make one hell of an explosion.'

'That's exactly what I want,' David said.

David gave Gordon further instructions where to meet

him, some way out of town, before hanging up. Gordon's coming to him simplified matters, gave him longer to prepare his own car for the explosives. Before he could set to work, however, Ned called. He had heard the news, wanted David to come home immediately. David had to laugh.

'But you said I couldn't come home until I got my man,' David said. He hung up. He did not blame his boss for what had happened to Sandy. He blamed himself and God. He felt like God as he began to carefully undo the seams of his upholstery. He had the power of life and death in his hands. And he was choosing death. He worked through the night; he wanted nothing to appear amiss. He wept only once, when he thought of her. But otherwise he didn't even let her name enter his mind. He could grieve later, he thought, if he was still alive. Either way, he didn't care.

Gordon arrived two hours after sunrise and gave him the goods. David thought of that famous line from *Apocalypse Now*. 'I love the smell of napalm in the morning . . . Smells like victory.' David held the hard red sticks up to his nose as he transferred them into his hacked-up back seat. Gordon watched, worried.

'You must be in deep shit,' Gordon said.

'Yeah, I suppose. But now I can just blow my way out.' David picked up the box of detonators and tossed them in the front seat. 'I really appreciate the fireworks, buddy. If anyone ever steals your wife again, just give me a call. I'll find her for you.'

Gordon blocked his way as he went to leave. 'You have to tell me what's happened. If you don't – I can see it – you're going to die.'

David stopped. 'So I die. So what?'

Gordon shook his head. 'You can't say that. You saved my wife's life. You have talents few people possess. You still have other people's lives to save. You have to let me help you.'

David didn't know why he listened to him, except for the hard fact that once he had Failla alone, he would need backup transportation to another place in the desert if he was going to play Good Godfather/Bad Godfather the way he envisioned. In the end, he told Gordon everything that had happened. He kept his voice calm and conversational as he spoke, which seemed to frighten Gordon more than if he had broken into hysterics. Finally, it was decided. Gordon would follow him far enough into the desert to where he could see the explosion. David believed that would leave Gordon at a safe distance.

There were two messages on David's machine when he returned to his apartment. One from Ned – which he fast forwarded over – the other from Failla's wiseguy. Drive here, turn there. Follow the dirt road, then make a left. Look for the squat hill. Come alone. We'll be waiting for you at exactly sunset. David wrote it all down, then tore up the directions. He had an excellent memory. A long memory with a short fuse, as they say.

Gordon watched as David outfitted his car for its last day on Earth. A black SC400 Lexus with leather interior, David had been driving it for two years and hated to see it not collect on his insurance policy. He quizzed Gordon as he worked about the power of the shock wave the bomb would generate, the range of the scrap metal from the blast. Of course, David knew the answers to most of his questions better than the contractor. But the talk helped pass the time. Certainly, David was not in the mood to sleep.

Close to sunset, the two of them drove into the desert, in separate cars. David left Gordon behind at the start of the first dirt road. Gordon had binoculars with him but David did not think he would need them. The evening desert air was as dry as table salt and as still as David's hands. He had no fear because for the first time in his life he had no expectations for his own well being. He didn't even care if he drew in another breath, or let the one inside his chest out. His tastes in what constituted a good time had simplified. He just wanted to torture Failla to death.

They waited for him at the base of a hill that resembled a garbage heap bulldozed over with cat litter sand. They had one vehicle – a black limo as impenetrable as an army tank. A gorilla with silver sunglasses stood outside the car. David was happy they had brought the armoured monstrosity. Otherwise, the gorilla might have signalled for him to park at a distance, afraid he might drive by and open fire. But secure inside his plated cocoon, Failla was only too happy to let him park beside him. A mile back, David had pressed the button that activated the timer. By his best calculations, he had five minutes before his Japanese made sports coupé revisited Hiroshima. David grabbed the manila envelope and tiny cassette player and quickly stepped out of the car before the gorilla could reach him. The windows on the limo were pale orange mirrors of the fading sun. The orange reminded David of Sandy but only for a moment. The gorilla had a gun out.

'Put your hands in the air,' he barked.

'Fuck you,' David said. 'I'm unarmed.'

Odd, the gorilla didn't trust him. David was thoroughly frisked, and his cassette player and manila envelope examined, before the limo windows came down. Failla stuck out his fat face. David noted Failla had company, one of his underbosses and possibly the *consigliere*. Ned would get his wish after all, David thought. The family would cease to exist.

'Get in,' Failla said pleasantly.

'If you wish,' David said easily. 'But you might prefer to listen to what I have alone.'

Failla glanced at his partners. The seed David had planted the previous evening had sprouted. '*I'd like to but my answer would not be appropriate, given the situation.*' Failla was worried how high up the mole might be. The Don nodded to the gorilla. Again, David was frisked, his

47

balls squeezed so hard he had to restrain himself from kneeing the guy in the face. The gorilla moved to the car, searched it quickly, found nothing amiss. He nodded to his boss. Only then did Failla get out of the limo. David noted the bulge under his suit coat. Failla pulled himself up on the sandy ground like an obese coyote that had delusions of being a grisly.

'Let's go for a walk,' Failla said.

'I want my money first,' David said.

'You'll get your money,' Failla said.

David put a hand on the Don's chest as he went to step by. The gorilla didn't like that, but then again, David didn't like the gorilla. Failla was unperturbed.

'First,' David repeated. 'Bring it with you. I want to see it.'

Failla was amused. He snapped his fingers. A bulky black briefcase was handed out from the bowels of the limo. David hoped they kept the window down, let in a little fresh air, a little Lexus shrapnel. Not that it would matter with his car so close to the tank. Failla held onto the briefcase. He pointed to the curve of the hill.

'Over there,' he said.

They walked approximately a hundred and fifty yards away from the others, a reasonably safe distance in David's estimation. Still, they were close enough for Failla to be startled when the timer kissed the big twelve. Clearly, Failla was not afraid to be alone with him now that he knew he was unarmed, and had no backup in the neighbourhood. Failla trusted in his own weapon, his bulk, his balls. Also, the gorilla still had his gun out. David figured Failla's goon squad had earlier searched the area for other FBI agents, hidden weapons. That was the beauty of his plan. His weapon was parked in plain sight. The plan had come to him the instant he learned Sandy was dead. Such was the perverse nature of the creativity of a killer. A pool of blood could serve as a muse. David thought of himself as a killer then. He was no longer concerned about the Constitution, the Bill of Rights or the RICO. They halted beside a cactus that looked like its last watering had been at the hands of a Spanish missionary.

'Who's the mole?' Failla asked quickly.

David held up his hand. 'I have brought tapes of conversations the FBI has of you and your people. I want you to listen to the first one and the answer will be obvious.'

Failla was impatient. 'Why don't you just tell me?'

Because there was no highly placed mole. But David didn't want to explain that at the moment. He nodded to the tiny cassette player. 'Just listen. It's better you hear the truth for yourself. Then you'll have no doubts.'

'But if it's a conversation where I was there, then I've already heard it.'

'You heard the man who has betrayed you, Mr Failla. But you didn't see who he was. Give me three minutes and you'll understand what I mean.' David paused. 'But first show me the money.'

Failla opened the briefcase. One hundred packs of hundred dollar bills. A hundred bills per pack. They looked crisp but not clean. Not to David. He knew how they had been purchased, with blood and pain and death. Yet he picked one out and studied it in the fading light and smiled in satisfaction. To his surprise, it was the genuine article.

He played Failla a tape of one of the first conversations they had received from the bugs. The one where Failla made several references to the execution of Gary Garrott. Failla listened closely, his impatience fading. Even if he couldn't hear a mole in the room, he knew such a tape would not sound pretty in court, especially if the body was found. David hardly listened. He counted the seconds, a hundred and eighty of them. He shifted to the side, putting Failla between him and the cars. Once again he thought of the power of the shock wave, what it would feel like if the fat fuck landed on him.

There was an incredible explosion.

The flash of the bomb was brilliant, almost blinding. Even David had under-estimated the sheer strength of two hundred pounds of dynamite. He had hoped the bomb would tear the limo in two pieces, turn it over maybe, kill the occupants. But the limo and Lexus detonated as one unit. The black orange ball of flame momentarily took the shape of atomic dimensions, a mushroom cloud. The gorilla vanished into a barely glimpsed image of flying pieces of dark meat. The cars were no more cars.

A thick hand of compressed air hit both Failla and David. But David had the near three hundred pounds of the Don to shield him from the shock wave. Failla fell towards him as if kicked in the lower spine. David caught him as he fell, in both arms. Then he rammed his right knee up into Failla's face. Something cracked, something splattered. Failla dropped to the ground. Almost casually, David leaned over and removed the gun from Failla's coat. He frisked him quickly then took a step back. Failla groaned, his face covered with blood.

'She was my girl,' David said. 'You killed her. I'm going to kill you.'

Failla opened his eyes, saw he was covered, and sighed. 'Shoot then.'

David picked up the briefcase. He would keep the money for his troubles. 'No. My friend is coming for us in a few minutes. After I drop him in town, you and I go deep into another part of the desert. My friend smokes – he carries a Bic lighter. I'm going to borrow it from him. They don't cost much, you know, maybe fifty cents. But they can be used as horrible instruments of torture.' David paused. 'You will feel a hundred times the pain she felt before you leave this world.'

Failla was afraid. 'But you're FBI.'

David shook his head. 'I'm not one of the good guys. Not any more.'

David buried Failla later that night, in a shallow grave. Still using Gordon's car, he drove part way back to Los Angeles and checked into a hotel off interstate 15. He slept twelve hours straight. Only once did he awaken, to a nightmare where he heard Failla's screams echoing over an endless black desert. It was a nightmare he was to often have, as the years passed.

There was a hearing, of course, after all the shit went down. In real life guns were not fired and bombs did not explode without plenty of second guessing and paperwork. But from behind the scenes Ned helped him and the hearing took on an unreal flavour. It didn't even focus on the deaths of Failla and his men, but rather on his relationship with Sandy and the money missing from Failla's casino. Officials were always more interested in illicit sex and missing bucks than whether you got the job done or not. But with Ned's help the board bought the story that Sandy had been his informant, nothing more. How awful it was to publicly deny any interest in her. And as far as the money was concerned, they couldn't prove anything until they found it, or he began to spend it. Even Ned was not sure he had stolen it.

He retired after that, sort of. He told Ned to plant him a corn field somewhere. Ned shipped him off to a small town in Iowa, Burkesville, where he was the only FBI agent for fifty miles around. Ned knew what he had done; the whole Los Angeles office did. But nobody said anything directly to his face. They were all a little afraid of Dirty Dave after that, and a little proud. But there was no pride in his pain. There was nothing left in his life except time to kill. He never stopped missing Sandy.

Seven years in Burkesville was like seventy years elsewhere. People moved as slowly as growing stalks, and consequently committed few crimes worth his attention.

His big case the first year there was when a guy shot his wife for sleeping with his brother – shot her twenty times in her bare ass with his BB gun. It was the gossip on the town square for three months. Things picked up after that, but not much. David liked that just fine. It was not – with a million in cash under his bed – that he had to work.

In the end, though, he knew the call would come.

Yet he first heard about the Angela Moore case, not from Ned, but from the newspapers. Pretty eighteen-year-old homecoming queen kidnapped out of her own home in the middle of a slumber party with friends. The guy just knocked on the front door and grabbed her. The stuff of a national tragedy. Angela's picture was on the cover of *Time*, but her friends didn't even get a good look at the jerk. One said he was blond, the other bald. In either case, Angela was gone and it didn't look like she'd be coming back. The latter was David's professional assessment. A week had elapsed and the kidnapper had made no ransom demands. The papers had all kinds of experts quoting odds on whether she was dead. A couple of people in town asked David to do the same thing. He ignored them. What were the odds that Sandy would have died? Fate spun an odd shaped roulette wheel.

Ned did ring, however, when he got a call from the kidnapper. Seemed Angela was still alive, after all, but in dangerous company. Ned had come up against the worst slime the world had to offer in his years with the Bureau, but David believed this was the first time he had ever heard Ned scared. The kidnapper had called Ned directly.

'You have to hear this guy's voice to believe it,' Ned said. 'He sounds like Charles Manson after electroshock. He kept tickling Angela the whole time we talked, and she kept crying. I don't know what he was tickling her with. He doesn't just want money.'

David understood. 'He wants to play.'

'Yeah. I think with us and Angela both. But he is making

monetary demands.' Ned paused, his voice becoming passionate. 'I need you, David. I need you to talk to him, to catch him. We can't let this girl die.'

'I'm the last person you should call.'

'No. What happened before – you're the only person I can call. You can save her, I know you can. Please, David, for her sake.'

David had to close his eyes, for all the good it did. The image of Angela's face remained in his mind – her innocent brown eyes, her happy dimples – as did the thought of what her captor probably did to her after he finished talking to Ned. David knew he was the best, knew Angela deserved that, as did everyone. It was just that David thought his involvement could seal her fate. He had started out wanting to save people and had ended up burning off a man's penis in the desert, while the man cried to Mother Mary for him to put a bullet in his brain. He was a monster, there was no doubt about that. But that did not mean he was the right man to go after a monster.

'What's the guy asking for?' David asked finally.

'A quarter million in cash.'

'That isn't much. I have that. I can give it to him.'

'Ned paused. 'The money's not a problem. He is. He calls me instead of the parents. He strings me out, talks about the weather and razor blades in the same breath. Jesus, the President called me last night about Angela.'

'Does he want a quarter million, too?'

'David, she'll die. She'll die without you. Can I put it any plainer?'

'What if I come back and she does die?'

'What kind of question is that? If she dies then she dies. At least we would have tried. Come back to me, David. It can help you, you know, to save her.'

'Help me forget? I don't think so.' David looked around his office, four blank walls cut out above a bankrupt savings and loan. His eyes came to rest, not on Angela's or Sandy's picture, but on a Bic lighter a cop had left on his desk yesterday evening. He picked it up, struck the flame, stared at the quivering orange, saw a Jack-o-Lantern grin at him from behind it. Trick or treat.

'David.'

'All right.'

'You'll help us?'

'Yes.' He let the flame die. 'I'll try to help all of us.'

The Bureau's code name for the guy who kidnapped Angela was 'Pokey'. When David listened to the conversations Ned had with the suspect, it sounded as if Pokey were jabbing Angela with a sharp object. David agreed with Ned's assessment of Pokey's disturbed state. He was definitely not just in it for the money. Curiously, Pokey sounded old as well as unstable. Few kidnappers were above fifty. Reviewing the tapes, David tried to get a fix on what Pokey really wanted. The talks were so brief; it was not possible to get a trace on the line.

Pokey: 'I have the girl. I have the goods. She's being a good girl. You want to hear her? Know that she's alive?'

Ned: 'Sure. Let me talk to her.'

Pokey: 'I didn't say you could talk to her. [Angela cries in the background.] There, that's her, you can ask her mother and father. Shut up, Angie. Now! I read in the paper you want her back.'

Ned: 'We would like it if you could return Angela to us. What can we do to make that happen?'

Pokey: 'I need money.'

Ned: 'No problem. We can get you money. When would you like it?'

Pokey: 'Soon.'

Pokey hung up. The next call was the next day.

Pokey: 'Do you have my money?'
Ned: 'We can get it for you. How much do you want? Where do you want it delivered?'
Pokey: 'A quarter million. Can you get that much?'
Ned: 'No problem. We give you the money and you give us the girl. How about that?'
Pokey: 'I have to give her back? I don't want to. I like her. I think she's beginning to like me.'
Ned: 'We can talk about that. Where do you want us to put the money?'
Pokey: 'In my piggy bank.'
Ned: 'OK. Where is it?'
Pokey: [Laughs] 'In a wet place.'

Pokey hung up. But the same time, the next day, another call.

Pokey: 'I have chosen a place for you to bring my money. I want her father to bring it. I don't want any-one else around. If my instructions are not followed, Angie will cry for a long time. She misbehaved once and I made her cry. She's not quite the girl she used to be, if you know what I mean.'
Ned: 'We want her back unharmed.'
Pokey: 'It's a little late for that. But I can assure you she still works.'
Ned: 'We just want her back. You can have the money. Would you like hundreds? Twenties?'
Pokey: 'Hundreds. I'll call you soon with the details. [Angela cried in the background.] I have to go. My baby needs changing.'

With Ned, sitting in his boss's office, David listened to the tapes over and over again, trying to construct a psychological composite of the enemy.

'I think we should believe him when he says he doesn't want to give her back,' David said. 'Why didn't you make that a condition of the transfer of the money?'

'I mentioned it enough times. But I did not try to pin him down because of what you just said. He doesn't want to give her back.'

David shook his head. 'You hope to catch him at the pick up? That's the wrong strategy with this guy.'

'Why?' Ned asked.

'We both agree he's old. That means he's waited a long time to pull off a stunt like this. He laughs but he also takes what he's done very seriously. He expects you to take him seriously. I think you're missing that. These points seem contradictory but they're not. It's all a game to him, but you have to play by his rules. If you make a deal with him and don't keep your end of the bargain, he'll make us pay for it by either hurting or killing Angela.'

'You want us to just give him the money and hope he returns her?'

'It might not be a bad idea,' David said. 'What's a quarter million?'

'It's more than the family has, a lot more. We'll be using the Bureau's money on this one. The President of the United States said it was OK. Do you think Pokey has a partner?'

'No. *Angie* is his alone. I think that's clear.'

'But if he has no partner, and he comes for the money, we'll catch him.'

'Not necessarily,' David said. 'You may think you smooth-talked him, Ned, but he controlled the conversations. You can't just go by what he says – he's intelligent. I suspect he'll force us to deliver the money in an interesting way.'

'Do you want to talk to him next?' Ned asked.

David was doubtful. 'You already have a relationship with him. He specifically called you. I'm a stranger to him.'

'But you're quick on your feet. I want you to talk to him. If he objects, I can always pick up.' Ned paused. 'Why do you think he calls us instead of the family?'

'It's another example of how intelligent he is. He knows we're here. He's saying he's not afraid of us.' David shook his head. 'I hate cases like this. Already I can tell, he'd sooner kill her than return her.'

'Don't tell the parents that. I haven't told them about his "Not quite the girl she used to be" remark.' Ned looked ready to spit. 'What do you think he meant by that?'

'Oh, you know. He cut off her ear or something. He personalized her. How are the parents holding up?'

'Good. Both are hopeful,' Ned said.

David didn't know if that was such a good thing.

Pokey's fourth call came two days after that, in the early morning hours. David took it; he had been sleeping at the office for lack of a better place to rest. Ned stood close by while David introduced himself.

'I'm special agent David Conner. I've been put in charge of this case. But if you would like to talk to Ned, he's here. It's up to you.'

The voice was raspy, pleased. 'David Conner? Haven't I heard of you?'

'I don't know. Have you?'

'You were in the papers years ago. You rescued other people that have been kidnapped. You're a hero.' Pokey chuckled. 'I like that, talking to a hero.'

'Good. Let's discuss business.' David wanted him to know he didn't see it as a game. The fact that Pokey was aware of him spoke of his extensive knowledge of the FBI. David had been mentioned in the papers only once, over ten years ago. He purposely avoided publicity. 'Where do you want us to bring the money?'

'There's a phone booth in Abolene Oregon, at the corner of Main and Lincoln. Be there at sunset tomorrow. You and the father. I will call and give more instructions.

The father alone is to deliver the money in a waterproof briefcase. If an attempt is made to capture me, Angie will cry again. Understood?'

'Yes. When we deliver the money, you will release Angela. Understood?'

'I didn't say that.'

'I did. I mean it. Otherwise, no money. Do we have an agreement?'

Pokey laughed. 'We'll see.'

He hung up. Again, there had not been enough time to trace the call. Pokey had each of the conversations timed. Ned nodded his approval of the way David had handled the call. David was in no mood for praise.

'He didn't agree to bring her,' David said.

'You can't force him. Do know anything about Abolene?'

'Yes. It's in northern Oregon, a lumber town, population around five thousand. Lots of trees and rivers in the area.' David paused, thinking. 'I wonder if the rivers are the reason he wants the money in a waterproof briefcase.'

'Really? Throw a briefcase full of money in a river and it would just sink.'

'Yes,' David said. 'But it would be easy to make the case buoyant. He might instruct the father to do so tomorrow afternoon, at the last minute.'

'You really think he will have the father throw the money into a river? That's a great way to lose it.'

'I think it is a strong possibility. One thing for sure, he sees the briefcase getting wet. Also, don't forget, the money is secondary to him. His plan is clever, if that's what it is. The woods are thick in that part of the state. He could wait downstream at any point for the money to come to him. We would be hard pressed to stake out every river in the area. Not without his knowledge.'

Ned was adamant. 'But we have to make an attempt to capture him.'

David nodded. 'I agree. But notice he said I was

to accompany the father. In a sense, he's giving me permission to come after him.'

'You'll never be able to stake out a river by yourself.'

'I realize that. We'll have to outfit both the father and briefcase with a directional beeper. We can follow Pokey that way.'

'You will need backup. You can't do this yourself.'

'I want two hundred agents for backup. A swat team for that matter. But I don't want them in the immediate vicinity. We mustn't spook the guy. We'll have everybody stationed nearby. You heard Pokey's warning. He meant it, he'll make Angela cry.' David made a fist. 'But only if he gets back to her.'

Ned stared at him. 'You can't kill him. You have to bring him in.'

'You put me in charge. I'll do whatever is necessary to save her.'

The next morning David sat in the front seat of a Jeep Cherokee beside Mr James Moore. The man was old to have an eighteen-year-old daughter, perhaps sixty, but with a full head of silver brown hair and a beefy body that looked as if it could take a hard punch. Their breath came out in white clouds. Mr Moore was nervous, but he was not afraid, not for himself. A quarter million in real cash sat on David's lap. He patiently explained how the directional beepers worked.

'It's crucial that after you give him the money and he has left,' David said, 'you turn off your beeper. The one in the briefcase and the one in your shirt broadcast at a different frequency, but it's not that different. If you don't turn off your beeper, you may confuse us. There's a famous case in FBI annals where a man forgot to do just that and his wife died as a result.' David pressed the top of the gentleman's pocket. The device appeared to be an ordinary pack of cigarettes. 'You press the top of the pack and the beeper is activated. Press the bottom and it's turned off. Is that absolutely clear?'

'Yes. What if he discovers the beeper in the briefcase?'

'I intend him to discover it. That's why I have placed a second beeper inside one of the packs of money. It's very small. He would have to search every pack to find it, and he won't have time, not right away.'

Mr Moore's lower lip quivered. 'Do you think he'll have Angela with him?'

'No. He never said he would bring her. But she won't be far.' David paused. 'Is there anything else you want to ask me? Once he calls, neither of us will have much time to talk.'

'What will he say?'

'He'll direct us to some place in the area. Listen closely to what he has to say, he may not repeat it. But don't worry. I'll be in the booth with you. If you miss something, I'll catch it.'

'Why does he want you there?'

'Because he's a fool,' David lied. Pokey wanted him around to add spice to the chase. But who would turn out to be the hound? Who the fox? David suspected Pokey had the unexpected up his sleeve.

'Will he try to kill me?' Mr Moore asked.

David hesitated. 'He might kill you.'

Mr Moore nodded quickly. 'It's all right. I would do anything for my daughter.'

David squeezed his hand. 'I'll bring her back to you. I swear it.'

They shut themselves in the booth a few minutes before sunset. Downtown Abolene was a corner gas station and a coffee shop. The evening light, filtered through the surrounding forest, was a haunting glow of orange and green. Pokey did not keep them waiting long. Mr Moore answered on the first ring. David put his ear to the phone.

'Listen,' Pokey said. 'Strap something to the briefcase to make it buoyant. A couple of boards will do. Take Tattler Road north out of town five miles to Mercury. Make a left. Mercury dead ends in the trees. Follow the path off the end of the road that leads to the river. Place the suitcase in the water and leave the area immediately. Do this now. I won't wait long.'

Pokey hung up. Mr Moore stared at him in surprise. David had not told him that this would be the probable scenario. 'Where am I going to get a couple of boards?' he asked.

'I have them in the jeep,' David said. 'Let's go.'

David followed Mr Moore towards the drop off spot, in a separate jeep, but did not turn onto Mercury. His maps showed another road and path that led to the river, two miles downstream. It was David's hope to come upon Pokey from behind, as the guy reached to snatch the briefcase from the river. David radioed Ned of his plan, once more cautioning his boss and the waiting agents to keep their distance.

The river was called Wild Current. David was displeased to see it deserved its title. He had hoped for a little creek that would not be able to carry the briefcase far. In reality the river was many feet deep, at least a hundred feet wide, and it flowed as if the Indian monsoon had just passed over. It could not be crossed without a raft of some kind. How would Pokey fetch the money from the river, David wondered? Perhaps he would have a long net of some kind? Cautious, staying in the shelter of the woods, his gun in one hand and his scanning device for the directional beepers in the other, David hiked upstream. He watched on his scanner as Mr Moore reached the river and let go of the briefcase. For a minute the two beepers in the briefcase, and the one in the father's shirt pocket, separated. Then Mr Moore's went off.

'Good,' David whispered.

Now the two beepers moved towards him at brisk speed, one flashing red on his miniature screen, the other, the tiniest one in the money, green, each overlaying the other. The two miles between him and the beepers was quickly cut to one mile, then a half mile. David's heart pounded when, one quarter mile upstream, the beepers halted in place.

'I've got him,' David whispered, excited.

Not yet. A quarter of a mile upstream the river narrowed in a stony gorge. The walls were sheer granite; David saw no way to hike down to the spot where his scanner said the briefcase must be, where Pokey must be. From behind a tree, David searched the riverside with a pair of miniature binoculars. The problem was there was no riverside. Yet the briefcase had halted. Had the flotation boards snagged on a protruding branch? Damn, he couldn't even spot the briefcase. Yet his scanner maintained it was still in the middle of the river, dead centre in fact, only two hundred yards from his position. The evening light was failing swiftly, but he still should have been able to see it. For one of the few times in his life, David was utterly perplexed.

Then the twin dots, red and green, began to crawl towards the opposite side of the river, and David understood. Even with no briefcase in sight. David had anticipated the unexpected and still it had caught him by surprise.

Pokey had snagged the case from the *floor* of the river. He must have donned scuba gear after calling them. Undoubtedly, he had previously prepared the river bed with strong ropes and cables to hang onto. David watched in horror as the twin dots reached the edge of the river and continued *through* the seemingly solid granite wall. Pokey had known of this spot for a long time, David thought. He understood the second dimension to Pokey's escape route. A cave emptied into the river at this spot. Another time of the year, it was probably visible, but not now.

David watched as the blinking dots accelerated at speed, away from him. Pokey had reached dry land, removed his fins, dropped his tanks. He was on the other side of an impassable river, on the backside of the far granite wall. To put it bluntly: he was getting away, and there was nothing David could do to stop him.

At the moment. The directional beepers had a range of three miles, four if conditions were ideal. David hastened back to his car. Now he had no choice. He had to call for reinforcements. Carefully, he outlined to Ned what had happened. Ned was still optimistic.

'We can flood that part of the forest with our people,' Ned said. 'We'll get rafts if we have to. As long as he has the beeper, we have him.'

'He's smart,' David warned. 'He'll drop the briefcase soon. He might even find the other beeper and destroy it. We must move fast.'

Pokey moved quickly. Fortunately, as David had run downstream to his car, a quarter of a mile away through the trees, on the other side of the river, Pokey had done likewise. Unfortunately, when David paused to report to Ned, Pokey gained substantial ground on him. Still, David was fast and in excellent shape. He believed he could catch up with the guy. Especially since, according to his scanner, Pokey was veering back towards the river. The move surprised David until he saw the twin lights pause up ahead beside the water. He would have given a lot to have been able to see his adversary at that point, even with his binoculars. But there was a curve in the river that blocked his vision. Yet David did not feel he needed to see Pokey to understand what he was doing, especially when the two coloured lights separated and the green dot began to race down the river, while the red remained where Pokey had paused.

'A boat,' David whispered to himself. 'He has a boat.'

The kidnapper had transferred the loot into the boat

and left the briefcase lying on the shore. Again, David had no choice. On foot, he could not possibly keep up with a boat being swept along by that current. Pokey would be out of range in minutes. David raced back to his car, scanned the map, and felt a burst of relief. The river flowed parallel to Tattler Road. At the very least, he should be able to keep Pokey in range for some time, even if he couldn't drive his jeep through the trees to the river to intercept him. Momentarily leaving the woods and pulling onto the main road, David radioed Ned and explained the new twist. Ned's optimism remained high.

'As long as the green light blinks,' Ned said, 'we know where the money is, and we know where he is.'

'Yeah,' David agreed, feeling far from certain, even as he raced a parallel course to his adversary, his fellow agents converging on his course. Pokey had considered every angle, David thought. The time of day, the amount of light – enough illumination to snag a floating object, not enough to be spotted underwater. The cave, the bend in the river. The directional beeper in the briefcase. What a brilliant mind. Yet why hadn't Pokey considered the possibility of a second beeper? Clearly, he understood FBI procedures and technical capabilities. He had his boat, he was moving fast. But with all that he was only postponing the inevitable. There were too many agents in the area. The net was tightening. Soon he would be squeezed out.

But that gut feeling was back.

David glanced at his scanner. Already he had moved out of range of the red light, the briefcase, the one Pokey had left beside the river when he had jumped into his boat. It was no surprise to David that he was receiving no signal from the red beeper. But what if he were to turn around, drive back to the other beeper? He should receive a signal from it then. It had been working when Pokey had left it. There was no reason to think it would not be working now. Of course, that would be insane, to turn around. He was closing on his adversary. To turn away from him now, after having come so far, would be madness.

Yet the feeling inside would not go away.

The certainty, that he was being played for the biggest fool of all time.

A hundred agents are after the green beeper. If I turn around, it will make no difference. I do not have to be there to read Pokey his rights. I just have to be there when Angela sees her father again.

David slammed on the brakes and spun the car in the opposite direction. It took him fifteen minutes to reach the point on the road where he should have been a mile from where Pokey had dropped the briefcase.

But there was no red light blinking on his scanner.

There was nothing. David called Ned.

'Did you send an agent to fetch the briefcase?' David asked.

'No,' Ned said. 'Do you think that's necessary?'

'Why don't you. For my peace of mind.'

'It's done.'

David rang off, consumed with the horrible suspicion that Ned and his men were chasing a decoy. Pokey had not climbed into a boat. He *had* found the second directional beeper. He had sent it downstream while he . . . what? Where was he now? David felt panic rising. Pokey could be anywhere.

Think man! Think of everything he's shown you.

All right, David told himself. Stay cool. Pokey had wanted to meet up here in Oregon. Why? He probably was calling from here all along. He had to be familiar with the area. Indeed, very familiar because he knew about the cave. He couldn't have just stumbled upon the thing. He must have grown up around here, and been to the river in the middle of summer, when the river was low and part of the cave was visible. David decided to accept that as fact one. He didn't have time for doubts. OK, what was fact two? Pokey could scuba dive. Perhaps he had been taught around here, in a lake or something. It might be possible to search through the records of every diving shop in that part of Oregon, see if anyone remembered instructing . . . Wait a second! It was simpler than that! Pokey had been underwater when he had grabbed the briefcase. He must have rented air-filled tanks in the last few days. Today even, probably locally.

David got on the line to the Portland office and asked them to get him a list of the five closest diving shops to Abolene. They were back to him in two minutes. There was only one diving shop close to Abolene, in Farside, twenty miles away. It was actually a sporting goods store, but they sold and serviced dive equipment. David called them. This is the FBI. Believe it, buddy. Did you refill a tank for an older guy in the last two days? You did? This morning? Do you have his name? Sampson Pincher? Do have his address? No? How about his diver's ID? Do you have the number? A PADI card number 9102027320? Excellent. Thank you for your time.

David called the Portland office back. Ring PADI and get the last address of this guy. Quickly! They called David back in ten minutes. Sampson Pincher, it turned out, lived ten miles outside of Abolene in the woods, in the other direction, away from the river. David took the address and thanked the Portland office for their help. He did not bother to contact Ned. If Angela was in the woods with Sampson, he didn't want a swat team breaking branches at his back while he snuck up on the house. Just the three of them would be just fine, he thought.

David *knew* Sampson was Pokey. What he did not know was how loyal the guy at the sporting goods store was to his customers. Not for a moment had he thought that he had to order the store clerk not to call Sampson and warn him that the FBI was curious about his air tanks. But it was these little details that made the world such a fucked up place to live in and raise a family. The store clerk and his conscientious customer neurosis was every bit as fucked as the fact that Sandy Quin's office happened to be one of the few offices in all of Las Vegas with a balcony that overlooked the hotel fountain.

Parking at a respectable distance from the Sampson residence, David crept through the woods towards the lone dark house that sat in the middle of the thorny meadow like the witch's house in every fairy tale that had ever been written to give children nightmares. The light in the west was almost gone but there was a moon. He was more than a little surprised when a shotgun blast burst from one window and the bark on the tree beside his head splintered. David fell to his belly behind a clump of weeds that looked like poison ivy.

'How the fuck did you find me?' a voice called out, the same voice as Pokey's.

'How the fuck did you know I would find you?' David called back. Sampson had obviously been waiting for him with shotgun in hand.

'The sporting good store called!'

'That was nice of them!'

'What are we going to do now?'

'Let Angela go! Then we can do anything you want!'

'Fuck you!' Sampson fired again. The round tore over David's head, causing him no personal damage but inspiring him to back up another thirty yards from the perimeter of the meadow. He realized that Sampson had no idea he was alone. The guy probably assumed his cabin was surrounded. David wondered if that might not be a bad strategy, to bring in the swat team. Yet his gut feeling screamed *no*! It didn't matter. After ten minutes of wasted observation of the house, David realized he was no longer alone in the woods. Silent as a small army of trolls wielding axes, agents with high powered rifles equipped with infra-red scopes were spreading out around him in the trees. Ned appeared by his side.

'Where did you come from?' David whispered. 'Did the Portland office call you?'

'We had a directional beeper on your jeep.'

'You bugged me? Goddam you, Ned. You don't trust me any more.'

'Quite the opposite. If we screwed up, which we did, I trusted you would be the first to figure it out. I also trusted that you would want to try to save her alone.'

'For good reason. This guy will kill her if we piss him off.'

Ned was impatient. The last few days had been hard on him. David had to remind himself that the man was near seventy. 'What do you suggest then? That we back off? He has his money. Now he'll kill her.'

'He doesn't care about the money. It's a play piece on his FBI game board. He's upset that we've caught him, but he's happy about it too. Now he gets to barter with us, face to face. I have to go in alone. I have to talk to him.'

'He might kill you before you get to the door.'

'It wouldn't surprise me one bit.'

'How do you know he wants to talk to you?'

'He likes to talk. He just couldn't on the phone because he knew we would trace him.'

'Why don't we tell him that he's surrounded and that he should surrender?'

'That won't work. Don't even try it. He'll make *Angie* cry.'

Ned considered. 'I don't like this. You're taking a big chance with your own life.' He paused. 'You haven't become reckless, have you, since Sandy?'

David kept his voice even. 'I just want to get the girl back to her family.'

'Why don't I go in?'

David chuckled. 'He would definitely shoot you before you got to the door.'

Ned was insulted. 'Well, if you're going in, tell me where you've got Failla's loot stashed. I'm about to retire. It won't do you any good if you're dead.'

'So you did know I had his money?'

'His casino receipts show he withdrew a million in cash before he went to meet you. Ten thousand hundred dollar bills.' He added, 'But I never showed the people at your hearing those receipts.'

'Are you the only one who saw those receipts?'

'Yes.'

'You're the boss. Why didn't you turn me in?'

Ned sighed. 'You know why.'

David understood. He was the son Ned never had. But he was not the good son. He kept breaking things, like his heart.

'It's under my bed in my apartment in Iowa. I haven't spent a dime of it.'

Ned was anxious. 'I was only joking. You didn't have to tell me.' Ned put his hand on David's shoulder. 'You be careful. Your life is as important as Angela's. Don't trade yourself for her.'

'I wouldn't think of it,' David lied. It was his main option. 'Do me one favour, Ned. While I'm in there, keep the boys on the swat team back.'

'I'll do what I can.'

David called out to Sampson. Let's talk face to face, work out a deal. Sampson was interested. But he wanted David to approach wearing only his shorts. David didn't complain, although the evening air was brisk. He was happy he had put on underwear that morning. Then he remembered that he hadn't even gone to bed the previous night.

The log cabin was rectangular, plain, a smoking chimney at one end, a propane tank at the other. The shadows clung to the structure like black halos did to TV evangelists. Walking towards it, arms up in the air, David wondered what it would be like to take a round of twelve-gauge shot in the belly. Talk about a gut feeling – that's what had got him into this situation. Yet, despite his gruesome thoughts, he found he was not afraid for his own life. What a brave man, he thought. Definitely, there were occasions when suicidal tendencies came in handy. He stopped at the door and knocked. Sampson called for him to come in.

The interior of the cabin was hot. Sampson had a fire going that was large enough to cremate a body. Perhaps, before David had showed, that's what he had intended to use it for. Or maybe Sampson had caught a chill during his dive. The crackling orange light flooded the cramped front room. The furniture was old, pieces given away free after a garage sale. Sampson sat on the floor with Angela, near the fire. David understood. Sampson had drawn the curtains on the front windows but the side windows were uncovered. Sampson was probably aware what excellent shots the FBI had.

Sampson looked like a messiah for the homeless. His long white hair fell over his barrel chest like strands of broken kite string. His face was sun worn, lined; it looked as if he used a burning pan instead of a hand mirror to shave in. In the light of the fire, his eyes were twin rubies stolen from a voodoo doctor's private deity. His brown leather coat was dirty, his blue jeans patched. The shotgun in his hand, however, looked clean enough. He pointed it at David.

'Sit on the floor and keep your hands where I can see them,' he said in Pokey's raspy voice.

'All right,' David said, going down on his knees, a position in which he could spring up quickly if he had to.

Angela was dressed much like her captor: blue jeans, a leather coat. The clothes were oversized and probably belonged to Sampson. Her long brown hair was clean, remarkably shiny for a captive, and there were no marks on her face. A pretty girl with a nice figure, she had a pouting nose and well defined cheekbones. Yet the innocent brown eyes that had stared out from the cover of *Time* had seen too much in the last few days to ever be innocent again. A bloodstained bandage covered her right hand. David glanced at the glass jar on the mantelpiece above the fireplace, the one holding the thumb. David was not sickened but relieved. He had feared much worse. Yet he knew there was still time for that. Angela stared at him with a hope so great it was close to despair.

Sampson smiled. He needed dental work. 'How did you find me?'

David explained. Sampson listened closely, and with approval. He nodded as he described his call to the sporting goods store. 'Freddy called me after you called him,' he explained. 'I've bought stuff from him for years.'

'I will have to meet this Freddy,' David said.

Sampson chuckled. 'But don't be too hard on him. He ran his motorcycle into a tree when he was sixteen, hurt his head. He's pretty stupid.' Sampson smoothed his left hand over the twin barrels of his shotgun. Briefly, David wondered if he had reloaded.

'Why didn't you flee when Freddy called?' David asked.

'I was doing just that when you appeared. I almost got you, didn't I?'

David shrugged. 'It looks like you have a second chance.'

Sampson was amused. 'Where do we go from here?'

'Do you want to surrender?' David asked.

'No. You have to get us out.'

'I can get you out. Not her. She has to stay.'

'No way,' Sampson said flatly. 'I give her up, I'm as good as dead.'

'You're wrong. Listen to my proposal. This cabin is surrounded by a swat team. That's a fact. You know that. But if you let her go right now, I can give her instructions to carry to my boss to allow you and I to leave here without interference.'

'Your swat team will try to take me out before we reach the car,' Sampson said. 'That's a fact.'

'Not if you and I are close together, walking under a blanket. In that situation, they will not be able to get a clear shot at you. They won't risk my life to kill you. They'll let us go, and once we're on the road, we can drive all the way to Canada if you want, or Mexico if you prefer. You can let me go once you're out of the US. I'm serious when I say I'm the only one who can get you out of here.'

Sampson studied him. 'I see that you are.' Then he shook his head. 'But I don't want to leave Angie. She must come.'

David shook his head. 'They will not let her come. It doesn't matter what I tell them. They will open fire, risk killing all three of us, before they let you take her again. That is another fact.'

Sampson considered. 'Getting to the car and on the road will be the most difficult part. We'll compromise, you and I. The three of us will leave together, under a blanket, and then, once we are out of the woods, I will release Angie. They can follow us that far to be sure I keep my word.'

'But they will not let you put her in the car. They will shoot you first.'

Sampson showed anger. 'As we leave here, you will explain the situation to them. You will tell them they have no choice.'

David relaxed a notch. Sampson was accepting his basic proposal. 'It would be better if you allowed me to explain the situation to them ahead of time.'

'No. I don't want you out of my sight.'

'Why not?' David asked.

In response Sampson withdrew a hunting knife from his back pocket. The fiery light in his eyes shone with cold malice. 'I told you not to try to capture me. You disobeyed me. I told you what the penalty of disobedience would be.'

Angela trembled; tears ran over her cheeks. Her eyes – they went to the knife, to David, pleading, imploring. He knew if he failed to save her those eyes would haunt him for the rest of his life.

'Please,' she whispered to him.

David spoke quickly, firmly. 'The time for that nonsense is past. You have been caught. I can help you escape. If you hurt her any more, they will never let you go, even if I ask them. Put away your knife.'

Sampson grinned, a steely affair. He scratched the blade over the barrel of the shotgun, aggravating their taut nerves. 'I have so little of Angie to take with me. Just a finger. I need more to remember her by.'

Angela broke down then, sobbing. Like a cornered animal, she made a useless try for the door. It was only then David saw that her ankles were bound together. She got nowhere; her face slapped the floor. Sampson reeled her back in by her hair. He pressed her cheek to his, the knife to her face.

'I think I'll take your nose,' he said to her in his hellish voice. 'Better to smell you with my dear.' He stuck the tip of the blade in her right nostril, which trickled blood from her fall.

'Wait!' David said. 'I'm the one who disobeyed you. Why don't you take my nose? It's nicer than hers anyway.'

Sampson was not interested. 'You're a guy,' he said.

Angela's terror-stricken eyes would not leave David. Instinctively, he climbed from his knees. Sampson shook his shotgun. David sat back down. He would not be able to save the girl if his intestines were hanging out. At the same time, he could not sit and watch as her face was carved up. Desperately, he struggled for the perfect thing to say. But what could you offer a madman that wanted a girl's nose?

'Take her other thumb,' David blurted out.

Sampson paused, the blade still up Angela's right nostril. 'Why the thumb?' he asked conversationally. David replied in the same tone.

'The nose will not come off cleanly. You'll be left with a mess of tissue that won't resemble anything. But if you take the other thumb, you'll have a nice matching pair. You can put the left one in your jar with the right one.'

Sampson raised a bushy eyebrow. 'You have a point there.' He turned to Angela. 'What do you think, my dear?'

Angela shook her head minutely. Her eyes went right back to David. Why was he offering the lunatic parts of her body? Why couldn't he save her? David wished he could explain that the world did not always offer a choice between good and evil. Usually, if you lived long enough, the choices were between bad and worse. Personally, he would rather lose another thumb than his nose. But he didn't know what to tell her so he spoke to Sampson instead. In doing so, he betrayed the last vestige of hope in her eyes. The fireworks were still a few minutes off, but it was as if she died as the words came out his mouth.

'Cut the other thumb off and let's get out of here,' David said.

Sampson obliged him. He worked slowly. Angela screamed all the while. David stared at the floor and listened to his heartbeat, the wind through the trees, the breaking of branches as the swat team shifted uneasily in the woods. With Angela's cries, David knew any possibility of him being allowed to escort Sampson and Angela away from the cabin had vanished. They would try to take Sampson down before he reached the car, blanket or no blanket. Still, David wanted Sampson to bring the blanket. David believed it could come in handy. He had a change of heart as he listened as Angela's wailing died in a shocked gulp. He would escort Sampson no further than the front door. He would rest his chances – and Angela's – on his trained reflexes rather than a sniper's sweaty trigger finger. And who knows, maybe Angela's thumb could be sewn back on if they got her to a hospital in time.

Time was a reason for his change of heart.

That, and the fact that he wanted to kill Sampson with his bare hands.

Sampson bandaged Angela's gory wound with an oil-stained rag. He stood up cautiously, still crouching, and undid the binds on Angela's ankles. She was a sack of potatoes dripping carrot juice. Sampson had to pull her to her feet. He gestured to David with the tip of his shotgun.

'Grab that blanket there,' he ordered. 'We'll put that over us.'

David stood. The blanket was caught beneath the corner of a wooden rocking chair. It looked as if a dog had slept on it. David pulled it free and slowly stepped towards Sampson and Angela. They had the fire at their back, two twisted figures in silhouette. Sampson was no fool; he continued to keep his head low, his shotgun poked in Angela's side. Yet David thought him the biggest fool to ever cross his path. Because he had tortured a young woman in front of him and David had this thing against guys who did that. Guys like that really pissed him off. Just look at his past. David would have liked to have enlightened Sampson about Failla right then. Sampson didn't know he wasn't the only lunatic in the room. David approached to within six feet, holding the blanket open in front of him with both hands.

'Let's do it,' Sampson said.

'Let's do it,' David repeated. He threw the blanket towards Sampson and took a quick step to the left. Sampson did exactly what David thought he would do, what normal reflexes demanded when an enemy threw up a screen. As the sheet lazily floated towards Sampson, threatening to cover his head, he turned his weapon away from Angela and fired at the blanket. Before he'd had time to recover from the recoil and understand that Special Agent Conner was not standing behind the ripped blanket with a hole in his body, David struck from the right side. His left foot lashed out, striking Sampson's hip, sending the guy crashing into Angela. The two fell to the floor, the shotgun to the side. David went for the weapon first, not Angela. He honestly believed that once he had the shotgun everything would be all right.

It should have been true. Nine times out ten it would have been.

Sandy should have escaped Failla. Ninety-nine times out of a hundred.

Sampson scampered to his feet. Angela got up a bit slower, but had some life left in her, after all. She broke free of Sampson's grip and retreated towards the fire to form the tip of their unstable triangle. By then David had retrieved the shotgun and had it pointed at Sampson's chest. Slowly, deliberately, David cocked the hammer. How tempting it was, the thought of squeezing the trigger.

'Fuck,' Sampson said bitterly.

David smiled. 'Fuck you.'

A bullet whizzed through the uncovered side window. Glass cracked and fell to the floor. Sampson doubled up and dropped to his knees, leaving only Angela and David standing. David understood in an instant that a member of the swat team had finally got a good sight on Sampson and rolled the dice. For a moment, that seemed OK. Sampson was bleeding from the left armpit and although it was clearly not a fatal wound, it was nice to see the guy hurt. Yet Angela was staring at David again. Those imploring eyes– where did they come from? She was saved. She could have her thumb sewn back on. She could return to being homecoming queen at her high school and next year go to college. Later, she could marry a doctor and have two beautiful kids, even learn to play the piano. You could play the piano with nine fingers, David told himself. Then he noticed that there was a hole in Angela's brown leather jacket, above her heart. It was such a small hole, it didn't look that important. As if in a dream, she slowly raised her right hand and covered it. See, now it's gone, David thought.

Wishful thinking.

Blood gushed around her fingers.

Her head swam to the side, her eyes dimmed.

'Oh God,' David cried, barely catching her as she fell. 'Jesus Christ.' He laid her on the floor, one hand behind her head, the other holding the shotgun. He moved his free hand to press on her wound, felt a thick sound of liquid beneath her coat. Her eyes stared up at him, at the ceiling, the sky beyond. 'No,' David whispered.

Yes. She was gone.

Sampson giggled. David glanced over at him.

'I won't even get murder one,' Sampson said. 'I didn't kill her. I'll be out in five years, eight at the outside.' He paused to snort. 'Ironic, isn't it?'

David let go of Angela and stood above Sampson. He placed the barrel between the man's eyebrows. 'You will not be out in five years. You will not leave this cabin.'

Sampson laughed. 'What are you going to do, shoot me?'

'Yes,' David whispered.

Sampson was afraid, as Failla had been afraid, in the end. Indeed, he said the exact same words. 'But you're FBI.'

'Yes. But with me it stands for Fire Between the I's.'

David shot him between the eyes, took off the top of his head. Then he carried Angela out of the cabin, past the swat team, who waited with their smoking guns, to Ned. He asked his boss where Angela's father was right now. As pale as the moon, Ned told him Mr Moore was at the hotel where they had stayed the previous night. David nodded. He carried the girl's body to the jeep. He rested her in the back seat and drove her home to Mr Moore. He kept his word to the man, yeah, brought him back his dead daughter. His word was as good as gold. False gold found on the bottom of cold streams. He had almost thrown the sack of ransom money in the fire. But it belonged to the government, not the mob, and he couldn't be bothered stealing it either. All the money in the world couldn't bring either of them back.

There was another hearing. Why did he kill Sampson? Was it necessary? He mumbled his answer, stared at the far wall, the TV cameras. He was a celebrity. They let him go – can't reprimand a hero and enjoy the public's support. They recommended counselling, however. Dirty Dave needs a wash. So he went out and bought himself a bottle, and overslept his counselling appointment by two days. No one cared. He was quitting anyway.

David Conner awoke in the middle of his late night flight to Idaho from a bad dream. Like an old war wound, he knew the nightmare well. Hotel fountains spouting orange blood. A fat man crying in a barren desert. A young girl's eyes piercing through a fiery sky. David signalled for the flight attendant, asked if she could please bring him a drink. He would have preferred a sleeping pill. The alcohol left a bitter taste in his mouth. He never was able to go back to sleep. He just sat and stared out of the black window.

CHAPTER THREE

Lucy and Vera Temple walked their mountain bikes down the last portion of the unpaved path. They had left Camp Paradise twenty minutes ago; it had taken them that long to ride and walk through the woods to reach the only road that connected them to civilization. Paradise was located on a mesa-topped mountain named Flattop, at an elevation of four thousand feet. The road passed by the camp three miles to the south. When their group had come to Paradise, three days earlier, they had had the advantage of Dr Henry's four wheel drive truck. It was the only vehicle besides their bikes that could tackle the rough path that wound between the camp and the road. But since then Dr Henry hadn't let anyone borrow the truck. Dr Henry had even taken to sleeping in it, under the stars. Lucy thought he had a fetish about the stupid truck, saw it as the all powerful male lover he had yet to find. Dr Henry was unabashedly gay.

'I heard the reporter's supposed to be cute,' Lucy said to her sister, who walked her mountain bike a few feet in front of her.

'Who told you that?' Vera asked over her shoulder. 'Dr Henry?'

'Yeah.'

'He's never met him. He's never even seen his picture. He just talked to him on the phone.'

'Dr Henry can tell a lot by a guy's voice,' Lucy said. 'I think he had his EEG wires hooked up to the line. Ran a brain wave coherence program on the guy. Said the reporter operated from a purely primal level, pure sexuality.'

Vera shook her head. 'All that information on a guy from ten words spoken over a static filled phone line? I swear, sometimes Dr Henry thinks he knows more than the Big Mind.'

'Vera. Sometimes Dr Henry thinks he *is* the Big Mind.' The path widened. Lucy caught up with her sister, skipping as she manoeuvred her bike over dirt bumps. The day was bright and warm, the sky the colour of the sea as seen from the moon. Summer was not far away, Lucy thought happily. She loved the hot months the way most people loved a long massage, the heat sinking into her bones, the cool sweat on her bare arms. Speaking of summer – below them, close to the road, June Lake came into view. Lucy was inspired. 'Why don't we go for a swim before the reporter gets here?' she said.

'We didn't bring our suits,' Vera said.

'It doesn't matter.'

'How do we know the reporter's not here already?'

Lucy nodded to where the road met the path, the spot where Dr Henry had told the man to meet them. 'I don't see him. Do you see him? No? Well, that probably means he's not here.'

Vera frowned. 'But what if he shows up while we're swimming?'

'Then he'll see us naked. He'll get all excited and probably want to have sex. But because we look exactly alike he won't know which one of us to jump. So he'll probably just have to have us both at the same time!'

Vera stared at her, incredulous. 'You are sick.'

'I'm not. I'm just horny. I haven't had a guy since Neil, and he didn't count.'

'What was wrong with Neil? You went with him for six months.'

Lucy laughed. 'I never told you this. He was so afraid of

catching HIV or herpes or whatever that he always wore *three* condoms whenever we made love. Do you know how long it takes to put on three condoms? His dick was so insulated I always felt like I had a plastic pear inside me.'

'You mean a plastic banana.'

'No! A pear! That was the other thing wrong with Neil!'

Vera was disgusted. 'You can't seduce the reporter, no matter how handsome he is. Professor Spear brought us here for an important purpose. He paid for this trip out of his own pocket. We have work to do.'

'You may have work to do. I'm here to relax.'

'We're having a session as soon as we get back,' Vera said.

'We are? But we had one this morning.'

'Yes, but this morning you kept interrupting the Big Mind to ask what the reporter was like. We didn't do any real work.'

They reached the edge of the lake. Lucy set down her bike and undid the buttons on her yellow blouse. She took off the tiny gold crucifix she always wore and put it in the blouse pocket. It had been a gift from her mother. If she had wished, she could have worn her white shorts into the water. They were as skimpy as a bathing suit. But she loved to swim naked, in a cool lake, especially with a cute guy. Not that she was a tramp. She enjoyed infuriating her sister with her loose tongue, but in reality she had only slept with five guys in her life. Not many, she thought, for a twenty-eight-year-old redhead.

'I thought what the Big Mind had to say about him was interesting,' Lucy said, finishing with her blouse and kneeling to untie her tennis shoes. 'Did you notice it repeated how brave and resourceful the man was? How he'd had a life rich in excitement but also filled with sorrow?'

Vera nodded. 'He's probably been all over the world on assignments. But I still wish he wasn't coming this week.'

'Why not? The Big Mind said he's important. That he can help us more than we can imagine. It also said we can help him. I'm glad he's coming. I would like to get some real recognition for Spear's work outside of New Age magazines.'

'Then we'll never have any peace.'

Lucy kicked off her shoes. 'Yeah, but we'll have more dates. Just think how many guys will want to go out with a modern day witch?' Lucy pulled down her shorts and mooned her sister. 'Especially with an ass like this?' She skipped into the water.

'Don't drown!' Vera called.

'You can always save me!' Lucy called back. *Jesus, it's cold*. She ran in quickly and, as soon as it was deep enough, dove underwater. The jolt of the frigid water sent her heart hammering. She screamed as she resurfaced, kicking fiercely. June Lake was a rough circle, perhaps a half mile across. It had been her intention to swim across and back, but with her skin already turning blue she wondered if she would make it. Vera waved and Lucy waved back.

'Ah,' Lucy moaned in pleasure a few minutes later. A warm patch mysteriously appeared, the water at least fifteen degrees higher than the rest of the lake. Rolling onto her back, she decided she would try to stay in it as long as possible. Relaxing, with only the blue overhead to fill her vision, she felt unconnected to her body. Yet the feeling was no stranger to her. In the presence of the Big Mind, she often felt as if the physical plane was nothing but a drawing sketched on a canvas much larger than the sky. She had objected to Vera about another session but they were really no work at all. They often brought deep peace.

Lucy had discovered both her sister's talent and her own while working her way through undergraduate school at Stanford doing part-time massage therapy. She had a state licence in massage; she charged forty dollars an hour for her services, although from a fellow student she often accepted half that. Any new thing caught her attention; her list of body techniques was consequently impressive. She knew shiatsu, Swedish, polarity, Raki, applied kinesiology and educational kinesiology. The latter two systems were related in the sense that they both used muscle testing, but were also quite different. Applied kinesiology, or AK, operated under the theory that every organ in the body had a muscle that corresponded to it. For example, the stomach could be tested by holding the arm straight out and turning the palm away from the body. The tester would then say 'Resist' and pull down on the arm. If the arm muscle locked, the stomach was probably fine. However, if the muscle failed to lock and the person could not resist then there was either something wrong with the muscle or the stomach. If the stomach was affected, the muscle was always weak, although the reverse was not true. Lucy often used AK at the end of a massage to balance a patient's major muscles and organs. Most people enjoyed the AK more than the massage itself.

Educational kinesiology, or EK, also used the locking of muscles to learn things. But whereas AK was directed at diagnosing and balancing the body, EK employed the body as a kind of living ouija board. If a question was asked and the arm was tested and the answer was no, the muscle would go weak. If the answer was yes, the muscle would remain strong. That was the theory at least, and Lucy had had good successes with it. Occasionally she might ask if a person's stomach was upset due to stress in school, or if it was a relationship problem. The accuracy was rather high, yet it was not a hundred per cent, and that bothered Lucy. Periodically she would test out the EK theory by asking questions she already knew the answers to. For example, 'Am I working on a girl?' 'Is this person an alien?' Sometimes the person's arm would remain strong when she asked if they were a robot. That made no sense to her.

Then, one day, a girl told Lucy to ask her body if she was pregnant. Before Lucy could move the arm into position, she knew the answer. It crystallized in her mind, not in the form of words, but as an unmistakable certainty. Yes, the girl was exactly nine weeks pregnant. Lucy blurted the fact out. Her patient was surprised, but not as surprised as Lucy was when the girl returned and informed her that she had been right. Nine weeks pregnant, exactly. Not ten or eight.

After that, Lucy discovered she did not need muscle testing to get answers. They just popped in her mind. She also noticed that if Vera was in the room, her accuracy was much greater. In fact, if she focussed her attention on wanting to know something, Vera had an involuntary habit of stopping what she was doing and going still. At such times, Lucy would feel as if an invisible thread connected them. And an answer would come, once again, not a voice, simply a certainty of what was true. Lucy was both delighted and frightened. They were both majoring in psychology and planned to go on to graduate school; neither had a desire to become professional psychics. But each time Lucy gave a mysterious answer, another new referral came. Soon her 'massage' business was booming and she hardly had time to study.

At the end of their senior year at Stanford, Professor Spear gave an open talk on campus on his theory of 'genetic memory'. Lucy had heard fascinating things about him through the grapevine and dragged Vera to the lecture. Spear spoke of how he used a technique of 'mutual hypnosis' to take small groups of people to a heretofore unobtainable level of consciousness where they were able to tap into the racial memories stored in the DNA. Lucy found his lecture both enlightening and confusing, the latter because even though Spear used many New Age phrases he was clearly an atheist. His past lives had nothing to do with reincarnation. Indeed, he angered a few people in the audience when he denounced such 'delusionary' practices as past life regressions. He even made several pointed remarks about the 'stupidity' of modern religions. He was a clearly a man who didn't care what others thought, yet at the same time a person who railed against all forms of human ignorance.

Lucy did not agree with everything he said but she was anxious to meet him. His grey hair was wild, his dark eyes riveting. For a man who believed in nothing spiritual, he gave off an amazing amount of charismatic energy. After the talk, Lucy dragged Vera with her to the front. To her surprise, Spear gave her a few private minutes to explain her experiences with AK. She even told him how Vera improved her accuracy. Spear was interested. He gave them his home number, asked them to call him.

He believed they could be ideal candidates for his practise of mutual hypnosis.

Two years later, they were still chasing memories.

Spear had not wanted the reporter to come. But the Big Mind had insisted. Yet Spear did not always listen to what their group channelled, not when it disagreed with his theories. For the Big Mind said they *were* spirit, souls evolving back towards the divine. Even to Lucy, a fan of the Professor's, Spear's relationship to the Big Mind was at best curious. He was a disciple without a master. An astronomer who trusted the stars, but not his own telescope. Spear used the Big Mind but did not have faith in it. The Big Mind did not seem to mind.

'Lucy!' Vera called.

Lucy shifted from her back, looked towards shore. She was surprised to see how far out she had drifted in a few minutes. Did this lake have a current? Then again, time often escaped her when she was daydreaming. In sessions with the Big Mind, a million years could pass in a flash. Vera was anxiously pointing to the side of the lake. Lucy shifted her view to find a man taking pictures of her with a sophisticated camera. Could that be the reporter? The primal sex maniac? Quickly, Lucy swam towards shore, away from him, hoping he would avert his head when she climbed out of the water, give her a chance to get dressed. Vera moved between her and the man.

'I hope he's not a pervert,' Vera said.

Lucy had her back to both of them, pulling on her shorts. 'Has he put away his camera?'

'Yes. But he's coming this way.' Vera paused. 'He doesn't look like a reporter.'

'What does he look like?'

'Trouble.'

Lucy threw on her blouse, the material clinging to her damp skin. Finally, she turned around. The reporter, wearing grey slacks and a long-sleeved white shirt, strode towards them. His gait was smooth, graceful, but Lucy noted that he moved like a man who was used to being in command. She was perceptive when it came to such matters. He had an athlete's body. His features were dark, mysterious, but also a little weary. The Big Mind was right, Lucy understood. He had seen a lot in his life, much of it unpleasant. Yet he smiled as he came closer, a small black suitcase in one hand, his camera dangling around his neck.

'Hi,' he said. 'I'm David Nichols. Are you two the welcome committee?'

'Yeah,' Lucy said. 'Where's your car? We didn't see you drive up.'

He nodded down the road. 'I hid it off the pavement under a bunch of trees. I was told by the gentleman I spoke to this morning that I wouldn't be able to drive it to the camp. It's a rental – I don't want anyone to steal it while I'm here.'

'That was smart thinking,' Lucy said. She stepped forward and offered her hand. 'I'm Lucy Temple. This is my sister, Vera. We're students of Professor Spear's.'

'Hi,' Vera said softly, also offering her hand. 'Why were you taking pictures of my sister, Mr Nichols?'

The question did not disturb him. 'David, please. The lake looked so inviting with Lucy in it – I wanted to record the scene for posterity. I meant no offence.'

Lucy chuckled. 'It's no big deal. Just don't let *Time* magazine publish it. OK?'

'Sure.' He nodded to their bikes. 'Is this how we get to the camp?'

'Yes,' Lucy said. 'It's too bad we only have two. But I'll be happy to walk with you . . . David.'

'You can take my bike,' Vera said quickly. 'I don't want to return to the camp right away.'

Lucy was concerned. Vera had been having nightmares since their arrival in Idaho. Lucy slept in the room beside her and had twice heard Vera wake up moaning. But Vera had no explanation for the bad dreams, and offered no details of their contents. Lucy was puzzled. The camp was as comfortable as it was beautiful. Indeed, Spear had chosen the spot because of its serenity. Over the last couple of days, Vera had gone for long walks away from the camp and seemed unusually preoccupied.

'You're the one who told me we have a session scheduled for this afternoon,' Lucy said.

Vera crossed her hands over her chest as if she were cold. 'I'll be there. I just want to be alone for a few minutes, that's all.'

'You should keep your bike,' David said. 'I'll probably run it into a tree anyway.'

Vera studied him. Lucy knew her sister was even more perceptive than her when it came to people, except perhaps when it came to men. Vera had not had a boyfriend in ages.

'Are you sure?' Vera asked. 'It's a long walk to the camp. I'm used to it but you might find it strenuous.'

'I look forward to the exercise after my plane ride.' He

nodded to Vera. 'It was nice to meet you. Really, Vera, you're one of a kind.'

Vera had to smile. 'We're not so similar as we look. You'll learn that soon enough, I think.'

Lucy set off with their visitor, walking her bike beside him, despite his protests. 'The path only worsens the further you go,' she said. 'I don't mind walking.'

'I'm confused,' David said. 'This area's beautiful. I'd imagine it would be a favourite vacation spot. Why is the camp so difficult to reach?'

'It's got two strikes against it. It's old and it's small. It was built before the first world war and can hold only fifty people. Most groups looking for such places need more space. As a result, it hasn't been booked in years and the path hasn't been kept up. At least that's what Professor Spear says. Did you know he grew up around here?'

'I'm afraid I know little about your mentor, Miss Lucy.'

She laughed. 'You make me sound like the woman in Dracula.'

'Funny you should say that. That's exactly what I was thinking. Can you read minds? Are you a good witch or a bad witch?'

'Why,' she said, taking the tone of Dorothy in *The Wizard of Oz*, 'I'm not a witch at all!' She paused. 'I guess we must seem like a bunch of nuts to a big reporter like you.'

'I have an open mind.'

She eyed him from the side. 'Except when it come to stuff like this?'

He shrugged. 'Well.'

'You just need educating, that's all. By the time you leave here, you'll be a believer.'

'Is that what you are, Miss Lucy? A believer?'

'In a manner of speaking, yes. I believe we're all born believers.'

'Not me.'

'I don't believe you! Isn't there anything that fills you with awe?'

He hesitated. 'Beautiful redheads swimming naked in mountain lakes.'

Lucy blushed. 'I pray you were gentleman enough to avert your head as I climbed out of the water.'

'Only long enough to fit a more powerful lens in my camera.'

'Did you really take a picture of me naked?'

'Of course, I'm a reporter. I need a complete record of what goes on here.'

The blood in her cheeks sizzled. She was not the exhibitionist she pretended to be. 'Then I can only hope you were able to maintain a steady hand as you shot the picture.'

David smiled. 'Your sister thinks I'm a pervert.'

Lucy shook her head. 'Vera always takes a while to warm up to people. Also, as far as anything remotely sexual is concerned, she's pretty conservative.'

'Hmm. Doesn't seem that she inherited the quality.'

Lucy shook her head. 'You know, Mr Nichols, you've known me ten minutes and already you're embarrassing me.'

'I'm deeply sorry, Miss Lucy.'

'And stop calling me that!'

David laughed. 'Tell me about your group.'

'Are you starting work so soon? Are you going to pull out your recorder?'

'I don't need a recorder. I will remember every word you say.'

Lucy glanced over, caught his face in profile. He had a gift for making conversation, and there was nothing fake about him. Yet the things he said – it was as if he was unattached to the present situation. She didn't know if that was because the rest of his life had been so intense or if she was simply boring him. He wasn't boring her, however. Not with that body.

'You know, you don't act like a reporter,' she said.

'What do I act like?'

'A spy.'

He liked that. 'Maybe I am a spy. Maybe the FBI sent me here to see if your Big Mind knows next week's lottery numbers.'

'So you've heard about the Big Mind?'

He nodded. 'I've done a little research on you, not much. I have a lot of catching up to do if I'm to write an article on you. Go ahead, tell me about your group.'

'Well, first there's Margaret Farrow. She's not someone that channels the Big Mind, but she's been with Spear since he started his research into the field. You'll love her. Officially, she's Spear's assistant but she's more like our Mum. She cooks for us and takes care of us when we're sick. Margaret's one of the few people I've ever met who honestly seems to have no ego. She's just there for you. But don't get the impression she's dull. She has a mischievous sense of humour. The other day, when we first arrived here, she planted a boom box with a tape containing weird African animal sounds in the woods. She set it to go on at three in the morning. Scared the hell out of the whole group. Even Spear was up running around in his underwear.'

'She sounds like my kind of person,' David remarked.

'She's also crippled.'

'Seriously? How does she do all these things?'

'Her handicap don't slow her down one bit. She's an inspiration to us all. Wait till you see her in action. Then there's Dr Henry Deering. We just call him Dr Henry. He's not a member of the channelling group either, but he's been studying the lot of us for the last year. He's a medical doctor and also has a PhD in neurophysiology. He's an expert on brain waves. He's brought lots of EEG equipment with him. He specializes in how the three levels of the brain interact with each other. He's gay and real out front about it but not in an obnoxious way. He's the funniest guy you'll ever meet. But like Margaret, he'd do anything for you.'

David shrugged. 'I have friends who are gay. Sometimes I've thought of becoming gay myself.'

Lucy paused. 'Really?'

'What's the matter? Are you homophobic?'

'No. It's just that . . . It's just that you don't act gay.'

'That's because I'm a spy, Miss Lucy. I have to be careful how I act.'

Lucy frowned. 'Are you pulling my leg again?'

'What does your intuition tell you?'

She burst up. 'It's not working right now!'

'I'm teasing you. Tell me more about the others?'

She shook her head again. 'You are a character. OK, next we have Panda Gopal. He's from India. We call him our sage, although he's not much older than me. He has an extensive philosophical background. He's quiet, gentle. Unless you're talking about God, he won't say much.'

'How did he meet Professor Spear?' David asked.

'He had a dream about him and went looking for him. Next there's Tom Forester. He used to be a long distance truck driver. You know what it's like driving cross country? That endless line in the middle of the road can be hypnotic. To make a long story short, Tom always wanted to be a country western singer. He would sing at the top of his lungs as he barrelled down the highway. Not only that, he would tape himself, and then listen to the tape afterwards to see how he sounded. Well, one time he was playing the tape back and he heard this guy saying all this esoteric stuff. The problem was the guy was talking in his voice! He was the guy! Apparently, Tom had spaced out and gone into a trance and channelled a being on the other side.'

'On the other side of what?' David asked.

Lucy hesitated. 'The other side of death's door.'

'So what you're saying is that a ghost spoke through him?'

'It wasn't a ghost but an angel.'

David nodded. 'I see.'

'Oh brother, I'm doing a terrible job of explaining how respectable we've become. Spear's going to chew my ass off. Forget what I just said. Let me finish describing our group. There's Jon Horst, he's from Sweden. He used to have a magic show there where he bent spoons and stuff like that. The thing is, like Uri Geller, he could really do it. But Jon's always wanted to be an actor. Arnold Schwarzenegger is his hero. He came to the States looking for a Hollywood agent and met Spear instead. He hopes to use our work as a platform to riches and fame. He's excited you're here. He's probably going to corner you and show you a few of his psychic abilities.'

'Do you think his abilities are genuine?'

Lucy considered. 'Is this off the record?'

'Whatever you say, I will keep in the same safe place as your nude photos.'

She giggled. 'I think Jon used to possess all kinds of psychic abilities. But since meeting the Big Mind, those abilities have faded. I don't even know if he can bend spoons any more.'

'Why?'

'The Big Mind thinks those abilities are a waste of time.'

'What is the Big Mind?' David asked. 'Is it a being that you channel?'

'It's not a being *per se*. It says that it's what we are, our true self, our higher self. I know that must sound abstract, and it is, but once you've personally experienced the Big Mind coming through, it's hard to doubt its authenticity. But you've raised another point. We don't actually "channel" the Big Mind. By that I mean we don't go into a trance and leave our body and become unaware of what we are saying. The Big Mind says that channelling as it's usually practised destroys mind body coordination and does not develop a person spiritually.' Lucy paused. 'What I just said is true except for Vera. When the Big Mind comes through, she's gone. She remembers nothing of what is said, and she never speaks for the Big Mind herself.'

'Then why is she a member of the group?' David asked.

'Her presence allows us to experience the Big Mind that much clearer.'

'Forgive me, I think I'm missing an essential point. How do you contact the Big Mind? What did Professor Spear teach you that allows the group to function as a unit?'

'We call it "mutual hypnosis" for lack of a better expression. Say for example someone hypnotises you. He or she has you take a few deep breaths. You relax, imagine yourself sinking down – all the usual things. If the hypnotherapist is experienced, you'll settle into a restful state of consciousness. But that particular state has its limits. The therapist is speaking to you from the waking state. You're not in the waking state. If I may use an analogy, it's like he's on the surface of the lake, while you've plunged twenty feet under. He cannot communicate with you clearly. Granted, you can hear him clearly, but your mind is not at the same level. Does this make sense?'

'Sort of. Go on.'

'Spear taught us a technique whereby we take *each other* deeper. We don't use suggestion the way ordinary hypnosis does. Our individuality ceases to dominate. Like I said, we're still there. We're alert, we know what is happening around us. But a larger presence floods our souls. It fills the room like the aura of a magical being. It connects us, and at the same time, it's this connection that allows it to come through. There is group coherence, literally – Dr Henry has discovered that our separate brains begin to produce the same wave patterns. It's as if the group functions as one big brain, giving rise to a higher state of consciousness. That state is the Big Mind. When it's there, you know things you wouldn't otherwise know. You feel centred, free, like you're soaring through uncharted realms of existence. Yet, at the same time, it all feels perfectly natural. Like the Big Mind says – the experience of it is nothing more than the experience of our own inner nature.'

'But from what I've read, Professor Spear is an atheist. Like most scientists, he says consciousness is dependent on the human nervous system. When we die, we're dead. That all this past life regression stuff is doing, at best, is tapping into genetic memories. Otherwise, he says, it's illusionary.'

Lucy nodded. 'That is his opinion and I respect it. Certainly his work with us has shown that most of the past lives we pick up are related to our ancestors.'

'Most? Not all?'

'Sometimes we pick up lives – we don't know where they came from. Many are so ancient it's impossible to say whether they're related to someone in the group or not.'

'Who taught Professor Spear this technique you describe?' David asked.

'He learned it in Africa.'

'From whom?'

She hesitated. 'I don't know. He never talks about who taught him.'

'Aren't you curious about the source of the technique you practise? What if it came from a witch doctor at the head of a tribe of cannibals?'

Lucy laughed. 'I am curious but you can't press Spear for information he doesn't want to give. You can't joke with him the way you're joking with me. He won't like it. He dislikes it when the Big Mind jokes with him.'

'The Big Mind jokes? I'm gaining more respect for it all the time.'

'It's hilarious. It even told us a dirty joke the other day! Of course the joke came out of my mouth so maybe its source is a little suspect. I'll tell it to you later, when I know you better. But I must warn you, Spear didn't want you coming here, not now. If he's less than open, understand why.'

'What's so special about now?' David asked.

'We've been running into a wall for the last two years. We regress back along a particular genetic line, and if we're lucky, we eventually end up in the Stone Age, always in Africa. It's a trip being in the mind of those people because they're half human, half ape. Their thought processes are slow. They stare up at the moon at night and wonder why the lit portion keeps changing. They think there's really lots of moons.'

'And you're actually in their mind?'

'Yes. It's hard to believe, I know, but you're right there. You feel what they feel. You see what they see. But it's as if from a distance. The peace of the Big Mind smooths out the experience. For example, if someone's about to be killed, you're afraid but it's like it's happening on a movie screen.'

'But if they are killed, then how do you have their memory in your genes? It couldn't have been passed on at that point.'

'That's a perceptive question. Actually, we've never experienced the death of an ancestor in our regressions. If you think about it, that adds weight to Spear's perspective. But let me continue with this wall that we hit and why Spear's upset you're here now. Spear calls it the "Rational Thought Barrier". He says that it's difficult to regress prior to two million years because back then there *was* no humanity. In that realm, the age of the missing link, before men were men and women were eating apples off the wrong trees, we cannot go. At that point in our evolution, we weren't capable of storing memories, not in the sense that we do now. Therefore, there's nothing to remember. Yet, at the same time, he says there is a way to go back before then, way back, sixty million years in fact. He says he's done it before. He plans to show us the technique during this retreat.'

'Another technique he learned in Africa?'

'I believe so. He said the one time he did it was with a group in Africa. Why do you keep asking about Africa?'

'Just curious. Again, I'm confused about a couple of things. How can any mind-altering technique, no matter how powerful, allow him to help you regress to a time when there were no people? Sixty million years ago there were dinosaurs still walking around.'

'I don't know,' Lucy said.

'Have you asked him?'

'Of course. He says he'll show us. He's not one to boast. If he says we can regress back that far, then he has done it before.'

'Has he ever explained with whom he's done it?'

'No.'

David scratched his head. 'All this is new to me. It takes time to absorb. I'm confused how specifically the Big Mind helps you regress?'

'While the Big Mind is present, our consciousness is more unbounded. We just slide backwards. It's easier to do than to explain.'

'Essentially you use that state of consciousness as a springboard into the past?'

'A springboard, yes,' Lucy said. 'That's an astute analogy.'

'Thank you. I liked your one about women eating apples off the wrong trees. Tell me, what does the Big Mind say about your research into the past?'

'That it's a waste of time,' Lucy said.

'Really?'

'Actually, the Big Mind says it's foolish. That we would be better not doing it.'

David halted on the path. 'Then why do you do it? If you have such faith in the Big Mind?'

'Spear wants it done. He wants to prove the authenticity of the theory of genetic memory. If he's successful, it opens up a whole new dimension of what we as human beings are. And the research is fascinating. Don't get me wrong, the Big Mind does not oppose him. It opposes nothing. It embraces everything. But it often says the past is a lower state of consciousness. It's into the present moment. Be in the present moment. Live life now, fully. Drop all regret and anger about the past. Don't be anxious about the future. The past is dead and tomorrow will take care of itself. The Big Mind says this repeatedly.'

'Sounds like good advice. Maybe you should listen to it.'

Lucy eyed him again. 'Is there nothing in your past, Mr Nichols, that you would rather not drop?'

She may have hit a nerve. He lowered his head. 'There's parts I would like to save. Parts I would like to forget.' He shrugged. 'But it happened. It's done.'

She reached over and touched his arm. 'I'm sorry.'

He looked up, smiled quickly. 'What are you sorry about, Miss Lucy?'

'I don't know. For asking you such a personal question.'

'That's fine,' he said smoothly. 'You can ask me whatever you want. As long as I can do the same in return.'

'Deal,' she said. 'But I'm still sorry.'

'About what?'

She smiled. She liked him. 'That I never met you sooner.'

CHAPTER FOUR

They were in Paradise Camp before David realized. It wasn't exactly like stepping into Girl Scout Land. Lucy had been right; it was tiny, and spread out. In fact, it seemed as if it had been purposely designed so that no visitor would be able to see two buildings from any place in the camp at the same time. They passed a small redwood-coloured dorm on the right, but it was hidden by the trees before they caught sight of the stone chapel. David was amused that a place as rustic as the camp would even have a church. He said as much to his guide.

'Professor Spear says that, eighty years ago, in this part of the country, they would put up the church before they built the kitchen,' Lucy replied. 'That tells you what their priorities in life were.' She nodded towards the chapel. 'See the stained glass windows on the sides? It's fortunate this camp has been almost forgotten. Those windows are precious. If vandals knew about them, they would be gone in a week. At certain times of the day, when the sun peeks through the trees, the coloured light floods the interior of the chapel and you feel like you've fallen into a kaleidoscope. We hold our sessions in there. Dr Henry has all his equipment set up on the altar.'

'I smell food but don't see a kitchen,' David said.

'It's behind the chapel, down the slope fifty yards. That's where the other dorm is as well. You can stay there, or in the one we just passed, the sorority house.'

David stared into her soft green eyes. One of the things about Lucy Temple that he liked already was that she was not self-conscious of her beauty, which was not the same as saying she was unaware of it. She knew how to flirt with the best of them: bat her long lashes, toss her head of red curls, and giggle. She loved to giggle. Yet even her flirting had a natural quality to it. On the long road to the camp, he found himself forming one opinion of her and then discarding it ten minutes later. She spoke of reliving the lives of cavemen, which made her sound like a New Age flake. Yet in the same breath she could expound on the fine details of computer programs that correlated brain wave activity. The world she had grown up in was so different from his own – an academic spiritual wonderland where the only time someone was tortured was during finals – that he realized his usual standards could not be used to judge her. He liked that about her as well.

Still, he did not believe she had been back in the Stone Age.

'I assume the women are staying at the sorority house?' he asked.

She blushed; she did so often, her many freckles lighting up like shy fireflies. 'Yes. But there's a room there that's available.'

'Then that's where I'll stay.'

'Are you sure? For the purposes of your story, it might be better if you room closer to Professor Spear and Dr Henry.'

'I'm sure, Lucy,' he said.

She was pleased. 'Good,' she said.

A tall burly gentleman in his mid-forties appeared. David remembered him from the stolen video tape – Tom Forester, long distance truck driver, channeller of country western angels. He had on khaki shorts, hiking boots, nothing else. From the film of sweat on his hairy pectorals, it looked as if he had been working, or working out. Despite his powerful stature, he was obviously a 'good old boy', the kind of teddy bear lonely women loved to meet at bars when they were drunk. His handsome face was lost in too many pizzas and second helpings but his blue eyes possessed a certain clarity and charm. He ambled up to them as if the war on crime had already been won and the sun only went down at night so he could sleep.

'Howdy,' he said, his fat hand already out. 'Name's Tom Forester. Are you the famous reporter?'

'I'm David Nichols.' He shook his hand. 'I don't know how famous I am, but yes, I'm here to write an article about your group.'

'For *Time* magazine?' Tom asked.

'That's the plan,' David said.

Tom whistled. 'Wow, that's big time. Will we be on the front page?'

David smiled. 'I can't guarantee that. But I hope it will be a substantial piece.'

Tom pointed to the camera around David's neck. 'Just so long as I get my picture in the magazine. My momma thinks I'm wasting my time with all this consciousness stuff. She wants me to work on my musical career. Hey, you wouldn't happen to have any AA batteries on you, David? My compact disc player died the day we got here.'

'Our only electricity comes from a gasoline generator Spear and Henry brought with them,' Lucy explained. 'That's another reason you might want to stay at their dorm. They have lights at night, we don't.'

Tom chuckled. 'But you don't need lights for everything.'

David smiled. 'Well said, Tom. I'm sorry I don't have any batteries of that size.'

'Gosh darn,' Tom said, truly disappointed.

'Tom,' Lucy said. 'Do we have fresh linen for Mr Nichols?'

'Am I in charge of housekeeping?' Tom asked.

'You were when we got here,' Lucy said.

Tom considered. 'We have some but I don't know where

it is. I'll have to look around.' He stuck out his hand. 'I can take your bag, David, put it in your room for you.'

'That's all right, thank you,' David said casually. 'I've carried it this far I feel like it's become an extension of my arm.' In reality, he did not want anyone to touch his bag because he was packing a special FBI cellular phone, an ultra-portable laptop computer, and his 10-millimetre semiautomatic pistol.

Tom withdrew his arm. 'Suit yourself. I'll go try to find some sheets and towels. I warn you, every mattress in the camp is about as firm as my ex's tits. Best you put your mattress on the floor of your room if you don't want to wake up with an aching back.'

Lucy took a step away. 'I'll go with you, Tom. I think I saw linen on a top shelf in the kitchen. I'll need you to reach it.' She patted David on the arm. 'Stroll around, try to figure out where everything is while it's bright and sunny. I warn you, at night, without a flashlight, you can't walk ten feet without running into a tree. Everybody knows you're coming so if you meet anybody just introduce yourself. Say, "Hi. I'm the famous reporter!"'

'Watch out for Henry, though,' Tom said seriously. 'That guy likes men.'

Lucy socked Tom. 'Don't listen to him, David. Henry only pinches Tom's butt because he gets such a reaction out of him. Tom's such a redneck. Henry's cool.'

'I am not a redneck,' Tom said, offended.

'Yeah, you are,' Lucy said. 'You're neck's getting red right now.' Then, to show she was only teasing, she grabbed Tom's arm. 'Come, let's not air our dirty laundry in front of our guest. Wander around, David, but don't wander too far. The woods are filled with lions and tigers and bears.'

'Oh my,' David said softly watching them leave. He wondered what it would be like to be a part of a close-knit academic group that worked on nothing more threatening than past lives. Somehow, he couldn't imagine it for himself. Yet he was sorry to see Lucy leave. He hadn't encountered such a sweet sexy woman since, well, Sandy. But he didn't want to think about that, not now. He appreciated the Big Mind's advice about dropping the past. He just wished he could follow it.

David heard running water off to his left. A short hike brought him to a stream and a flowered meadow. Beside the water sat Margaret Farrow in her wheelchair. David had imagined her older and more decrepit, but she appeared to be in her late thirties and, with the exception of her handicap, healthy. She wore her long brown hair in twin pony tails. Her round face was wholesome rather than pretty, a tomboy who should have been playing basketball with the guys rather than confined to a chair. That was the world for you, David thought. It didn't care whom it paralysed. Margaret wore green slacks, a yellow tee shirt with a picture of a whale on the back. On her lap was a half completed green and white sweater, a ball of white yarn and long knitting needles. Hearing his footfall, she stopped working. He expected her to look over, but all she did was stare down at the running water.

'Hi, Margaret,' he said when he was about twenty feet away.

She finally looked over, the reflected sunlight glittering in the water behind her like a million shards of glass. 'You must be David,' she said.

'Yes, David Nichols. Lucy brought me here. I'm the reporter you probably heard about.'

'Come closer. Sit on the grass near me. Don't you love the smell of these daisies?'

He approached and knelt down. The spot she had chosen to knit in was idyllic. Along most of the path to the camp, Lucy and he had been in shade. But here the sun was as bright as it was in the desert. Oh, there was that thought of Las Vegas again. He would have to watch that. The Big Mind might notice.

'Yes,' he said. 'They're quite lovely.'

Margaret studied him, as he did her. Her face was remarkably smooth and youthful for someone who had suffered the traumas she had. For some reason, he liked her immediately, something he seldom did with anybody.

'Have you travelled far today?' she asked in a pleasant voice.

'Yes. I was on a plane part of the night and then had to take a car up from Boise. I've been on the road a few hours.'

'You must be exhausted.'

'No, surprisingly, I'm not. The air here is invigorating.'

'But you must be hungry?'

'I could use a bite to eat.'

'We'll go back to the camp in a few minutes and I'll fix you lunch.'

'That's not necessary. I can just scrape together something.'

'You're a bachelor, I can tell. You're used to taking care of yourself. But I enjoy cooking. I was just thinking what we should have for dinner this evening. Before you arrived, I thought I should ask you, our guest.'

'Anything's fine by me. I'm not fussy.'

'What is your favourite meal, David? In the whole world?'

He had to chuckle. 'You won't be much impressed if you cook regularly. I love roast turkey and mashed potatoes and gravy and stuffing.'

Margaret nodded. 'The way your mother used to cook it?'

'Yes.' His mother had died while he was in high school. Cancer. 'She used to cook it whenever it was a special occasion.'

'Today is a special occasion. You're here. And guess what?'

'What?'

'I just happened to have picked up a turkey on the way up here. I'll take it out of the freezer as soon as we go back and you'll have your favourite meal tonight. How does that sound?'

'Really, Margaret, you don't have to trouble yourself. I'll eat whatever everyone else is eating.'

Margaret smiled. 'Tonight everybody will be eating turkey. It's no trouble at all. I get to eat it as well. I love turkey.'

'I would have thought you were all vegetarians,' David said.

'Vera is, she's the only one, besides Panda, who doesn't count because he's a Hindu. Tom still eats hamburgers. I bought some of them as well, to make them for him. Did you meet Tom?'

'Yes. He's a friendly fellow.'

'Yes, he is,' she said softly.

'Is there something wrong.'

'No. Why do you ask?'

'I don't know,' David said. 'I was just wondering.'

'Do you want to ask me some reporter questions while you've got me alone?'

'Only if you don't mind,' David said. 'We can always do it later.'

'I'm so busy cooking and cleaning, there might not be a later. Ask, I don't mind.'

'Very well. Who's that sweater for?'

'Lucy. She catches a chill easily.'

'How did you meet Spear?'

'I met him at the hospital after I awoke from my coma.'

'You were in a coma? When?'

'Eleven years ago. I was in an accident. The doctors tell

105

me I was probably hit by a car, but I don't know for sure. I have no memory of how I was hurt. I have no memory at all of before I was hurt.'

'Are you serious? But what about your family?'

'I don't know if I have any family. I hear the surprise in your voice, but it's true. Total amnesiacs are rare but you have the genuine article sitting in front of you. When I came out of the coma, I was paralysed from the waist down, and a nonentity.'

'That must have been terrible for you.'

'Not at all. I didn't have to relearn to speak or eat or any of those things. I remembered what it's like to change the car oil and mop the floor, and even how to work a word processor. But awakening again after being unconscious for two months was like a rebirth for me. I awoke free, content. I feel that way now. There's no reason to pity me, David.'

'I don't pity you. I admire you. Do you remember what you looked like?'

'Like I do now.' She laughed. 'I'm not blind, you know. Why do you ask that question?'

'It just popped out of my mouth. I'm sorry if it offended you.'

'No offence taken.'

'But what I specifically meant was, do you remember how you used to dress? How you used to wear your hair? How you used to walk?'

She was thoughtful. 'No. I don't remember any of those things. Your question *is* interesting. I may look different. Maybe if my husband met me today – if I had one – he wouldn't recognize me.'

'When you awoke did you have on a wedding ring?'

'No. But it looked as if I had worn one most of my life.'

'I'm still amazed no one came looking for you.'

'The doctors and the police believe I may have been

injured some distance from where I was found, which was in a garbage dump behind a grocery store. For all I know I was on the east coast before I was hit. But Professor Spear came to check on me. He was in the room across the hall. He was a patient, like me. He had just returned from Africa and had a terrible fever. He padded over to meet the famous patient without a past. We got talking and he told me of his desire to form a special group of sensitive people to peer back into the past. When I was ready to check out, he offered me a job. I had nowhere else to go so I took it.'

'What do you think of the work he's doing?'

Margaret paused. 'It's full of possibilities.'

'Do you believe his theory is correct? That we carry the memories of our ancestors inside us?'

'I believe we are many wonderful things inside. The past as well as the future.'

'Does the Big Mind ever predict the future?'

She smiled, yet there was a hint of sadness in the expression. 'I think the Big Mind knows the future.'

'But has it ever said something was going to happen and then it did happen?'

'I don't know, maybe a few times.'

'Can you remember any specific instances?'

'You're asking me? The woman without the memory? You should ask Lucy. By the way, what did you think of her?'

'She seems like a nice young woman.'

'I think you two are going to get along great.'

'Are you a matchmaker on top of all your other duties?'

'Yes. I love romance.'

'Are you married? I mean now?'

'No. Do you want to marry me?'

He chuckled. 'Maybe we were married once, in a past life. Maybe our ancestors were married. Sure, I'll marry you if the turkey tastes as good as you promise it will.'

She nodded. 'Then we have a deal. But Lucy will be jealous.'

'No. She hardly knows me.'

'Yes, she will. I guarantee it.'

'Are you psychic as well, Margaret?'

'No. I'm just silly. You don't have to marry me unless you want to. But I think you're going to end up with Lucy. Yes, that sounds right. Or maybe Vera. Did you meet her as well?'

'Yes. I don't know if she took to me as well as her sister.'

'Oh, but Vera's prettier.'

'But they're identical twins,' David protested.

'Even identical twins can be told apart. I cut their hair. Vera's is longer and softer. Look closely next time and you'll see the difference. Lucy eats too much junk food. I know, I cook her cakes and cookies all the time. What you need is a hybrid of Lucy and Vera. That's me.'

David shook his head. 'I think I need to discuss this with the Big Mind.'

'You'll have a chance this afternoon. I hear Spear plans a session.'

'Margaret, can I ask you a couple of questions about Spear?'

'Sure.'

'After the two of you left the hospital, did he form a group right away?'

'No. He was too ill and too upset over the death of his wife. It took him time to regain his strength. The same with me. My spine was broken. The bones took a long time to heal. I was not able to get around in a wheelchair for several months.' She shrugged. 'We took care of each other during that time.'

'Was it Spear who gave you the name Margaret?'

'You are perceptive. Yes, of course, I woke with no name, none that I could remember. He just started to

108

call me Margaret as some way to address me. I didn't object. It was better than being "she" or "you" all the time.' Margaret paused. 'Margaret was his wife's middle name.'

'Did he ever talk about how his wife died?' David asked.

'No. Except to say that she passed away in Africa.'

'Do you know what he was doing in Africa?'

Margaret paused. 'I get the sense that you have studied his background. Do you know what he was doing in Africa?'

David decided to take a chance with Margaret. He trusted her, and in his business he trusted few people. Yet what did he trust her with? For her to keep his confidence over Spear's? That was asking too much, yet he did not feel she would spy on him for anybody, including her mentor. Besides, even if she did, many of the things he knew about Spear could have been discovered by an industrious journalist.

'I know he was studying the Dogon people,' he said.

'Do you know what is special about the Dogon people?'

'They were connected with the ancient Egyptian culture. And that culture appears to have had contact with alien beings.'

Margaret stared at him. 'Why alien beings, David?'

'I read a paper published by two French anthropologists that describes the Dogons' knowledge – and theoretically the ancient Egyptians' knowledge – of the star Sirus and its white dwarf companion. Knowledge that only modern astronomers have been able to prove accurate.'

'Did you believe the paper?' Margaret asked.

'I did not believe that the anthropologists were lying. But that's not the same as saying I think aliens from the Sirian star system visited here thousands of years ago. Do you believe the article?'

'I haven't read it,' Margaret said.

'Did Spear ever discuss the Dogon people with you?'

'Briefly, a few times. No one in the group here knows much about his experiences in Africa.'

'Why is that?' David asked.

'They have not probed into his past as you have.'

'But haven't they asked him where he obtained his mind- altering techniques?'

'Oh, sure. He says he learned them in Africa. He just doesn't go into details.'

'Do you know why his sister-in-law went insane in Africa?'

'Where did you find that out? I don't believe that's been published in an article.'

'I have my sources. All reporters do. I take it no one here except you knows about the wife and sister-in-law?'

'That's correct,' Margaret said. 'The sister-in-law might be another question you want to put to him. But not right away. Let him get to know you first.'

'Over turkey?'

'Yes. People are more inclined to share secrets while they're stuffing themselves with stuffings.'

'Does Spear have secrets? What did he tell you when he discussed the Dogon people?'

She regarded him gravely. 'That there never were any aliens.'

'How did he explain the Dogons' knowledge of the Sirian system?'

'He said it was the past. The ancient past.' Margaret looked past him then. 'Let's get back to the camp. I have things to do in the kitchen.'

David stood quickly, took hold of the rear of her wheelchair. It was purely manual; she had no special battery or motor installed. 'Let me help you,' he said.

'Thank you. I would have had a devil of a time getting up the hill without your help.' She glanced over her shoulder, up at him. Her eyes were unusually kind, but in that moment, it was as if she were blind. Or else she was seeing right through him. He didn't know which image disturbed him more. All he knew is that he felt the same chill he had experienced when he had studied the picture of Spear's wife, and the sister-in-law. She added, 'Maybe I shouldn't say that while we're here.'

'Say what?' he asked.

'The thing about devils.'

David smiled. 'You surprise me, Margaret. You believe in devils?'

She turned back around, away from him. 'I would rather believe in aliens.'

CHAPTER FIVE

David met Jon Horst while wheeling Margaret up the slope to the camp proper. Apparently Jon had come to get her. Once clear of the incline, Margaret bid David farewell, wheeling her chair vigorously over the mat of pine needles in the direction of the kitchen. David could see at a glance why Arnold Schwarzenegger was Jon's hero. Although fifteen years younger than the Hollywood star, they had similar builds and complexions, and even, to the unsophisticated, similar accents. Not that David would ever mistake a German upbringing for a Swedish one. He remembered from the file Ned had given him to study that Jon had been born in Stockholm. Clearly Jon had worked long hours in the gym to establish the similarities with his idol. Yet Jon's face lacked Arnold's power. David would have hated to break it to the guy that – even with the sloppy way he walked – he wasn't in Arnold's category. Jon seemed friendly enough, however; they all did at the camp. David was looking forward to meeting the master asshole himself, Spear, just for variety.

David and Jon shook hands and introduced themselves. David was distracted; a part of his mind was still with Margaret, the odd things she had told him, and the strange matters she had hinted at. She had cleverly avoided certain topics, but he had not been fooled. Spear was not chasing aliens, never had been. His fascination with the Dogon people and his interest in genetic memory were tied together, in the past. David had his own interest piqued. He was actually looking forward to the session with the Big Mind, that is if Spear allowed him to attend.

'Did you know I was the first one Spear chose to make a permanent member of his group?' Jon asked.

'I thought Margaret was.'

'Margaret's our cook. She's a wonderful woman but has no special abilities. Do you want to know how Spear found me?'

'Sure,' David lied.

'I was working a club in Hollywood called the Magic Parlor. Spear was in the audience enjoying the night out. He had not come there to see me, not in a professional capacity. I was doing tricks with a pack of cards. Picking them out of people's ears, making a queen of hearts change into a jack of spades – the usual things you see magicians do. Then I pulled a trick nobody else can do because it involves real magic, and Spear spotted that. On the other side of the stage, I had a woman draw a card and look at it and then put it back in a pack she held in *her own hand*. Then I told her what card it was, just by reading her mind. I had her do this ten times and I guessed the correct card all ten times. What do you think of that?'

'She wasn't working for you?' David asked.

Jon was disappointed in him. 'She was picked randomly from the audience. But I understand your lack of enthusiasm for what I just told you. If you were a magician you would know that not being able to touch the cards makes it impossible to use sleight of hand. Spear understood that. He knew immediately that I had psychic abilities.'

'But if you have such abilities,' David said, 'why don't you go to Las Vegas and make yourself a fortune?'

'I'm not interested in that,' Jon said, indignant.

'But I understand you want to be an actor.'

'Who told you that?'

'Lucy.'

'She shouldn't have told you that.'

'Is it true?'

Jon hesitated. 'Yes. I would like to act. I'm not ashamed of it. I'm a very good actor. But I don't see what that has to do with going to Las Vegas.'

David put his hand on Jon's shoulder. 'Jon, movies are made with money, lots of money. Las Vegas is full of money. Go there and load up on the stuff and you'll have plenty of producers and directors in Hollywood ready to cast you in the starring role.'

Jon blinked. 'In what film?'

David laughed. 'It doesn't matter! You can write the screenplay if you want! They'll let you. They'll let you sleep with your choice of romantic leads as well.' David patted Jon's shoulder and took his hand back. 'As long as you've got the money.'

Jon thought about it a moment then shook his head. 'It would be unethical of me to use my God-given abilities in such a manner. I can't do it, I won't do it.'

'Then you may as well forget about becoming a Hollywood star.'

'Why?' Jon asked.

'Because it just doesn't happen in real life. No one gets discovered any more. I can't even get discovered.'

Jon was interested. 'Are you an actor too?'

'Jon. I'm always acting.'

To David's relief Dr Henry Shayer came by right then. He carried the linen for David's room and offered to escort him to the women's dorm. David accepted, saying a hurried goodbye to Jon. Dr Henry, as he preferred to be called, was a handsome man with a tad of a British accent. David remembered from Ned's files that Dr Henry had won a Rhodes Scholarship to Oxford. So the guy was no dummy, even if he did, as Tom said, like guys. David found him effeminate but charming. He was one of those rare people whose normal expression was a grin. He was short, five foot six in shoes, but appeared as fit as David, although he must have been ten years older. He wore a doctor's white coat over a nice pair of black slacks and a red silk shirt.

'Was Jon hitting on you for space in your article?' Dr Henry asked.

'I think he was warming up to the topic,' David said.

Dr Henry waved his free hand. 'Jon's all right. He's just young, full of dreams. I have a few of those myself. I want to be the first gay black man to win the Nobel Prize. But I do wish Jon would concentrate on our research. He's not like the others. He doesn't feel he gains anything substantial from the sessions. Lucy and Vera are both working on their Masters degrees in psychology, in conjuction with the work they do with Spear. This is class for them – they get credit. Panda is here because when he sits with the Big Mind he feels the presence of God. And I think Tom stays around because of Margaret's cooking. But Jon has no such focus. He's anxious for the group to become famous for fame's sake.'

'Is he an integral part of the group?' David asked.

'Oh yes. Spear wouldn't have him here if he wasn't.' Dr Henry nodded to the redwood dorm on their left, so wrapped in branches it looked as if it had been built by a hobbit. They headed up the rickety steps, leaving prints in the dust. 'They tell me this is your room here, at the end. That means you're rooming with the ladies. Tom didn't scare you away from the other dorm by telling horror stories about me, did he?'

'Well, I think Tom's from the old school.'

Dr Henry laughed. 'I only tease him about how cute his ass is because he's so uptight about homosexuals. Otherwise I wouldn't say boo to him.' Dr Henry reached out and opened the door to the room. David wondered who was next door. Dr Henry added, 'He does have a cute ass, though.'

'So do you,' David said.

Dr Henry glanced over his shoulder, lit up. 'Do you think so, David?'

'Absolutely. It's just not as cute as Lucy's.'

'I heard you took a picture of her while she was skinny dipping?'

'Several.'

Dr Henry approved. 'I'm glad *Time* magazine sent you instead of a stuffed shirt. The Big Mind won't even talk when one of those is around.'

They entered the room and now David finally felt as if he was back at camp. There were two sets of bunk beds – four mattresses altogether – stuffed into a wooden box too small to swing a bottle of beer in. There was a bathroom, however; he had it all to himself, missing tiles and all. The slender shower stall looked as if it had been designed to keep out and humiliate the chubby kid. David had been fat as a child. Too much turkey stuffing. He had only lost weight when his mother had died.

'Isn't this cool?' Dr Henry asked after a moment of silence.

'It's way cool,' David said, setting down his bag on one of the lower bunks. It looked as if he would have to put a couple of mattresses on the floor to get a decent night's sleep, if not all four of them. He didn't mind; he could sleep standing up, or he could not sleep at all. It didn't matter much one way or the other, the way his bad dreams sucked his energy lately. Dr Henry went to make up one of the bunks with the fresh linen but David shook his head. 'I can get that,' David said.

'Just trying to be the proper host,' Dr Henry said. He glanced at his watch. 'We have a session starting in about thirty minutes. You're welcome to sit in on it.'

'Would it be possible to meet Professor Spear before then?'

'No. He specifically told me he would talk to you after the session. He wants you to get a taste of what we're doing here. He feels it will make you more open to his ideas.'

'Are you open to his ideas?' David asked.

'I endorse them a hundred per cent. I think Professor Spear will win the Nobel Prize before myself, once the scientific community fully understands what he is saying.' He added, 'I hope your coming here this week will help speed up that process.'

'But I understand Spear is not excited about my being here.'

'He is and he isn't. He wants publicity, he simply wants it a few months from now when the two of us have completed our research. But the Big Mind said you were to come so here you are.'

'Lucy told me you specialize in how the three levels of the brain interact with each other. What exactly does that mean?'

Dr Henry set down the linen. 'How well do you know the working of the brain?'

David shrugged. 'Assume I know nothing.'

'To understand the brain and my association with Spear you have to understand how the human brain evolved on Earth. Take a fish. A fish has a spinal cord and a little swelling at the front end of the spinal cord, which is its brain. Its brain weighs no more than a gram or two. Fish are pretty stupid. But even their small brains have the same major divisions as the *core* of our brains. Like us, they have a hindbrain, a midbrain and a forebrain. Five hundred million years ago there were fish swimming in our primeval oceans with these same basic parts already in place. What's fascinating is to study the development of the brain from fish on. Three major steps in evolution have occurred since then, and each time a new layer of the brain has been added. Yet the old layers have remained. They still have to be taken into account. Do you understand?'

'I'm not sure. Tell me more.'

'The principal modern exponent of the view I am discussing is Paul MacLean. He was chief of the Laboratory of Brain Evolution and Behavior of the National Institute of Mental Health. He developed an amazing model of the brain structure and evolution that he called the "triune brain". I have already mentioned that our core brain is similar to a fish's core. It contains the basic machinery for reproduction and self-preservation. Our heartbeat and blood flow and respiration are controlled by the core of our brains. A fish only has this core, but we have three layers built on top of it, three different mentalities you might say, with which we view the world. When the fish moved to land, reptiles evolved what is called the reptilian complex or the R-complex. Reptiles to this day have it, as do mammals and humans. MacLean was able to show that the reptilian complex plays an important role in aggressive behaviour, territoriality, ritual and the establishment of social hierarchies. I see your knowing smile, David. Yes, much of our modern society is characterized by the influence of the reptilian complex. Have you noticed how often a murderer is described as "cold blooded"?'

'Yes,' David said softly.

'Perhaps we describe such people instinctively, knowing that the side of a man that commits murder comes from the complex developed by cold blooded reptiles. Myths are replete with references to reptiles as evil. There's dragons, of course. The knights of the round table were always off slaying some fire-breathing monster. Then there's that most famous reptile of all, the serpent in the Garden of Eden, who offered Eve the knowledge of good and evil. But I have to wonder if the knights of the round table, in their search for the Holy Grail, were really searching the depths of their souls, the depths of their brains. If the myth of Arthur and his men isn't a profound allegory of human evolution. Why were Adam and Eve driven out of the Garden of Eden? Because of a stupid apple? Or was it because they had finally accepted what the master reptile had to offer? That part of themselves that was capable of unspeakable acts.'

'Your ideas are interesting,' David said honestly.

'They are not my ideas. MacLean developed them. Give credit where credit is due. I merely run with them as far as history and literature are concerned. The next level of the brain development was the limbic system. It covers the reptilian complex the way the reptilian complex covers the brain core. It probably evolved a hundred to two hundred million years ago. We share it with other mammals. It appears to be the seat of most of our emotions. The pituitary or 'master gland' is an important part of the limbic system. The pituitary controls the entire endocrine system and modern scientists have documented how even slight changes in the endocrine system affect moods. Thus the popularity of drugs like Prozac, which largely act on the limbic system. "Friendly behaviour" started with the development of the limbic system. Mammals and, to a lesser extent, birds are the only organisms to devote a lot of attention to taking care of their offspring. If you were to ask me, I would say the seat of love in man is in the limbic system.'

David smiled. 'What about the heart?'

'The heart is a pump. I don't care what the Big Mind says.'

'What does the Big Mind say about the human heart?'

'That it's the throne of the seat of the God,' Dr Henry said.

'I'm confused, Dr Henry. From several of your earlier comments I thought you respected the Big Mind. Yet you sound so much like a traditional scientist. Where do you stand on this great presence the group says it channels?'

'I am an agnostic. As far as God and the Big Mind are concerned. Many times I've heard it say things I know the people in the group could not possibly know. Unlike Spear,

I feel we as human beings probably do possess non- physical means of obtaining information.'

'Huh?'

'My experience with the group has led me to believe the human brain is sensitive to energies scientists have yet to acknowledge exist. For example, there is Krilian photography. For centuries saints have said we have halos around us. Now it looks like we do. That's a fact – it can be proven. But what energy is our aura composed of? Why does it seem to change with our emotions? Are other people sensitive to that energy? Can they pick it up from a distance of ten feet? From around the world? Does that energy respond to more than emotions? Can that energy transmit specific information over a distance? These are questions I ask myself. Especially when the Big Mind says that there is going to be bloodshed in the Middle East tomorrow and then the next day a madman walks into a mosque with an automatic weapon and blows away dozens of innocent people.'

'The Big Mind has made such predictions?' David asked.

'Yes. A few, not many. It does not often talk about tomorrow.'

'Does Spear share your interests in other forms of energy?'

'No. He's obsessed with genetic memories. We work in parallel, not in concert. He gives me a group of sensitive individuals who become something greater than the sum of their parts when they sit together with their eyes closed. I give him hard scientific measurements to back up his theories. EEGs that indicate that the group is experiencing a state of consciousness that the group members, as individuals, cannot experience. He takes us into the past. I measure how the past is perhaps located deep inside our brains. Yet we're still on the surface, all of us. In time as well as anatomically. The third layer of the brain is the neocortex. It is the most recent development. It probably appeared tens of millions of years ago, but its development was greatly accelerated when humans came on the scene two million years ago. More advanced mammals have it. Relatively speaking, ours is the largest, although an argument can be made that dolphins' neocortexes are as powerful. But the point I'm making is that our group has never been able to regress more than two million years, and then only on rare occasions. I don't know where Spear would place our genetic point on the path, but I say we're still stuck in the neocortex.'

'What does the neocortex do for us?'

'Many things. It would take me hours to explain everything. Much of our sensory and speech capacity, even the use of our hands, is controlled in the neocortex. But more important it gives us the ability to experience abstract thought. The neocortex is what makes us human.'

'It keeps the wild animal and the evil reptile inside us outside the door?'

'Very nicely put, David. You make an excellent student.' Dr Henry glanced at his watch again. 'But if you will excuse your teacher he has to finish checking his equipment. The session will be in the chapel. Why don't you freshen up and relax for twenty minutes and then come over? Everyone should be there. Have you met Panda yet?'

'No.'

'He's a wonderful man but his English is poor. Except for when he speaks for the Big Mind. Then and only then is his English fluent.'

'What does that tell you about *his* brain?' David asked.

'I don't know. I haven't figured it out yet. But if he says little to you, understand why. He's not being rude.'

'I won't take offense. Thanks for the lecture. I hope the information comes in useful in my article.'

Dr Henry was at the door. 'I appreciate you listening to

me. I know once I start talking I'm hard to shut up. See you soon.'

David saw him out. 'I'll be there.'

David closed the door behind Dr Henry. He was not able to lock it, the latch being broken. Sitting on one of the lower bunks beside his black leather suitcase, he opened it and removed his cellular phone. He checked the time – twelve forty-eight. His boss should still be on the flight to Florida. It was not necessary for him to check in. He had nothing special to report. Yet there were a few minor points he wanted to discuss with Ned. He pushed a button that automatically dialled the number. Ned answered immediately.

'Hello?'

'Hello. This is your favourite field reporter calling you from the green mountains of Idaho. What is the Big Mind? Why does it want me here? I don't know and I don't care. Lucy Temple is beautiful, she swims naked, and I think she likes me. How are you, Ned?'

'I'm in first class.'

'We never fly first class.'

'I am treating myself with the Bureau's money. I figure I deserve it. Do you know how much alcohol you can drink for free in first class if you want to?'

'Yes. I do know. I have treated myself with the Bureau's money for years.'

Ned sighed. 'I hope this call isn't being bugged. It sounds like you're having fun. Have you met Spear yet?'

'I will in a few minutes. I've talked to most of his people. They're a curious group. It's hard to tell the true believers from the damned. They seem to like me well enough.'

'I told you that you were perfect for the assignment. I'm scheduled to speak to Professor Buckley this evening at the University of Florida. It should be interesting.'

'Ned, Spear has an assistant named Margaret Farrow. She's been with him from the beginning of his research into genetic memories. You didn't have anything in your files on her.'

Ned was surprised. 'She didn't come up in our research. That's odd.'

'Maybe it's not so odd. She only met Spear after emerging from a three-month long coma, with no memory of her past. Margaret Farrow isn't her real name, but it might be a lead with which to start a file on her. She's a paraplegic, supposedly a great cook, and a hell of a nice woman. See if the boys in the home office can dig up anything on her. I'll find out what hospital she was in during her coma.'

'That would help,' Ned said. 'She sounds like an interesting woman. Did you join Lucy Temple on her nude swim?'

'No. But the day's young and the night is long. Anything is possible. Isn't it great we're quitting? We can break all the rules and it doesn't matter.'

'You have always broken the rules, David. Call me tonight after eleven my time. I might have some information for you.'

'Have you made arrangements to see the sister-in-law tomorrow?'

'It's being arranged. Mental hospitals are not easy places to get into.'

'Or to get out of,' David added.

'Touché. The flight attendant is about to serve dinner. Steak and potatoes and steamed carrots, cooked to my specifications. Anything else?'

David hesitated. 'Ask Professor Buckley what the Dogon people knew about the brain, and the evolution of man.'

'Why?'

'I'll explain later. But be sure to do it. It could be important.'

'Important? Are you becoming a believer, David?'

'No. You forget, I'm already firmly entrenched in the other group.'

They exchanged goodbyes. David put away his phone and used the restroom. Returning to his bag, he checked to make sure his official FBI gun was still in place. In addition to his 10-millimetre semiautomatic pistol he had brought a snub nose Colt .22 revolver that fitted inconspicuously beneath his trousers leg. He had worn it entering the camp but now took it off and put it inside the bag. There was nothing dangerous here, he thought.

David heard approaching steps. Standing, he peered out his cloudy window. Vera was returning from her long walk. She entered the room two doors down from his. Two minutes later he heard a toilet flush, then she reemerged and headed in the direction of the chapel. On the walk up the path, Lucy had confided that her sister had been having nightmares since coming to the camp. Twice, Lucy said, Vera had awoken moaning in pain. Lucy had also said that of all the members of the group, Vera was the most intuitive.

David wondered what the young woman was dreaming about.

He decided to hang on to his .22, after all. What the hell.

CHAPTER SIX

David had not been in a church in two decades. This one was so small it felt like a confessional booth, and instinctively he thought of his many sins. He had been raised a Catholic, before he realized when his mother died that guilt did not vanish with absolution, it only changed clothing. He had been at a swimming meeting when she passed away. Counting the space on the twin rows of dark wooden pews, David estimated the chapel could hold forty adults, maybe sixty boy scouts. The floor was smooth grey marble tiles, the walls thick slabs of unpolished quarry rock. As Lucy had said, the stained glass windows gave the chapel its magic. On one wall Satan tempted Jesus, on the other side Jesus ascended into heaven. David found the stained glass window behind and above the altar curious. Here Jesus simply sat by a stream by himself, lost in thought. It was nice to see Jesus taking a break. It was through this window the afternoon sunlight poured, sending all the colours of the tranquil scene over the pews. David was not such a sceptic that he did not believe that places had vibes. He would have been the first to say the church *felt* peaceful. Someone had lit a stick of incense. The back doors lay wide open, the fresh mountain air brushing his cheek with each stir of the green trees outside. All in all it was a nice place to hold a seance.

The group was gathered on the altar. Professor Spear and Margaret had yet to appear. Dr Henry was busy wiring up Lucy, Vera, Jon, Tom and Panda to his

EEG and EKG machines. David had met Panda briefly. Seemed a nice enough fellow, although he was obviously very shy. He was shorter than Jon, not to mention Lucy and Vera. He had long black hair and the lovely dark eyes so many Indians were known for. His manner was reflective, pious. By the way the others deferred to him – giving him the nicest chair, falling silent when he entered – David recognized him as possibly the invisible leader of the group. He sat with his eyes closed while Dr Henry wired him up.

'Do I look like the wife of Frankenstein or what?' Lucy asked David, referring to the electrodes attached to her scalp and chest. She sat in the chair closest to the front pew, where David had chosen to place himself, after first noting where Lucy was sitting. She still wore her white shorts from that afternoon, although she had changed her yellow blouse for a blue sweatshirt, a tiny gold crucifix around her neck. The chapel was a bit chilly. Vera sat to Lucy's left, absorbed in a science fiction novel. She had not looked up since he had entered the chapel.

'Dr Frankenstein was the man who created the monster,' David said. 'Not the monster himself. So you could easily be his wife.'

Lucy was surprised. 'You mean all these years I've been calling that monster Frankenstein and I was wrong?'

'Yes,' David said.

'What was the monster's name then?' Lucy asked.

'I don't know. I think he was just the monster. It's been a long time since I read Mary Shelley's book. But I recommend it highly. It's a masterpiece.'

Lucy glanced at her sister. 'Did you know that?'

'Yes,' Vera said, her eyes not leaving her book. 'Everybody knows that.'

'Oh.' Lucy turned back to David. 'Margaret was looking for you. She wanted to feed you. Where were you?'

'I just came from my room,' David said.

Lucy brightened. 'Guess who you're rooming next to?'

'That silly redhead who swims naked in mountain lakes?'

Lucy frowned. 'Yes. *Her*. She's rooming next to that pervert with the *powerful* lens.'

'Are you implying that my camera is an extension of my penis?' David asked.

'She's a psychologist,' Vera muttered, turning a page. 'She sees penises everywhere.'

'I don't know,' Lucy went to answer him. 'I haven't . . .'

'Don't say it,' Vera interrupted. 'Remember, we're in a church.'

'Oh, I suppose.' Lucy smiled, tossing her head and her many lovely curls the way pretty girls were taught to do when they were young and they wanted Daddy to buy them something. She reached over and touched David on the tip of his knee. 'Guess what we're having for dinner tonight?'

'Turkey,' David said.

Lucy blinked. 'How did you know that? Did you talk to Margaret?'

'It just came to me,' David said. 'I love turkey.'

'I hate it,' Vera muttered.

'You must be psychic,' Lucy said seriously, eyeing him.

Professor Spear and Margaret Farrow entered the chapel. David knew Spear's face, of course, from the video tape and the photographs in Ned's files. Yet he appeared much different in person. The wild grey Einstein haircut was still there, as was the bushy moustache and even the rumpled brown coat he had worn on the tape. Yet he was taller than David had imagined, thinner. He in fact looked as if he had recently checked himself out of a hospital after suffering a high fever. His long fingers had a skeletal quality to them; the skin on his face and hands was like old cheese. Maybe he didn't like Margaret's meals as much as the rest. His demeanour was threatening but not arrogant. More than anything else he appeared intensely preoccupied. He nodded to David as he passed but did not stop to shake hands. David was not insulted. Margaret smiled at him as she wheeled herself towards the altar and that was all the warmth he needed, for the time being. It was nice to be around a group of young women who were not drinking hard liquor. Since arriving at the camp, he had not missed having a drink. A camcorder rested in Margaret's lap, and David realized she had shot the video he had watched at the LA office.

With Spear's arrival, preparations to start the session picked up pace. Dr Henry finished wiring up Panda and Margaret set her video camera atop a stand in the corner. The five members of the channelling group – David still thought of it that way despite what Lucy had told him – closed their eyes and began to take long slow deep breaths. Margaret peered through her camera lens, searching for focus. Dr Henry bent over a computer terminal beneath a holy picture and Spear leaned against the chapel's main cross, the nailed and bleeding feet of Jesus Christ pressing against the Professor's waist. David sat and watched and tried to feel for the presence of the Big Mind, but noticed nothing. The group continued to breathe in and out for several minutes and he had to stifle a yawn.

Then, in the same manner as on the video tape, each of them began to speak about the beauty of the breath, coming into the present moment and the dawning of unbounded awareness. All except Vera, who sat so still her breath could have ceased altogether. Yet, as before, she clutched Lucy's hand, and it was definitely Vera holding onto Lucy and not vice versa. Holding onto her twin sister as if she feared she was about to fall off a bottomless cliff.

Then there was a long silence where no one spoke.

'Ah. What is the program?' Panda said finally, his English much improved over twenty minutes ago, his voice clear, resonant. It was as if he spoke in a much larger sized room. The effect puzzled David.

'We have no program this afternoon,' Spear said in a surprisingly gentle voice. 'We let you decide.'

'Ah,' Panda said. Or was it now the Big Mind? David had to assume so. 'We have a visitor, do we not? David?'

'Yes,' David said, sitting up. 'I'm here.'

'How are you? How was your trip?'

'It was fine. I'm fine. How are you?'

'Wonderful. What would you like to do this afternoon?'

'Maybe ask some questions. Then regress into the past. See some dinosaurs.'

Panda, the Big Mind, chuckled. The faint echo quality in Panda's voice continued.

'If we see dinosaurs, they might see us. They might be hungry. It might not be such a good idea. But ask your questions. I enjoy questions.'

'Who am I talking to right now?' David asked.

'Ah. No one, everyone. A window into eternity, a blank wall. It is all the same. Words cannot describe me. I can only be described by negation. I am not this, I am not that. It is a paradox. It is confusing. I don't even know who I am. I am the Big Mind. That is as good a name as any. Who are you?'

'David Nichols.'

'Ah. Is that who you are? Who is David? Is he these clothes you wear? This body? This personality? I don't think so. Those things will fade away in time, but you and I, we're timeless. We have that in common. I think I must be you. Or at least your friend.'

'I am curious if you have any individuality?'

'Yes and no. I adopt individuality for the purpose of

this communication. The same way a wave rises from the ocean to take the surfer to shore. Then, when it has finished its task, the wave dissolves back into the ocean. Do you surf? Swim? You're from California, you must be a good swimmer. I see that. You have been treading water a long time. Take the next wave in, David. It's coming soon.'

David took a moment to absorb the response. He had almost made the Olympic swimming team. Did the Big Mind know that? Or was it just a coincidence? David's curiosity jumped a notch.

'What is your purpose in contacting this group?' David asked.

'I am the group. There is no contact. I am always here. They simply become aware of me when they sit like this and settle down.'

'But are you here to help them?'

'Yes. I help all living beings. I bring love, peace, expansion. Did you know it is the nature of life to expand?'

'It seems that it is the nature of life to suffer,' David said.

A chuckle. 'Suffering can be expansive. Why should you run towards the sun when you sit in a bright room? The darkness makes you crave the light. But for you, I understand, it has become old.'

'Yes,' David said.

'What do you want? What do you really want to ask me?'

'Proof that you exist. That there is a Big Mind.'

'The only proof is in your experience. How do you feel now?'

'Fine. I feel the same as I did when . . .' David stopped. He suddenly realized he felt exceptionally fine, as if the fatigue of his journey had been lifted in one swoop. He wondered if he was the victim of subtle suggestion but couldn't remember the Big Mind saying anything suggestive. The Big Mind waited.

'Yes?'

'I feel refreshed,' David said. 'Relaxed.'

'Good. I am relaxed as well. Another thing we have in common. See, we must be the same. You want a miracle, I understand. People always do. But miracles sneak up on you when you least expect, and usually pass without your knowing. Life is a miracle. I lied to you a moment ago. Every time I speak, I lie a little. I don't mean to but it happens. Words conveys so little. The purpose of life is unknown. It's a mystery, and you know mysteries can be lived, but never explained. Do you understand?'

'I think so. You are talking about a state of life beyond words?'

'Yes. It is like that. The Big Mind is pure silence. Your inner nature is silence. How can you talk about silence? It is not possible. Still, we sit and talk together because it is fun.'

'I read a book this group published that contained transcripts from several of your talks. In it you mentioned top secret projects the government is working on. Cold fusion. Jet planes capable of flying into Earth orbit. Technology that can transform nuclear waste into harmless isotopes. You say the government had already developed these things?'

'Yes.'

'Is that true?' David asked.

'Yes. You know it is true.'

David hesitated. For the first time he considered it possible the Big Mind *could* see through his disguise. Just as quickly he dismissed the idea. He was a master at undercover work. No one knew anything about him unless he wanted them to know.

'What do I know?' David asked, a note of challenge in his voice.

'Many more things than you let on. *You* are mysterious. You play that role. But it keeps you at a distance from those around you, those who love you. You believe you must stay distant or your love will injure you again as it has injured you in the past. But no love is ever lost. How is it possible? Does death destroy it? There is no death. The form may change but the essence is never lost. Can any wave, no matter how big, dry the ocean? I tell you seriously, the next wave comes soon. It can take you all the way to the shore. Yet your eyes stay fixed on the horizon. One miracle is not enough for you. You keep waiting for another, and another, the perfect wave to arise out of the darkening sea. But time goes by, the sun nears the horizon. Your life passes. What are you waiting for, David?'

Despite his resolution of a moment ago, David felt strangely moved by the words. The Big Mind spoke in a delightful rhythm that magically disarmed. Yet he had trouble hanging onto what was being said. The comments were like lines drawn on water; they existed only for the moment, in the room and in his brain.

'Honestly,' he said. 'I don't understand this wave I keep missing. I don't understand this shore I'm supposed to reach.' He added, 'Could you please explain it to me?'

'The shore is the shore. It is covered with sand. It is very sandy. That is what you miss most. That is what haunts you. I tell you it is still there. Angels guard the sandy shore. The waves do not wash it away. Yet the angels haunt you as well. Your past is a shark that circles beneath your feet. You worry it will bite, that you will bleed. You think you bleed now. That your blood stains both the sand and the angels. That is maya – an illusion. Drop your guilt. Come into the present moment. It is eternal, as all the angels in heaven and all the particles of sand on all the shores in the world are eternal.'

David had to take a moment. Why did it keep bringing

up sand? Why angels? Was it talking about Sandy and Angela? That was not possible, he thought. They were dead. They only lived in his memory. He didn't want to drop that. Then he would have nothing. He realized he was trembling and had to will himself to stop. He lowered his head as if in shame.

'I appreciate you answering my questions,' he said. 'Thank you.'

'Ah. What next?'

Spear straightened himself. 'Mr Nichols. You said you wanted to observe the group regress into the past. We cannot visit the dinosaurs you mentioned but perhaps we can show you another slice of history. What is your preference?'

David looked up and met the Professor's eye. 'I have always been interested in ancient Egypt,' he said. 'Pre-dynastic Egyptian culture.'

Spear in turn met his stare, his eyes cold, and amused. 'Very well.' He spoke to the group. 'Let us regress. Follow *all* the genetic chains.' Spear's gaze returned. 'I see your surprise, Mr Nichols. But yes, everyone sitting here had an ancestor in ancient Egypt. An amazing coincidence, wouldn't you say?'

David shrugged. 'It's remarkable.' Spear saw that the Big Mind had rattled him, David realized, and wanted to take the opportunity to underline the fact. Of course, with his request, David suspected he could be asking to see Spear's dirty laundry. When David just wanted to know if aliens helped build the pyramids.

What happened next differed from the regression David had witnessed on the video tape. With the exception of Vera, each of them began to talk again. Yet they did not simply slip into a lifetime in ancient Egypt. They jumped around, seemingly into their own gene structure as well as into different bodies. David found the shifts disconcerting, as well as the continued resonance of the voice of whoever was speaking. He could not understand why even simple-minded Jon sounded as if he were speaking from a deep well, with the voice of Thor, or at the very least with the voice of a large and wise man. Yet when they slipped into a life, they did not adopt a particular accent or language, which David found a relief. He assumed the Big Mind – since it was so big and smart – automatically translated for them.

Jon: 'The molecule is an almost endless spiral. We walk the five billion blocks of nucleotides. We carry the code, our way is clear. The human taxa is complex but it is not the first. The structure is binary. We see yes, we see no. We feel plus, we feel minus.'

Lucy: 'My lord and master, the king, draws his sword. I am to be knighted. The king thinks I am brave. He is wrong. All I feel is fear of the impending battle. I know I will die.'

Tom: 'Mutations in the gametes, in the eggs and the sperm cells, are all that matter for the survival of the race. Radioactivity mutates the cells. Cosmic rays alter the building blocks. Sometimes the nucleotides simply fall apart. The patrol work to repair the damage but some destruction must be left so that the body can evolve. As we walk the spiral, we skip over the damage, over the genes that bring change. Because we choose to go back, not forward. It is our choice. We feel it is right.'

Panda: 'The water is as blue as my mother's eyes. She carries a basket of bread to feed the lepers who rot by the shore. My own fingers crumble in my hands, yet my mother says I will be well because she loves me. I love her too much not to believe her.'

Lucy: 'The line of time is not linear.'

Tom: 'It is not a circle.'

Jon: 'It is a spiral.'

Panda: 'It stands before us.'

The room fell silent. David stared at the back of Lucy's

head; he could not turn away from it. Because even though his eyes told him her red curls had not smoothed out or darkened, and her skin had not changed to black, and her sweatshirt had not been transformed into a long red robe, *something* in the room kept trying to tell him *something* different. Something that didn't show up on video tapes even upon close examination.

'Isis,' Lucy said.

Jesus Christ, David thought, and not without a sense of irony. For from the point of view of the woman who now sat in front of him Jesus hadn't even been born yet. No matter how hard he tried, he could not free himself of the illusion that he was *staring at an Egyptian priestess*. Especially when Lucy turned her head to the side and he saw her ancient profile, carved from the stone wall of a secret pyramid long buried beneath desert sands.

She was very beautiful. This dead person.

'Ast and Asar,' Lucy said softly. 'Isis and Osiris. It is said Set is the brother of Osiris but that is a poor metaphor. The night is not related to the day. It is said the black rite is the highest initiation, and that is a danger. Isis is not the bright star in the sky. Isis is not the statue on the altar. Isis is the star above the head. Isis is the celestial, from where the Goddess pours down the healing white light. The inward breath takes me up to Isis. The outward breath pours her grace down upon me. In between the breaths I silently utter her sacred name. She warns me:

'"*Do not take the initiation, child. Do not stare in the mirror. There you will only find the corrupt past – the black one, the old one, the horror of Set.*"

'I listen to the Goddess. I flee the temple without my sister. At night I walk along the river. I am alone but I feel the eyes of the serpent follow me. They think they fool us with their human bodies but their eyes are never the same after the black rite. I have only the light of Isis to protect me. They are many and I am only one. The night grows darker and I feel them close. I begin to run, I am afraid. But I am more afraid to become like them and never see the face of Isis. I heard the hiss of their breath in my ears. They have caught me. Their invisible claws scratch my skin. I am thrown to the ground. Later, I see their faces. They force me to look into their eyes and I am sick on the sand.

'They have brought my sister. She cries for me to help her but I cannot. They hold my face under the river until my chest burns. Then they lift my head up and order me to stare into the mirror. They say they can force me against my will. I pray to Isis for help and she hears my prayer. White lights pours down upon my head and Isis speaks to me.

'"*Only human eyes can see Set. If not for my light in this land, the curse would spread like a plague. That is why they need the mirror that reflects no colour. Do not look into it. Offer your eyes to me, child, and they cannot use you. Fear not – the eyes with which you will behold me can never be destroyed.*"'

Lucy's head dropped. She finished the tale in a frail whisper. 'I shake free of them. I raise my hands and dig my fingers into my eyes. Warm blood soaks my cheeks and my vision fails. There is pain and I hear my sister scream. They take her away and I never see her again. They leave me alone, bleeding by the river, and I never see anything ever again.'

The session suddenly ended, without a soothing period of transition. David was confused for a moment until he saw that Vera was responsible for the group leaping out of the trance. Her eyes were open and there were tears on her cheeks. Everyone stared at her and David would have given a pretty penny to know what they saw. He no longer trusted in the regularity of human perception, and he had his reasons. Even though the illusion of seeing an ancient priestess had left him, he had to blink and rub his eyes to convince himself that the tears running down Vera's face were not in fact drops of blood.

CHAPTER SEVEN

Ned Calendar sat in the back row of Anthropology 111 in a large theatre type classroom located on the University of Florida campus and thought what a lousy teacher Professor Carl Buckley was. The class went from six to nine in the evening, and although he had missed the first half of it, Ned would have thought that after an hour of listening he would have at least had some idea what Buckley was talking about. True, Ned understood that the title of the course was Ancient Greek Culture, but Buckley seemed to be discussing how to tear down a Parthenon rather than how to build one, or better yet, something about the famous scholars who had taught there. Buckley did not help matters by keeping his substantially sized bald head glued to his notes while he spoke in a monotone that would have put a hyperactive arcade figure to sleep. Around him, Ned noticed several students dozing. It looked like an old habit with some; they didn't even bother jerking their heads upright once they were down. Despite his rare glances at his students, Buckley might have been aware how little attention he was receiving from the audience. Certainly no one was interrupting to ask questions. At twenty to nine – twenty minutes early– Buckley abruptly closed his notebook and dismissed class.

'I will be in my office to ten if anyone needs help with their paper,' he called out as the students – specifically those who had been comatose a minute before – charged for the doors. Two minutes after dismissal, Ned was alone in the classroom with the esteemed Professor. True to his old habits, Ned had not called to warn the Professor that he was coming. Ned had a theory about informants: the more nervous they were, the more they said that they later regretted. Of course, he did not classify Buckley as an informant just yet, but had already decided that he was not going to say goodbye to the man without getting a better explanation for the death of Penny Spear than the LAPD had received. Ned walked down the steps that led to counter where Buckley was collecting his papers with the simple-mindedness of a Disney character trying to look cute.

'Professor Carl Buckley,' Ned said when he was maybe twenty feet away. 'We have to talk.'

Buckley finally looked up, startled, a fox caught with a Foster Farm Chicken in his greedy paws. Should have left those USDA approved babies alone, Ned thought. Now the US government was required to send in the FBI. Already, instinctively, he knew that Buckley had secrets to hide, and not the wit to do it. Buckley was a fat man with a body the shape of a stuffed laundry bag. His cheeks and jawline were one smooth slab of twitching flesh. Honestly, Ned could not understand how a man like this had survived sub-Sahara Africa for six months. Maybe the years in between had been hard on him. Or maybe, with his Professor's meagre salary, he was simply no longer able to afford his Slim Fast. Buckley eyed him warily.

'Who are you?' he asked.

Ned took out his FBI badge, flashed it so quickly a video camera couldn't have recorded whether it was silver or gold and put it back in his pocket. 'Ned Calendar, Special Agent in Charge of the Los Angeles branch of the FBI. I'm here to question you about your activities in Mali Africa with Professor Stephen Spear, and about the death of his wife, Penny Spear. Would you like to talk here or in your office?'

Buckley drew in a breath and swallowed. He lowered his head and shuffled his papers. 'I cannot talk now. I have students waiting for me in my office.'

'I doubt that.'

Buckley glanced up, fearful. Now that was a new emotion, Ned thought. Fear was not the same as anxiety. Fear often came when there was a victim involved, and a victimizer. Which was Buckley? Ned believed he would find that out as well.

'What do you want?' Buckley demanded, meekly.

Ned shrugged. 'I told you. To talk. Let's go to your office. I think you will be more comfortable there.' He turned towards the door. Buckley hesitated, then began to follow.

'Am I under arrest?' Buckley asked.

'Not yet,' Ned said reassuringly.

Ned found the walk across campus refreshing. He enjoyed Florida, the tropical air, the beaches, the flapping white sails on the many boats. Not Miami, though, the criminal element, and he knew it was an odd prejudice for a man who had worked for the FBI in Los Angeles for the last thirty years to have. He didn't like crime, period, and occasionally wondered why he had spent his entire life pursuing, not something he loved, but the destruction of an element he loathed. Yet his career was over with, as was most of his life. It was too late now to second guess his choices.

Ned did not feel the same about David Conner and his career. Yet he was not simply upset that David was retiring. He wanted David to get away from it all, as desperately as he wanted David to fulfil his destiny. David was one of the few people Ned had met in life who he believed to have a destiny. The power to save life or destroy it. He had only worked with David a short time when he realized that if he pointed this incandescent ball of energy and intelligence at a problem, it would either be quickly solved or explode in unforeseen directions. That is what he had loved most about David, that he allowed no major case to sink into a mire of inconclusiveness. He wanted David to retire for his own mental health, and he wanted him to stay on to save that kid or that wife that no one else could save. If only David had been able to save Angela Moore. Maybe it would have made the incident with Sandy Quin bearable. Maybe not.

Ned had tried to keep his promise to David to hold back the swat team. But Angela's screams as her thumb was dissected from her body had wrung the men's nerves taut, and Ned could not blame the young man, Special Agent Mike Clancy, for taking the shot at Pokey that his scope gave him. To this day Ned did not know if David realized that Clancy had twice tried to commit suicide since the death of Angela. It was not exactly news that Ned thought would cheer David up. Of course, David would probably smile and point out that no member of a swat team should have trouble blowing his own brains out.

And what of Sandy Quin? That had been his own call for sure, although David had never blamed him for her murder. Over the years Ned had repeatedly reviewed what had gone down and he supposed he would not stop until the day he died. Yet, logically, he could not fault his decision back then. Had Failla discovered a single bug, he had planned to bring Sandy out of Las Vegas immediately. If only David had not insisted on saving the movie theatre owner, Holt, Failla would not have been tipped off. Then, if only David had managed to reach the hotel two minutes earlier, and caught Sandy before she fell. Ned supposed David did know that Mr Holt had later been found guilty of murder in the first degree. Sandy's life for that of a con.

What scale of justice must David have struggled to balance to even stay with the Bureau, especially with a million dollars in cash under his bed? Ned supposed David had remained because of Angela, knowing an Angela would come. But now that she was gone, he was going as well. It was sad, Ned thought, the whole story, and with just a little luck it could have been so incredible. David could have been a legend. Now he was only a phantom hero who had failed to bring back the girl, spoken of in whispers around the water cooler. Dirty Dave – Ned hated the nickname.

And he tried not to think about what David had done to Failla. Ned preferred to remember the greatest agent he ever had as the son he never had. If he had found Failla's body in the desert, he feared that would have been impossible.

Ned was excited about this case. He had been a philosophy major in college and had always been interested in spiritual matters. He was not into traditional religions but he often prayed when he was alone in his office late at night. God was an important part of his life. He was also something of an ancient culture buff, and a lover of astronomy, so the mystery of the Dogon fascinated him from many directions. He was happy that David had taken to the enigma surrounding Spear's group. Anything to make the poor guy forget the last couple of months.

Buckley's office was unimpressive, four sparse walls that sat above a greasy cafeteria, and looked out over a huge tree that virtually covered the window with its hungry branches. So this is the expert Professor Spear chose to accompany him to Africa, Ned thought. Teaching general ed classes and stuffed in a closet without a broom. The more Ned studied the man, the more convinced he was that a past trauma had caused him to fall. Buckley had followed him across the campus like a dog wearing a shock collar. As soon as they were both seated, Buckley quickly tried to profess his innocence of any wrongdoing. Ned cut him off with a raised hand.

'You will tell me everything about your trip to Africa. You will start at the beginning, skip no parts in the middle, and give me a detailed ending. If you don't do this you will annoy me, and when I'm annoyed I cease to be your friendly neighbourhood FBI agent.'

Buckley stared at him. 'What do you do?'

'I take out my handcuffs. I take out my gun.' Ned leaned forward and smiled. The gesture on him was not as disarming as it was on David. He had grown too old. When he grinned he just looked unstable. 'Would you like to see them now?'

Buckley sat back. 'No. I can tell you about the trip. I have nothing to hide.'

Ned sat back and relaxed. 'We all have something to hide, Professor. By the way, I know about the Dogon people and their special knowledge of the Sirian star system. I have read Marcel Griaule and Germaine Dieterlen's paper. You don't have to review their discoveries, but I don't want you to skip any points that relate to how the Dogon came by such remarkable knowledge. I do hope I make myself clear.'

Buckley looked at him in a new light, and with even more fear. Ned sensed he was rearranging the story he had been about to tell him. 'That's very interesting. Few people are aware of that paper.' He cleared his throat. 'That gives you a sound understanding of why we wanted to visit the Dogon people. My specialty is ancient Egyptian culture. That's why Spear contacted me to accompany him. That, and the fact that we used to teach together at Stanford.'

'So the two of you go way back?' Ned asked.

'Yes.'

'How do the Dogon relate to the ancient Egyptians? Specifically?'

'I can best answer that question by explaining how the Sumerian culture relates to the ancient Egyptians. You may not be familiar with the Sumerians. They gave rise to the Babylonians, what is commonly called "the cradle of civilization", in the Mesopotamian region. But let me start out by saying that phrase is a misnomer. The Sumerians had a highly developed culture in their own right. Now I speak of approximately four to five thousand BC. At the same time the Egyptians also had a flourishing culture. That these two cultures were connected, indeed, that they had a single sudden origin is in my mind beyond dispute. But that is not a sentence I would utter among my colleagues at this university.'

'Why not?' Ned asked.

'With the exception of a few brave souls, most anthropologists do not feel that the Sumerians and Egyptians originated together. But I can support my belief with hard facts. Basic Egyptian astronomy and Sumero astronomy are identical. Twelve months composed of three ten-day weeks each, resulting in thirty-six constellations. That adds up to three hundred and sixty days, and in each culture the five left over days were considered sacred. In fact, these five days are also important in Mayan astronomy. But I don't want to get into that now or we'll be here all night. Later, of course, the Egyptians adopted a calendar that related more specifically to the sun, but that was not for another two or three thousand years.'

'This is all very interesting. But what does it have to do with your expedition?'

'The point is that civilization itself rose remarkably fast, in different parts of the world, but in a similar fashion. For hundreds of thousands of years we wandered around in caves and then in the space of a few centuries our ancestors had a highly developed understanding of astronomy. Naturally, the French anthropologists' paper describing the Dogon's knowledge of astronomy interested us. I thought to myself, even before we left for Africa, this tribe lives in Mali today. But was it possible that thousands of years ago they had direct contact with the Sumerians and the Egyptians? Spear impressed upon me the Dogon's strong oral tradition. Their spiritual knowledge is passed down from father to son in a very secret and exact manner. It was my hope to learn more about the connection between the Egyptians and the Sumerians through the Dogon.'

'What did Spear hope to gain from the expedition?' Ned asked.

'He was more interested in how the Dogon knew that Sirus has a white dwarf companion. I was curious about that fact as well, but, as I say, it was not my primary reason for going to Africa.'

'I notice you use the word fact. After being with them for six months, you still believe that they knew about a star system many light years from here?'

'Yes,' Buckley said. 'The evidence is indisputable. They also knew about the four primary moons of Jupiter and the rings around Saturn, objects that can only been seen with a telescope. They have drawings of these planets and stars. I have seen them with my own eyes.'

'How do you explain their knowledge?' Ned asked.

'The Egyptians and the Sumerians gave it to them. The Dogon are excellent librarians, but I do not believe the knowledge originated with them. However, I should hastily add that it is possible that the Dogon people could be an actual offshoot of the ancient Egyptians. I think that is likely, in fact.'

'Then let me rephrase my question. How do you explain how the Egyptians and the Sumerians obtained this knowledge?'

Buckley hesitated. 'I can't.'

'You're going to have to do better than that.'

Buckley gestured helplessly. 'How would you explain it?'

'I don't know. But I did not spend six months in

a boiling desert researching the matter. Is it possible that the Dogon were contacted by an alien civilization thousands of years ago?'

Buckley smiled. 'I hardly think so.'

'Why not?'

'I don't believe in UFOs.'

'Yet you're positive that the Dogon's astronomical knowledge is accurate. You and Spear must have a theory, Professor. Tell me it and quit beating around the bush.'

Buckley lowered his head. 'I honestly don't know how they could know such things.'

'Why do you avert your eyes when you're being honest with me, Professor?'

Buckley's head snapped up, a hint of anger in his face. 'Spear knew them much better than I. Why don't you ask him these questions?'

'Perhaps I will. Later. Tell me about Spear. Tell me what it was like to live in Africa with him and the Dogon. Tell me about his wife, Penny, and his sister-in-law, Frances. I am curious about all these people.'

'Only three of us – Penny, Spear and myself – went to Mali first. Frances came later, at Spear's request. We went at the worst time of year, the beginning of summer. I wanted to go in the fall but Spear was insistent. When he gets something in his head, it's impossible to change his mind. That's his major weakness, his stubbornness. I didn't like that about him. I didn't like several things about him.'

'Such as?' Ned asked.

'He was always the boss. He might listen to your opinion, if he was in the mood, but if he didn't like what you said it was as if you had never spoken to him. It just vanished from his mind. My credentials were every bit as good as his. I should have been treated as an equal on the expedition, but I was not.' Buckley sighed. 'Except by Frances.'

'The sister-in-law?'

'Yes. She always treated me with respect. She was also an anthropologist, but more of a specialist in North American Indians.'

'Were you romantically involved with her?' Ned asked.

'I liked her. She liked me as well, you know, but as a friend.'

'Did that upset you? That you were only friends?'

Buckley's pride was evident. 'Of course not. We were both professionals.'

'I see. When did Spear bring her over?'

'In September. Three months after we got there.'

'But why bring her to such a harsh place at such a hot time of year? If the Dogon were not even indirectly related to her field of expertise? Did she want to come?'

'No. She hated it there. We all did, except for Spear. The heat's impossible to describe. Even in the dead of night you feel as if your skin is ready to dry up and flake off. The bugs never leave you alone. I would spray my body from head to toe with repellant and they would still bite me. Frances in particular suffered from the insects. She was there less than a week when she was bitten on the head by a poisonous spider. She almost died. There was no medical doctor in the area, and even the local Dogon medicine man wouldn't help us.'

'Why not? Are the Dogon a cruel tribe?'

'Not at all. I complain about how difficult the conditions were, but the Dogon are exceptionally friendly. They have an age-old tradition of non-violence and hospitality.'

'Then why wouldn't they help Frances with her spider bite?'

Buckley hesitated. 'Because she was Penny's identical twin sister.'

Ned felt as if the light in the room had dimmed. Naturally, he remembered that Spear had twin sisters in his channelling group. Still, why the instinctive alarm? Ned actually felt a wave of dizziness with Buckley's remark. Because the last time Spear had been around twins one of them died and the other went insane? Maybe the Professor just had a thing about twins, Ned told himself. There were far worse fetishes. Yet he had to wonder what Spear did with them when he had them alone, in the desert, in the mountains.

'What did they have against twins?' Ned asked

'They see them as evil. When they're together.'

'Did they see Penny as evil as well?'

'Yes. Once Frances arrived, they avoided her like the plague. The Dogon have no identical twins in their tribe.'

'But surely they must. They are human beings like us. Identical twins must show up every now and then. Wait a second. You're not saying they kill the twins as soon as they're born?'

'No. They have too high a regard for human life to do something barbaric like that. But they separate twins at birth. The Dogon are actually made up of three tribes, spread over considerable distances. If identical twins are born, they send one of the twins to one of the other tribes. Someone is assigned to take care of the child. But for the rest of their lives, the twins are never allowed to meet. When the Dogon saw Penny and Frances together, in their minds, they were seeing something unnatural.'

'But once the twins are separated, they don't see the individual people as evil?'

'That is correct,' Buckley said.

'Why is that?'

Buckley hesitated, making an effort not too look away, Ned noticed. 'I don't know,' he said finally.

Ned was impatient. 'I don't understand any of this. You

and Spear and Penny had been with the Dogon for three months. You must have known this fact about them. Why did you bring over Frances?'

'Penny and I did not bring over Frances. Spear did. He did so without our prior permission. God knows how he talked her into coming. And Penny and I did not know about the Dogon's fear of twins.'

'But Spear did?' Ned asked.

'Yes. Look, I have to admit something no reputable anthropologist would be proud to admit. When it comes to learning foreign languages, I have difficulties. But in that department Spear is a genius. He picked up Sanga quickly, and some Wazouba, spoken by the most remote of the three tribes. Because of that he was on friendlier terms with the Dogon than myself. He often gave their priestesses and priests small gifts. He spent long nights walking and talking with them. They liked him – he had them fooled. He learned many things from them that I never learned. That was another one of his faults. Spear was not generous when it came to sharing secret knowledge. He does not pursue scientific knowledge for the sake of science alone. He is also driven by the desire to be the main instrument of truth. His ego knows no bounds.'

'OK, he's an asshole. We've established that. Why did he brings Frances to Mali if he knew it would spook the Dogon?'

'I think he brought her there for that very purpose.'

'What do you mean?' Ned asked.

'He wanted to scare them. He wanted to show them that he had power. Anthropologists the world over will tell you that what most primitive cultures fear, they also most respect. Perhaps it's not so strange. We're not so different in the West, if you think about it.'

'But why do the Dogon associate identical twins with power?'

Ah, that was the nerve. Twins and power. Buckley began to perspire.

'I don't know,' Buckley said.

'Why did Spear want to scare them? What was he trying to scare out of them?'

Buckley considered, his fat neck twitching. 'I don't know.'

'Professor, if you say that one more time you are going to piss me off. Did Spear speak of his theory of genetic memory while he was in Mali?'

'It was while we were there that he began to formulate it.'

'Did he in fact formulate it? Or did the Dogon give it to him?'

'I . . . I'm not sure. They might have. Even if they had, Spear took credit for it.'

'So he did talk to you about the idea?'

'Yes,' he said quietly.

'When? Specifically? When Frances arrived?'

'I believe it was just before she arrived that he began to discuss it.'

'Professor, it seems clear to me that Spear's theory of genetic memory and the existence of identical twins are intertwined, at least in Spear's mind. Would you agree with that much?'

'Maybe,' Buckley admitted, shifting in his seat, probably wishing it would teleport him into another building away from the merciless FBI agent who drew his salary from the very taxes that came out of the Professor's monthly cheques.

'Then you should also agree that he brought Frances to Mali to be with Penny because he planned to do *direct* research into his theory of genetic memory, which the Dogon both believed in and feared. Am I correct?'

A bullseye. Buckley almost fainted. Panic entered his voice.

'How can I answer these questions? I'm not him. You'll have to ask him.'

'Oh, I will definitely ask him. But you can answer these questions as well as him because you were there and you're an intelligent man and you have a goddam PhD. Now, is there or is there not a link between identical twins and the uncovering of genetic memories?'

'I don't know!'

'Damnit, you're lying to me! I warn you, I am not the LAPD. I don't listen to a vague tale about a wild animal killing a woman and driving another insane – which you told them – and then close the case. We're talking about a possible murder here, and you're a suspect until you convince me otherwise. How did Penny die? Why did Frances lose her mind?'

Buckley was having trouble breathing. His fat face had swelled up like a red beetroot that had been genetically regressed from a future vegetable dynasty. Ned feared he might have a heart attack on the spot. Maybe he had pushed the guy too hard, he thought, at least for the time being. Interrogation had to be accomplished in waves, hard hits followed by soothing words, or even breaks. Clearly something dreadful had happened in Africa that had scared the hell out of Buckley and yet the Professor was still trying to hide it. This, despite Ned's confident opinion that Buckley had not been personally responsible for the death of Penny or Frances' mental breakdown. From the look and sound of him, the worst that Buckley could destroy would be a double-decker hamburger at McDonald's. Buckley bent over as if he might be sick on the top of his desk. Ned worried he'd had a large dinner.

'An animal got her,' Buckley mumbled into his trembling hands.

'Which one?' Ned asked dryly.

Buckley drew in a shuddering breath. 'Penny. She was killed by an animal.'

'What was the animal?'

'I don't know.'

'What happened to Frances?'

Buckley shook his miserable head. 'I don't know.'

Ned remembered David's questions. 'What did the Dogon know about the human brain?'

'A lot.'

'Would you care to elaborate?' Buckley didn't respond. He sat up and blinked as if he were a little boy who had just been told his favourite TV program had been cancelled. Ned added, 'What did they know about the evolution of man?'

'A lot.'

'They weren't so primitive after all, were they, Professor?'

'No.'

Ned stood. 'Frances Cumberly is locked in a sanatorium in South Carolina, in a small town called Salutory. She's been there for twelve years, since you left Africa. Did you know that?'

'Yes.'

'I'm going to visit her right now.'

Buckley jerked involuntarily. 'Now?'

'Yes. I was going to go tomorrow but after listening to you I feel impatient to speak to her.' Ned paused. 'Do you have a problem with that?'

Buckley paled. 'But it's so late. It's dark.'

'I am not afraid of the dark, Professor. Are you?'

Buckley suddenly reached across the desk and grabbed Ned's hand. 'Don't go there, please? You don't want to go there. She can't speak. She's too far gone. There's no reason to go there.'

Ned noticed how damp the man's grip was. And how Buckley was no longer worried about himself, but about the mean FBI agent who one minute ago wouldn't stop tormenting him. Ned gently unwrapped the man's fat fingers and wiped off his own hand on his trousers leg.

'I have to go,' Ned said. 'When I am done speaking to her, I will return. I know your home address. I don't need a lot of sleep. I may come in the middle of the night. Be there.'

Buckley's face crumpled in despair. 'If you do see her, for godssake don't be alone with her. Have someone around, a couple of strong men. And don't look directly in her eyes. Be sure not to do that.'

'Why not?'

Buckley trembled. 'Because she's so horrible.'

CHAPTER EIGHT

'At last we meet,' David Conner said to Professor Stephen Spear.

They sat in what must have been the camp manager's office. Given the dimensions of the retreat centre, the room was spaciousness itself, with the obligatory moose head on the wall and a half dozen logs burning in the brick fireplace. The warmth and light of the latter was welcome; behind Spear, outside the screen-covered window, the evening shadows lengthened the green arms of the trees into dark outlines of would be trolls. David had waited the better part of the day for the meeting. After the afternoon session, each of his attempts to talk to Spear had been rebuffed with the word that the esteemed Professor was resting. David thought Spear looked pretty fried for a man who had napped all day.

The only effort Spear had made to personalize his office was a two foot green iguana, which crouched in a straw-littered glass cage off to the left and stared at David as if he – and not the turkey in Margaret's oven – was the feast they were all waiting for that evening. David had to assume the lizard was a pet of the Professor's since it could not be native to the area. The realization did not exactly make David view the man with greater warmth.

'I'm sorry to have kept you waiting,' Spear said. Once again David was struck by the gentleness in the man's voice, at odds with his dark eyes, as emotionless as a pair of shrunken cue balls. Spear had traded in his rumpled brown coat for a neatly pressed green sweater, although his grey hair still looked as if he combed it with a shorted wire. Spear added, 'It's been a difficult week, coming up here and all.'

'That's a pity,' David said. 'Since I understand one of the reasons you brought your group here was for the serenity of the location. I was told you grew up around here?'

'Yes, not far from here.'

For some reason, David was reminded of Pokey Sampson. Knew the area of his birth well. All the hidden caves and crevices. Had probably fantasized about that trick in the river since the time he was a teenager. David brought out his miniature cassette recorder, which all good reporters were supposed to carry. He set it on the desk between them.

'Do you mind if I record this conversation?' he asked.

'That depends.'

'On what?' David asked.

'On what you ask me.'

'Does it matter what I ask? Your answers are your own.' David reached over and put the recorder back in his pocket. 'But we can save the official record until later, if it makes you more comfortable.'

Spear shrugged. 'What brings you to our retreat, Mr Nichols?'

'Curiosity. I'd like to ask you a few questions.'

'I believe it will be more than a few, gauging from your questions this afternoon.'

'Naturally, before taking on this assignment, I acquainted myself with your past achievements. I know of your interest in the Dogon people and their connection to the ancient Egyptians.'

'Africa is long ago and far away, Mr Nichols.'

'David, please. I believe your present work is influenced by your experiences in Africa. For example, you went to Mali primarily as an anthropologist. But since you returned you've branched out into what I think we would both agree is parapsychology.'

'I had a doctorate in psychology long before I received my degree in anthropology. But let us not quibble over the past. What is your point?'

'Did the Dogon people give you the technique of mutual hypnosis?'

'The technique existed in the West before I went to Africa.'

'But not as you practise it. I have studied the literature on the subject. Nowhere is there an example of such collective group consciousness used to project into the past.'

'Do you believe it is only a projection?'

David paused, decided to give an honest appraisal. 'I admit I came here ready to dismiss the whole idea. But after this afternoon, I don't know. I was impressed with many of the things the Big Mind said. Also, when Lucy spoke for that Egyptian woman, it was as if . . .'

'She was the woman,' Spear interrupted. 'Even her appearance seemed to change in your eyes. We have all had that experience. I call it "genetic transference". Of course, Lucy's appearance had not changed at all. If you study Margaret's video tape you find no Egyptian woman in it. But at the time of the session, in that group state of coherence, consciousness is fluid. There are fewer boundaries between each of us. You experienced Lucy as she was experiencing herself.'

'And you wouldn't call that a spiritual experience?'

Spear snorted. 'That type of interpretation is New Age rubbish. I have fought against it for the last twelve years. People who are desperate to give a spiritual slant to every incidence of expanded awareness are sad souls indeed. I use the pun intentionally. With their frantic search for God they deny the glory of humanity. We are remarkable beings. Contained within our DNA is the secret of how life began on this planet. We can probe that secret using altered states of awareness, which are also, ultimately, a product of that same DNA. What I am trying to do with my work is to give a new meaning to human potential. Not redefine it in a modern religion which doesn't even have the decency to call itself a religion.'

'I spoke to Dr Henry today and he explained to me a bit about the evolution of the brain,' David said. 'He said your probe into genetic memories related to his probe into deeper layers of brain functioning.'

'That is an oversimplification. It is not as if more ancient memories are stored closer to the core of the brain.'

'Yet the core of the human brain is oldest, evolutionary-wise. I understand fish had it. Then the three layers that were built up on top of it – each layer corresponds to a different leap in evolution. There is the reptilian complex, the limbic system and the neocortex. With your genetic regressions, are you trying to tap into these different layers of brain functioning?'

'I believe I have already answered that question.'

David smiled. 'I'm sorry, I must have missed it. What was your answer?'

'No. We are not trying to regress into the limbic system or the reptilian complex. These levels of brain functioning are with us now. There is no need to go into the past to find them. Every human who walks this planet is a savage animal and a cold reptile. It is only because we have trained ourselves with our highly developed neocortexes to suppress these areas of functioning that we have been able to develop a civilized society.'

'Then you do believe each level of the brain has specific emotional and psychological characteristics associated with it? I know the theory is debated among scientists.'

'My answer to your question is yes,' Spear said.

'A moment ago you used the word suppress. Do you,

Professor, believe we are suppressing a portion of our potential as human beings?'

'We are suppressing the bulk of it. At the beginning of this interview you referred to me as a parapsychologist. That is not a title I willingly adopt, but for the sake of this discussion you can call me that. Because I have seen with my own eyes people bend spoons without touching them. Or read the pictures on cards that other people held in their hands two blocks away. I have also seen people remove deep and long lasting pain just by the touch of their hands. Now, understand me clearly, none of these things are miraculous. None of them means that there is a beneficent God in heaven watching out for us. They are normal human abilities. Abilities we should all have. They are built into us. That is the goal of my research. To give back to man what he has lost.'

'So you believe people had these abilities in the past?' David asked.

'I didn't exactly say that.'

'You implied it, Professor. Did we or did we not have these abilities in the past?'

Spear considered. 'Perhaps.'

'Have you been able to rekindle them with your genetic regressions?'

'I'm not sure I understand your question.'

'Have you found a culture in the past that possessed these abilities? For example, the pre-dynasty Egyptians?'

'There are signs, of course, that they had such abilities. You heard an example of that this afternoon.'

'You refer to how the young woman was pursued by bodiless eyes and held down by invisible arms until the evil priests arrived on the scene?' David asked.

'The woman in question saw them as evil. For all we know, she could have been the trouble maker.'

'Yet she did not seem interested in having the others' abilities.'

'I cannot comment on her personal interests,' Spear said.

'I am reminded of a remark Dr Henry made today. We were talking about the structure of the human brain and he said, "Yet the old layers have remained. They still have to be taken into account." I didn't understand what he meant at the time but the longer I stay here the better idea I get. Also, a comment you made a moment ago interests me. You said, "It is only because we have trained ourselves with our highly developed neocortexes to suppress these areas of functioning that we have been able to develop a civilized society." I am not misquoting you, am I?'

'No. What's your point?'

'Just that these remarkable abilities we might have possessed in the past – maybe we lost or suppressed them for good reason. Maybe they had a way of fucking up society, if you will excuse my Egyptian.'

Spear frowned. Or perhaps it was closer to a glare. It was hard to tell in the shifting orange light of the crackling logs. The iguana was still staring at David. He had to resist the urge to walk over and open its cage and throw it in the fire. He had never cared for lizards. They reminded him of the desert, Las Vegas. He wondered if there were dinosaur bones buried in the sands surrounding sin city.

'Your comment reveals the bane of every true scientist the world over,' Spear replied in a measured tone, not so gentle now. 'That is fear. Space is unknown. The bottom of the ocean is still largely unknown. The future is unknown. The bulk of the past is unknown. What is unknown, not understood, is feared by most people. But that does not mean it's evil. When we began this discussion you said you were here because you were curious. You have been here only one day. Aren't you still curious? Wouldn't you have us go ahead with our work?'

David met his gaze. Spear had a bit of a megalomaniac

in him. He liked to try to stare people down, an easy thing to do with those two black holes in his head. David replied in the same measured, slightly condescending, tone.

'I would urge you to go ahead with your work only after a close examination of your past efforts in the same direction,' he said.

Spear was startled. 'What do you mean?'

David smiled. He had just been fishing for a reaction and was happy to get one. 'We haven't talked about your experiences with the Dogon in Africa. I would like to know if they were aware of the phenomena of genetic memory?'

Spear found the question insulting. 'I did not steal the theory from them, if that's what you're implying. Besides, I have never said the idea originated with me. But I am the first one to prove its validity.'

'I'm afraid you didn't answer my question, Professor.'

'The Dogon have a mystical tradition that does seem to incorporate elements of the theory of genetic memory.'

'Do they sit around in groups like you guys do and delve into the past?'

'Not exactly.'

'What do they do different?' David asked.

Spear was still annoyed. 'For one thing they don't have redheads in their groups.' He added, 'I don't understand the purpose of your question.'

'My purpose should be apparent, but let's move on. Do you have a special technique for bypassing what you call the rational thought barrier?'

'Who told you about that?'

'Lucy. She said you're planning to have the group regress beyond primitive man during this week's retreat. Is that correct?'

'Lucy shouldn't be talking about such things. We have never regressed that far before.'

'But are you going to make the attempt while we're here?' David persisted.

Spear was a long time answering. 'That remains to be seen.'

'You had a Professor Buckley, your wife, and your sister-in-law with you while you were in Mali. Is that correct?'

Spear's guard was up. He was wondering how this annoying reporter could know so much. 'Yes,' he said carefully.

'How did your wife die, Professor?'

Spear sucked in a breath. Sounded like a hiss. Might have been the iguana doing his yogic breathing. For a moment David had trouble telling the master and his pet apart. Spear shifted in his seat and it sounded as if it were about to crumble beneath him.

'My wife died in an accident,' Spear said finally. 'The details are not pertinent to this subject matter. I will not discuss it.'

'Why did your sister-in-law go insane? Was that an accident?'

Spear stood. He was remarkably tall, when you were looking up at him. 'Really, these questions are getting too personal, and have nothing to do with our present research or hopefully your article on our research. I will not answer them. My wife's death is still a painful memory for me. I do not need to have it stirred by your prodding, especially before dinner. I'm going to eat now. You are welcome to join me if you agree to stop asking abusive questions.'

David stood as well. 'I apologize if my questions caused you pain. That was not my intention. I'm simply doing my job. But I do have one other question, if I may ask it?'

'Yes?'

'Is it your belief that the ancient Egyptians were contacted by an alien race?'

'No.' Spear stepped around his desk. 'Are you coming with me?'

'Yes.' David gestured to the iguana. 'What's her name?'

'*His* name. It's Frank. I've had him for the last twelve years.'

'I see,' David said.

David did not sit next to Spear at dinner. Actually, the Professor collected his food and retreated back to his office. Frankie had probably put in an earlier request to his master for a drumstick to chew on. Maybe not. David remembered that reptiles liked to eat living things, when they could get hold of them.

Well, he ended up asking Margaret to marry him. He had to; the food was that delicious, and then some. Unfortunately for David's stomach, he had second and third helpings and was groaning before dessert, a German chocolate cake topped with vanilla ice cream, appeared. Margaret had accomplished the impossible. She had made the mashed potatoes just like his mother used to, and David had never met a woman who could do that. Even Sandy had made lousy mashed potatoes. Margaret accepted his wedding proposal but immediately wanted a ring to make it official. David then backed off, laughing, noticing Lucy frowning in the corner.

After dinner, with the exception of Spear, the group stayed at the dining room table to gossip. David felt at home with them. Indeed, he thought he was going to miss them when he said goodbye. To liven things up, he challenged Jon to a game of poker but the Swede declined, citing moral qualms about such a low life game. But he did agree to bend a few spoons for David.

'You'll bend them right here in front of me?' David asked. 'Using your mind?'

Jon nodded nonchalantly. 'Of course.'

'You won't touch them?' David asked.

'I will touch them only lightly, with my fingertips,' Jon said.

'Come on, Jon,' David prodded him. 'Why do you have to touch them at all if you're going to bend them with the power of your thoughts?'

'I don't like having my spoons ruined,' Margaret said, sitting on David's right, Lucy on his left. Jon ignored her. He handed David a soup spoon.

'Feel this,' Jon said. 'It's stainless steel, of high quality and thickness. If I were to hold this lightly between my index finger and my thumb, and it were to melt down before your eyes, would you be impressed?'

David checked out the spoon and found it normal in all respects. 'Do it first and then ask me.' He gave the spoon back to Jon.

'We should hook the dude up to the EEG,' Tom said.

'He'd probably short it out with that kind of cosmic energy going through him,' Dr Henry said. He reached over and tapped Tom lightly on the arm. 'Speaking of which, you had high theta waves going on inside your head in the session this afternoon. What were you thinking about? Your old rig? A night out with those good old country boys down in Oklahoma?'

Tom quickly withdrew his arm. 'I was thinking about the Egyptian priestess, like everybody else. Besides, you shouldn't be discussing my private brain waves at the dinner table. What kind of doctor are you anyway?'

Dr Henry grinned. 'Sue me, Tom.'

'Quiet, everybody,' Jon said, closing his eyes, lightly massaging the point on the spoon where the handle joined the cup between his two fingers. 'I have to concentrate.'

'I suppose there's a first time for everything,' Lucy said, amused by the psychic demonstration. To her left sat Vera, quietly finishing her cake. She hadn't taken any turkey, but had eaten a small amount of potatoes and vegetables. David had been happy just to see her at the meal. He had been concerned about her after the session, especially when she had left the chapel quickly without speaking to anyone. But she seemed all right now.

'That's one of my favourite spoons,' Margaret said.

'We can always bend it back,' Lucy said.

'Would everybody please shut up?' Jon asked, his tanned forehead wrinkled. The gang left him in peace for a few minutes. Jon continued to work the spot on the spoon as if hoping it would climax. Then, much to David's surprise, the spoon magically began to sag in front of his eyes. The thing drooped as if it were roasting in a furnace. Jon opened his eyes and smiled.

'No sweat,' he said.

'Let me see that,' David said, swiping the spoon from Jon. By golly the spoon was hot. David was dumbfounded. 'How did you do it?'

Jon revealed, 'I was born gifted.'

'So was everyone,' Lucy said. She swiped the spoon away. 'David, did you know that you can do what Jon just did? I can teach you how to do it, in a few minutes.'

'I don't think so,' David said. 'I don't have soldering tips for fingernails.'

'You don't need them,' Lucy said. 'All you need is to work the spoon as Jon did and have an off focus that it's getting hot.'

'What's an off focus?' David asked.

'You focus while you look the other way,' Vera muttered.

'You concentrate but you don't strain yourself,' Lucy said. 'Margaret, give me your spoon.'

'No,' Margaret said.

'I have a spoon,' Panda offered, searching the area of his plate, unsuccessfully. It seemed as if Margaret had grabbed it just before he spoke. Panda hadn't had any turkey either, of course, but had eaten plenty of everything else. David wondered where the little guy put it all.

'You can have mine,' Dr Henry said, taking the one besides Tom's plate.

'That's mine,' Tom said.

Dr Henry was sweet. 'I was using it before you.'

Jon shifted uneasily. 'This is not something everybody should attempt. It could be dangerous.'

'Bullshit,' Lucy said, accepting the spoon from Dr Henry. Closing her eyes, she began to rock it lightly between her thumb and index finger. 'It's getting hot already,' she muttered a minute later.

'But hot enough to melt?' David asked. Offhand he did not know the melting point of steel, but figured it must be hotter than two sweaty fingers could produce – by a few hundred, if not few thousand, degrees. Yet, to his astonishment, two minutes later, Lucy's spoon sagged the same way as Jon's. She opened her eyes and handed it to David. It was *real* hot.

'No sweat,' she said sarcastically, giving Jon a dirty look.

'I did it in less time than you,' Jon said defensively.

'How in Christ's name did either of you do it?' David asked.

'It's done by focusing one of those strange forms of energy inside us that science doesn't yet understand,' Dr Henry explained. 'Somehow, by bringing the attention to the fingertips and wishing for heat, the body produces a current that loosens the molecular structure of the steel. Actually, I don't even know if the rubbing motion is necessary for it to work. I think the focus is enough.'

'You've seen people do this before?' David asked.

Dr Henry nodded. 'I was once at a party of little kids and I handed out a bunch of spoons and asked them to give it a try. Without exception they were able to bend them with the tips of their fingers, even though I have never been able to do it. As Lucy and Vera explained, the trick is to focus on heat without focusing too hard. Children have a knack for that.'

'I never knew you guys could do it,' Jon said.

'Ah ha.' Lucy pointed a finger at him. 'You didn't know anyone else was *gifted*? What would the Big Mind say about your ego, huh? That it was *fully* inflatable?'

'I was impressed,' David muttered.

Lucy shook her head. 'You're a smart guy, David, but you're also too materialistic. There's a whole world going on around you that you never look at. Wake up and smell the coffee. Grab yourself a spoon. Seriously, give it a try.'

Margaret sighed and handed her own spoon to David. 'Just promise me you'll try to straighten it out when you're done with it,' she said.

David held the spoon warily. He thought he might have been more comfortable handling a jagged edged hunting knife that he wasn't required to bend, just stick in some bad guy maybe.

'I don't know if I was meant to channel unexplainable energies,' he said.

Lucy patted his arm. 'Just do it. I promise Satan will not enter your body and possess your soul. I will stand guard.'

What the hell, David thought. He closed his eyes and began to lightly rub the bend in the spoon between his thumb and index finger. He thought of heat flowing from his hands into the metal. He thought of all the others staring at him with smirks on their faces. After a few minutes, the spoon was no hotter. He opened his eyes and set it down.

'Nothing happened,' he said.

'Too much heat,' Panda said, touching his forehead.

'He's saying you were straining,' Lucy explained. 'You can't try. You have to let it happen.'

David felt like he was back in kindergarten. 'How do you try not to try?'

Lucy picked up the spoon and offered it. 'Do it again. I'll rub the back of your head while you rub the metal. You'll be relaxed and attentive at the same time.'

'This is getting kinky,' Dr Henry said. 'The whipped cream will come out next.'

'I bought some whipped cream,' Margaret said.

Once more David closed his eyes and set to work on the spoon. With Lucy's delightful fingers digging into his neck muscles and stroking the back of his skull he did begin to feel kind of hot, but he had to wonder through which part of his body the warmth flowed. A few minutes went by. The session with the Big Mind had given him a boost of energy but the caressing relaxed him to the point where a fifteen year backlog of fatigue started to pour out. His head fell slightly, and he had to catch himself to sit up straight, and to remember to keep rubbing the spoon. In the middle of all this someone let out a cry of pleasure. His eyes popped open. Around that table, except for Jon, they were all grinning.

The spoon had melted in his hand.

He dropped it on the table. It was not that the thing was that hot; it was just unnatural, in his mind.

'Wow,' he said.

'Our new high priest,' Lucy said, leaning over to give him a congratulatory kiss on the cheek. 'Oh Master, teach me the ancient secrets. Let thine eternal power enter into my bosom.'

Tom nodded to Dr Henry. 'Definitely time for the whipped cream,' Tom said.

'I can't believe I did that,' David said, enjoying Lucy's closeness. Her hand continued to rest on the back of his head. He chuckled as he stared into her lovely green eyes, and wondered where he had seen them before. They looked familiar. Must have been a past life. 'How do I know it wasn't your touch that didn't make it all possible?'

She flashed a nasty grin. 'You might always wonder, David.'

The dining hall had a storage room as well as a kitchen. It was in the basement at the end of a steep ten foot flight of stairs. Together, Tom and David carried Margaret and her wheelchair down into the cool damp room. She preferred to put away the food they hadn't finished herself, she said. While Tom and Dr Henry cleared the dining area, and the rest washed and dried the dishes in the kitchen, David assisted Margaret with the odd placement she couldn't reach. David had known a few handicapped people in his days but none impressed him as much as Margaret. It was as if the life she had lost in the lower half of her body had simply shifted to the top half, and doubled her vitality. She pushed and spun her wheelchair about the cramped storage area as if she were an MTV extra on a skateboard.

'I know I've told you already,' David said, putting away a box of flour. 'But I wanted to say again how good the mashed potatoes were. I wish I could take you home with me.'

'You had your chance,' Margaret replied, sealing the unused salad fixings in plastic wrap. 'You chickened out.'

'I saw a dark cloud forming over Lucy's head.'

'I told you she'd get jealous. It's just as well. If you ate my cooking all the time, you'd get fat. Besides, you know the secret to those mashed potatoes you liked so much?'

'What?' David asked.

'It's a little butter and milk. I made them very plain. The others weren't so crazy about them as you. But I knew that about you from the moment I saw you. You like plain food. You would drive most women who can cook crazy.'

'Am I that transparent?' David asked, not worried by the idea. Margaret stopped what she was doing to study him.

'No,' she admitted. 'I agree with the Big Mind. You're a mystery man.'

'What makes me so mysterious?'

'If I told you then it wouldn't be a mystery Did you enjoy the session this afternoon?'

'Very much. Except at the end when Vera got upset. I was worried about her.'

'I know you were.' Margaret was thoughtful, sad even. 'I worry about her as well. She's such a beautiful girl.' Margaret briefly closed her eyes and rubbed her head. 'She's very sensitive.'

'Is something wrong?' David asked, taking a step closer.

Margaret blinked and shook her head. 'No. Everything's fine.' She returned to her lettuce and tomato. 'Are you going to take the Big Mind's advice?'

'I might if I understood how to translate it into practical terms,' David said honestly. He still didn't believe the intelligence of the universe had spoken to him that afternoon, but he continued to remain deeply affected by the encounter. The Big Mind had touched a sore spot inside, and made it hurt worse. Yet, ironically, there had been relief in the midst of the pain that he couldn't explain to himself. Sandy and Angela were still dead, and he doubted if he would ever be able to drop how they had died, and his role in their ends. Yet, after the session, it was as if the tragedies – in particular, Angela's – had occurred longer ago than they had before the session. Unfortunately, not so long ago that they felt like incidents in another life. If reincarnation was a reality, he thought, he was glad it was arranged that they forgot what had happened the last time around. He sure as hell didn't want to come back as an FBI agent.

'Oh, I think it was very practical when it came to giving you advice,' Margaret said.

'That I should be happy? What do I do to be happy? It skipped over that small detail.'

'It pointed you in a direction. Besides, happiness doesn't come from doing this or that. Or even from thinking happy thoughts. Happiness is what we are, inside.'

'Happiness may be what you are, Margaret, but I'm afraid to say you're in the minority. You have to multiply yourself.'

She smiled, such a kind expression on her face. 'If there were too many of me, just think how congested the malls would be at Christmas with all the wheelchairs.' She threw a carrot at him. He caught it easily. 'Go see Lucy. She's waiting for you. I can manage down here. Tom and Dr Henry can lift me back out when I'm through.'

'Isn't she still doing dishes?' David asked.

'Lucy never does dishes. She's too lazy.'

David stepped for the steep stairway. A thought made him stop. 'Margaret?'

'Yes?'

He glanced over his shoulder. 'Do you have any idea at all who you were before your coma? Any image – even a faint image – from before the hospital?'

She looked at him a long time before answering. 'When I awoke, I remembered the sun and the moon and the stars. Mostly the stars.'

'Is that all?'

'Yes,' she said softly. 'That's all.'

CHAPTER NINE

Ned Calendar chartered a private plane to Salutory, South Carolina. The evening was clear and the visibility excellent. The pilot chatted nonstop beside him about how his wife was cheating on him with a guy who designed clothes store mannequins for a living. But he couldn't leave the fucking bitch because of the kids. The pilot's name was Ed Barnsdale and he sounded as if he enjoyed his kids about as much he liked finding his wife's lover's used condoms under the bed. Ned advised him to talk to an attorney and not an FBI agent.

Salutory had its own airport, one of those narrow country affairs where the runway was mowed rather than paved. Ned thought he saw a couple necking on the nearby grass as they set down but could have been mistaken. Ned could have had a local agent waiting to take him to the mental hospital, but he took a cab instead. As he climbed out of the plane, he told Ed not to go far.

The sanatorium, as they drove up, looked like a prison that had been dropped from a great height. The building was a squat, rectangular; the bars on the windows looked as if they had been welded on while the patients inside screamed to get out. There was no landscaping except for a few scraggly bushes that would have been better off with a nice layer of asphalt at their roots. It was a cheery place. He told the cab to wait as well.

The head physician in charge of the night shift was expecting him. Ned had pulled strings to get in to see Frances Cumberly at such an odd hour. That was another good thing about retiring. He could call in all the favours he wished like there was no tomorrow. The way Professor Buckley had gripped his hand before he left, maybe there wouldn't be. Not that Ned was afraid of an insane woman who had been locked up for twelve years.

Dr Simon Goldberg was younger than Ned had expected. He looked like a nerdy first year medical student who didn't wash his hands after gross anatomy. The lenses on his glasses belonged on the new and improved Hubble telescope. He even had a few zits left over from college all-nighters fuelled with chocolate bars and girlie magazine posters. But by golly was Simon happy to meet a genuine FBI agent, especially at one in the morning.

'Did she kill somebody?' he asked when Ned explained that he was there to see Frances Cumberly.

'Not that I know of.' Ned paused. 'Has she killed someone while she's been here?'

'She might have done if she had had the chance. We have her on heavy Thorazine, wrapped in a straightjacket in security isolation. The whole ten yards.' Dr Goldberg flipped open the folder in his hands. 'Would you like me to review her medical records with you?'

'Yes. Please.'

'Frances Cumberly. Forty-four years of age. Primary diagnosis: acute schizophrenia. She thinks she is the direct descendant of an ancient godlike race. Has delusions of supernatural powers – telekinesis and mental telepathy and such – but has never demonstrated any paranormal abilities, although she is extraordinarily strong. Perception of reality is intermittent. Spends the majority of her time wrapped in hallucinations. Has failed to respond to traditional psychotherapy or even repeated shock therapy. Prone to exceptionally dangerous outbursts of violence.' Dr Goldberg closed his folder and looked at Ned as if he should be impressed they had such an interesting patient. 'Are you sure you want to interview her?'

'Yes. Have you woken her?' Ned asked.

'We didn't have to. She doesn't sleep much. I have gone to the liberty of having two orderlies chain her down for your visit. While you are here, I am responsible for your safety.' He added, 'I must also be present during the questioning. Hospital rules.'

'Why is it a hospital rule?' Ned asked.

'It's for your protection as well as hers.'

'But if she's in a straightjacket and chained down, I should be safe. And I doubt my questions can harm her more than twelve years of Thorazine has, not to mention all the voltage you've run through her brain.' Ned paused. 'I'll speak to her alone.'

Dr Goldberg did not persist. If anything he looked relieved. 'Very well. Let me show you to her room.'

'Just a moment. You mentioned she has a *primary* diagnosis of acute schizophrenia. Does she suffer from anything else?'

'Yes. She has severe psoriasis. It has failed to respond to treatment. For hygienic reasons, we keep her completely shaved.'

'When did this start?' Ned asked.

'She's had it since her initial breakdown, twelve years ago.'

'I see,' Ned said.

Dr Goldberg led him to Frances' room, which in reality was a padded cell fresh out of One Flew Over The Lobotomy Nest. The room's only illumination was a dull red emergency light on the ceiling, encased in hammer-proof plastic. Ned requested more light before he was shut in the cell but was told that was not possible. Frances, it seemed, straightjacket and all, had managed to break every light that had ever been installed in her room. She didn't mind the red night light, however. Ned felt as if he were being shut in a volcanic cave as Dr Goldberg wished him happy hunting and closed the door. Dr Goldberg insisted the door be closed. As one last tiny bit of medical history, the good doctor added that Frances had once escaped her cell and gouged out and eaten both the eyes of a severely retarded twelve- year-old boy. Wonderful, Ned thought.

Besides being dark and claustrophobic, the cell was permeated by a peculiar odour. To Ned it smelled like a tropical rain forest after a fire. The odour was specific to the room; the rest of the hospital was simply stuffy. Ned wondered at its source.

There were no chairs available. Ned sat on the floor across from the bunk bed bolted into the wall, a toilet and sink on his right. Frances leaned upright against the far wall as if she had been fixed there by a spear. In combination with the sober red light, her straightjacket and bald head made her look like a mummy dug from a burning tomb. Her expression was grotesque. Had the electroshock destroyed the nerves in her face? Left them permanently firing in a pattern of pain? Her mouth was twisted in a voracious maw, her nostrils peeled back like mucus-dripping snouts. Her eyes, as Buckley had forecast, were the material of nightmares. A speck of gold glowed in the centre of each. Beneath the overhead light they looked like twin pools of steaming blood, where the treasure of an entire life had ages ago boiled and drowned. Her long pointed tongue raked the air in search of invisible flies. The hiss of her breath was the death rattle of a cobra pit.

'Frances,' he began. 'My name is Ned Calendar. I'm an FBI agent in charge of finding out the truth about what happened to you and your sister in Africa. I'm here to ask you a few questions.' He paused. 'Do you understand me?'

The gold eye dots swelled. Her head continued to bob from side to side but it steadied somewhat in his direction. 'I understand,' she said in a snake's voice.

Ned swallowed. Jesus. She needed a fucking exorcist, not Thorazine. That was the trouble with psychiatrists today, he thought. They were never trained in the dark arts. He felt for his gun under his coat and was happy she was chained down.

'Do you remember what happened in Africa?' he asked.

'No Africa. One land.' Her head perched forward. 'Come closer.'

'I'm comfortable where I am. Do you remember your sister?'

'Yes. The mirror. We came out of the mirror.' She hissed. 'Hungry.'

'You and your sister came out of the mirror?'

'No. The mirror. Want to bite you.'

Ned felt inspired. 'Who is *we*?'

'We are your master. Made you. Came before you. We can do anything.'

Ned took his wedding ring off his finger. 'Do you know what this is?'

'Yes.'

'This is a ring. If you can do anything, make it disappear.'

'No. The mirror's cracked. No power.'

'What is the mirror? Was it in Africa?'

'No Africa. One world. Sister cracked. No power.'

'Your sister was related to the mirror?'

'Yes. Cracked.'

'When it cracked you lost your power?'

'Yes.'

'When she died?'

'Yes.'

'Did you lose your mind when she died?'

Her head stretched towards him an almost impossible length. It was as if she were an ostrich with silly puddy for a cervix. 'No. Hungry. Feed me. Give me arm.'

'I would like to keep my arm, thank you. How did she die? Did you kill her?'

'No.'

'Who did kill her?'

'Don't know. Dead. Power dead.'

'Frances, do you remember your name?'

'Yes. Zenath. Master of Frances. We made you.'

'Zenath exists in the past inside Frances?'

'Zenath now and past. Zenath hungry. Water. Thirsty.'

Ned went to get up. 'You want a glass of water?'

'Yes.' The maw twisted into the facsimile of a grin. 'Then meat. Blood.'

Ned sat back down. 'I'll get your water later. Let me understand you. Zenath existed in the past. Is she an ancient ancestor of Frances?'

'Yes. Ancient. One land. We were the masters.'

'Were you the Dogon?'

'No.'

'The ancient Egyptians?'

'No. Before the warm ones came. We were there.'

'Are you saying there existed a race of people before the Egyptians?'

'No people. Only masters. People are food. Come closer.'

Ned felt a cold wave, a damp hand rising from below, from a place where things that were best left buried had been stirred as if summoned. He couldn't believe the thing sitting in front of him had once been a friend of Professor Buckley's, or anyone else's friend for that matter. He couldn't stop staring at her. She had some kind of hold on him.

A race more ancient than mankind dreamed?

I am talking to a schizophrenic. I must not forget that.

Yet everything she said, no matter how absurd, rang true. Why?

'But I don't want you to eat me, Zenath,' he said. 'I won't come any closer.'

'Oh.'

'What kind of race are you from, Zenath?'

She might have bitten her own lips or tongue. Blood trickled out her mouth and onto her straightjacket. The gold in her eyes liquefied. 'Beautiful. Powerful. Intelligent. We are your masters. We come for you.'

'You come for us? Out of the past?'

'Yes.'

He discovered he was trembling. He couldn't make himself stop.

'How do you come? Through the mirror?'

'Yes. Hungry. The past burns.'

'Why does past burn?'

'We burned it. Everything black. Cold. No food.'

'Did your race destroy itself?'

'Yes.'

'How?'

'Hunger. Power. Hate.'

'Did you hate each other?'

'Yes.'

'Why?'

'No why. Nature. Power. Hunger.'

'Do you hate people?'

'Yes.'

'How long ago did your race live?'

'Ancient.'

'Did you have an advanced civilization?'

'Yes.'

'More advanced than humanity's?'

'Yes. More power.'

'Was your race able to travel to the stars?'

'Yes.'

'Did you ever go to Sirius?'

'Blue white star. Bright. Yes. Three stars there.'

'Not two?'

'Three.'

'You come from the past into the present through the mirror?'

'Yes.'

'Is the mirror constructed of identical human twins?'

'Yes. Perfect.'

His heart pounded. That was the key, he thought. Then he recalled his vow to not be influenced by her insanity. But who was the real patient here? He thought he would go nuts just looking into her eyes. He wished he could stop looking at them.

'Like Frances and her sister?' he asked softly.

'Yes. Came through that mirror.' A satisfied hiss. 'Swallowed Frances.'

'Was Penny swallowed?'

'She died. Mirror cracked.'

'Are you able to come into the present through the process of genetic regression?'

'Yes.'

'Did Professor Spear guide his wife and his sister-in-law through this process?'

'No. Zenath did.'

'Did the Spear help?'

'Spear is food. Ned is food. Come closer.'

'I will come no closer. What's special about identical twins that you can manifest in our time through them?'

'Perfect reflections. Mirror faces mirror. No holes. No cracks.'

So that was it. Logical. Genetically identical twins could not be told apart. The coherence between them during mutual hypnosis would be flawless. How did this thing– he had ceased to think of it as human – know that?

'Genetic regression works perfectly when only identical twins are used?' he asked.

'Yes.'

'Did the Dogon know this?'

'Yes.'

'Did the ancient Egyptians?'

'Yes.'

'Did you manifest in that time?'

'Yes. Powerful. Spread from mirrors. Ruled people. Ruled land.'

'If you were so powerful, how did you lose your power?'

'Don't know. The future.'

'What about the future?'

'Poisonous. Danger.'

'What do you mean you spread from the mirror? Can people other than identical twins manifest your race in our time?'

'Yes. Need mirror. Short time. Control brain. Heat core.'

'You can alter people's brain and they become like you?'

'Yes.'

'But you lost your power when Frances' sister died?'

'Yes.'

'Did you alter anyone before you died?'

'No answer.'

'You don't know?'

'I know. No answer you.'

'Why not?'

The thing giggled. 'You are food!'

He fought to get a grip on himself. It was tied up. He had the gun. He was safe.

'I may be food but you're locked in a mental hospital. Do you know that?'

'Yes.'

'Can you break out of here?'

'No.'

'Zenath is trapped? You don't sound so powerful.'

'Another mirror. Another Zenath.'

He spoke with conviction he did not feel. 'I don't think so. Only the Dogon and Spear know how to bring you alive. And the Dogon know you're dangerous and keep twins apart. And I will stop Spear. The knowledge will be lost. Zenath will be forgotten.'

It continued to giggle. 'I will touch you.'

Ned put his gun away and stood. 'No, you won't. Even if everything you say is true, which I doubt, you'll never get close to me again.'

'Oh.'

Ned stepped for the door. 'Zenath, before I leave, describe to me what your race looked like?'

In response the thing suddenly sucked in a deep hissing breath. Ned heard a mighty ripping sound, but it took him a second to understand what was happening. By the time he did, it was too late. The monster had torn a large hole in the straightjacket. It lurched forward. Ned tried to back away but a crushing grip closed on his right wrist. He momentarily lost his footing as he was yanked towards the cackling beast. It raised his right hand towards its bloody teeth, its long tongue darting out in anticipation. Ned thought of the retarded boy and his missing eyes as he struggled to reach his gun with his left hand. The stench from the thing's mouth made his head spin. Smelled like a corpse found in a cesspool in deep Amazon land. Ned's terror was a black wave sent crashing from the nightmares of human infancy. It washed away all reason. The situation was primeval. The thing was hungry and he didn't want to be its food. He tried to shout for help but nothing came out his mouth.

Jesus help me!

The thing licked the back of his hand with a tongue made of scratchy reeds and slowly looked over at him. Truly, Ned thought, something deep in its brain ignited in that moment, burning through its optic nerves, bringing a hot sheen to the coldness of its dragon eyes.

'I look like this,' it said.

Ned got out his gun. He pressed the barrel to the thing's temple. 'Let me go,' he croaked. 'I'll blow out the core of your fucking brain, you goddam witch.'

The thing was pleased. Slowly, delicately, it licked his hand again. Ned didn't know why he didn't pull the trigger. He knew it could take off his fingers in one bite. Perhaps it had him hypnotized. He felt his will belonged to another. Yet it didn't put his flesh in its mouth, and in a strange sense this disturbed him more than if it simply bit him, especially after all its talk of hunger. He realized then that its craving was not primarily physical.

It wanted something else from him.

It moved his hand to the top of its bald head and stroked his finger over its sickening skin. Psoriasis, my ass Ned thought.

The thing had scales.

'I feel like this,' it said.

'Oh God,' Ned whispered.

It was a reptile.

How ancient was ancient?

The thing grinned. 'No God.' It shoved him back. Ned almost fell as he hit the opposite wall. Fortunately, it was padded or he would have been knocked out. Then the devil only knew what would have become of him. He had dropped his gun but quickly scampered to pick it up. That is how he felt; like a beast raised for food grovelling at the feet of its master. Even as he levelled the pistol at the thing, it was still in control. 'I will touch you again,' it said.

Ned left then, quickly. In the long sanatorium hallway, Dr Simon Goldberg wanted to know how his interview had gone but Ned was in too much of a hurry to tell him. He ran to the cab, and once inside it he yelled at the driver to take him to the airfield. Ned rolled down the window, wanting to vomit. He felt as if he had absorbed a large portion of Frances Cumberly's psychosis during his brief time inside the sanatorium. He wondered how Dr Goldberg coped so well, but perhaps the prize patient had put on a special performance for his eyes only. Or perhaps the good doctor knew which patients were best left alone. No wonder the man had been relieved not to accompany him into that cell.

At the airport, Ned ordered Ed Barnsdale to spare no fuel getting him back to Miami. He had to talk to Professor Buckley immediately. He had to confront him with the evidence. What was left of Frances had exploded his belief system. He had to ask the learned Professor if it was not all just some bad dream. Or if humanity was in fact cursed. Cursed by a prehistoric past where no angels had ever roamed.

CHAPTER TEN

Lucy Temple and David Conner drifted on a starry lake. Lucy rowed gently, lest the ripples completely ruin the reflection of the black dome. They sat facing each other in the boat but the darkness was so thick her date could have been a shadow. She liked to think of him that way – as a blind date, an enigmatic stranger who had just happened to show up at her door, which David had done only thirty minutes ago. They had not hiked to the lake where they had met, but rather to a smaller pond behind the camp. Here the water was warmer; she hoped they could go for a swim. In her bag she had brought two towels as well as a high powered flashlight. No bathing suit, though. Now all she had to do was get his clothes off.

'Did you know this boat would be here?' David asked, leaning back, relaxed, his outstretched legs near her own.

'Yes. Dr Henry and I found this spot yesterday.' She added, 'The water is clean here.'

He yawned and stretched his arms upwards, his head tilted back. 'I don't know if I've ever seen so many stars in the sky at once. Do they have more of them in Idaho than the rest of the country, do you think?'

'We're a long way from a major city. Even a smattering of indirect light can ruin the constellations. Guess how many *individual* stars you can see in the sky with the naked eye? I am not talking about the fuzzy light of the Milky Way.'

'I would guess *billions* and *billions*,' David said, imitating Carl Sagan from the *Cosmos* TV program.

'A little over two thousand,' Lucy said.

'No way. I see more stars than that.'

'You just think you do. Two thousand is a lot of stars. There are only two thousand stars of a magnitude six and less. The human eye can't see anything fainter than that. Trust me, I grew up playing with telescopes. I wanted to be an astronomer when I was young.'

'And now you're old, Lucy.'

She smiled. 'Do you think of me as a little girl?'

He continued to stare at the sky. 'No. I think you're an alien. Strange words come out of your mouth at odd times. Where's Sirius? Is it up now?'

'No. It's a winter star. But that blue star you see directly overhead is important. It's named Vega and it's twenty-six light years from Earth. I read an article once that said it might mark the limit of man's universe. If the speed of light is the maximum we can hope to achieve, then a man could conceivably travel to Vega and back in fifty-two years. But he would use up the majority of his adult life.'

'Don't you believe in the possibility of warp drive?' David asked.

'I told you, I'm a born believer. I don't rule it out.'

David pointed east, just above the trees. 'What's that star there? It's bright.'

'That's the planet Jupiter. And that's Mars over there. It's not nearly as bright but it has that wicked red colour. I used to dream about travelling to Mars when I was young. I wanted to be an astronaut as well.' She paused. 'You know, I'm always telling you about myself but you never say anything about your past. Why is that?'

'I told you, I'm afraid you're an alien. I don't know what you'll do with the information.' He gestured to the sky as a whole. 'How did the ancients see so many constellations and gods and goddesses up there? I don't see any. What do you think they were smoking?'

Lucy laughed softly. 'Many of them stared at the sky every night. To them, it was a big part of their life, as it should be. We forget how small the Earth is in the greater scheme of things. They let their imaginations flow. The stars spoke to them.'

'You believe they channelled the myths?' David asked.

'I don't know. Maybe,' Lucy said. 'The word channelling can be applied to so many different states of mind. All I know is I loved those myths as a child. But many of the stories we classify under Greek mythology actually came from the Egyptians. Professor Spear explained several examples to me: Jason and the Argonauts, the Golden Fleece, the great god Hermes – all those legends came from the Egyptians.'

'What about Zeus? Was he really Egyptian?'

'The Egyptians worshipped their queen before their king.'

'Isis?' David asked.

'Yes. She was *the* Goddess.'

David sat up, making the small boat rock. Lucy stopped paddling; she had been going in circles anyway. He touched her bare leg, and she liked the feel of his fingers. It had been too long since she'd had a real man touch her. Yet it was not as though she just wanted to seduce him. His attraction for her was complex. She had only known him twelve hours but already felt as if he were a large part of her life. Of course, anybody else would say she was just riding high in the infatuation phase. He could not be that important to her life because she knew so little of his life. Yet, deep inside, she felt she knew David Nichols. Not that the Big Mind had endowed her with cosmic intuition when it came to men.

Lucy had joked that morning with her sister while discussing her last boyfriend, Neil Hardell, but her remarks about his need for three condoms and HIV phobia had just been a smoke screen. The truth was much darker.

Unknown to Vera, her six month relationship with Neil had been highly damaging to her psyche and her body.

And he had seemed like such a nice guy.

She had met Neil at a health food store located near the Stanford campus, which most would have classified as a safer place than a bar in downtown Oakland. She had gone there for a glass of fresh carrot and celery juice, a daily ritual with her. Waiting for her vegetables to finish pulverizing, she noticed the long-haired blond guy with the bare back that looked as if it had just climbed off a surfboard. He was scrutinizing the vitamins. It didn't appear as if he could tell a B-complex from a herbal laxative. Since the only help in the store was making her drink, she asked him what he was looking for. He was kind of cute, a little sloppy maybe. He smiled when he saw her. Great mouth, lots of white teeth.

'I'm looking for something to straighten out my glands,' he said.

'What's wrong with your glands?' she asked. He looked as healthy as a porpoise.

He leaned closer, very close. Maybe he liked redheads, she didn't know.

'They never go to sleep,' he confided in her.

She didn't have sex with him on their first date, but they made love most of the second. Never had she felt the way that she did in Neil's arms, so much like an animal that for a time she saw the big three – sex, food, and sleep – as the be all and end all of human experience. When they were together even the simplest act of getting undressed or eating a candy bar was coated with a silver lining. They spent most of the time in his bedroom, the music blaring and the grandfather clock ticking loudly in the corner. They ordered out for pizza and when he ate it off her belly she came before he could burp. It was the kind of love affair she had always dreamed of, sort of.

It was a dream. What she didn't know at the time

was that from the word go Neil had been feeding her X&L, candy flips, a combination of LSD and ecstasy that produced a long lasting psychedelic trip with soft, loving edges. Later, a million times later, she was to ask herself how she didn't know that she was drugged. That was one major drawback with her research into heightened states of awareness. She regularly drank her raw juice and did her deep breathing. She was a natural kind of girl; she thought she was tripping on a natural high. Love and sex with a tanned California babe. It was way cool. She saw Neil every night. How was she to know he was a drug addict? He never smoked anything, much less drank. How was she to know *she* was ingesting illicit chemicals? By the depression that flattened her like a falling safe whenever she was away from Neil too long? That, she passed off by blaming her messed up period – which had never been messed up before – and true love. She was such a fool.

He told her the truth in his own subtle way when, after a month of dating, he offered her a X&L pill instead of grinding it up and mixing it in with her Pierre. She flipped, screamed at him for two hours straight. How dare he fuck with her body and mind? What a scum bag. Piss off, buddy, no way am I going to keep seeing you. I would just as soon call the police and have you arrested. Yet, her haughty words aside, she eventually took the pill and spent the night with him. Just this one last time, she swore to herself. One last good fuck for the road. But the road Neil Hardell had put her on created a weary spiral. There was every bit as much uphill as there was downhill. She was an addict for his body as much as his pharmacy. At least, she thought, he didn't charge her for the stuff.

Of course, that financial arrangement didn't last.

Things probably would never have gone as far as they did if she had been having regular sessions with the Big Mind during that time. Unfortunately, Spear was in Europe travelling and they had curtailed their meetings for several months. When he returned, however, and the group sat to contact the Big Mind, it immediately launched into a stern lecture about her behaviour. Yet it respected her privacy. Even when it had finished speaking and she was left sobbing in her seat, no one knew what her problem was. Vera, of course, knew there was something wrong. She had known for a while, she said. They were too close to hide things from each other. Yet, even if Vera knew there was a serious problem, she did not know the specifics, could not imagine them really. The hardest thing Vera ever took was Tylenol. Somehow, Lucy brushed off their questions. It's nothing, it's personal, it's over. Vera was not so easily placated but Lucy made up a convincing story about how awfully she had been treating others lately. Vera bought it. Lucy did confide in Spear, however. He'd been around; she trusted him to understand what she was going through and not judge her. And he was wonderful about the whole thing, but firm as well, like the Big Mind. Quit being a baby. Stop seeing the asshole and stop taking the pills. You'll be your old self in a month.

Easier said than done. The truth is she didn't want to stop sliding and grinding to sensual heaven every night. Plus when she halted the X&L for even two days, she got terrible headaches and felt suicidal. She made discrete inquiries about what she had fallen into. Psychotherapists she knew personally swore LSD and ecstasy were not addictive. They were nuts! By its own nature every chemically induced high had to be classified as addictive if the person in question wanted to keep getting back to the high. She could have written a dissertation on the subject. Candy flips – at night she dreamed about going trick or treating to Neil's apartment. She did not listen to the Big Mind or to Spear.

Naturally, she travelled the usual route of all respectable addicts, but perhaps in a shorter time. She lost weight, skipped classes, had her spending money confiscated, looked like shit, and fought with her pusher and her boyfriend which – lucky her, 'cause it saved her the driving – were the same person. Despair was her new identical twin. Something a little harder from Neil's personal medicine cabinet that could close her eyes a little longer began to look attractive. On top of everything else, the Big Mind was not talking to her any more, although it continued to allow her to sit in on the session. Remarkably, except for Spear, no one knew she was a wreck. But with each passing week she sensed the presence of the Big Mind less and less in their sessions, and it was that loss more than anything else that made her weep. Because she felt as if she were losing her soul as well as frying her nervous system. But maybe the despair was a friend in disguise. Certainly the Big Mind allowed it to build to breaking point without intervention.

During one session, when they were sitting silently and breathing, she prayed to the Big Mind to give her the strength to get away from Neil and quit the drugs. Nothing sensational happened. The hand of God did not zap her with golden light. Yet from that moment on she felt a quiet certainty that everything would be all right. After that session, she marched over to Neil's apartment and told him that she wouldn't be needing his stupid pills or his stiff dick any more. He took it all right. She suspected he had another girl in the back room when she gave notice.

She was fine in less than a month. From then on her faith in the Big Mind was unshakable. Literally, she believed it had saved her life.

Now David Nichols sat before her. In the dark. In her boat. She wanted to kiss him. Hadn't kissed anybody since silver-lined Neil. She had a feeling, with David, that she wouldn't need drugs to swoon. God, she thought, he was so handsome, even though she could barely see him.

193

'What was your question?' she asked.

'I didn't say anything,' he said. 'Are you hearing voices again?'

'I don't hear voices. What were you going to ask?'

'About Isis. I love the sound of that word. It's followed me throughout the day.'

'Isis is one of the words in the mantra the woman in ancient Egypt meditated on. When I was in her mind, I understood the technique she used. It was very powerful. It brought the flood of white light from the chakara – the centre– above the head.'

'Is there really such a thing?' David asked

'Yes. It is subtle but real. I experienced it today.'

David shook his head. 'You scare me sometimes, you know that? I don't know how many of you there is in there.'

She smiled uncertainly. She didn't want to scare him away but she also wanted him to understand her for what she was, no pretences. Neil had never been interested in her work, just her body, her money, and her hands to rub his bony back. What a sick relationship they'd had, she thought sadly. She wanted so much more.

'There's just me in here,' she said softly.

His fingers played with the skin on her knee. 'At the moment, Lucy. But in the session this afternoon, were you really in that woman's mind?'

'Yes. I experienced what she did. But, like I told you earlier, it was as if from a distance. I did not suffer as she suffered.'

'But Vera did.'

'Perhaps. Vera's Vera. She's very sensitive.'

'That's the second time I've heard that about her tonight.'

Lucy paused. 'I know this will sound silly to you as a reporter who is used to hard facts, but when I was with that woman I felt as if I was with my sister.'

'You mean you think it was Vera in a past life?'

She pursed her lips. 'I had a powerful feeling that I knew and loved that woman. Even when the session was finished, I couldn't free myself of the conviction of kinship.'

'What was the black rite?' David asked.

'I don't know. Something awful that permanently altered a person.'

'Do you think it was real?'

Lucy shuddered at the horror of the woman's thoughts when she had contemplated the secret initiation. Yet there had been awe inside the woman as well when she reflected on how her meditation on Isis' name helped prevent the black rite from spreading over the land. Lucy wondered if she could practise the technique the woman had used, if it would work in their modern time. Just the memory of the white light had been wonderful beyond compare.

'Yes,' she replied. 'I think it was completely genuine.'

'Hmm.' David was thoughtful. She put her hand over his hand on her knee.

'Now you tell me a few things about how you feel.'

'About what?' he asked.

'About what's happening right now?'

He was amused. 'Nothing's happening. It's very peaceful.'

'Are you teasing me?'

'I wouldn't think of it, Cleopatra.'

'Yeah, right, I believe you. Have you any family, David?'

'My father's still alive. He has Alzheimer's. He doesn't recognize me.'

'I'm sorry.'

He withdrew his arm and shrugged. 'It happens. He's been that way a long time.'

She missed David's hand. 'Do you have any brothers or sisters?'

'No. No ex-wives or kids either. There's just me.'

'That must get lonely. I don't know what I would do without Vera. Both our parents are dead. They were killed in a car crash when we were seniors in high school. Since then, Vera and I have grown extremely close, although we always talked to each other.'

'Was it difficult growing up with an identical twin sister?'

'Many people ask me that. Really, it was the most wonderful thing in the world. Even though we're quite different personality wise, Vera understands like no one else can.' She paused. 'I should say, she understands most things about me.'

'But not your dark side?'

She laughed softly. 'You are perceptive, Mr Nichols. You should be the psychologist. Yes, absolutely, I do have a dark side. And I must warn you, it comes out most forcibly in the dark.'

He sounded interested. 'How does it do that?'

In response, she took his hands and raised them to her lips and lightly kissed his knuckles, the tiny crucifix hanging from her neck brushing against his fingers. 'There,' she said quietly. 'I have made the first move. Now you can do what you want and you will still be considered a gentleman in the eyes of the universe.'

He scooted closer and touched the side of her face. He seemed to stare at her for an eternity but what he saw of her in the dark was a mystery. His hand was nice and warm, however.

'You're very dear,' he said finally.

She smiled nervously. 'Is that a no?'

'You don't know me.'

'You don't know me.'

He brushed her hair back. 'I'm not what I appear.'

She grabbed his hand, kissed it again. She was dying

for him to kiss her. 'I know, you're a spy. Your real name's James Bond.'

'Close.' He brushed her hair aside again. Was it in her eyes? Was there something she wasn't seeing? 'Close,' he repeated.

There was a sad note in his voice. She froze. '*Are* you a spy?'

The question floated in the air between them and into the starry heavens. The gods debated it. The goddesses said it could not be so. They tossed it back to the Earth for denial. David's whole body seemed to sigh, although he didn't speak. She reached over and caressed his face.

'I don't care about things,' she whispered. 'It's you I care about.'

He shook his head. 'It isn't that simple, Lucy.'

'Why not? I'm a simple girl. You don't have to tell me anything you don't want to.'

He drew in a breath. 'I must be insane talking about this.'

'The stars can do that to you late at night. Make you silly.' She waited. 'David?'

'I can't believe I am talking about this.' He struggled with himself. 'It must be because I'm quitting.'

'Quitting what?' Lucy asked.

'My name's not David Nichols. It's David Conner.'

'That isn't such a big change.'

'I'm not a reporter.'

That startled her. 'What are you? A cop?'

He moved away from her. The boat rocked. The stars on the lake surface shifted position. He spoke to the water, to the sky, at the same time. 'I'm an FBI agent. I was sent here to see how your group knows so much about what's happening inside our government. Several of the Big Mind's comments were too insightful for the powers that be.'

Lucy tried to absorb the information. The only problem

was, there was no place inside her to fit it. She had never met a spy before. No matter, she tried to tell herself, he was trying to be honest with her. Yet she was confused.

'Are we going to be arrested?' she asked.

He chuckled dryly. 'No, not that. Government agencies are not as evil as they're portrayed in movies. We're just a group of men and women who are trying to do our jobs. We mean you and your friends no harm.'

'But why didn't you just tell us what you wanted at the start? We have nothing to hide.'

David hesitated. 'You may not. I'm not so sure about Spear.'

'What do you mean? Has he broken the law?'

'Not that I know of, but let's just say he has a complex past. Look, I'm only telling you these things because I trust you, Lucy. I shouldn't be doing it.'

'Wow. I don't know what to say. Are you on duty now? Is that why you can't kiss me?'

'It's not that way. I appreciate all of you here. You most of all. Just because I'm an FBI agent doesn't make me any less human.' He lowered his head and added, 'I hope it doesn't.'

'Then why can't you kiss me?'

He was taken back. 'You still want to kiss me? After I've lied to you?'

She didn't have to consider long. 'Yes. I understand your position.'

'Really?'

'Well, maybe not. But as long as you're not here to hurt us, I don't mind. David, please.' Leaning far forward, she came to rest on her knees between his legs. His nose was two inches away. She rested her hands on his strong shoulders. She wondered if he could fight like the heroes in the spy movies. The thought was sort of stimulating in a non New Age fashion. She added, 'Tell me what's really bothering you?'

He frowned. 'Haven't I said enough?'

She ran a hand through his hair. She wanted him so bad! Could they do it in the boat? Would it sink? Would she care? 'No. You're afraid to get close to people. The Big Mind said as much this afternoon. What happened? Did the bad guy get away once and steal your heart?'

The moment the question was past her lips she regretted it. He stiffened.

'Twice,' he whispered.

'Jesus, I'm sorry. I'm an ass. What happened? I mean, you don't have to tell me. Was it terrible?'

He looked weary then, even in the dark, an outline of a myth best left untold. The stars seemed to weigh down upon him. He took a long time to reply. 'Did you hear about the Angela Moore kidnapping?'

'Sure. Who didn't? It was in the papers and on the TV every day. Did you work on that case?'

His voice was strained. 'I was in charge of the case. I dealt with the kidnapper directly.' He coughed. 'That night, I was the one who went in the cabin for her.'

She took her hand back and put it to her mouth. She had read what had happened, the whole country had. 'Oh God. You were *him*? You poor dear. But what happened wasn't your fault. Someone fired their rifle when they weren't supposed to. You tried your best to save her.'

He buried his face in his hands. 'You don't understand. I was responsible for her safety. I had her life right there in my hands. Everything was under control. And I let it, her, slip away. Her father was waiting for her back at the hotel and I let her die.'

'But that's ridiculous! You can't blame yourself. You did what you could. You risked your life for her life. No one could ask you to do more.'

'It doesn't matter how hard I tried, Lucy. I learned that a long time ago. All that matters is that they're dead.'

Carefully. 'They?'

He slowly sat up. 'There was another person I allowed to . . .' He stopped himself, shaking his head. 'It doesn't matter. It was long ago. This case was last month. Angela should have graduated from high school this month. Anyway, you're right. It happened. It's done. I'm not God, I can't control fate.' He paused. 'Still, I should have been able to control myself.'

'What do you mean?'

He took a painful breath. 'I mean my dear Miss Lucy that the newspapers seldom get the whole story. Angela was dead and the kidnapper was injured. The swat team had stopped firing. Still, Special Agent David Conner was upset. He didn't like the way things had gone, not at all. He wanted a little payback, for himself as well as for Angela and her family. While the kidnapper lay helpless on the floor, he took a shotgun and put the barrel to the motherfucker's forehead and blew his brains through the hard wood floor and into the mud beneath the cabin.' He chuckled bitterly. 'He didn't even read the guy his rights.' David tossed something in the water, a small stick perhaps, and watched as it sank. He glanced over at her. 'Do you still want to kiss me?'

Lucy wept. 'You have been so hurt. Do you even want my love?'

He stared at her a moment, then up at the sky, then back at her. 'Yes.'

Lucy hugged him. 'Then yes, David, I want you.'

CHAPTER ELEVEN

When Professor Carl Buckley answered his apartment door, it didn't appear as if he had just jumped out of bed. Since leaving the university campus he had changed into wide red sweat pants and a bulky white sweater that made him look like a department store Santa Claus who had received an electric shaver for Christmas. Even with the eighty degree night air, the guy was dressed for the next Ice Age. Behind him Ned could hear the TV on loud. Sounded like a Shirley Temple movie. Grandfather! Grandfather! I just remember that you abused me while I was in the womb. Buckley looked psychologically abused. The dark bags under his puffy eyes drooped like misplaced silicon implants.

'You saw her?' he mumbled.

Ned nodded. 'I saw her. May I come in?'

Buckley let the door drift open. There was alcohol on his breath. 'Please do. Don't mind the mess. It's the way I feel.'

A minute later they were seated in Buckley's small but smartly furnished living room. Actually, the place was not that messy, except for a few misplaced books and magazines. But perhaps the Professor had been referring to the half empty bottle of Seagram 7 sitting on the coffee table when he had excused the place. He offered Ned a drink, which was the best offer Ned had had all night. They drank to each other's health. How different the meeting was from the earlier one. The time of pretence was over and they both knew it.

'Did you know,' Buckley began without prodding, staring at the residue of whiskey left in his glass, 'that human beings are born with three instinctive fears. They are afraid of the dark, of falling, and of reptiles. After seeing Frances, don't you find that interesting?'

'Yes,' Ned said grimly. 'She scared me.'

Buckley was drunk but nowhere close to falling over. The altered state seemed to broaden the range of his personality. He was a lot less nerdy, more sure of himself. His face had stopped twitching.

'I knew she would,' he said.

Ned sighed. 'Before we begin, can you just tell me if it's real?'

Buckley reached for the bottle again. 'Yes. It's more real than either of us want to believe.'

'Do you know that Spear has a channelling group with twins in it?'

Buckley swallowed directly from the bottle. 'Yes. Since Africa, I have followed his career from afar. I have written him letters warning him but he ignores me. I know it's only a matter of time before he tries another experiment.'

Ned shook his head. 'I'm not ready to talk this way. I still cannot believe that an ancient super race of reptiles once ruled the Earth.'

Buckley looked at him with something akin to pity. 'Then why are you here?'

'I told you. Because she scared me. She wasn't like a normal crazy person. She wasn't like a person at all. Do you know she almost bit off my hand?'

'Ouch.'

'Is that all you have to say?'

Buckley spread his hands. 'Do you want me to talk about Africa? About lizard monsters? The combination of the two?'

'Explain to me how such an advanced civilization could

have existed in the past and we know nothing about it? I just don't buy it.'

'Yes, you do. You bought the whole farm when you went up to Salutory. You see, I've been to the sanatorium since Africa. I know what you saw. You just want me to give you reasons to believe Frances is another mental case rotting away in some delusion. She's not. She's not even a *she*.' Buckley burped. 'She's an *it*.'

'But there would be ruins of their ancient cities,' Ned protested. 'Some sign that they had been here.'

'Not necessarily. You're not an anthropologist. I am. In daily life you're used to thinking in years, at most decades. Until I met the Dogon, I was accustomed to thinking in terms of thousands of years. That's a long time. The average person cannot really imagine a thousand years, never mind eight thousand years, the length of human history. They think they can but they can't. You have to mould your point of view over a lifetime to develop that kind of perspective. Yet eight thousand years ago is nothing compared to sixty million years ago. It's a drop in the bucket. The world has changed a lot since the great reptiles were here. Continents have come and gone. Mountain ranges have risen and fallen. Oceans have been born and dried up. Why do you think the remains of a civilization would be lying around for us to simply pick up? We would be lucky to find anything. Besides, they burned it all down when they destroyed themselves. If we went searching for a clue of their existence, it would be a search for ash. That's all they left.'

'How do you know that for sure?' Ned asked.

'Didn't Frances mention their Armageddon?'

'She did say that they had destroyed themselves.'

'They destroyed themselves and practically everything else on Earth. You must have heard the old riddle. What happened to the dinosaurs? Why did they suddenly vanish after millions of years of good living? There's lots of theories floating around that explain their extinction. The most popular is that an asteroid or comet hit the Earth and stirred up so much dust in the atmosphere that the sun was blacked out for several years and all the vegetation died. I believed that theory myself until my vacation in Mali.'

'They did not have a war that blocked out the sun for years,' Ned complained.

'Perhaps not. But I think they had a war that liberated as much energy as a collision with an asteroid would have done. I'm sure they scorched the world in their fury. This race went to the stars. We can hardly get back to the Moon. They controlled physical energies that we can't even conceive of. They had *mental* powers we have never even dreamed of.'

'How do you know that?' Ned asked.

'I saw a demonstration in Africa. That may be another answer to your first question. Because they were so highly developed mentally, I don't even know if they required extensive cities. For all I know they teleported themselves to the neighbouring stars without the use of a spaceship at all. Of course, now I'm just speculating.'

'You speak of how developed their minds were. But it's my understanding that reptiles are stupid. Their brains are supposed to be small compared to the rest of their bodies. Dinosaurs in particular were supposed to be idiotic.'

'I'm not saying this super race was made up of gigantic dinosaurs like you see in the movies. On the contrary, I believe they were approximately our size. There are various evolutionary reasons why our size is conducive to intelligence. We are large enough to have developed brains, but we are not so big that we couldn't acquire hands that can carefully manipulate the environment. The use of our hands stimulated the growth of our brains. We did not get smart until we stood up. Still, you make a good point. The reptilian complex is only one layer above the core brain. We have the limbic system and the neocortex in addition to what reptiles have. Our brains are much more evolved, much more complex. How could they be so smart? I pondered that question myself after I returned from Africa. I did research into the field. Spear has a respected neurophysiologist – Dr Henry Deering – working with him now. I read his published papers and talked to other experts in the field of the evolution of intelligence. Then it occurred to me that I was looking at the situation backwards.'

'What do you mean?' Ned asked.

'I was trying to understand how they could have been smart like us, when they were here before us. A more realistic approach would have been to try to understand how we were smart *like* them. But an even more accurate approach was to accept that their intelligence just wasn't the same as ours. What I mean by that is that we judge intelligence largely by the ability to solve logical problems, retain information, and see the relationships between various situations. But since they only had the layer of the brain above the core to work with, I reasoned that their intelligence was basically *instinctual*. They did not sit and discuss things as we do. They acted, but not randomly as animals and other reptiles do. Their instinctual capacity was so great that they invariably moved forward – perhaps even unconsciously – developing a more and more advanced understanding of the universe and themselves. I know that sounds paradoxical but that is only because we examine them as human beings must – from a human point of view. We cannot see them as they saw themselves. I believe they lacked our self-consciousness but were far more perceptive.'

'They couldn't have been that perceptive if they wiped each other out.'

Buckley chuckled. 'That's a weak rationalization when you consider how close we've come to wiping ourselves out. Anyway, you forget a fundamental point. For all their power, they were still reptiles. Excuse the cliché, but reptiles are cold-blooded. They're aggressive, dominating, but unemotional as well.'

'Aggression is not an emotion?'

'Our society labels it as one but in reality emotion is a product of a level of brain functioning that reptiles do not possess.'

Ned strummed his knee with his fingers. 'I still can't believe this. Everything I have read on prehistoric creatures states that their brain size – never mind if it was instinctual or logical in functioning – was simply too small to support intelligence.'

'You did not read enough. Scientists have discovered the fossils of a man-sized dinosaur that resembles an ostrich. It had a large brain, relatively speaking. It was not as large as ours, and I'm not saying it is the remains of one of our super beings. But this creature could have been related to them. It's very possible in fact. Few people know that birds are the descendants of dinosaurs. Ostriches have hands, four fingers on each. As I have already stated, hands are crucial to the development of intelligence. You must drop the concept that we *have* to be the first intelligent race here on this planet. The idea is egotistical, and not based on the scientific facts that you think it is. The Earth has been around for four billion years. Human beings have only been here two or three million years. That's nothing. Plenty happened before we got here. God only knows how long they were in charge. God only knows how long we will be.'

'Do you believe in God?' Ned asked.

Buckley took a sip from his bottle. 'No.'

'But after Africa you believe in the devil?'

'I don't know what I believe in.' Buckley's expression was ironic. 'High powered weapons, maybe. If even they could stop those things.'

'I don't understand that remark. Maybe I will after you explain what happened in Africa. But before we move on, I want to point out that Frances displayed emotion. She giggled several times while I was there and seemed to take pleasure in my discomfort.'

'It was a cold pleasure, I'm sure. Besides, whatever's inside her is inside a human body. She may be a hybrid of what they were and what Frances was. Or else . . .' Buckley trailed off.

'What is it?' Ned asked.

'It's possible that only a portion of the reptilian intelligence in her genetic past was able to come through. Or perhaps, I should say, only a portion was able to remain in our time.'

'Is that another insight Africa gave you?' Ned asked.

Buckley gave him a dark look. 'You think I'm a fat fool. When you came to my class eight hours ago, you had me shaking in my shoes. I know that. I was scared. But not for the reasons you thought. The FBI can't do shit to me after what I've been through. I just wanted to tell you that up front.'

'You're drunk,' Ned said.

Buckley laughed proudly. 'You'll get drunk with me when I'm done. Then you'll fly to Washington DC and try to talk Congress into exterminating the world's population of identical twins. They won't listen to you, though. From experience I can tell you that ahead of time. From now on, whenever you see twins together, you'll think of death. You'll never be the same after you hear what I have to say.'

Ned crossed his legs. 'I'm here to listen, Professor.'

The reference to his respected title seemed to cheer Buckley somewhat. He set down his bottle and began where he had left off, before the addition of his lies.

'As I said, before Spear brought Frances to Mali he began to talk about the idea of genetic regression. At the time he was spending time with a Dogon priestess. Her name was Kalu and she was something to look at. Thirty years old, tall as myself, with black hair down to her knees. She wore it in stone braids and often covered her face with red and black paints. Kalu was a wild woman, high up in the tribe, but not entirely trusted either. Penny didn't like her. She could see that her husband had more than a scholarly interest in her. Spear was wooing Kalu for secret knowledge, giving her small gifts and coins, when he wasn't fucking her brains out. Kalu told him things she wasn't supposed to tell any outsider. Spear confided in me when it suited him, which was not often. One night, however, after Frances had arrived and recovered from her spider bite, Spear and I got drunk and he told me more than he intended. That was the first time I heard about the *Listeners*.'

'Who are they? The reptilian race?'

'No. The Dogon called them the *Setians*. The name is virtually identical to the brother of Osiris, Set, who is an Egyptian God, and the supposed brother-in-law of the Goddess Isis, the highest of all Egyptian deities. The Dogon word for the Listeners was actually the *Hotri*, which means "to listen" in Sanga. Spear called them the Listeners because naturally he thought in English terms. And to the Dogon that's what they were, an inner circle of initiates who were able – through a technique we would describe in the West as mutual hypnosis – to listen to the inner voices of the distant past. They had to listen closely, I thought, to regress through their genetic codes back to the lives of ancestors. Spear confided that he had seen them in action and that the knowledge they accessed about ancient cultures was genuine. Even though he was drunk, Spear spoke with authority. I was intrigued. With his background, Spear could tell real information from garbage. If he believed they were seeing back in time, I couldn't dismiss the idea.'

'Did he invite you to observe these initiates regress?' Ned asked.

'No. He said they wouldn't let me be there. They only trusted him. He was a jerk about the matter, as usual, but he did have a point when he said that my observing the initiates wouldn't do any good since I couldn't understand what was being said. Let me go on. The reason he was courting Kalu so fervently was to obtain the details of an even deeper secret. You see, she had told him about the super race of reptiles and the reason the Dogon were so fearful of having identical twins in the same proximity. Spear told me about the Setians as well, just before we went to bed after that long drunken night, but I didn't give any credence to the idea. Who would? And Spear himself laughed as he said it. I had no idea he was already convinced of the validity of everything Kalu said.'

'Why would a highly educated man like Spear be so quickly influenced?'

'You jumped pretty quick after you visited Frances,' Buckley observed.

'You enjoy the fact that she shook me up. I think you wouldn't have minded seeing me lose a few fingers as well.'

'I tried to warn you.'

'That you did,' Ned agreed. 'Please continue.'

'To answer your question, I don't know. It could have been a combination of factors. When you're living in that part of the world, so isolated from civilization, you're much more likely to believe things you never would consider in America. I know that must sound naive but it's completely true. The deserts of Mali have a hypnotic quality in themselves. Sometimes when I stared up at the stars at night through the swarms of buzzing insects I wondered what the hell had gone on in Africa before man had arrived on the scene. As Spear began to talk openly of the Setians with me, I began to listen. And as

I already mentioned, Spear had seen genetic regression in action. He was an anthropologist. He could question the Dogon's information, see if it matched our knowledge of the ancient Egyptians. He was able to validate it directly. That's an important point to remember.'

'So the Dogon are descended from the ancient Egyptians?' Ned asked.

'Probably. We were never able to establish that as a fact. If nothing else, they were connected to them. The Dogon initiates were able to go back to the days of the construction of the earliest pyramids. When they need to know something, they search for the answers in the past. According to the Dogon, there are many huge structures we don't know about buried under the desert sands. To find them would be a major archaeological discovery, yet in Spear's mind, it paled in comparison to what he was digging out of Kalu. Before Frances arrived on the scene, Kalu had already told him that the way the larger pyramids were built was by the use of mental powers reawakened from the ancient past. She said when a human was transformed into an Setian, he or she could do anything.'

'Do you believe that?' Ned asked.

'You should probably hold that question until I'm through. But I'll say now that it would solve the central mystery of the pyramids. I'm sure when you were going through grade school you were given texts that showed coloured drawings of the how the Egyptians built the pyramids. Rolling the large stones on trees – two dozen smiling slaves pushing from behind. The idea is patently ridiculous. Today, even with our most sophisticated heavy equipment, we could not build the pyramids. We simply cannot lift a rock the size of a small house and fit it into a space cut to within a centimetre of accuracy. There is not a crane on the Earth that can do that. That's a fact. So how did those rocks get up there? Kalu said when you became a Setian, you could just float them into the sky as if they were kites.'

'Kalu knew about the pyramids?'

'Yes. And she had never been to Egypt. Nor had she ever spoken to a white man before she started sleeping with Spear. Like the other Listeners, she knew of them from the past.'

'Earlier this evening you mentioned how our civilization sprung up all of a sudden. I would assume now that it's your belief that it was handed to us by the – at least partial – re-emergence of the super race from the past?'

'Correct. The ancient Egyptians' knowledge of astronomy was staggering. The Mayans', also, was very sophisticated. The average person has no idea how much these people knew.'

'Do you believe that the Mayans also stumbled upon the doorway to the past?'

'The question is intriguing. But I wonder if it happens simply by chance. Maybe there is something built deep into our genetic code that comes out when identical twins are together. That pushes them, so to speak, to experiment.' He looked over at Ned, pale. 'I wonder if the Setians cursed us somehow.'

'*I will touch you again.*'

Ned shivered. 'Cursed us and said that they would one day return?'

'Yes. It's not an idea I like to contemplate in the dark.'

'I understand. Did Kalu warn Spear about the dangers of trying to reawaken the Setians?'

'I believe so. But he promised her so many things that she kept telling him more secrets. He was going to take her out of Africa. He was going to buy her a house by the ocean. She would wear beautiful clothes and have sparkling jewellery. He filled her head with so much nonsense that she forgot her sacred vows. Finally, maybe two months after Frances arrived in Mali, Kalu told Spear the big secret. How identical twins could punch through the memory of the dawn of mankind and reach all the way back to the time of the Setians.'

'There is a specific technique?' Ned asked.

'Yes. Like most profound secrets, it's very simple once you know it. The twins have to sit close together facing each other – their knees touching, their hands clasped – and stare into each other's eyes. They must synchronize their breath so that one inhales while the other exhales. Then they must lead each other back in time.'

'How do they do that?' Ned asked.

'Through suggestion. But the process is much more profound than ordinary hypnosis, or even, for that matter, mutual hypnosis. Suggestion plays only a small part in it. Once the process starts, it goes by itself. The understanding of the breath is crucial. The Dogon do not see the breath as something that travels in and out of our lungs. They believe that there is an energy associated with it. When we exhale, that energy goes out from our bodies. When we inhale it comes back in revitalized by the elements in the air. The energy goes out further when we breathe hard. That's the reason, they say, we get tired when we exercise. When the twins sit together and breathe in this manner, they function like a single organism, as one nervous system, one big mind.'

'The being Spear's group now channels is called the Big Mind,' Ned said.

'I know. I have read the books the group has published. The coincidence is disturbing. Let me continue. That the twins stare into each other's eyes is also critical. In the usual meetings, Spear told me that the Dogon initiates always kept their eyes closed while regressing into the past. But with identical twins their focus on each multiplies the power of their mental coherence manyfold. Spear likened it to two mirrors set each in front of the other. The reflections go back and forth, down into an infinite tunnel. Think about it – sixty million years back in time. That's as good as infinity to the human mind, don't you agree?'

'Frances mentioned a mirror to me several times,' Ned said.

'I'm not surprised. She's the only one alive on this planet who I know has looked into it.' Buckley's head hung heavy. 'And look what it did to her.'

'I'm sorry. As we analyse this, I forget that you were close to her.'

Buckley coughed deep in his lungs. 'I wanted to be a lot closer. You were right when you implied I hoped for a romantic relationship with her. I was a lot thinner when I was in Africa. I had a great tan. But she wasn't interested and I could understand that. Still, she never ceased to be a close friend until the night Spear opened the black door. Frances and I would often swim together in a lake far from the main tribe. Afterwards we would lie on the stones naked and talk about being back home. I felt close to her then. It was like we had a satisfying physical relationship, although we never made love.'

'What about Penny? What was she like?'

'Very quiet, reserved. I think Spear had ground down her own natural personality over the years of their marriage. Penny did not have Frances' sense of humour. She seldom started a conversation. She was a good person, though. She never gossiped, never had an unkind word to say about anyone, except Kalu. Near the time of the big catastrophe, Spear didn't even try to hide his affair with the priestess. Even the Dogon – liberal by nature – had to wonder at him. They feared Penny and Frances but they meant them no harm either. Secretly, I think, they worried what Kalu was telling Spear. The knowledge of Setians, how they could be invoked, was their deepest taboo, as well as their greatest insight. They understand the workings of the breath and the genes and the evolution of the brain like no one in the civilized world. And here the world sees them as savages.' Buckley paused. 'How did you know to ask me about the brain and its evolution earlier?'

Ned was not worried Buckley was going to warn Spear. 'I have a partner with Spear and his group now. He's undercover – they think he's a reporter. He told me to ask you those questions.'

'What prompted him to say that?'

'I don't know.'

'Hmm. I would advise him to grab one of the twins and get the hell out of there.'

'I thought the same thing myself. I'll call him after we finish. Please continue.'

Buckley reached over and touched his knee. He spoke seriously, as he had when he had warned him to stay away from Frances. 'Are you sure you want me to? It gets ugly from here on in. You might not want these things put in your brain. Once there, they're hard to forget.'

'If what you say so far is true, then they're already in the brain. Just buried.'

Buckley sat back. 'Very well, don't say you weren't warned.' He drew in a shuddering breath, showing signs of anxiety again. 'Frances and Penny heard from Spear about the Setians and how identical twins could supposedly regress into the past. The women had wondered why the Dogon were so frightened of them. But Spear gave them his version of the Dogon's fears, passing them off as childish. It was a challenge for him, I'm sure, because he had to give the idea of regression enough weight for the women to be curious, but not provide so much detail that they became concerned for their own safety. Now you must be wondering what kind of monster would risk his wife and sister-in-law for the sake of a scientific experiment. In defence of Spear, I think he honestly believed the Dogon were exaggerating the dangers. Remember, he had observed many genetic regressions with his own eyes, and the initiates always came out of their trances smiling. So the women went back further in time, he said to me. It was all in the mind. Nothing could physically harm them. They would be fine, he assured me, and it would be exciting if it worked. He had us all excited at the prospect. Also, he promised Penny and Frances if the experiment was successful they could leave Africa the following week. That was incentive enough for all of us. Believe me, you cannot imagine how nice it is to have a bathroom and a kitchen when you've done without them for as long as we had.'

'Was Kalu present when you did the experiment?' Ned asked.

'Yes. Penny didn't want her there but Spear insisted. Kalu was stoned that night. Besides being a horny priestess, she was addicted to a leaf that grew in the vicinity called Posos. The Dogon, as a general rule, were opposed to their people taking psychoactive substances, but I think it must be clear by now that Kalu never followed the rules. She was a liberated woman. Posos was usually smoked. It worked something like mescaline, from what Spear said. I think he was high a lot of the time he was off with Kalu. But he was clear headed the night as we hiked up towards Lucian Point. Lucian is a Sanga name for demons. The hill was called that because it had once been an active volcano, and the smell of sulphur fumes was still strong in the area. It isn't much of a peak – it rises at most two thousand feet above the desert plain – but its tip is black with tar and smells awful. It can appear intimidating when viewed from a distance. I had been to it once before with Frances to swim in the naturally heated sulphur baths, but since it was so hot in Mali all the time, we had no incentive to return. The place gave me a headache, to be frank, but Kalu said it was a powerful spot to perform a Setian regression.

'Frances and I trailed the others as we climbed the rocks. The moon was out, three-quarters full, and there was plenty of light to see by. I remember Frances talking excitably about where we could eat when we got back to the States. I know that it must sound odd that before an important experiment we could be thinking about food, but none of us saw the trial as a life-changing event.

'Finally, we arrived at the sacred spot. It was on a flat stone ledge that overlooked the pools I mentioned. A cave led away from the ledge, deep into the hill. I shone my flashlight into it but did not explore further. A lion in that area would have been rare, but Spear and I each carried a high-powered rifle, just in case. Kalu was laughing and flirting with Spear, annoying Penny. The sisters were both panting from the long walk. I have to admit I needed to sit down and rest myself. Only Spear was clear headed and bursting with enthusiasm. Back in those days, he had almost unlimited energy. It was one of the qualities that made him such a good anthropologist and at the same time an egomaniac. He wanted to get started right away.

'The women sat crossed-legged together on the rocky ledge, facing each other, their knees touching, their hands clasped. Earlier Spear had gone over the secret instructions with all of us. I remember how the moon shone straight overhead. It illuminated the entire plain with silver light, and it was easy to imagine we were back in time sixty million years ago. I half expected to see a dinosaur raise its curious head from around the wall of the cliff that shot up another three hundred feet above the ledge. Once again, I emphasize how powerfully hypnotic parts of Mali can be at night. And we were at a spot where, according to Kalu, the Dogon themselves had long ago awoken the beast inside. I noticed as the women sat and began to breathe in rhythm together, that Kalu fell strangely silent. She fingered an amulet the Dogon occasionally wore around their necks to ward off evil, a gold coloured string necklace with a single snake tooth at the end. The Dogon do not ordinarily believe it takes evil to combat evil, but I guess when it came to the Setians they made an exception.

'Kalu fidgeted nervously as the women began to whisper to each other about going back in time, back through the Middle Ages, the Roman Empire, the Grecian civilization, the ancient Egyptians. The sound of their voices changed as the process proceeded. They spoke more softly, yet their words echoed into the night. I had the impression that they spoke to each other from a great distance, even though they had unconsciously leaned forward to the point where their noses almost touched. I sat to the side, near the cave entrance, Kalu close on my right. Spear knelt on the ledge beside the women. He couldn't take his eyes off them. Nor could any of us. Their forms seemed to shimmer beneath the moon. I had trouble focusing on them and had to rub my eyes to convince myself I wasn't hallucinating. For brief moments I imagined I could see through them. It was as if they had fallen into another reality. I remember having the thought that maybe history didn't exist in the past, but in another dimension that followed alongside us as we moved forward as a race, just out of earshot, just beyond the horizon, laughing at us, knowing that it would once more catch up with us when it suited its needs.

'After perhaps thirty minutes the women fell silent and nothing seemed to happen for a while. I noticed they didn't blink, hardly appeared to breathe. Yet if nothing was happening outwardly, plenty must have been changing on the level of their consciousness. As an FBI agent, you must have had the experience of arriving at the scene of a crime not long after someone's been violently killed.

Unfortunately, I've had a similar experience. Before my trip to Africa, I once visited a 7-Eleven late at night just after it been held up. The owner of the store had been killed, and although the police and paramedics were already present, the body was still lying on the floor in a pool of blood. The feeling about the store was devastating – the pain, the tension, the loss. It lingered for months. I got so I never went back to the place.

'That night, on that rocky ledge, as the women sat facing each other like two ghostly statues, the feeling in the air altered in a similar painful way. It was as if a silent swarm of insects came between us and the moon. The light seemed to dim. The sulphur fumes could have worsened – suddenly I was having trouble breathing. The tension in the air was unbearable, as thick as rotting molasses. I thought if I tried to stand I would fall over. Yet there was nothing physically present. To a remote TV camera, nothing would have changed. It was all on the feeling level. The vibration was like spider's web. I felt as if we had already taken a wrong turn. Now all we could do was wait for the monster to arrive and slowly devour us. Kalu began to sob quietly, then steadily louder. I wanted to cry myself but didn't want to draw the attention of the women in my direction. There was no question in mind that whatever had come to that cursed point, had come especially for them. It was as if a huge black fathomless pupil formed in between their rock-still forms.

'Yet maybe Spear was immune to the bad vibes, I don't know. Kalu's sobbing annoyed him. I think he was afraid it would disturb the women. He motioned for me to take her away. I wanted an excuse to leave. Suddenly I wanted to get out of that place more than anything I had ever wanted before in my life. Like I said, however, it was hard to move. It was as if my body had gained an extra two thousand pounds. Somehow I managed to get to my feet. Stepping past the opening of the cave, I pulled Kalu up as well. She clung to me like a terrified child. Her Posos high was gone. Patting her on the back and rubbing her head, I tried to comfort her, but it was no use. I knew I had to get her away from the women like Spear wanted. Carefully, leading her as if she were blind, I began to retrace our steps down the side of the cliff.

'We were maybe a hundred yards away when Kalu suddenly broke free of me and looked back up at the stone ledge. One of the women had turned and was staring in our direction. The other had her back to us. To this day I don't know which one it was. I know that must sound odd but they were both dressed the same that night – in khaki shorts and tee-shirts. To be honest, I don't think it mattered which one it was. In my opinion, for both of them it was already too late.

'Then the madness began. I could feel the gaze of the woman as if she projected a green laser light from a black crystal buried deep in her cranium. It brushed past me as it settled on Kalu. She was really staring at her, the high priestess who had sold her secrets for the lies of a power-drunk American. Kalu's sobs ceased and her shoulders slumped as if the carcass of a large animal had been thrown over her back. Yet she continued to look up the cliff, her head pulled slightly forward as if she were a puppet dangling at the end of twisted string. Her body jerked spasmodically, compelled by an external source. Spear was on his feet now, trying to get a better view of what was happening. I was about to hike back up and demand he stop the experiment when Kalu broke from my side and took three long strides and dove head-first off the side of the cliff. She did not scream as she fell and somehow, for me, it made the shock of her suicide that much more tragic. She was just gone. I heard her body as it struck the rocks below. It broke with a moist crushing sound. Then there was nothing, no movement at all. I knew she was dead. For all her crazy ways – or maybe because of them – I knew Kalu loved life dearly. It had been no suicide. The woman had made her do it. Slowly, she turned their head once more in my direction. I had seen enough. I didn't give her a chance to get a fix on me. Turning, I fled down the side of the cliff. Christ, I never ran so fast in my life.'

Buckley paused to wipe the sweat off his brow. 'I suppose you'll think of me as a coward. I had left my partner alone with two dangerous females. I had left the women themselves – I had not even made an attempt to snap them out of their trance. I ran and walked almost all the way back to the Dogon camp, a distance of five miles. But you have seen Frances with your own eyes. You must have an inkling what she was like that night. Maybe you can understand why I kept going. Yet no matter how bad Frances seemed to you at the sanatorium, the two of them that night were a thousand times worse. The mirror was not cracked. It blazed with cold fire. They had power. I didn't think anything could stop them. I assumed Spear was a goner, maybe that whole section of Africa too.

'I neared the Dogon camp close to dawn. With the coming light, I was suddenly plagued by doubts. What if Kalu had survived the fall? What if I had left her injured on the rocks when with some first-aid she could survive? I questioned what I had witnessed. So much of the experience was purely subjective. Penny and Frances were my friends. They couldn't have changed into two creatures from a super race of extinct reptiles. Such things did not happen in the real world, I told myself. My steps faltered. I was exhausted, but did not feel I would be able to rest at the camp without knowing what had eventually transpired on the rocky ledge. After a brief period of internal debate, I turned and headed back towards Lucian Point. The sun rose as I closed on the tar scarred slope. It shimmered in the orange morning light like a volcano on the verge of erupting.

'Between the hill and the camp was one of those pools where I told you I used to go swimming with Frances. It lay a quarter mile off to my left, to the west, in a cluster of large granite boulders and a low lying sandy bluff. Even over such a distance, I heard human cries. It sounded like frightened children. My heart pounded in my chest. I looked up at the hill and stared at the sun. Now I doubted my doubts. Maybe I am a coward at heart. But people were in pain, I told myself. I had already fled once that night. I could not run away a second time. I don't know where the courage finally came from. Once more, I changed direction and ran towards the pool.'

Buckley sighed and shook his head. 'I shouldn't have bothered. What I saw next, it's difficult to repeat even after all these years. I found a mother and her two children. They stood at the edge of the pool, their bare feet in the water. The mother held a spear in her hand, pointed at one of the women. I think it was Frances. I'm pretty sure it was. She wore her hair a little longer than Penny did. But I couldn't swear to the fact. It might have been Penny. It doesn't matter, really. I peered at the four of them from behind a boulder. The mother was trying to defend her children from the women. They were clearly terrified of her. I don't know what Frances had done before I arrived to invoke the fear. Maybe she hadn't done anything. The sight of her was horrible enough. Yet I must emphasize that physically she looked only slightly different, a bit more wild. It was the black aura that radiated from her. She stood shaking like a being possessed by demons. Her eyes were as empty as a snake's. She hissed as she stalked the mother and her children. But she was not afraid. It was if she was playing with her prey for the sport of it.

'The mother could take no more. She flung the spear at Frances. I mentioned their mental powers earlier. Here was my first clear demonstration of them. The spear splintered in midair. It exploded as if detonated from inside. The debris didn't even touch Frances. At that the mother charged her. What a brave mother she was. Frances struck her on the side of the head as if the mother were a paper doll. I heard bones break. The mother collapsed in a pile in the shallow water.

'Frances turned her attention to the children, two young girls approximately six to eight years of age. Clearly they were of a mind to flee. They knew their mother was dead. But the older girl could not move. It was as if her feet were glued to the shallow bedrock. I know what you must be thinking. That she was too terrified to move. That was not the case. As Frances came closer and the little girl drew back, the older girl yanked with all her strength for her feet to come free. But they were stuck because the monster was holding them in place with the power of its mind. The little girl backed in my direction, unwilling to leave her sister but not willing to charge the beast. Here was my chance to redeem myself, I thought. Frances was not looking in my direction. I jumped up from behind the boulder and grabbed the little girl. She went to scream but I smothered the sound by putting my hand over her mouth. Quickly, I ducked back down. I turned the little girl's head away so that she wouldn't have to watch but I felt compelled to see for myself what my dear friend had become. What Spear had changed her into with his mad thirst for secret knowledge.

'Frances came and stood beside the older girl. The poor thing was so terrified she couldn't even scream. She trembled as Frances stroked her long dark hair. The Dogon women have the most beautiful hair in the world. There are so many good things about them. I wish we had been able to honour their knowledge and not steal it. I wish we had been able to bring them something other than pain and death. To this day I wish I never stayed to watch what Frances did to that little girl. But I did stay, and what I saw – I will never forget it till the day I die. I still wake up every night thinking about it.'

Buckley stopped to cry. Ned didn't know what to say. He didn't know what to believe, except that the Professor was making none of his story up. No human being was that powerful a liar. Buckley reached over and poured himself another drink. Not all the whiskey made it in the glass, past his trembling lips. He stared down at the floor as if the poor Dogon girl buried beneath his carpet.

'Frances killed the girl?' Ned asked delicately.

'Yes,' Buckley whispered. 'She ate her. She ate her alive.'

Ned was sick to his stomach. 'Oh God.'

'She started with the girl's right shoulder and kept feeding. There was so much blood. The entire pool turned dark. The girl died slowly. Standing up, her feet fastened down in the red water.'

'But you saved the little girl?' Ned said.

'Yes. I did that. She was a beautiful little girl. As beautiful as her sister.'

Ned remembered he had said the same words to David. 'You did the best you could.'

Buckley sadly shook his head. 'We were anthropologists. Other people might think the Dogon were savages but we knew better. We lived with them for half a year. We knew they were one of the greatest people to walk the Earth. Yet we ignored their warnings about the danger of awakening the Setians. We passed them off as superstitious fools. We behaved like the ignorant white men that we were. We murdered that mother and that girl as surely as if we butchered them with our own knives.' Buckley looked at him. 'You can see why I've become the way I am. A fat and frightened caricature of the picture of the man on the passport I took to Africa. I wasn't always this way, though. I want you to know that. I was a great scientist once.'

'Don't be so hard on yourself. You did more than most men would have done under similar circumstances.' Ned added carefully, 'What became of Spear and Penny?'

Buckley nodded, getting a grip on himself. 'I ran with the little girl back to the path that stretched from the Lucian Point to the Dogon camp. There I set her down and told her to run and get help. She was scared but she was a smart child. She set off at full speed. Then I turned my attention back to my original destination. I had little hope of finding Spear alive or Penny unchanged, but now I was determined. The desecration of the girl had given me resolve. These things could not be allowed to invade the village unchecked. I started towards the peak. I prayed that Frances' hunger was satisfied for the time being and that she wouldn't come after me.

'Now my strength began to fail me. I had been going all night with nothing to eat or drink. My vision swam as I climbed the path that led to the sulphur baths and the cursed ledge. Several times I was forced to stop and rest. Everywhere I looked I saw blood. I reached the spot where Kalu had fallen and saw that she was beyond my help. At least it had been quick for her, I thought.

'Near the top I found Spear lying unconscious on his back at the edge of the ledge where we had performed our experiment. His breathing was erratic and he burned with fever. I had a hard time awakening him. But once he was up he seemed alert enough. His eyes were strange though. The whites had turned yellow and his pupils were completely dilated. Yet there wasn't a mark on him. He gripped my arm, and despite his fever, his hands were cold. It might have been from lying so long on the hard stone.

"What's happened?" he demanded.

"Frances is on the loose. She struck down one woman and ate a small child." I wept. "What's happened to them? What are we going to do?"

'Spear was grim. "We know what's happened," he said. "We were warned. Was she headed in the direction of the Dogon camp?"

"Yes," I said. "I don't know what can stop her. She can move things with her mind, make them explode."

'Spear stood. He grabbed me by the shoulders. His eyes were freaky but they were clear as well. His thoughts were way ahead of mine. He was a brilliant man. I hate to acknowledge that after all the pain he caused but it's true. While I was falling apart in my boots, he was making plans. He said, "I know how to stop them. But we must act quick. First the hunger is there, but then the need to reproduce will dominate. We can't let it go to the next step. Then we'll all die."

'The way he said the word "all" I knew he meant the entire human race would perish. Kalu must have explained to him in detail how the Setians reproduced. Spear clearly implied to me that twins would no longer be necessary from that point on. Any human could carry the Setian consciousness. He handed me my rifle and urged me to hurry back to the camp and try to slow her down. In my anxiety to get away from the women, I had left the weapon by the cave entrance. Spear had his own rifle as well. I asked him what he was going to do but he wouldn't answer me.

'"Never mind," he said. "Just try to stop her from killing anyone else."

'"But will the gun stop her?" I begged.

'He shook his head. "No." He hugged me then, something he had never done before. "Go my friend. Go with luck. Wish me the same."

'What could I do? I wished him luck. I didn't know what he was doing, where he was going. But as I scampered back down the hill, I thought I saw him enter the cave. It struck me then that he had never confirmed that it was Frances I had seen. It might have been Penny. Or maybe Penny was in the cave. I was never to know for sure.

'On the long road back to the Dogon camp, I came across a cluster of tribesmen. They carried spears and bows and arrows and were gathered around what I assumed was Frances. Her clothes were torn, soaked with blood. She grovelled on the ground as three strong men tried to pin her down. To my immense surprise they seemed to be getting the better of her. Yet even then I knew she was not the beast I had watched eat the child at the pond.'

'So it was Penny you saw the first time?' Ned asked, becoming confused.

'I'm not sure. It could have been, but I still believe I saw Frances in both cases. But what I'm saying is something different. The woman the Dogon were trying to pin down did not have the power of the woman at the pond. She had lost it in the interim.'

'How?' Ned asked.

'I don't know. Spear said he knew how to stop it. Apparently he did stop it. But he never explained to me what he did. Later, I was able to establish for a fact that it was Frances that the Dogon had captured. She was strong but they were able to control her.'

'But what about Penny? How did she die?'

'Once again, I don't know. Spear only told me that he killed her. Since he had his rifle with him, I assume that he shot her.'

'But he told you bullets wouldn't stop them?' Ned asked.

'I know. Yet he did stop them. I never saw Penny's body. He buried it somewhere up on Lucian Point. I can only take his word that he killed her. He was as anxious as myself to stop them from hurting anybody else. Obviously Penny did not return with us to the States. For that matter, I did not return with Spear. I accompanied Frances back on a separate flight. A French physician travelled with us. She was tied down and heavily sedated, unconscious actually. It was the only way to transport her. I was there when she was checked into Salutory. Since then, I have been up to see her twice. I don't know why I go. Frances is gone forever.'

'But Frances still possesses supernormal powers. With my own eyes I saw her rip through a straightjacket. Her doctor said it took three strong men to hold her down when she escaped from her room.'

Buckley shook his head. 'Neither of these is a demonstration of supernatural power. It is not abnormal for an acute schizophrenic to demonstrate tremendous strength. It took three Dogon to hold Frances down. Note also that when you were with her she broke the straightjacket but not the chains that held her to the wall. Believe me, before Spear did whatever he did, a hundred men could not have stopped her. She is still horrible, true, but only a shadow of what she was immediately after the transformation.'

'I'm frustrated by your account,' Ned said. 'You leave many loose ends. You must have spoken to Spear after all these events?'

'Only briefly, when he returned from Lucian Point. He told me that Penny was dead, it had been stopped, and to tell the authorities it was a wild animal that had caused all the problems. Then he collapsed. He had a high fever, a hundred and ten degrees. It should have killed him. The Dogon medicine men treated him with special herbs. They helped transport him to the Ivory Coast. After all the heartache we had caused them, they still wanted to help. From there Spear flew to a clinic in Spain, and eventually to another hospital in California. I tried to visit him during his convalescence but he refused to see me. As I mentioned, I have since written him a dozen times but he never writes back.'

'Didn't the police question you concerning Penny's death?' Ned asked.

'You know that they did. You wonder why I agreed with Spear's lie? At the time I felt I had to. I didn't want to go to jail. What purpose would that serve? I didn't want to plant suspicion in the authorities' minds. I went along with Spear's account, just as I went along with him that night he talked us into going up to Lucian Point.'

'I understand,' Ned said, and he did. He probably would have done the same.

Buckley grimaced. 'What was I to do after such a nightmare? I couldn't tell anyone about it. They would never believe me. I did my research, as I explained to you, trying to grasp the nature of Setians. But it was purely intellectual research. I don't think my theories help anyone nowadays, certainly not the victims of our experiment. Maybe they can help you. That is my hope. My own mental state was fragile for a long time after Africa. I couldn't sleep unless I had a light on. I had no money, and I couldn't even teach. Eventually, however, my strength returned. I landed the job at the university. I know my students find me a bore but it pays the bills.' Buckley shook his head. 'If only they knew what Professor Buckass had gone through. Maybe they wouldn't use my class periods to nap.'

Ned took a minute to absorb it all. 'Now what?' he asked finally.

Buckley nodded. 'That's the important question, isn't it? I guess you know why I decided to tell you what really happened.'

'You want me to stop Spear? You want the Dogon's knowledge to die with you two?'

'To die with us three.'

'I don't know,' Ned said.

Buckley leaned forward. 'You said it yourself, he's got another pair of twins.'

'I can't arrest him based on what you've told me tonight. You know it would never hold up in court.'

Buckley stared at him with something that might have been hope if it hadn't held such a disturbing edge. 'I'm not asking you to arrest him,' he said seriously.

Ned shook his head firmly. 'We don't do things like that.'

Buckley accepted his reply without surprise. Still, he wanted something more than words from the bigshot FBI agent. Perhaps it was the chance to sleep one whole night without waking up in cold sweats. Ned noticed two night lights on in the living room.

'But you do believe me, don't you?' Buckley asked. 'What I've told you?'

Ned shrugged. 'It's hard to believe.'

'Do you?' he persisted.

Ned thought of Frances' eyes. The way the gold in the centre of her pupils liquefied before igniting. The stench of the ancient forest. Her last words to him, especially those.

'*I will touch you again.*'

'I believe the inexplicable happened to you and your friends in Mali,' Ned replied.

Buckley's grin was bitter. 'What if the inexplicable happens to your friend while he's with Spear and the next pair of twins? What if he gets a high fever, and is never the same afterwards?'

'*Yes. Need mirror. Short time. Control brain. Heat core.*'

Ned shivered. 'Do you think one of the women tried to alter Spear?'

Buckley sighed. 'I don't know. Perhaps it's true their hunger had to be satisfied first, as Spear told me. But who knows what he *really* did in that cave with his wife? Who knows what she did to him? Spear stood face to face with the horror of the Setians, but he hasn't given up trying to bring them back. You think about that when you tell me you can't stop him because the facts won't hold up in court. Because what comes next– it won't be so easy to stop.' Buckley nodded gravely. 'If he awakens them again, and they do have a chance to multiply, then they might just wipe out the entire human race.'

CHAPTER TWELVE

David Conner dreamed of the past and the future. He was scuba diving in the deep end of the Silver Shamrock hotel swimming pool in Las Vegas. He sat on the bottom and watched as the rising bubbles from his regulator tickled the bellies of the brown bodies of the people swimming above him. It was not bad being under water except for two minor concerns: he knew his air was going to eventually run out, and he knew it was going to be dark soon. He was more worried about the dark than the air in his tank, however, and for that reason he did not want to return to the surface. He believed when night came, it would get real cold.

After some time a pretty woman in a one piece orange bathing suit swam down to see him. She looked like Sandy but a part of him knew that was impossible because Sandy was dead. But the other part – the larger section of his dream mind – was happy to see her. He reached out and she clasped his hand and they smiled at each other under the water, her blonde hair floating above her head like sunlight blowing in a turquoise wind. She was so close, and he wanted to kiss her, but he had the stupid regulator in his mouth and was afraid to take it out.

Sandy blew bubbles in his direction, kisses that raced to the surface faster than he could follow. He knew she had to return to the surface soon herself, to breathe, but he was worried about the approaching cold. He wanted to protect her from it, keep her close. That was the only reason he continued to hold on to her hand, even when she stopped blowing her bubbles and began to struggle. He didn't want to hurt her. He loved her, for Christsakes. But he held onto her just the same because it seemed the lesser of two evils. Even when her eyes pleaded with him that she couldn't stay any longer and she began to thrash and her face turned blue. He held onto her until her expression went blank. Her eyes dimmed; the lights went off and no one was at home. It was weird, it was tragic, and it made no sense at all, but it was only then that he could finally let go of her. Sandy's body floated to the surface and drifted lazily above his head. Everyone else in the pool got out quickly he felt bad, real bad.

A while later another girl dove down to see him. She had long brown hair and wore blue jeans and a brown leather coat. He thought it was pretty weird that she didn't have a bathing suit on, but he was happy to see her, at least at first. It had got kind of lonely sitting on the floor of the pool with Sandy's body floating overhead. It took him a moment to realize it was Angela. He knew she was dead as well and for that reason he didn't offer his hand. Yet she took it anyway; she hung onto it tight. He didn't want that. He had seen what happened last time. But for the life of him, he couldn't shake free of her. Not until her eyes clouded over as Sandy's had and she ceased clinging to him. Like Sandy, Angela's body floated to the surface, where he had to look at it all the time.

He felt miserable. He noticed his air gauge sinking towards zero. He knew if he stayed where he was, he would drown. Still, he feared to brave the surface, especially with the two bodies floating there. It almost seemed as if death was the preferable option. It was a dilemma of the worst kind, and he couldn't see a way out.

It was then a third woman dove down to see him. He recognized her immediately – Vera,and she was naked. Her red hair floated above her head like the flames of a dragon; her green eyes sparkled like lost emeralds. He knew it was her and not her sister because he had made love to Lucy once long ago and Lucy had a scar on her right hip that Vera didn't have. There wasn't a mark on Vera; she was perfect. Swimming straight for his face, she pulled out his regulator and began to kiss him hard. For a moment, he forgot everything except how nice it was to have her mouth on his. He even forgot his need to breathe. But then her tongue slid in his mouth and he shook in horror. It was forked; she had the tongue of a snake. It slid around the inside of his mouth like a tapeworm crawling through the intestines of a corpse.

He felt nauseous. He tried to draw back but she gripped his head with both hands and she was very strong, much stronger than himself. He didn't know how to get free. He only knew that he had to get her tongue out of his mouth. Closing his eyes, he bit down as hard as he could. Cold acid burned the inside of his mouth and he gagged. He opened his eyes and saw Vera floating before him with red blood dripping from her open mouth. He assumed she would be furious with him but she was not. Her arm was outstretched and a crooked finger with a long sharp nail pointed at him. Her mouth twisted in a grotesque smirk. You're mine, she seemed to say. You stayed under too long.

Then the light started to fail.

David whipped his head upward. Far beyond the surface and the dead bodies, somewhere out in deep space, he could see as a huge taloned hand moved over the face of the sun, devouring it as if it were just another solar system along the way to the centre of the Milky Way, swallowing humanity's only source of light and life. It happened so fast; he had no chance to react. The sunlight failed; the pool turned dark and cold. The floating corpses halted in place. A splinter of ice formed on the surface; it cracked down to the floor of the pool like a splinter in a pane of thick glass, sharp and dangerous. Vera froze before his eyes, her floating blood now a permanent stain for the darkness to peer through, a stained glass window hung before a devil's tabernacle. He reached to put the regulator in his mouth but was too late. His arm was frozen in place, his eyeballs. He could not turn his gaze away from Vera, and he knew, as the world turned as black and cold as an asteroid tumbling aimlessly through space, that she would always be before him, for all of eternity. The curse was old, the pain raw. He was an Egyptian mummy stored in a pyramid raised on the spilt blood of tortured slaves. No Goddess waited to take him to the safety of the other side. His soul was entombed with a monster.

David Conner awoke to silent darkness. He heard his heart beating, that's all, the endless rhythm of circulating blood, the pulsating veins, a red drum set beside a narrow stream in a forgotten forest. For a moment he imagined his mother was near. Yet the external silence did not last. The night thawed, he became aware of the falling rain, and remembered the clouds that had swept in as Lucy and he hiked back to the camp from the lake, hand in hand, eager to make love. With the rain he heard the gentle rise and fall of her breathing as she lay naked beside him on the bunched mattresses on the floor of his room. She had stolen his blankets; his legs were cold. But then he remembered his nightmare, and everything was cold. It had been like no dream he had ever dreamt before. So real, a memory arisen from a mangled strand of DNA. He did not want to know what his ancestors had suffered. He did not want to meet what his children would see. The pain of his life was all he could bear.

I won't have children. I'll never have a wife. Who would take me?

Yet she said she loved him. What could that mean? He

had known her for only a few hours. Was it possible to
love someone that quick? Was it possible after ten years?
What was time but a measure of mistakes. He had not told
her that he loved her but he felt something for her that
he thought had died forever when he had found Sandy's
body splattered on the front steps of the Silver Shamrock.
It was a wonderful feeling. Why couldn't he let it be?
The wave had arrived. The sandy shore waited. Angels
stood guard. It was safe to love her, the Big Mind had
promised him.

David turned over and peered at her face in the dark.
Even in shadows, it was wrapped in innocence. She had
a glow about her, a warmth; it was as if her flesh healed
him where it touched him. There was passion, too. Even
now he felt the moist warmth radiate between her legs.
Never had he made love to a woman for so long, with such
abandon. What had Vera thought, two doors down? Vera,
who Lucy said slept lightly. Yet her sister's proximity
had not prevented her from moaning in pleasure. Lucy's
affection for him possessed her to the core. She let it; that
was her special ability, to give herself over completely.
She let go and trusted that everything would be all right.
That was what he loved about her most of all, and what
worried him as well; that she was trusting in him to make
everything perfect, as had Sandy and Angela.

Loved about her most of all.

He had not said it aloud, he reminded himself. Only
thought it. It did not count.

His cellular phone beeped softly. Lucy stirred; she
sighed and rolled over. David sat up, picked it up quickly.
Lightning flashed in the distance as he pushed the talk button. He counted to himself but the thunder never came.

'Hello?'

'David, I need to talk to you,' Ned said.

'I'm not alone.' He paused. Lucy's breathing was deep,
regular. 'It doesn't matter, she's asleep.'

'You're not going to believe what I have to say.'

'Bad news?' David asked. He glanced at his watch. Five-fifteen in the morning.

'It's not just bad. It's a nightmare.'

David thought of his own nightmare. 'I might believe more than you think. Talk.'

'You know the story of the serpent in the Garden of Eden?'

'Yes.'

Ned sounded scared. 'I think that story had a lot of truth in it.'

David listened to his old partner for well over an hour: the meeting with Buckley, the visit with Frances, the real talk with Buckley. Ned often quoted Buckley and Frances word for word and David remembered the phrases well. He had always had an excellent memory, particularly when it came to bad news. Oddly enough, nothing Ned told him surprised him. He recalled his own dread when he had first seen Frances and Penny's photographs. In the pictures they looked dissimilar, but subconsciously he must have realized they were identical twins, and connected their fate to Lucy and Vera. With Spear and Dr Henry and the Big Mind, he had been chipping away at the same mystery Ned had pursued. Good old Frank the iguana – Spear was a lizard lover from a long time ago. Yet when his partner finished, David was left with the big question: did he believe any of it? A long silence settled between them.

'Are you still there?' Ned asked finally.

'Yes.'

'What do you think?'

'Her eyes were that weird?'

'God just doesn't make them like that. They looked like something dug out of a futuristic robot's head with a pair of pliers.'

'Maybe they are from the future. Maybe these people

236

aren't regressing at all, but looking forward. Maybe the Flintstones were more prophetic than we realized.'

'David, I'm serious. You've got to get out of there. Get your girlfriend out as well. Which one are you with?'

'I don't know. It's hard to tell them apart.'

'David!'

'I'm with Lucy. I don't know what I can tell her. She has a lot invested in Spear and she just met me. To tell her to throw it all away on the ravings of a broken down professor on the other side of the country – that's asking a lot.'

'David, remember how you begged me to get Sandy out of town and I wouldn't listen to you? Well, you were right and she died. I fucked up. But now I'm begging you to get out, and take the girl. Buckley wasn't raving. He had seen people eaten alive and he was scared.'

David glanced down at Lucy. He couldn't imagine her or Vera harming anyone. Still, Ned did not panic easily and the way his boss sounded, it could have been him who had been in Africa instead of Buckley. Besides, Spear gave David the creeps anyway. The guy looked like someone who'd had the core of his brain cooked with laser eyes. David would just as soon get Lucy away from him – if she would come with him. Big if, and then what? Was he going to ask her to move in with him? He would have to start picking up after himself, couldn't leave his pizza boxes lying on the floor for a week at a time. He might have to stop drinking, not that he enjoyed it anyway. Life could get complicated. But he supposed he could worry about those things later.

'I'll leave here today with Lucy,' he said. 'You have my word. But I'll have to tell her some of what you told me to get her to leave.'

Ned hesitated. 'Does she know you're FBI?'

'Yes.'

Ned sighed. 'Be careful what you say to her.'

'I understand. You sound like you're on a plane. Going somewhere?'

'Denver.'

'Why Denver?'

'It's on the way to Idaho. It's the only flight I could get so early in the morning. I want to make sure you get the girls out of there. I might even arrest Spear – I'm thinking about it.'

'Why don't we just kill him? Save the taxpayers the money.'

'You joke, but after what I've seen, I've thought about it. Buckley asked me to waste him. I think Spear's a menace to humanity.'

David chuckled softly. 'This doesn't sound like the boss I said goodbye to in Los Angeles. When do you arrive in Denver?'

'In two hours.'

'Call me from there if you wish, but I'll be out of here before noon. Honestly, Ned, you don't need to come up here. It's not an easy trip. The camp's in the middle of nowhere.'

'If you and the girl leave the camp immediately, I won't bother with the flight. Don't wait until noon.'

'As soon as Lucy wakes up, I'll have her to pack. By the way, did you find out anything about Margaret?'

'I haven't checked with the office lately. It's still too early there – I'll call them as soon as I get to Denver. What's your interest in her?'

'There's something about her that fascinates me. I can't explain it.'

'She's not another Frances, is she?' Ned asked.

'No. She's very kind.' David paused. Lucy stirred again. 'I have to go. Happy flying.'

'Next time we talk I want you to be on the road to Boise,' Ned said.

They exchanged goodbyes. David stared down at Lucy,

the curl of her red hair over her pale ears, the way she pursed her lips while sleeping like a young child. The intensity of his feelings for her shocked him. If there was even a remote chance she could be harmed using Spear's mental techniques, he wanted her as far from the guy as possible. He wasn't about to lose another woman to bad timing. Sliding back onto the floor beside her, the wooden floor creaking beneath the worn mattresses, she turned in his direction. What a wonderful thing her warm skin was. Maybe there was a God, after all. Her sleepy green eyes blinked in the poor light, although it was not nearly so dark as when Ned first called. It would be a grey and wet morning.

'Were you gone?' she whispered.

'Secret agent business. I had to use the bathroom.'

She smiled. 'You're cute. I was dreaming about you.'

'Was it a nice dream?'

She frowned. 'I'm not sure. I don't remember it that well. There was some kind of eclipse, and it was dark and cold. I don't know where we were.'

David stiffened, but he pulled her close. 'Go back to sleep, Lucy. We can talk about it when the sun's up.'

CHAPTER THIRTEEN

Ned Calendar found a private phone booth in the Denver airport and shut himself inside. Dialling his home office, he talked to a new receptionist and ended up with Special Agent Carol McCormick. Carol was a tough-assed chick out of Harlem, New York. He used her with the east side gangs, mainly to keep an eye on where they were getting their drugs. Not one of them dreamed she was FBI. She had a black belt in karate, could drink a bottle of tequila standing up and still blow it out of the air with one shot if it was thrown higher than the ceiling. David liked Carol as well; practising together at a dojo in the Valley, she once broke three of his ribs. Ned had put her in charge of investigating Margaret Farrow's past history.

'That woman's got no past,' Carol said. 'For all we can tell she crawled out of the ground a year ago. It's spooky. I spoke to her doctors and the police and they said they advertised her face across the country. Not a soul called in to claim her.'

'Did you run her fingerprints through the computer?' Ned asked. He assumed the police had got them; it would have been standard procedure with an unidentified comatose patient.

'Yeah, that's another weird thing about her. She ain't got no prints.'

'The police didn't take a set?'

'Oh, they took them all right. She just ain't got any. Her palms are as smooth as the palms on Michelangelo's *David*.'

'What? Her palms are featureless?'

'That's it, boss. I spoke to the medical examiner who printed her.'

'There must be some mistake. It's medically impossible not to have fingerprints.'

'I don't know. The medical examiner said he ain't never seen anything like it. He wondered aloud to me if she broke her back falling out of a UFO.'

'But you get fingerprints in the womb,' Ned protested.

'Maybe this chick ain't never been in no one's womb.'

'Carol.'

'Well, boss, she doesn't have a past. They dug her out of a garbage bin. God knows where she came from. And right away she hooked up with that weird Professor. You have to talk to the doctor at the hospital about them both. They're a pair, I tell you. If David's with them now, you tell him to watch his back. They might put a spell on him.'

'Do you have the numbers of the doctors who treated Spear and Farrow?'

'It was the same doctor who took care of them both, except for Farrow's back surgery. That was done by an orthopedic specialist. I haven't been able to locate him. I'll give you the doc's info. You call and talk to him yourself. He has a thing or two to tell you.'

Ned took down the information and rang off. He checked his watch – eight thirty-nine. It would be an hour earlier in Los Angeles, but doctors often worked from the crack of dawn. Ned rang Cedar Sinai in Los Angeles and asked for the internist, Dr Ralph Barnes, saying it was an emergency. The receptionist left the line to have him paged. Ned was on hold ten minutes before the man came to the phone. Ned introduced himself, told him why he was calling. The doctor sounded suitably impressed. He did not ask for his credentials – Carol had probably already scared him into being a believer. Dr Barnes asked the question they all asked.

'Have the Professor and Margaret done anything wrong?'

'That has yet to be established,' Ned said. 'We're doing background checks at present. I would appreciate it if you kept this conversation confidential.'

'No problem. How can I help you?'

'I understand you treated both the Professor and Margaret. Is that correct?'

'Not precisely. I was in charge of Professor Spear's care, but was only a consultant for Margaret. She had a serious spinal injury. While she was in her coma she developed a stubborn case of pneumonia. I was called in to treat it. She was under the direct care of Dr Ruth Thompson. Dr Thompson no longer lives in this area, but I could find a number for her if you want.'

'It's not necessary. My associate, Agent McCormick, has already told me of Margaret's lack of fingerprints. I understand you spoke to her. I want to know if you have ever seen such a thing in your experience as a doctor?'

'Personally, no. It confounded many of us here at the hospital. But I have read about such cases in the literature. They're very rare, but I can safely say Margaret is not alone with her smooth palms.'

'What creates the condition?' Ned asked.

'Medical science doesn't know, but it would appear to be an inherited condition.'

'You mean, it's genetic?'

'That's correct.'

'Did Margaret have any other conditions that medical science cannot explain?'

'No. But her complete amnesia in conjuction with her day to day clarity is also rare. When a person suffers loss of memory due to an injury of the central nervous system, they usually forget how to read or how to make coffee or even dress themselves. Margaret had a serious concussion as well as a broken back, but she was exceptionally clear after she awakened. I remember her tested IQ was in the genius range. Yet she had not a single memory from her personal life.'

'How do you explain that?' Ned asked.

'I can't. I'm not a psychiatrist. But in talking to psychiatrists here, they say it's possible her injuries were inflicted by someone close. That the trauma of the incident caused her to selectively block out her memory.'

'Did Margaret act psychologically traumatized?'

'No. Once she awaked from her coma, except for her loss of memory, she was one of the most rational people I ever met. Because of the severity of her injuries, she was here a couple of months and was well liked by the other patients. I got to know her quite well.'

'I was just going to ask you that. I'm surprised you remember the details of her case so well. You must see many patients each year.'

'Margaret was very special. I must tell you another unusual incident related to her. When she was first brought in, she was placed in a trauma wing for spinal injuries. You can imagine how when someone breaks their back they need special care. Often they are not even kept in a normal bed, but are fixed in the air with a combination of metal poles and pulleys and rods. The suspension allows them to be easily turned and cleaned without disturbing their healing bones. Anyway, Margaret was in such a wing throughout the bulk of her coma, along with perhaps two dozen patients. Now, none of the others were unconscious like Margaret, but the severity of their wounds was such that none was expected to walk again. Yet all of them did.'

Ned had to take a moment. 'What are you implying, doctor?'

'I'm implying nothing. I'm simply stating a fact. All the spinal injury patients that were roomed with Margaret made full recoveries. It's unprecedented in medical history.'

'But what did Margaret have to do with their unusual recoveries?'

'She couldn't have had anything to do them. Yet she was viewed superstitiously by the nursing staff as well as the doctors. We saw her as a lucky charm.'

'It sounds like you should have kept her as a patient,' Ned muttered.

'I had the same thought myself.'

'But she never regained the use of her own legs? I understand she's still paralysed from the waist down?'

'That's my understanding as well. We would expect her to remain a paraplegic. Her spine was severed at T6 – the sixth thoracic vertebra.'

'Did any of the patients roomed with her have severed spines?'

'I think a number of them did. But they didn't when they walked out of here. Don't ask me how.'

'I am asking you how, Dr Barnes. This woman had no fingerprints, no past, and she heals like a modern Jesus. I'm surprised you didn't keep closer track of her after she left the hospital.'

The good doctor sounded offended. 'Margaret Farrow is a private citizen like the rest of us. We're not the FBI. We don't keep track of people. Besides, no one is stating categorically that she had anything to do with the other patients' recoveries. Other factors could have been involved.'

'Such as?' Ned persisted.

Dr Barnes considered. 'I don't know.'

'Tell me about Professor Spear. I have heard he came to you with a high fever after being in Africa. What was his diagnosis and treatment?'

'I was his personal physician and I was never able to make a positive diagnosis. Initially we treated him for meningitis because he showed a definite swelling of the brain, which we attributed to infection. Yet he had no other signs of a bacteria or virus in his system, and we later decided he was suffering an injury to the soft tissue of the brain stem. His brain wave activity was extremely erratic.'

'By erratic what do you mean?' Ned asked.

'His EEG showed hyperactivity activity, even in sleep. It was as if his brain operated in high gear. He was literally burning up. The bulk of his treatment consisted in keeping him cooled with cold packs and on heavy anti-inflammatories. The man should have died. He had a fever of above a hundred and seven degrees for over a month.'

'Did he have an injury to the brain stem?'

'To be frank, I don't think so. We were just shooting in the dark with him. But I was glad to see him recover. I understand he and Margaret now work together?'

'Yes. While Spear was in the hospital, did he ever demonstrate supernormal abilities?'

'Pardon me?'

'Did he ever move things with his mind? Or show signs of unusual strength?'

'No. Not that I ever saw. May I ask why you ask that question?'

'It's a long story. Was there anything about Spear you found distasteful?'

'I'm afraid I don't understand your question. He wasn't the most personable man if that's what you mean.'

'Did he ever scare you?'

'Scare me?'

'Yes. You know, like the Bogeyman scares children?'

Dr Barnes was haughty. 'Why would I be scared of a patient, Mr Calendar.'

'I know one in South Carolina that would scare the shit out of you. But that's another story. Doctor, I want to thank you for your time. I know you must be a busy man. If there's anything else unusual that you can remember about Margaret or Professor Spear, please call the Los Angeles office of the FBI. We're in the phone book. Ask for myself or Carol McCormick.' Ned paused. 'Do you have anything else to tell me?'

Dr Barnes hesitated. 'Just that when Professor Spear was delirious with his fever, he often spoke in a foreign language.'

'He knows many languages. He had just come from Africa, where he spoke Sanga and Wazouba. That must be it.'

Dr Barnes was uncomfortable. 'I don't think so.'

'What do you mean? Did you recognize the language?'

'No. That's my point. It didn't sound like a human language.'

'Did it sound like an *animal* language?'

'Sort of. I know that must sound silly.'

Ned was afraid to ask. 'Did it sound like a language that a race of reptiles might have? Assuming of course, hypothetically, that there existed reptiles intelligent enough to develop a language.'

Dr Barnes swallowed heavily. 'Yes. He used to hiss a lot.' He added, 'It did kind of scare me every now and then.'

'I understand,' Ned said.

Ned said goodbye to the doctor. The conversation had not reassured him. He made a vow to himself that he would neutralize Spear, one way or the other. If he didn't he knew he would never be able to enjoy his retirement. If David got Lucy clear of the Professor's influence, however, he would have time to mount a legal case against the man. Perhaps he could get Spear for the murder of his wife, after all. It would be preferable to just blowing away the Professor. Ned had killed two men in his life – one a mob assassin, the other a kidnapper – and had not enjoyed the feeling. A long hot shower did not wash it away, nor did time. David understood that. It was one thing they wished they didn't have in common. Of course, both of Ned's victims had been trying to kill him at the time.

Close to three hours had elapsed since Ned had last spoken to David. He tried David's cellular number, let it ring for a while but got no answer. No reason to panic, Ned told himself as he set down his phone. David could have left his phone in his room while making preparations to leave. It was still early in the day. At the camp, David probably didn't carry the phone with him at all times. Still, Ned would have felt better hearing from his partner. He had a bad feeling about the situation, lizard monsters notwithstanding. Spear had sought publicity for years for his theories, and yet he had resisted the visit of a supposedly important reporter during this special retreat. He had also gone to extremes to isolate his group. David was not exaggerating when he said Camp Paradise was in the middle of nowhere. Ned remembered the map of Idaho. The place was about as far from civilization as a person could get and still be in the continental United States.

What did Spear need with the isolation?

Why had he hiked up to Lucian Point in the middle of a dark Mali night?

Ned checked the airline schedules. His Delta flight for Los Angeles left in forty minutes. Northwest, however, had a flight to Boise that departed in twenty minutes. Denver and Boise were approximately seven hundred miles apart; the flight was ninety-seven minutes long. If he reached David on the phone while he was in the air, it wouldn't be a major problem. They could always spend the day together in Boise and decide what should be done about Spear. It might even be better than trying to rendezvous in Los Angeles. But if he got on the flight to Los Angeles, and didn't reach David for the rest of the day, then he would go out of his mind with worry. That would not do.

Ned hurried to the Northwest counter and bought a ticket to Boise.

First class. Because he wanted the free booze. Needed it. '*I will touch you again.*'

What was the story with Margaret? Who the hell was she?

'*She's not a she. She's an it.*'

CHAPTER FOURTEEN

David Conner sat eating breakfast with Margaret Farrow. Or rather he ate and she served him, in between knitting the green and white sweater she had been working on when he had first met her in the flowered meadow. She had made the pancakes and, yes, they did taste exactly as his mother used to make them. The coffee, too, was much to his liking, although the same could not be said for the weather. David did not know if Idaho often got rain storms like this one, but if it did then it should have had a great lake of its own. The sky was not filled with grey clouds but black nozzles. He should have brought scuba equipment rather than his waterproof Patagonia green coat, which had not kept him from getting wet on his brief walk from the dorm to the dining area. Yet the thought of scuba diving was not a pleasant one this morning. The gloom of his nightmare continued to linger. He could not dispel the image of the blood freezing in place before his numb eyes, the scaled hand reaching out to smother the sun. Camp Paradise was no longer a happy place to be. Yesterday he'd had the boring concern of government leaks. Now he had to worry about super reptiles. The Vera in his dream had had a tongue like a snake, and that had been before Ned's call. He may not have believed what Buckley had to say but he didn't disbelieve him either.

'Can I get you more butter?' Margaret asked.

'You have done too much for me already. Sit and relax. I mean – I didn't mean that. I'm sorry.'

Margaret smiled, a ball of white yarn on her lap, her knitting needles in hand. 'I know I'm crippled. I'm not ashamed of the fact. It's the body God wanted me to have. He must have had his reasons.'

'But it didn't start out that way. Could God's reasons have changed?'

Margaret stared at him a moment. 'You know what you are, David?'

'What?'

'A deeply spiritual man whose head has chosen to be an atheist and whose heart still yearns for the divine.'

'I thought I only yearned for a good turkey dinner.' He shrugged, added, 'There's nothing spiritual about me.'

'I disagree. You care deeply about other people. You never think about yourself. You never make room for your own happiness. That can be a redeeming quality as well as a great failing. But I prefer to look at your positive side. You are the perfect servant. The Big Mind said it is only a servant who can become a master.'

David chuckled uneasily. 'You read too much into what the Big Mind said yesterday to me. I didn't even recognize the man it was talking about.'

Margaret went on knitting. 'I did. Did you see Lucy last night?'

'Yes.'

'Good.'

'Do you really think so?' He realized that he did want her approval.

'Yes.'

David didn't want to leave Margaret without saying goodbye. It was the main reason he had come to the dining hall. He had already explained to Lucy that they had to get out of the camp. As expected, she demanded an explanation and he had been forced to recount some of what Buckley had told Ned. Lucy had listened with great attention, and had badgered him for details as to exactly what the women had done in Africa that allowed them to punch through the rational thought barrier. But he had held back on specifics, afraid curiosity might get the best of her and she might experiment with her sister. He had *not* told her about the super reptilian race that supposedly ruled the planet sixty million years ago, but had simply said Spear's wife and her twin sister went insane and harmed a lot of people after fooling with mutual hypnosis on their own. He figured that would be hard enough to swallow, but his choices seemed effective. When he was finished, she agreed that they should go. Yet she had asked for a couple of hours to get ready. She pleaded that she had a lot of stuff to pack.

'I'm glad you approve.' He added as casually as possible, 'And I hope you won't hate me too much for leaving with her this afternoon.'

She did not act surprised, and he had thought the remark would floor her. Or rather, he had thought it *should* floor her. He was beginning to see that Margaret had a strong inner core, and nothing threw her off. She continued to knit.

'You're going to have trouble getting out of here with the path flooded,' she said.

'You're not upset that I'm ruining Spear's experiment?'

'It's his experiment. It's not mine.'

'But you must support it. You've been with him for so long.'

Margaret paused, thoughtful, her head lowered. 'I support the Big Mind. I *listen* to it. The Big Mind is never worried. But Spear is racked with concerns.' She shook her head. 'We see things a lot more differently than you think.'

'Can you continue your sessions with Lucy gone?' David asked.

'No.'

David felt bad. 'I have my reasons for leaving with her. I would like to explain them to you but I can't. Too many issues are involved.'

'That's all right.'

David stood. 'Margaret, it's hard to say goodbye to you. Why is that?'

She beamed up at him, her dimples showing. 'Because I'm so cute.' She held up the almost finished sweater in front of her face. 'What do you think? Will Vera like it?'

'I thought you said it was for Lucy?'

Margaret slowly lowered the sweater, her smile fading in stages. 'It's for one of them,' she said softly. 'I'm not sure which.'

David hugged her in farewell. He washed his dishes in the back and left the dining hall. Margaret had told him that Dr Henry had left at the crack of dawn in the four wheel drive truck to pick up supplies in Augustine, fifty miles away. He had set out before the heavy rain started, but she believed he was going to be forced to return. Apparently, ten miles beyond where the path to the camp met the road, the road frequently washed out. At least that's what Spear said, and he knew the area well. It was David's hope to use the truck to get back to his own rental car with Lucy and her things. But if the worst came to worst, he would carry her stuff to his car, or he might even be able to hike down and bring the car part way up the path. That might be more logical, if the muddy path gave him room to manoeuvre. He would only wait so long for Dr Henry. It was like a full eclipse morning; the sky was as dark as an evening on the moon. He had a bad feeling about the day and just wanted to be gone.

David went looking for Lucy. He wondered what she was doing.

But he didn't find her.

CHAPTER FIFTEEN

What David Conner did not know when he spoke to Lucy Temple early in the morning about the danger of her attempting a private regression with her sister was that they had done it before. After they had met Professor Spear and learned his technique of mutual hypnosis, it was one of the first things they had tried. It had worked well, in fact, better than the sessions with the others. But they had not continued to experiment with it because for some unknown reason Vera always got a headache when it was just the two of them. Lucy remembered – especially after talking to David – how Spear's jaw had dropped when they told him they had regressed alone together. He had quizzed them about their experiences, and when they were through had suggested they confine their experiments to the group. Yet he had not forbidden them to try it again. The prospect did not terrify him the way it did David. Lucy had to laugh at David's concern. No doubt he was an incredible spy, but when it came to research into the field of consciousness he didn't know tarot cards from a ouija board. She had done hundreds of sessions and never been harmed. She believed David simply disliked Spear, and wanted her to run away with him.

Not that the latter was an unpleasant prospect. She had not lied to David when she had agreed to leave with him in two hours. The night in his arms had opened a doorway inside her, and through it she saw a large part of her life that was not being lived. She saw a great man who deserved true love. David was like no one she had ever met before. A gentle soul with the heart of a lion, but a sad man who had lost more than he realized. She wanted to spend time with him, give him back what the rest of the world had wrestled from him. Faith in God, in love. She honestly believed she could love him for the rest of her life.

Yet Lucy had no intention of permanently abandoning Professor Spear. But she realized she had allowed him to dominate her life in too many ways. He had become a surrogate father for her and that was not healthy, not at her age. She still planned to get her degree and help establish his theories, but she was no longer going to jump every time he said the word. Leaving abruptly like this, she felt, would serve notice that she was her own person. He would be angry but the anger could serve to reinforce the personal step she was taking. Naturally, she planned to tell him her reasons for departing before simply vanishing. She did not want to be rude.

What about the things Spear had done in Africa with his wife and sister-in-law? Murdered her, his old partner had said. Sounded like a plot straight out of an unfilmed episode of *The FBI*. The idea amused Lucy as much as David's anxiety about the danger that lay beyond the rational thought barrier. She had heard enough about Buckley from Spear to know that he was nothing but a jealous academic. Even now he was still trying to tarnish Spear's reputation. Spear couldn't hurt a fly; she had known him too long to believe otherwise. Yet, at the same time, she believed Buckley had mixed truth in with lies. Most accomplished liars did, and many of David's remarks had sounded authentic. Buckley had spent a long time with the Dogon, and David had told her far more about the unique method of Dogon regression than he realized.

Lucy was much more experienced in these matters than David knew.

First, David had said that the twin sisters had flipped out when they stared into each other's eyes. It must be a salient point. Vera and she had never attempted to regress with their eyes open. Logically, it would seem that doing that would keep their attention focused outwardly, when they were trying to sink inside. Perhaps, however, the Dogon had insights into identical twins that no one else did. Certainly, if one tenth of what Buckley had said was true, then they had taught both him and Spear a great deal about the mind. That was one thing that did bother her about Spear, that he had never acknowledged the debt his theories owed to them. She knew he had spent a long time there. In fact, she hardly remembered him talking about the Dogon.

Second, David had accidentally revealed to her that breathing was crucial to the unique style of regression. In contacting the Big Mind, it was important that they all took long slow deep breaths together. It was difficult to reach a deep state otherwise. When she had pressed David about the specifics, he had thrown up his hands and said, 'I don't know! They did everything backwards. It was dangerous, that's all that matters.' To Lucy that meant the women had breathed in rapid rhythm, or opposite one another. One inhaled while the other exhaled. It would not take much experimentation to figure out which was the case.

And Lucy planned to do just that. Before leaving Camp Paradise.

She was not worried that she or Vera would go insane.

They could always stop if they felt uncomfortable with the technique.

They could just close their eyes and the Big Mind would come to their rescue.

Lucy found Vera in her bedroom, reading. Vera read two or three novels a week. Her special love was science fiction, but fantasy was a close second. Lucy, on the other hand, preferred movies to books. She was visual, liked action. Vera had always been contemplative by nature, even when it came to romance. But her daydreams of her knight in shining armour never materialized. And she was such a pretty girl, Lucy thought. As pretty as me! Vera had dated too male many students who had to stretch their student loans just to spring for popcorn. Lucy often thought Vera had to be with a strong man or nobody at all. Her thoughtful silences swallowed lesser souls. As Lucy knocked and walked in, Vera set aside her book and appraised her as if from an amused height.

'Don't say it,' Lucy said.

Vera raised an eyebrow. 'What was I going to say? Did you practise safe sex? Was he as good as *you* sounded? Are you getting married? Are you sore?'

Lucy closed the door and sat on the bunk bed opposite Vera's. Her sister had the heater way up. Vera was sensitive to cold. Lucy unbuttoned her coat.

'All of the above,' she said. Then she giggled. 'Yes, yes, yes, yes.'

Vera sat up. 'You're not getting married. You just met him.'

Lucy shook her head. 'Well, maybe not yes to that question. But he's adorable, really. I can't tell you how great he is.'

'I think you told the whole camp how great he was last night.'

'Was I that loud?'

'It's a quiet forest, Lucy. But don't worry. I don't think any of the men heard you.'

'But you think Margaret did?'

'Yes. Margaret hears everything.'

Lucy waved her hand. 'But Margaret doesn't judge. What are you reading? The Tao of Sex?'

Vera showed her the cover. '*Frankenstein*. Your boyfriend's favourite. I just happened to have it in my suitcase. But he's right – it's a masterpiece. I haven't read it since I was a child.'

'When I was a little girl I read Nancy Drew and you read *Frankenstein* and *Dracula*. I don't know, maybe we're not sisters. Have you ever thought of that?'

Vera picked her book back up. 'I think it's true how some people say sex destroys brain cells. You are living proof.'

'If they have to die, I suppose there are worse ways to kill them. Vera, put the book down. I have something important to tell you. David knows a great deal about Spear's past. He's researched him thoroughly. This morning he told me some of the stuff Spear picked up while he was with the Dogon people in Africa. Remember them? Spear mentioned them a couple of times but never went into detail.'

Vera frowned. 'I remember when he spoke about them he was always uneasy. What happened while he was with them?'

Lucy hesitated. She didn't usually lie to her sister, but didn't want to frighten her either. Then Vera would never be able to focus for a regression. For that reason, Lucy had decided to wait until after the regression to tell Vera she was leaving with David. Vera would be upset. Her sister's loyalty to Spear knew no bounds.

'Nothing in particular,' Lucy said. 'But Spear picked up a few tricks from them that he hasn't taught us yet. David just told me one. It involves the regression of identical twins, but with a new twist.'

Vera shook her head. 'I don't want to try that again. I always got such a pressure in my temples. I would have to take a Tylenol and lie down for two hours for it to leave.'

'This will be different. We keep our eyes open the whole time and stare at each other. Also, we breathe differently. Let's give it a try. It's supposed to be how the Dogon penetrated the rational thought barrier.'

'If Spear knows it, why don't we wait until he shows us how to do it properly?'

'That's my point. We've been with him all this time and he hasn't shown us. I wonder if he ever will. Come on, what can it hurt? Think how exciting it will be to go back before cavemen were even walking around.'

Vera considered. 'If we go back that far, into the minds of beasts, we'll lose our focus. We'll just dull out and forget what we're doing.'

'That won't be so awful. At least we will have tried. And who knows, maybe we'll see something we never expected? It's possible. The Big Mind says anything is possible.'

Vera thought a moment then chuckled. 'All right. But if we run into Fred and Barney, I'm going to scream. Do you want to do it in my room or in your room?'

'Neither. We might be interrupted. Let's go to the unopened dorm down near the meadow.'

Vera was doubtful. 'We'll be soaked by the time we can get there. And it will take a while for the heaters to warm up the place. I don't even know if the heaters work in that dorm. It doesn't look like it's been used in a long time. Do you have a key?'

'I have an umbrella. You can use it. I have a raincoat as well. The heaters work as efficiently there as they do here. It takes ten minutes to warm up one of these rooms. Also, I have a key. Tom gave it to me when I got here. He was afraid he'd lose it. Come on, let's go now while David's at breakfast.'

Vera got up slowly. 'Why are you so worried about David?'

Lucy smiled. 'How can I fly into the past when I'm moaning in the present?'

Minutes later they were headed in the direction of the unused dorm. Lucy found the short hike difficult, as did Vera judging by the number of her complaints. There were minor streams everywhere. Both their feet were cold and wet as soon as they left their dorm, even with their waterproof boots. Lucy hated to think what the deluge was doing to the path that led to the road. It was just a dirt trail; it would be a ravine by tomorrow if the downpour kept up.

Along the soggy road through the trees, Lucy thought of the night her parents died. Vera and she were eighteen, one month away from graduating from high school. They were both in bed asleep when the knock came at the door. The pounding was loud – sounded like thunder to half conscious ears; and their doorbell worked perfectly. Vera was slow to get up. She always took time getting out of bed in the morning, even when it was a bright happy morning. That night she clung to her blankets as if they were another body, while Lucy hurried to see who it was. Just the sight of the highway patrolman was enough for her to know Mum and Dad were gone. The cop didn't have to say a word. But he did anyway – a few choice phrases. A drunk driver had crossed the centre line, hit them head on. They had died instantly, *painlessly*. That word was to echo in Lucy's head for the next few days. Could any change as radical as death be painless? Could any afterlife deserve the name of heaven when the new residents must know how the ones they had left behind suffered? Lucy had been close to both her parents, and knew her mother especially would grieve over her daughter's grief. At least she and Vera had had each other to give them comfort. After those long dark days, there was nothing Lucy would not do for her sister.

Lucy had once asked the Big Mind about death.

It had just laughed. No such thing, child.

Thunder boomed nearby as they settled inside one of the off limit rooms, leaving their boots by the door. The heater creaked loudly as the electricity poured through its numb wires. The place was dusty but dry, and was surprisingly free of the mildew odour that afflicted several of the rooms in the other two dorms. Vera had brought a candle with her. She lit it and welded it to the top of a table with a bubble of hot wax. The orange flame stood by their sides, tall like the sail of a ship caught by the rising sun. Yet it smoked as well. Lucy had never seen so much black soot pour off a white drugstore candle. She mentioned the fact to Lucy as they both sat on one of the bunk beds. Vera stared at the candle as if it were a crystal ball.

'A candle is supposed to purify the atmosphere of negativity,' she said finally. 'Maybe there's lots of bad vibes in here that need burning up.'

'Maybe it's a cheap candle.' Lucy gestured for Vera to sit facing her. They fiddled around for a moment, trying to get comfortable on the exhausted springs and paper thin mattress, and ended up reclining on their knees. The little girl posture was easy for both of them; they were blessed with limber joints.

'What do we do now?' Vera asked.

Lucy reviewed the point about focusing on each other's eyes, and admitted her uncertainty about how they were to breathe. She half expected Vera to complain again that they should wait for Spear to show them precisely what the Dogon did, but apparently her sister was committed. Lucy presented her with the two options: rapid breaths, or alternate inhalation and exhalations. Vera feared hyperventilating. They decided to experiment with the latter method first. The mattress sloped slightly between them. They clasped each other's hands to help their balance, and because they always held onto each other during a session. It made them feel closer.

Lucy slowly exhaled. Vera slowly inhaled. Lucy smiled and blinked. Vera did likewise. It was not so bad, Lucy thought, staring at the person she cared most about in the whole world. She was not embarrassed, any more than she would have been embarrassed kneeling before a mirror. That is how she felt. Like she was opening herself to herself. They kept so few secrets from each other. At the time, it seemed a minor lapse that she had failed to tell Vera that what they were doing might be dangerous.

Lucy slowly inhaled. Vera slowly exhaled. Lucy felt a shift in the room even with the exchange of the first breaths. Curiously, it seemed an external phenomena. It was if the walls had closed slightly, and a damp wave had arisen from beneath the floor. Lucy shivered and wondered if the heaters were failing, even though she could hear them clearly as they protested the expansive quality of the energy pouring through them. Lucy felt no expansion herself, on the level of consciousness, as she almost invariably did the moment they attempted to contact the Big Mind. She wondered if the Big Mind were observing their experiment, but then chided herself for the naivety of the question. The Big Mind was omnipresent. Of course it was watching.

Lucy exhaled. Vera inhaled. Lucy became aware of the sheer blackness of her sister's pupils. Of course all pupils were dark on all people, but Lucy had never before stopped to consider how the world of colour was perceived through a tiny colourless circle. It was one of those paradoxes of nature that their genes seemed so fond of organizing. She noticed that Vera had not blinked in a couple of minutes and wondered if the same was true for her. She wanted to ask but found that she couldn't speak.

Lucy inhaled. Vera exhaled. Lucy felt a definite pull

inwards. But it was not a gentle expansive feeling like in a normal session. Rather, it was as if the very energy that gave life to her body was coming to a focus in her head. But not between her eyebrows as was often symbolically depicted with yogis in deep meditation in the Himalayas as a third eye drawn on their foreheads. This energy – it was actually more of a sensation of power–moved over her face from sense to sense. It was in her eyes, then her mouth. It crawled up her nostrils, where it burned slightly, like a firefly with parasitic tendencies. Her ears tingled; she heard an unpleasant ringing sound that only ceased when another wave of thunder shook the room. Lucy felt as each sense touched by the power then grew in intensity, in range. Particularly as far as her vision was concerned. She saw deep into Vera's pupils; they could have been bottomless.

And she knew her sister was experiencing exactly the same thing she was.

Lucy exhaled. Vera inhaled. Their breath was one rhythm, a single pulsation, although it pulled in opposite directions. There was no conflict. The heart had to squeeze the blood out before it could draw more in. Lucy felt as if she drew from Vera's life, and Vera in turn drew from her. Deep in her sister's eyes in a place of knowledge her genetic chain had never revealed to her before, she saw the Egyptian priestess whose mind she had entered the previous day. Only now she saw her from a different angle: what *would have* been the woman's fate had she failed to gouge out her eyes. In other words, she saw an alternative path for the woman, had she not listened to the Goddess Isis. A path where divine vision had never intervened.

Lucy inhaled. Vera exhaled. The priestess was forced to sit upright and stare into her twin sister's eyes. Cold blades were held at their throats. If they blinked, if they lost the rhythm of the breath, lost the focus, they were cut, not enough to kill them but enough to make them feel their own mortality. The blood was a reminder not to veer from the black rite. That was what it was all about. An occult path that led off the normal course of human evolution. Yet it was not a short cut into a realm of light and love, where mankind joined the angels on the joyful journey to God. But a detour that forced one back into a blasphemous history where the light of the Goddess Isis never shone. Only a mirror could turn away all light. Only a mirror could show what had always been present from the start, deep in the brain, waiting to crawl out of the ears and once again nibble on the flesh of warm mammals. Truly it was a wicked secret that only the conscious fusion of identical bodies and minds could open the pit to hell.

Lucy exhaled. Vera inhaled. Lucy did not want to see the end result of the black rite but felt as if her sister compelled her to watch. Yet with the thought came the understanding that her sister felt the same way. Forced to do another's bidding. That was the most frightening realization of all. As they came so close together, closer than two human beings had a right to do, *something* came between them. Something came *out* of them, and its will was greater than theirs combined. They had to watch; ignorance was not an option. Too late, Lucy realized she had made a serious mistake by not listening to David.

She found she could not stop the process.

Lucy inhaled. Vera exhaled. The Egyptian priestess stared deep into her sister's eyes. She breathed as her sister breathed. She moaned as – she moaned. The 'I' of the priestess began to dissolve, but it was not the extinguishing of small ego in exchange for spiritual realization. A greater ego flooded the hearts of both women. A single entity that required – at least for a short period – two nervous systems to support it in the new time. The influx of reptilian consciousness made the blood heat, the brain burn, especially at the core, where the forgotten powers had lain dormant for millions of years, just waiting for a fateful day to awaken.

Lucy choked. Vera choked. Lucy felt her own temperature soar as the priestess began to shake violently. The evil ones withdrew their knives. Fear was no longer necessary when mastery was all but achieved. The priestess' body convulsed as if caught in the throes of a viper's deadly venom. Then it went so still it could have been dead were it not for the agony that burned behind its eyes. Lucy felt that agony as well because she *was* the priestess. The foolish human who had not listened to the Goddess. The damned soul who had exchanged mortal eyes for a vision of the beast.

Lucy did not breathe. Vera could not. They stared at each other through pupils that had swollen to the size of black holes and saw as the priestess and her sister began to change. Yet ultimately only one body was required to carry the will of each member of the super race, the masters as they called themselves, who scorned their warm blooded hosts as simply fresh expressions of bloody meat. Only one nervous system in each set of identical twins had encoded in its genes the information that triggered the metamorphoses that supported the full possession. Yet such a wild genetic scheme was not nature's doing. It had been deliberately placed in the DNA by the race of reptiles when they saw their own impending doom. Because they did not welcome the end. They had no god but their own instinctual feelings of importance and so could not accept death. They hated the thought of the missed opportunities to feed, to conquer, almost as much as they hated each other. Their hatred reached even as high as the stars. And it was possible that somewhere far off in the shimmering mist of the Milky Way the old ones still lived. Still watched the cradle of their civilization and wondered when it would spawn a new generation of foes capable of doing battle with them.

Lucy went numb. Vera froze. Only one permanent host was required, although two nervous systems were needed to uphold the transition. To support the time between feeding and reproduction. The mirror required its own reflection to see past all limitations. The priestess watched as her sister shed flesh and grew scales, lost fingers and sprouted talons. Yet was the change physical? Or was it all just in the mind? And did it really matter anyway? The barren desert sprouted a tropical forest thick enough to bury an unborn civilization – ancient Egypt, lost to the spread of the black rite. Simultaneously, the dorm in modern Idaho changed to a warm cesspool of large lizards. Lucy felt slime seep over her legs and into her crotch. With the eyes that had been given to her by her mother and father, she watched as Vera's face followed that of the priestess's sister. Vera's lips split open and pulled back over a mouth that elongated into a hungry maw.

The priestess screamed. Lucy screamed.

No one heard her, though. There was no one to save her but herself.

The trial of the priestess was only an illusion. She had faced her fear and chosen the path of the righteous. What was left of Lucy's mind knew it had a similar choice. She could reach up now and rip her eyes from their sockets and break the spell. The transformation would be halted. Yet she was so afraid. No white light poured down to comfort her. The Goddess seemed distant. Tentatively, Lucy released her grip on her sister and raised her hands and touched her eyes. They hurt as she pressed down on them. They pleaded with her not to wound them. The cold gaze of the intelligence that filled the room penetrated the flesh of her fingers and mocked her attempt to stop it. It knew she was a coward, nowhere near strong enough to thwart the will of one such as it. It knew it had only to push a little harder from inside her brain and the hands that she sought to hold it down with would fall. And once that cliff was fallen from, despair would swallow her as surely as the desert sand had buried the greatest of all pyramids. She would plunge back in time to where thought became irrational and the whole world burned.

Yet a warm tear burst from Lucy's eyes as she pressed down. A star twinkled through the black sky that had roped the Earth for ten years after the final battle. The star was white in colour and shone with the grace of Isis.

'Vera,' Lucy managed to whisper.

Her sister smiled with human lips. But the hands that reached out to touch Lucy's hands were clawed. They tore into Lucy's flesh; casually ripped the skin off her palms as if shredding the indigestible greens off vegetables. Blood dripped from Lucy's hands and she moaned because she knew she did not have the willpower to tear away her vision and feel her empty sockets drip such blood. The thing inside Vera made a cruel hissing sound.

'Do it,' it taunted. 'Or don't it. We always give humans a choice.'

Lucy's tears came out cold. She would never be able to do it if she was given a thousand years. And that was nothing to these monsters. Their reach stretched over the millennia, as well as the light years. She was doomed. It lightly scraped Lucy's lower lip with a sharp nail.

'Nothing will stop us this time,' it said.

Lucy shook her head. 'Vera.'

The thing shook its head, as if it were indeed a reflection. 'It's too late.'

There was a flash of silent lightning. It hit with the power of the sky's wrath and yet was as cold as an endless Ice Age. Lucy's human eyes failed her. In quick succession she saw and felt: the ancient Egyptian priestess sitting blind and alone beside the Nile; a leper crawling alone on a crab-covered beach; a wild woman running naked from a large tiger. Next she entered a series of disjointed bodies where it was difficult to comprehend what was being done to her, except that most of it was painful. She was a powerful man raping a hairy woman. Then she lived in a cave, and had two children. When it was cold, they stayed close to the fire. They were always hungry. When the moon rose at night she stared at it and tried to remember something she knew that she had long ago forgotten. Something that had to do with the white light that shone from above.

That was her last rational thought.

Images poured in. A cauldron of biological soup stirred by an alien spoon. There was birth and death, heat and cold. Most of all there was feeding and famine. Never any peace, never any understanding of why things happened the way they did. Of course there was no why. The return road was not natural. And eventually, thankfully, there was no more questioning. Her mind went as dull as an animal's. Yet she could still see and feel things. She fell through a unsanctioned path of terrestrial evolution, towards a bright light she glimpsed like an afterglow of the Big Bang that had started the creation. Yet this explosion had sent a shock wave that had wiped out an entire race. Entering into it, she felt the agony of a million flames lick her from all sides. The race had not died easily. They would not be reborn without sacrifice.

Understanding returned. Of an altered nature.

A primeval world spread around her. All was still, for the moment.

She opened her eyes.

A hideous creature of extraordinary cunning *stood* before her.

'*Vera*,' she thought. It was not a human name to her any

271

more, simply a sound that she clung to without reason. The creature drew back its arm. '*Lucy and Vera.*'

A powerful blow struck the side of her head. Then everything went black.

CHAPTER SIXTEEN

Ned Calendar sat beside a crazy pilot as he flew from Boise, Idaho towards the small town of Augustine, which was located in the north-east portion of the state, approximately forty miles west of Camp Paradise and sixty miles south of the Canadian border. The reason Ned considered the pilot insane was because he had agreed to fly him to Augustine in the first place, when the sky was ready to split open and return Noah and his ark back to Earth. Plus the guy – his name was Gabe Steel, and it suited him – had worse marital problems than the infamous Ed Barnsdale, who was probably back in Florida right now searching under his bed for mannequins. After twenty years of marriage, Gabe had recently learned his wife was not only having an affair with the local high school football coach, but was also on intimate terms with a number of the team's linesmen. It seemed Mrs Steel taught a volunteer sex education class at the school, as well as American Literature. But Ned was having trouble sympathizing with Gabe's problems because it was taking everything he could muster not to throw up. They were not flying through a thunderstorm; they were trying to paddle through an electrical tidal wave. A bolt of lightning had already caused Gabe's instruments to fail for five minutes. Ned had forgotten how much he had agreed to pay the man to take him to Augustine, but whatever it was, it wasn't enough. The plane took a scary fall as Gabe gestured excitably about how one of the guys on the team had had the nerve to leave his football helmet in Gabe's closet.

'I mean, I can understand that she's an attractive woman,' Gabe said, a wad of tobacco in his mouth and nowhere to spit. 'I can see those young fellas wanting to bone her. But they should clean up afterwards. I wouldn't do that to a guy if I was screwing his wife.'

Ned felt as if he was missing something. 'Would you screw another guy's wife?'

'Sure. I've done it lots of times. I make sure they're clean, though. I'm no fool.'

'But you are upset that your wife is having multiple affairs?'

'That's what I'm telling you. I come home and she doesn't even try to hide it anymore. She's lost all respect for me. I don't think the marriage is going to work out.'

Ned had to wonder if commuter pilots suffered from special problems. 'Would you prefer her to hide it from you?' he asked.

Gabe shrugged. 'What you don't know can't hurt you. That's what I always say. How's your stomach feeling? Ready to hurl yet? Keep that bag handy. I don't want to have to clean up your mess. Last guy who threw up in my plane ended up having a heart attack as well. He was dead before we got back to the airfield.'

The plane dipped sharply. Ned felt a wave of nausea. 'I will try to keep that in mind,' he promised. His cellular phone rested on his lap. He tried David again, without luck. Why wasn't his partner answering? 'How long to Augustine?' he asked.

'Twenty minutes, if we don't crash first.'

'Is it possible their runway will be flooded?'

'Let's just say right now I wish this plane didn't have fixed landing wheels. I don't think they're going to help us much. We'll do a flyby, have a look down. We can always detour to Fallston. That's only thirty miles west. A regular crew services their field.'

'We won't detour unless we absolutely have to.'

'Better safe than sorry.'

'Better early than late. I have a car waiting for me in Augustine.' Ned paused. 'And I believe I have an old friend who needs my help.'

CHAPTER SEVENTEEN

Over an hour had elapsed and Dr Henry had not returned from his trip for supplies and David Conner had been unable to locate Lucy Temple and her sister, Vera. Impatient and worried, David had barged in on Professor Spear, who was reading and smoking a pipe in his office. But the man seemed genuinely confused as to where the women could be. David had decided it was not the time to confront Spear about his thorny past. He just wanted Lucy and a clear road back to civilization. Next, he had gone to Tom Forester for help. The ex-truck driver had suggested they check the unused dorm beside the meadow. There they found all the rooms locked up tight, and Tom said he was the only one with a key to the place.

'They must have gone for a hike,' Tom suggested.

'In this weather?' David asked, wiping the rain from his brow. The storm continued unabated but strangely enough the temperature had risen dramatically in the last hour, as much as fifteen degrees. The water on his face now felt as if it had fallen from a Hawaiian sky. Tom had noticed the shift as well.

'The cold has passed,' he said. 'And Lucy loves the rain. At Stanford, she's always out in it. I wouldn't be surprised if she talked her sister into taking a hike up to the caves.'

'Where are they?' David asked.

'Two miles north of here. I can show you if you're seriously worried about them.'

David considered. Lucy might have confided in her sister many of the things he had said about Spear. Vera could have taken the information hard. Spear was, after all, their personal mentor. For all David knew, Lucy had told Vera he was an FBI agent, although he had asked her to keep that little detail private. It was possible Lucy had suggested a walk to calm Vera down. Or else Vera had brought up the hike as an excuse to talk her sister out of leaving the camp so abruptly. He was not worried that they had gone off to practise forbidden Dogon rites. Lucy had not struck him as that impulsive, and in any case he hadn't explained how the regression was accomplished. Actually, he was more worried about how they were going to get out of the camp that same day. He felt pressured to check on his car, see if what was left of the path would allow him to move it closer to the dorms. He dreaded the thought of having to carry what sounded like five heavy suitcases all the way to the road.

'Tom,' David said. 'I know this is asking a lot but I would like you to see if they've gone to the caves. I am worried about them, but I shouldn't go with you. I need to check on my car.'

Tom was surprised. 'You're not leaving today, are you?'

'Yes. Something's come up. I have to go.'

'Do you have enough information for your article?'

David patted him on the shoulder. 'I have enough for many articles. Just find the women for me, Tom.'

David was a mile down the path when he remembered that he hadn't checked in again with Ned. He wondered if the lapse was entirely accidental, if he wasn't avoiding his boss with the secret hope Ned would freak out and fly up unexpectedly. It was not as if David was to the point where he felt he needed reinforcements, but odd portents disturbed him. There was the women's disappearance, of course, but more than that, as he headed away from the camp he felt, well, watched. Like many experienced agents, he had a sixth sense when it came to being stalked. He felt eyes on his back, and this particular set did not follow him kindly. He had his snub nose .22 revolver with him but not his 10-millimetre semiautomatic pistol. His favourite weapon was back in his room with his cellular phone. The .22 would not stop a grizzly, of course, nor would the 10-millimetre for that matter. Anyway, there weren't supposed to be grizzlies in Idaho. What the fuck was out there? He stopped and scanned the woods, his vision impaired by the merciless patter of rock-sized drops.

But there was nothing.

Portions of the path turned out to be no better than an overflowing gully. The more he saw, the less hope he had of bringing his car any closer to the camp. Yet he remained determined to leave. His sense of being followed stayed with him almost the whole way to the road, only leaving when the lake where he had met Lucy and Vera came into view. The disappearance of his stalker disturbed him more than the shadowing. At least when it was on his back, he knew it wasn't. up to mischief elsewhere. He tried to convince himself Ned's stories had gotten to him, that there was no one there. But his old gut feeling was back, and Rollaids were not going to make it go away. Maybe that's how the Big Mind communicated with him. So he didn't have higher intuition. God spoke to him the same way a hamburger did.

But God did not reply to his cry when he reached his black Infiniti rental.

The hood had been ripped open. The distributor cap and the carburretor were in ruins. The windshield was shattered; a gaping hole allowed the rain to pour through to the dashboard. The steering wheel had been literally torn out; it lay on the ground near a nearby tree stump. David studied the damage, saw no signs that a crowbar or sledge hammer or any other man-made tool had been used to destroy the car. He was perplexed until he remembered a line Ned had used to describe Frances' strength.

'*She tore through her straightjacket like it was made of newspaper.*'

The accumulation of water in the front seat was not that great, not considering how hard it was raining. Whoever had done this had been at most ten minutes in front of him. They had not wanted him to leave.

'They couldn't have tried it,' he whispered to himself. 'It couldn't be true.'

He had not *really* believed Buckley's tale.

For that matter, he had thought his old friend was exaggerating.

Not now. David spun and raced back to the path, two hundred yards down the road. To his immense horror and frustration, he saw that Dr Henry had returned and headed up the path while he had been preoccupied with the wrecked car. There was a fresh set of tyre tracks in the mud, replacing the earlier set that had all but washed away since the doctor had left that morning. David figured the rain must have drowned out the sound of the truck engine. Again, he thought miserably, it was all a question of timing, bad timing. He had missed Dr Henry by a few minutes. Now he would have to hike the entire three miles up to the camp. And what would he find when he got there?

'*Then she ate the little girl. Ate her alive.*'

CHAPTER EIGHTEEN

Jon Horst worried about his lack of a Green Card as much as his poor image. It was only because Professor Spear had used his influence to get him an extended student visa that he had been allowed to stay in the United States as long as he had, even though technically he was not enrolled at Stanford University. Jon was concerned that if Spear's theories gained notoriety as a result of David Nichols' article, many people would volunteer as research subjects and the Professor would no longer have a special need for him. Then he would probably have to go back to Sweden where he would be forced to give up his dream of being a famous actor and return to work as a lounge magician. Jon hated magic tricks. When you knew the secret of most of them, they seemed stupid. Besides, his skills were rusty and, outside of Las Vegas and a few other vacation spots, there was no money in it. Jon had a longing for the security he believed money could bestow. He had grown up dirt poor on a dairy farm outside Stockholm where the cows stared at him early in the morning like he was a sex offender. He hated the smell of their udders; he felt like an overgrown nurse in a pediatrics ward tending to infants who resented female breasts. To this day, he could not stand the taste of milk.

When Lucy had embarrassed him at the dinner table the previous night, he had been devastated. He had retreated to his room to try to figure out a comeback strategy. It was important that David Nichols not treat him as a fool in his article. Jon still had high hopes of using the reporter's influence to jumpstart his acting career. What none of them understood was that his gifts were genuine. When he was young, he had routinely bent spoons and forks *without* touching them. But the ability had atrophied with use. The more often he had done it, the less it worked. In the early days of his magic show, he had only resorted to the backup method of rubbing the metal between his index finger and thumb when his magic fingers took a leave of absence. As the years passed, however, massaging the spoons and forks became the norm.

At present he sat alone in his room with a half dozen forks and knives spread out on the table before him. He had specifically asked Margaret for spoons but she felt too many had been ruined the night before, and he could understand that. What he was trying to do was to get one of the utensils to bend, not even all the way. If one would just curl up at the edges without him touching it he would be happy. But these were American knives and forks, he thought. They didn't like foreigners without Green Cards. He had been at the task an hour and so far all he had to show for his troubles was a bad headache. He was thinking of returning to the dining hall and asking Margaret for some aspirin when he heard a knock at his door. Lucy poked her head inside before he could answer. She stared at him strangely.

'Hello,' she said. 'May I come in?'

'Yes,' he said, not rising from his seat. He assumed it was Lucy; she had on the tiny gold crucifix she often wore. Even after knowing the sisters for two years, he still had trouble telling them apart. He preferred Vera to Lucy, and the other night was a perfect example why. Lucy was always kidding him, trying to push his buttons. Vera was much more respectful. She knew he was destined for great things. Lucy sat across from him and stared at his knives and forks.

'What are you doing?' she asked.

He shrugged. 'Practising an old magic trick for fun. Nothing special.'

'Are you trying to bend the knives and forks with your mind?'

He flushed. 'No. I'm trying to eat a meal that's not there with my nose.'

She ignored his sarcasm. Leaning close to the utensils, she peered at them as if she were seeing forks and knives for the first time. 'Bend them for me. I will help you.'

He snorted. 'I don't need your help, thank you.'

She sat up and smiled mechanically. 'You look healthy, Jon Horst. That is good.'

'Huh?'

She reached across the table and took his right hand. Her skin was wet, cold. The texture of her fingers, of her palm, was odd; they felt *slick*. Her eyes focused on him.

'Bend the fork on the end,' she said. 'I want to see.'

Jon was annoyed. 'Well, I can't very well do it with you holding onto me.' He tried to shake her off, and to his surprise, failed to do so. He hadn't known she was so strong. 'Let go of my hand.'

'Bend the fork,' she repeated.

'Lucy?'

'Do it,' she hissed.

Something in her voice startled him, even scared him a bit. If the truth be known, lots of things frightened him. He had yet to get his driver's licence for fear he would get in an accident. And his health was a constant concern, particularly the threat of skin cancer. A cousin had recently got melanoma and died three months after being diagnosed. The sun was dangerous, the roads were killing fields. He resettled himself in his chair.

'Very well,' he said. 'I can try. You want me to bend the fork?'

'Yes.'

'You understand it's thicker than an ordinary spoon. I might not be able to do it.'

'Begin.'

'OK.' Jon closed his eyes. 'Give me a moment to mentally prepare myself.'

'Open your eyes. Look at me. Bend it.'

Jon opened his eyes. Lucy had leaned her head closer. She continued to stare at him and he wished she would stop. Her sense of humour irritated him but he would have welcomed it now. There was something wrong with her eyes, the dilated pupils – they looked as she had left them overnight in the freezer.

'What's bothering you, Lucy?' he asked.

She smiled again. 'I am hungry.'

'Why don't you get some breakfast? I'm sure Margaret will fix you something. We don't have a session scheduled until this afternoon.'

Her smile remained fixed, stuck. 'I will eat. Bend the fork.'

Jon drew in a breath. He tried to focus on the fork but found his gaze drawn back to her eyes. They were much greener than he remembered, and brighter, at least near the edges. There was also flecks of gold near the centres; they swam around the black pupils like expensive fillings cracked loose and spat into the watery vortex of an emptying sink. And the drain beneath them seemed so very deep.

'Jon Horst,' she whispered intently.

A surge of energy went up his spine; it rose like a magnetic column set vibrating by invisible cooper conduits buried in his sacrum. His back straightened with a jerk and he heard several vertebrae pop. A wave of blood rushed his brain. He felt momentarily dizzy and his vision blurred.

Yet the peculiar sensations passed as quickly as they had come. Lucy withdrew her hard stare and grinned easily. Jon let go a held breath and relaxed. What was that? He had no idea. But when he glanced down a beatific smile broke on his face.

He had bent the fork!

'I did it!' he cried. 'Look, Lucy I did it!'

'Yes.' She stood and went over to the door and locked it.

He laughed. 'What are you doing?' He couldn't get over how quickly his power had returned. Now, if only he could do it in front of David Nichols. He would be on the cover of *Time* for sure, maybe even in *People* magazine. All his relatives back home read *People*. Lucy returned and stood by her chair. She unzipped her coat.

'I do not want anyone to disturb us,' she said.

He blinked. 'What are you talking about?'

She tossed her coat aside and then reached down and in one fluid motion pulled her grey sweatshirt over her head. She wore nothing underneath. He had never realized her breasts were so nicely shaped. Her erect nipples made his smile grow larger. He sure had impressed her!

'We have to be alone,' she said.

He bobbed on the back legs of his chair. 'Are we going to make love?'

She unbuttoned her pants. 'I do not want to stain these clothes.'

He nodded quickly. 'I understand. We won't even wrinkle them. You can set them on that chair there. This is good, this is great.' He shook in wonder. 'Lucy, I didn't think you found me attractive.'

She pulled down her pants, underwear and all. Jon felt another wave of dizziness, this one pleasant. Her body was the stuff of choked chickens – flawless. She kicked her pants and panties into a pile in the corner. Naked, except for the tiny gold crucifix around her neck, she sat in the chair opposite him. Her eyes narrowed on his face.

'I am Vera,' she said.

He had to laugh. 'Really? Wow. This is turning out to be one incredible day. I always knew you liked me, Vera. Why did you pretend to be Lucy?'

'Confusion is our way. Cunning is our nature.'

'Oh. Some women are like that. Should I get undressed?'

'No. Put both your hands face up on the table beside the knives.'

He gave her an exaggerated leer. 'You really need another demonstration? Shouldn't I save my energy for better things?'

Her eyes went hard again. 'Put your hands on the table now.'

He hastily obeyed. He had never realized Vera was so moody. Well, that could be a good thing, in small doses. He had found unstable women to be the most uninhibited in bed. God knows Stanford was full of them, with all those exams they had to pass just to keep their fathers paying their tuition. He tried to joke with her.

'It's going to be hard to concentrate with you not wearing anything.'

'Look at me,' she said.

The gold flecks around her pupils drew his attention immediately, and it was odd because he did not like to stare at them. They appeared so unnatural, metal implants from a race of computerized wizards who used body parts to make fireworks. Yet they were preferable to her hollow pupils. He still could not understand why they were so dilated, and why when he looked into them he felt as if he were falling through uncharted space. He'd had a fear of heights since his father threw him in the air on his third birthday and accidentaly dropped him on the way down. He wished to God she would at least blink or something.

'The knives bend,' she said.

He stammered. 'You want me to try to bend them now?'

Her dark tongue moistened her lower lip. 'Jon Horst,' she whispered, exactly as she had the first time the energy had raced up his spine and he had performed his minor miracle. Only this time he felt the wind sucked out of him. It was as if a living vacuum had reached across the table and attached itself to his heart and lungs. His shoulders slumped, his head – he could hardly keep his eyes focused on her, like she insisted. He did notice her mouth, though – she was smiling again. He wondered if he had somehow done it again, moved the unmovable. His eyes flickered downwards.

The knives were bending!

Even as he watched, the blades magically turned upwards and around towards his open palms. He watched with the awe of a three-year-old child who had discovered that the new bump on his head allowed him to make all his wishes come true. This was unprecendented! Uri Geller had never bent two knives at once, and certainly not American brands.

'Do you see this?' he asked, excited.

'Yes. Your hands will not move.'

He hesitated. 'What?'

'Your hands will not move.'

Now that she mentioned it, he couldn't move his hands. He tried and it was as if the backs were glued to the table top with that kind of super glue that was advertised late at night, in between reruns of Korean sitcoms. The kind of glue that could lift up cars without breaking. That wouldn't have been such a bad thing in itself but the tips of the knives were steadily moving closer to the centre of his palms. And he realized that he didn't know how to stop them any more than he knew why a young woman who had only treated him with reserved affection for the last two years should be sitting naked across from him on a rainy morning in the mountains of northern Idaho. No, Jon Horst definitely did not understand why this same woman should be staring at him with eyes that would have been more attractive covered with rolls of masking tape, or better yet, gouged out and buried under six feet of mud. Jon began to perspire heavily.

'Stop them,' he whispered.

She got out of her chair and came and stood by his side. She was so close – her pubic hair touched his right bicep. He had to twist his head to look up at her. She stroked his hair.

'No,' she said.

He couldn't move his hands! The knives were coming! 'Please!' he cried.

She put her hand over his mouth, a hand that felt like a mermaid's mutated paw.

'I am hungry,' she said.

Oh God, he thought. He tried to scream but her slimy hand muffled the sound. Straining to stand, he found his ass was mysteriously fixed to the chair. The tips of the knives touched his moist palms. This could not be happening! He had done nothing wrong! He had not tried to remain in the country illegally! The blades dug into his flesh. Blood spilt out over the table top. Burning pain throbbed up in his arms and into his brain. His blood puddled and dripped on the floor. He heard his bones cracking. The knives dug through his skeleton and into the table top. Vera, her hand still over his mouth, leaned down and licked his right earlobe.

'I need you to remain still,' she said.

Jon felt a rough tug on his ear. Ignoring her instructions, fighting against the force of her grip with a terror that momentarily transcended even the power to bend spoons and forks and knives from a distance, he managed to twist his head to the right side. Her mouth was closed; she was chewing something and he couldn't see what it was. But he knew the blood that dripped out the sides of her mouth belonged to him. Taking a moment to work her teeth, she made a lumpy sound as she swallowed.

'You do not listen,' she said. 'But I understand.'

He understood as well. She had bitten off his ear.

Her free hand caressed the top of his head once more.

She closed her eyes, whispered in the stump she had left behind.

'You are healthy, Jon Horst.'

She licked him again. Opened her mouth wide.

'*That is good.*'

CHAPTER NINETEEN

The landing at Augustine proved uneventful. The asphalt field had a slight slant to it and no major puddles had accumulated. Gabe Steel put down his plane as easily as if it was a calm sunny day. Ned Calendar wished him luck with his wife and the football team and ran to the four wheel truck he had previously arranged in Denver to have waiting for him. The rental car man provided him with a detailed map of the area, pencilling in the most direct route to Camp Paradise. But the man was worried about two sections of the road.

'I used to go up to that camp when I was a kid,' he said. 'I know the road. It floods on days like this. I don't think you're even going to make it to the path. For sure, you won't be able to get the truck all the way up the path. It narrows the further you drive, and with weather like this it probably vanishes altogether.'

Ned looked up at the dark sky. 'Do you often get rain like this in May?'

The guy shook his head. 'I've lived here all my life and never seen a storm this bad – any time of the year.' He brushed the back of his arm across his face. 'But at least it's warm rain. Feels like it blew in from the tropics.'

'Yeah, it does,' Ned said, thoughtful.

Ned left the airport at high speed. The truck was a brand new Toyota, with only three hundred miles on it. He hoped it was specifically water-sealed like many modern vehicles. If he came to a washed out section – he was driving through it. He would drown before he turned back. The only reasons Ned could think of that would have prevented David from checking in were: his partner was physically unable to call; David wanted to scare him into coming. Either way Ned did not expect a Boy Scouts honorary welcome when he arrived at Camp Paradise.

The first danger spot the man had marked on the map turned out to be nothing. But when Ned reached the second flagged area, he reconsidered his vow to drown first. He was an hour from Augustine, well into the mountains and woods, on a broken down one lane road that had had the foolishness to dip down for fifty yards between two tree-clad hills. The half football field distance was definitely the low point of the forest, if not the entire state of Idaho. As a result it looked mighty deep. But exactly how deep Ned could not tell for sure. And the way the muddy water churned as it made its merry wave towards the plains, he was not about to wade into it and use his body as a measuring stick. Going around it, however, off the road and into the trees, was out of the question. Ned dialled David again, got no answer. He climbed out of his truck and stood looking down at the swimming pool. It did not remind him of the ones in Las Vegas, yet many aspects of the day did. Like the day Sandy died, time felt like an enemy. He remembered how close David had come to saving his girlfriend.

'Shit,' he swore, getting back in the truck. He would just have to see how efficient the Japanese were at making submarines. He backed up several yards and then ploughed forward, holding his breath.

He was slowed to a crawl almost immediately. Water offered a lot more resistance than air. He reasoned that the water could reach halfway up the sides of the engine before he was screwed, but maybe he was being optimistic. The sealing on the doors was sound but it wasn't up to the task he was demanding. He was a quarter way into the pool when he sprang his first leak. The next ones came hard and fast. Soon he had to splash down to find his accelerator and brake. His tyres vanished; he had to apply heavy thrust just to keep moving. The engine roared; it choked. The carburrettor coughed: mix air with fuel, not water with gasoline you stupid man!

Ned passed his optimistic limit and then some. The muddy wash swam over his hood, ruining the wax job. Water gurgled at the bottom on his driver's window. For two eternal seconds the current lifted him up and tilted the truck at an awkward angle and he was sure he was going to die. But the kick in the ass might just have saved his life. Close to the side of the road, his wheels momentarily caught on solid footing. He floored the accelerator. The four wheels dug in and he jumped forward through a series of spastic leaps. Then he was free of the pool, and feeling grateful.

'Goddam!' he exclaimed, pounding the steering wheel. That had been close.

He reached the path twenty minutes later. From talking to David before his partner had entered the camp, Ned knew David had planned to park his car at the foot of the path and have the people at the camp pick him up. Yet Ned did not see David's car right away, and even though he understood David might have stashed it nearby in the trees, he did not bother searching for it. All that mattered was to reach the camp as soon as possible. He turned and started up the path; it was like trying to drive up a polluted creek. Even with his four fat wheels and extra gears, he slipped repeatedly. He was on a roller coaster; the carnival operators were all smoking dope. He knew it was only a matter of time before he was forced to abandon ship.

That happened approximately a mile and a half up the path, at what should have been the halfway point to the camp. Another four wheel drive truck blocked the path. It had been abandoned, and Ned only had to look beyond it to understand why. A large tree had fallen across the path. It would be two feet from here on out. Fortunately he was in excellent shape. He wished he was wearing waterproof hiking boots, but his Nike walking shoes were stronger than what he usually wore to the office. He reached in his bag for his 10-millimetre semiautomatic pistol, checked to make sure it was loaded and stuffed it in his coat. He had not shot anybody in a long time.

He was climbing out of the truck when he saw the woman standing a hundred feet further up the path. The dark green hood of her coat covered most of her face, still, he caught a glimpse of red hair. Lucy or Vera Temple, he thought. Walking slowly towards him, she kept her head down as if deep in thought. It was odd how he had not seen her coming earlier, and he wondered if she had just stepped out of the woods and onto the path. He padded his weapon in his coat but did not take it out. Ten feet from him, with his heart pounding in his mouth, she finally looked up. Her green eyes startled him; they were so bright, so beautiful. No way she was like Frances, he told himself, relaxing. Not with that face of an angel. She smiled faintly but didn't speak.

'Hello,' he said. 'My name's Ned Calendar. I'm a friend of David's. Are you Lucy or Vera?'

She hesitated, glanced past him, then stared directly into his eyes. 'Lucy.'

'Where's David? Is he at the camp?'

'Yes.' She gestured over her shoulder. 'That way.'

'What are you doing out here alone? Are you looking for somebody?'

'Yes.' She stepped closer, throwing back her hood. Even with the dark sky, her wet hair shone like fire. 'I am looking for my sister.'

'For Vera?'

'Yes.'

'You don't know where she is?'

'No.'

'How long has she been missing?'

'An hour.'

'Do you want me to help you look for her?'

In response, Lucy glanced up and down the path, then stared at the two trucks as if they figured heavily in her answer. Then, to his surprise, she reached out and took his left hand. He had just climbed from the truck's heated cabin; his fingers were warm, but hers were as cold as wet stones. Her gesture was somewhat bold, yet she hung her head shyly.

'I feel like I know you,' she said.

He smiled. 'Did David tell you about me? I warn you, all of it's true.'

'Yes.' Releasing his hand, she nodded up the path. 'Go see him. I will be there shortly.'

'Are you sure you don't want me to accompany you? Hiking in a storm like this can be dangerous.'

She patted him on the shoulder. 'Do not worry. Tell David, I am coming.'

'All right,' he agreed reluctantly. 'Don't be long.'

She nodded and carefully replaced her hood over her head, using both hands. Ned started up the path. After about two hundred yards, he paused and glanced over his shoulder. He was surprised to find her still standing by the trucks, watching him. He waved, and she waved back. Apart from her great beauty, he wasn't sure if she was David's type. She seemed kind of quiet.

'*I feel like I know you.*'

An odd remark, to be sure. He was sure he had never met her before.

Ned quickened his pace.

CHAPTER TWENTY

David Conner was dirty and exhausted when he finally reached the camp. He imagined Dr Henry had not returned much ahead of him. He had been relieved to find Dr Henry's truck, albeit blocked by the tree, undamaged. With its four wheel drive, it was their best way out of the camp. Yet David had to ask himself if escape was now the priority. He needed to have a hard look at who he led to safety. Given that his rental car had been attacked by someone stronger than a normal human being, he had to face the fact that the situation might already be severely fucked. He found Dr Henry, Tom Forester, and Panda Gopal in the chapel. He didn't waste time on pleasantries.

'Did you find the women?' he blurted out.

Tom jumped up. 'No. They weren't at the caves. We've just been discussing where they might be.'

'Where is Spear?' David asked.

'He's in his office reading,' Dr Henry said. 'I saw him a minute ago.'

'Does he know Lucy and Vera are missing?' David asked.

'I told him we didn't know where they were,' Dr Henry said.

'What did he say?' David demanded.

Dr Henry shrugged. 'Nothing.'

David looked around. 'Where's Jon?'

'I haven't seen him today,' Tom said. 'Have any of you guys?'

No one had. David turned towards the church entrance. 'Show me his room.'

Jon Horst's door was locked. They called but there was no answer. David had had enough of the bullshit. The others jumped as he kicked in the door.

The room was empty. A small wooden table sat in the centre between the bunk beds. Bent knives and forks littered the top. David picked one of them up, noticing that the table top was badly scraped. There was an unpleasant odour in the air.

'Did Jon bend all these?' Tom asked, gesturing to the ruined utensils.

'Not with his mind,' Dr Henry said. 'Not with his IQ.'

David sniffed the air, fingered the bent knife. 'There is something wrong here.'

'Blood.' Panda said softly.

'Huh?' Tom said.

'He's right.' David exclaimed. He dropped to his knees beside the table, felt the wooden floor carefully with his fingertips; he put his nose to it. His nails picked up faint red scrapes. His nostrils detected death. He looked up at the others. 'Someone wiped up a puddle of blood . . .'

Dr Henry crouched beside him. 'Are you sure? I don't see it. I don't smell it.'

David showed him his nails. 'It was here, but was carefully removed.'

Tom paled. 'What do you think happened? Is Jon all right?'

David stood. 'I don't know, Tom. It doesn't look good. I just came from the road. My car's been sabotaged.'

'What are you talking about?' Dr Henry asked.

David found it hard to concentrate. Images of Buckley's story kept bursting in his mind over images of Lucy in his arms last night. He had to fight to stay calm, to take long deep breaths. Already, the others looked to him for direction.

'Somebody does not want us to leave here,' David said calmly. 'Their reasons may be dangerous to us. We must speak to Spear, but first I need to check out my room. I want you all to come with me. From now on, it's crucial we remain with each other at all times.'

No one asked him why. The trace of blood was self-explanatory. As a group, they hurried to the other dorm. There he found his door unlocked, when he clearly remembered having locked it. Upon closer inspection, he saw that his lock was in fact broken. Snapped by sheer force. Knowing that it was a waste of time, he searched his bag. He ended up throwing it against the far wall.

'Shit!' he swore.

'What's wrong?' Dr Henry asked.

'My cellular phone and my 10-millimetre semiautomatic pistol are missing.'

Their eyes swelled. 'What the fuck are you doing with a piece, man?' Dr Henry asked, not sounding like a Rhodes Scholar or effeminate homosexual. David whipped out his badge.

'I'm an FBI agent. I was sent here to check out your boss.' David bent over and pulled out his .22 from beneath the hem of his pants. They instinctively backed off. 'Trust me, he's got a rotten past. Come on, I want to talk to him.'

David burst in on Spear without knocking. Indeed, David was so tired of playing Mr Nice Guy that he grabbed Spear by the collar and thrust him up against a wall and buried the tip of his small revolver in the Professor's throat. Spear's pipe fell from his hand and smoked on the floor. Frank the iguana looked over but didn't say anything. David breathed fire on the Professor's clammy skin.

'I know everything that happened in Africa,' he said in a deadly voice. 'Buckley spoke to my partner. I know about the Setians, the secret of the black rite, the little girl your sister-in-law ate. I know why Lucy and Vera turn you on. But there's blood in Jon's room and I don't know where the women are. I'm worried about Jon. I'm worried about Lucy and Vera. But I'm not worried about you. If you should die from a bullet wound in the next two minutes, I won't shed a tear. Do you understand me, Professor?'

Spear regarded him with his dark emotionless eyes. 'You don't know half of what happened in Africa, Mr Nichols,' he said. 'Or are you going by another name now?'

David leaned closer, if that was possible. 'Where are they?'

'I don't know.'

David throttled him. 'What have you done with them?'

Spear choked. 'I never told them about the black rite,' he said quickly.

David released him. 'Damnit! I told them about it! I told Lucy! But I didn't tell her how to do it. You're the expert on these fucking techniques. Could she have done it with Vera without knowing all the details?'

Spear thought a moment. 'Jon's missing? There's blood?'

'Yes! Yes! Could they have done it?'

'Did you say anything to Lucy about them staring into each other's eyes? About the breath?'

David put his hand to his head. Could he have been the cause of it all? As he had been the cause of Sandy and Angela's deaths? 'I talked about those things. I tried to be vague.'

Spear was grim. 'Even a blunt key can open Pandora's box, once you know where to insert it. Yes, they could have done it. Who saw them last?'

None of the others had seen the women all day. 'I was

300

with Lucy this morning,' David admitted. 'It must have been three hours ago.'

Spear picked up his pipe, regarded it gravely. 'We have to find her before she makes another.'

David had been ready to blow the man's brains out a moment ago. Now he looked to him for reassurance. 'But they could be all right. It doesn't have to be like Africa all over again, does it?'

Spear nodded. 'It's possible Jon simply cut himself. The girls could be hiking. Lucy is addicted to the rain. She could have dragged Vera off.'

'I told him that,' Tom said anxiously, sounding like he wanted everyone to chill out and stop talking about black rites. Panda stood thoughtful, as if listening to strange sounds in the distance. Dr Henry was shaking his head.

'I don't understand,' he said. 'Are we afraid someone murdered the women? Or are we afraid they've murdered someone?'

David and Spear exchanged glances. 'Both,' Spear replied.

David jammed his gun in his belt. 'I want to return to the unopened dorms I was shown earlier. Let's go now. No, wait, let's get Margaret. Then we'll go.'

'It will be difficult to wheel her through the mud and rain,' Dr Henry said.

'We can carry her,' David snapped. 'I told you, we all stay together. I want no one out of my sight.'

'I haven't been able to find the key,' Tom said, embarrassed. 'I think I might have given it to Lucy to hold.'

David nodded. 'More reason for us to go there then.'

Margaret was in the kitchen peeling potatoes. She came with them without explanation. Didn't even ask about the gun in his belt. David helped wheel her through what was turning into a swamp. The rain had faltered; the damp was so warm it had begun to mist. The haze clung to the low bushes like a cloak thrown over a fallen warrior. How had the vegetation changed, he wondered, in the last sixty million years? How would it change in the next six years? He did not trust this storm, it did not feel natural.

David kicked in each door. Behind number four he found a burning candle and a fallen beauty. She lay stretched on her back on the bed across from the orange flame. He leapt to her side. Her breathing was ragged. Blood leaked out of her right ear. Her skin was the temperature of the room. Red and purple swelled from her right temple. But which Temple was it? Lucy or Vera? David turned to the others for confirmation even as Dr Henry attempted to gauge the severity of the wound. Tom was the only one to speak.

'It must be Vera,' he said. 'She doesn't have on the gold crucifix. Lucy always wears her cross.' Tom pointed to the ceiling, the wood tiles missing above the bed. 'It looks like Vera was trying to fix the ceiling and she fell. Or else she was trying to hide something up there.'

David looked up. 'Maybe.' He clasped the woman's hand. He had to tell himself it was Vera, the twin he had not made love to, particularly when Dr Henry's expression changed from cool professionalism to silent gloom. Yet David hated himself for wishing for one sister's wellbeing over the other's, as much as he hated her failure to respond when Dr Henry pinched her Achilles tendon. Dr Henry shook his head, and David thought the gesture should be outlawed among all physicians for all time.

'She's got a bad concussion,' Dr Henry said.

'How bad is bad?' David asked. The question summoned up his life, and God always gave him a hard answer. Dr Henry carefully probed the bone around the main swelling. The bump was as large as a flattened orange.

'Her skull's cracked,' Dr Henry said. 'We have to get her in the chapel. An EEG will tell me what we're looking at.'

'But should we move her?' David asked. 'It might cause her more harm.'

'We can't do anything for her here,' Dr Henry said. 'I have a med kit, various drugs. If I can figure out the extent of her injury, I might be able to give her something. We can lift the mattress as a whole, two of us on each side. David – is that your real name?'

He stared at her face. She looked so much like Lucy. 'Yes,' he whispered.

'David, if there is pressure on the brain due to swelling,' Dr Henry said. 'I can slow it down with steroids. But I can't risk giving her a massive dose without a few tests. And we can't move the equipment in here. It would take hours, and it wouldn't fit anyway. We must move her and we must move her now.'

'Do any of you have a cellular phone?' David asked.

'No,' Spear said.

David nodded and tucked her hand back in by her side. He stood. 'We'll move her. But let us cover her with a blanket first. I don't want rain to fall on her face.'

Or tears to fall from her eyes, he thought. He was ready to cry himself. But he knew he mustn't do that. He might be responsible for what had happened, maybe even more than Professor Spear. He had to remain strong to make it right. Yet his guilt would not leave him free to act. When he stared at her, he saw Sandy and Angela. When he brushed Spear's side, he felt Failla and Pokey near. Why, he could even hear Ned yelling to him. Telling him that the case was important, that no one could possibly get hurt.

'*David*!'

'Wait a second,' he muttered. 'That's Ned.' He looked at the others. 'My partner's here. He'll have a phone. We can call for help.' He stepped towards the door. 'I'll be back in a second.'

Tom grabbed his arm. He was scared. 'You said we have to stay together.'

David paused. Then he leaned his head out the door and cupped his mouth with his hands. 'Ned! We're here! Ned!'

Ned Calendar came stomping into view a minute later, looking soaked and tired. David was so happy to see his boss, he embraced him on the dorm porch. Ned seemed glad to see him as well, going by the number of times he slapped him on the back. But the moment they let go of each other, Ned's anxiety was apparent.

'Is this clan of the cave lizards or what?' he asked.

David shook his head. 'I don't know yet. Weird things are happening. Just inside this door one of the women is lying seriously injured. We don't know if it was accidental or if she was purposely knocked down. Christ, we don't even know if it's Lucy or Vera.'

'Lucy's fine,' Ned said. 'I passed her on the path about a mile and a half back. She's looking for her sister.'

David almost exploded. 'You saw her?. She's all right?'

Ned smiled nervously. 'Why, yes, she seemed fine.'

David paused. 'Are you sure she was *normal*? We have bloodstains in another room, and the occupant is missing.'

Ned hesitated. 'Well, she was worried about her sister. I don't know if she could be feeling normal. She seemed a little stiff. Is Lucy normally that way?'

David frowned. 'No. But these are unusual circumstances. Listen, do you have your phone with you? Mine is gone.'

'What happened to it?'

'Somebody stole it. They stole my gun as well.'

Ned snorted. 'That doesn't sound good. Yeah, I have my phone. It's back at my truck.'

'Why the fuck did you leave it at the truck?'

'Because the only one I wanted to call in this fucking state was you, and I was walking up the path to see you in person. Don't worry, I'll go get it. We can call for an ambulance helicopter. Not that I'm sure one will come out in this weather.' He turned. 'I'll be back soon.'

David stopped him. 'No. I don't want us to scatter while there are still so many unknowns. I will go for the phone after we move Vera into the church and Dr Henry performs an EEG on her. I want to search for Lucy as well.' He pulled out his .22. 'Do you have your pistol?'

'Yes. Of course.'

'Let's trade guns.'

'Why?'

'I'm a better shot than you. I deserve the fire power. Give me your gun.'

Ned handed over the 10-millimetre reluctantly. 'She has amazing green eyes.' He paused. 'Doesn't she?'

David sighed. 'They amazed me.'

They moved Vera to the church without mishap and rested her on the altar. Dr Henry wired her quickly, monitoring her heartbeat as well as her brain activity. Bumpy green lines traced across dark screens, falling stars on a rough road to extinction. The beep of her fluttering heart sounded like a broken answering machine. I'm not at home at present. Please leave a message and if I don't die I'll call you back. David fretted about the delay, but didn't want to leave until he knew whether there was hope for Vera or not. Bent over his instruments, Dr Henry did not look encouraged.

'Will she live?' David asked finally. It was the only question that mattered.

Dr Henry showed pain. 'I don't think so. Her EEG is virtually flat. The brain damage must be extensive.'

David had to take a breath. 'There must be something we can do for her.'

A tear ran over Dr Henry's cheek. 'She's not going to wake up.'

David felt great pressure on his chest. He looked over to Spear. 'Have you ever seen anything like this before?' he asked.

Spear was a carving on a mummy's coffin. 'Yes.'

David nodded. 'In Africa.'

Spear stared at Vera, lying like a sacrifice on the altar of a God who had forgotten his creation the day after he took off to rest. The Professor looked sort of dead right then, but what memory killed him most he did not say. He only nodded. Yes, in Africa. It all began in Africa.

David was bitter. 'Well, that's just fucking great. What does your experience do for Vera now? What does it do for Lucy?'

Professor Spear wasn't given an opportunity to respond. The doors at the rear of the church swung open, with fanfare, as if the arrival of the royal virgin bride had just been announced. Nature was impressed. Lightning flashed at her back; thunder sounded as she stepped forward. Her hair shone like an angry volcano, her eyes burned like cursed treasure. Her hood was thrown back, her arms swung loose at her sides. Yet it seemed, as she moved, that her feet never left the floor. They slithered over the stone slabs, newborn limbs rediscovering their way inside stolen goods. Her feet were bare, her stance arrogant; nothing in the church could threaten her, and she knew it. Her face was the worst nightmare of all. The beauty of lost love enthralled by the power of possession. She reached the altar. Taking her time, she scanned each one of them, looking for God only knew what. Her gaze came to rest on David, and he understood what it felt like to be stabbed in the heart, although no blade had ever broken his flesh. It had on the gold crucifix.

She smiled. 'Who wants to be first?'

CHAPTER TWENTY-ONE

David Conner took out his pistol and pointed it at her. 'If you try to harm any of us,' he said, 'I will kill you.'

No one moved, except their visitor. It s head rocked slightly from side to side in a gesture no human in a rational state of mind ever made. There was a blankness as well as a strength to its eyes. It was cunning; it knew how to manipulate them, that was obvious. But did it understand them? Perhaps it felt understanding was not necessary, not with its psychic powers. It radiated a field of energy around it that was as palatable as the buzz of a high tension wire on a foggy night, an invisible cyclone of astral pollution. No one in the chapel stared at it as if they were seeing a human being. Their combined fear, also, was a tangible element that the creature seemed to draw strength and satisfaction from. The fact that it had thrown off all disguise led David to believe it could not be stopped by physical means. Still, he clung to his pistol, putting pressure on the trigger as it slowly moved in his direction. The smile remained fixed on its face, a line scraped in bloodstained plaster.

'Will you kill me?' it asked. 'We sit below the human mind. We have only to glance upward and your thoughts are visible.' It shook its head. 'You will not kill me.'

'For the love of God, shoot it David,' Ned pleaded, which was an ironic plea indeed. He, too, had his gun out, and pointed at the creature's back. Yet he had not fired 'It's not Lucy. It's one of them.'

The thing ignored Ned. It continued to stare at David,

and he in turn at it. He did not have to look deep into its eyes, however, to know the danger of probing its black soul through such uncensored windows. But already it had him under a spell. He wanted to shoot and he could not shoot. He could not add the two extra pounds of pressure to the trigger necessary to send the bullet hurtling into its heart. There was no aversion, no threat of disobedience, he simply lacked the will to carry through with the act. He suspected that it came at him from inside as well as outside. That the core of his brain was keeping him from firing as much as its psychic forcefield. It was a truly scary thought.

It moved closer, to his side, and went up on its toes. He felt its breath on his cheek, cold as a fossil found beneath Arctic snow. It was older than that, though, more ancient than the last hundred Ice Ages combined. It stared at him with eyes that had seen a million species rise and perish. He wondered if its mind had always been there, inside them, within all its thorny descendants, witnessing their trials, mocking their dreams, knowing that one day it would reawaken and wipe them all out as easily as it had wiped out its own civilization. The thing seemed pleased at his unspoken insight

'We are you,' it hissed softly. 'You simply buried us. You forgot us. You lost all power.' It leaned forward and kissed his cheek. 'Who am I, David?'

He drew back in revulsion. His vision blurred with tears. 'You are not Lucy,' he cried. God it was so horrible! Its smile widened.

'I am not Lucy,' it agreed. 'But you will join with the body of her sister. The fire of her brain will burn yours. You will remember what you lost.' It turned and gestured to the rest of the group. 'You will all burn. Or else you will serve as food.' It paused and touched its stomach. 'Jon Horst.'

David struggled to move; it was hard enough to breathe,

to think. It said it was not Lucy. Assuming it had no need to lie, that meant it was Lucy who lay nearby dying, her brain haemorrhaging. A silent cry wailed deep inside him, bringing a wave of darkness he knew only too well. He had to struggle to hold it at bay, knowing he could not give in to despair. Why hadn't it simply killed Lucy? It must have known they would find her.

'Why must you awaken?' he asked. 'You have powers we lack, true, but you have no wisdom, no compassion. You destroyed yourself last time. You will only destroy yourself again, and take us with you.'

Its eyes returned to his face. It seemed to reflect on his words. 'Your young awake when they are hungry. It is the same with us.'

'But it's humanity's time,' he said. 'Your time has passed.'

'Our destiny has arrived.' It raised its hand when he went to speak again. 'We do not talk. We do not discuss. We do what we do.' It surveyed them. 'Who will be first?'

Big surprise: there were no volunteers. David wondered if he had it alone, if he could fight it more effectively. A foolish thought, he knew, but one he felt was required of a supposedly brave man. Feeling like he was throwing his body in front of a speeding train to try to keep it from derailing, he spoke again.

'I will go first.'

The monster was amused, cruel. 'You will be last. You will hear each of the others scream. And you will pray for their screams *not* to stop. Because each time they do stop, another portion of your precious humanity dies. I know your mind, your deepest fears. You will pray for help, David Conner, to a god you know is not there. And he will not listen.'

'It doesn't matter what I believe,' he said, sick of its

arrogance. 'It only matters what is. You were beaten before. You will be beaten again.'

It reached out and took the gun from his hand. 'Not by you,' it said. Then it turned abruptly, as if feeling a disturbance at its back, and moved towards Spear. He did not fidget at its approach, but rather, focused on it intently, his dark eyes narrowing. Yet his mental efforts did not slow down its approach. In a mocking gesture, it tapped the top of his head with the butt of the pistol. 'You will not stop us again, either. You earned the honour before. You will be first.'

With that remark Spear's face suddenly changed. For a moment he could have been the one possessed by an intelligent reptile born of a super race. A cold rage flared from his mouth and nostrils. He raised his arms and shoved it hard in the chest, and to everyone's immense surprise it toppled backwards. Yet he did not try to press his advantage. Instead, he turned towards Lucy. Poor Lucy, who lay flat on her back on the altar, oblivious to the fading twilight of the human race. Spear leapt in her direction.

He did not make it. The creature recovered with blinding speed. In a move too swift for the human eye to completely follow, it lashed out with an arm and struck Spear on the side of the neck. He did not simply crumble, but went flying across the floor, his head smacking the cold grey marble tiles with a series of sickening thumps. In a crumpled ball, he came to a halt close to David's feet. David felt his paralysis momentarily lift. He knelt by the Professor, cradling the man's head in his lap. Blood poured from the wound to Spear's temple, and from the tilt of his neck it looked as if several cervixes had been crushed. He was not going to make it and he knew it. He spoke with great weariness, painful regret.

'I wasn't going to do it,' he whispered. 'Believe me, I had decided not to do it.'

David nodded and leaned close. 'I believe you, Professor. But how do we stop it? How did you stop it before?'

'You see,' Spear said, blood leaking out his mouth. 'My wife was fine.'

'What do you mean?'

'Penny was fine,' he gasped.

Those were his last words. Spear's eyes lost their focus. They rolled up into their sockets and the whites stared at David as if challenging him to guess what the dead man had been about to say. David became aware of the redhead with the bad attitude standing above him. For some reason, he didn't feel like looking up at it.

'Ned Calendar will be the first, instead,' it said. 'You may both remember, I promised to touch him again.'

CHAPTER TWENTY-TWO

They heard when Ned began to scream. They were locked
in the storage room, beneath the dining hall. It had put
them there: Margaret, Panda, Tom, Dr Henry, David,
and even poor Lucy. It had smiled when David had
swooped his injured love into his arms upon the order
to leave the chapel. It had not tried to stop him. 'I know
you will take good care of her, David Conner,' it said.
Not that there was anything he could do for her. David
cradled Lucy in his arms as Tom angrily punched out
the tiny windows near the ceiling of the storage area.
It was through such openings that they heard Ned's
cries, and David wished Tom had not bothered inviting
in the sound. A kitten could have crawled through the
shattered windows, not much else. Also, unfortunately,
the storage room door was not the kind to respond
to a stiff kick, especially with the heavy wooden bar
applied from the outside. Breaking out was not the key
to salvation, anyway. They would have needed a cloaking
device that shielded their minds as well as their bodies
to hike out of the camp without the creature knowing.
Bummer, David thought, and soon there would be half
a dozen of them for the world to contend with. How
had the Egyptians stopped them? The white light of
Isis? Somehow, David couldn't see her materializing in
the next so many minutes.

But he had been wrong before.

*'You may both remember, I promised to touch him
again.'*

The remark was interesting. It carried with it profound philosophical implications. Was the creature that had possessed Frances the same one that was inside Vera? Or were they simply related? Go back that far in time and probably every human on the planet had some of every Setian that ever lived inside them. Clearly, Frances had allowed Ned to escape knowing that it would just catch him again, later, and do worse things to him than just bite off his hand. The truth was probably that no individual Setians were returning to the modern world, just the collective reptilian spirit. Certainly, though, once they had taken over enough human bodies, and staked out fresh personalities, they would start fighting again. The thing that was inside Vera didn't act like a team player.

David could not forget the look on Ned's face when they had said goodbye. Two weeks more and his boss would have been retired, fishing on some stupid lake with some stupid dog sitting beside him. But he had wanted to get into the field one last time, have a final taste of the action. Good God, David grimaced internally, it sounded like the thing was skinning him alive. How could a grown man scream like that and not die in the next breath? David clenched his eyes shut as he stroked Lucy's back. She was getting cold and he didn't want her to get cold. Corpses got cold.

Ned had looked to Margaret, not to David, when they were being led away. 'Can you do anything?' he asked her. She shook her head.

Why had Ned turned to Margaret?

David opened his eyes and looked over at the crippled woman. She was knitting her sweater. The balls of yarn and her needles had been tucked in the rear bag of her wheelchair when they had gone for her in the kitchen, just before discovering Lucy.

'Isn't it a little late for that?' he asked dryly.

She looked up and snapped a thread in her hands. 'No.'

David sighed and hung his head. 'Fuck.'

Dr Henry knelt nearby. 'We have to talk. We have to figure out where it's vulnerable.'

'It isn't vulnerable!' Tom cried, pacing restlessly. 'That's the problem! It can do anything! We're all going to die!'

'Shut up and sit down,' Dr Henry said.

'We're going to die screaming like him!' Tom moaned.

'It isn't killing him,' David said quietly, squeezing Lucy tighter. He had already given the others a condensed version of what had happened in Africa. They had not enjoyed the story. 'It's changing him, making another like itself.'

'How does it do that?' Dr Henry asked.

David snorted. 'You're the expert on the brain, you tell me. But I think it stimulates the reptilian complex layer somehow, perhaps by the power of its attention. Spear had a violent fever when he returned from Africa, after combating it last time. I think it tried to change him there, but was interrupted for some reason.'

'Is that how Spear was able to resist it briefly?' Dr Henry asked. 'He had a trace of its power?'

David nodded. 'It's possible. You guys knew him better than me, but he always struck me as someone that had a part of his brain burned out. Anyway, he wasn't able to resist it long.'

'But Spear did confront it and stop it in the past?' Dr Henry asked.

'Yes,' David said.

'But how did he stop it?' Dr Henry insisted.

'I don't know. That's what I tried to ask him. You heard him. All he said was, "My wife was fine. Penny was fine."' David was thoughtful. 'His wife had not changed.'

Ned let out a particularly frightening wail, it echoed

through the trees like the sound of a wounded animal, as the rain settled to a soft warm patter. David wished it would just hurry up and be over with. But he would not pray to God for it to end. The creature had him pegged. He didn't believe there was anyone above or below to listen to his prayer. Two feet away, sweat glistened on Dr Henry's forehead, but the Rhodes Scholar was not ready to quit yet.

'What do you mean, the wife had not changed?' Dr Henry asked. 'I thought that they regressed together? I thought that's what allowed this thing from the past to awaken? Identical twins working together.'

'They were . . . like this,' Panda said, sitting in the corner. He nodded and clasped his hands together. Then he yanked them apart. 'Then . . . like that. Weak.'

David studied the quiet Indian man. 'What are you saying?'

Panda didn't have the English, not without the Big Mind to help him. He gestured with both his hands in front of him, then pressed them together. 'Right holds . . . the left.'

David gasped in understanding. 'They need each other! They needed each other to bring it into this time, and in the same way it needs them to *exist* in this time. At least until it can make another. That's it.'

Panda nodded.

'I'm not going next,' Tom said. 'I don't want to go next.'

'What do you mean, *exist* in this time?' Dr Henry asked. 'It's already in our time. I want to know how to get it back to where it belongs.'

David shook his head. 'No. You misunderstand what it is. It's not just a being from the past. It's a part of what we are today. It said so itself. We can not send it back in time to where it belongs. We can only hope to bury it again in our time.'

'Splendid!' Dr Henry said impatiently. 'I can live with that. How the fuck do we do it?'

David went to answer but a lump in his throat stopped him. He paused to stroke Lucy's red hair. It was so beautiful, maybe not as long and fine as Vera's, but close. He was careful not to touch near her head wound. He didn't want to hurt her. Yeah, he had heard that one before, and that was the cosmic joke, wasn't it? The Big Mind had set it all up; it knew the punch line. It had said as much in the session. Another wave on the horizon, David. You see it coming, you had better move fast. He had wanted to save Sandy and Angela from death, but that hadn't worked, and now Lucy was dying in his arms. Now he only had a few minutes left to be with her. Now, in fact, it seemed he couldn't even have those. *Now*, David, the present moment is the place to be. He didn't buy that. The wave was cresting. Ned's screams were beginning to subside. Soon it would all be over.

He understood how Spear had stopped it the last time.

He understood a lot of things.

David turned to Margaret. Another piece of yarn snapped in her hands.

'Who are you?' he asked.

She set the sweater aside. 'Margaret is as good a name as any.'

'I don't even know who I am. I am the Big Mind. That is as good a name as any. Who are you?'

Ned had turned to Margaret for help because he knew something about her that no one else did. A crippled woman with no past, David thought. But Ned must have found something in her past that made him believe she could stop a seemingly omnipotent monster. Who was Margaret anyway? Why had she suddenly entered Spear's life after he returned from Africa? Who had sent her? How did she know how to cook just like his mother?

Why did everyone love her so much? They were all scared. Why wasn't she scared?

'*I support the Big Mind. I listen to it. The Big Mind is never worried*.'

The Dogon had called their high initiated the Listeners.

'Who are you?' he repeated.

'Let's have a session with the Big Mind!' Tom suddenly cried. 'It will help us! It will tell us what to do!'

David let go of Lucy's hands and raised his arm. 'Relax, Tom, we don't need a session. We have the Big Mind here. We've always had it here. The same way we've always had the creature with us.' He paused. 'Isn't that true, Margaret?'

'What are you talking about?' Dr Henry demanded.

'Sh,' David said. 'Let her answer. You will answer me, won't you, Margaret? You answered all my questions yesterday afternoon, in the session.'

She stared at him, her face kind as always. 'It's up to you. It's always that way. You have free will. You can chose what you will.'

'What are the choices?' David asked.

'To go forward. Or to go back. Spear always wanted the past. He thought the real power resided there. He did not believe in the future, in the spirit of man. What do you believe in, David?'

'Is that what the Big Mind is?' he asked. 'The future?'

Margaret shrugged.

'No, answer me,' David insisted angrily. 'It looks like we have the devil in the past, and humanity's in the middle. Are you an angel? Is that what we're to become?'

'I'm not getting this, man,' Dr Henry said.

'I just don't want to get eaten,' Tom said, holding his belly, no doubt thinking about Jon Horst and his bad karma. Margaret again reached for her yarn and knitting needles. But the yarn snapped again in her hands.

'I understand the symbolism,' David said. 'You can stop doing that.'

Margaret stopped and waited.

'What is she doing?' Dr Henry exploded. 'How do we stop it?'

'It's very simple,' David said. 'The creature was able to enter our time through a unique portal in consciousness, constructed of the fusion of two identical beings. It's only that fusion that sustains it in our time, at least until it can make another of its kind. While the twins are linked, the portal stays open. But break that link, snap it the way Margaret keeps snapping her green and white threads, and the portal closes. Spear must have understood that.' David paused. 'I know what happened to his wife in Africa.'

'What?' Dr Henry demanded.

'Spear said she was fine. She couldn't have changed as Frances changed. Like Buckley, Spear must have got away from Frances when he saw what was happening, and then later returned for his wife. But maybe Frances zapped him a little before he escaped, I don't know. She could have been adjusting to the transformation, and not at her full power. Anyway, when Spear returned, he probably carried Penny into the cave. Buckley saw Spear go in there. Perhaps Frances had knocked Penny out as Vera knocked Lucy out. We know for a fact that it was not Frances who killed Penny. No, that wouldn't do. Frances *needed* Penny, and Vera did not kill Lucy because Vera *needs* Lucy. That's why it smiled when it said, 'I know you will take good care of her.' It wants Lucy here with us. It wants us to keep her alive until we're all changed. Then it won't matter. By that time the portal will be split wide open. Then Lucy can die.' David paused. 'But Penny died in Africa too early for the creature's tastes. It was early because Penny was specifically killed in order to stop it.'

'Who killed her?' Dr Henry asked.

'Spear did.' David chuckled. 'Here I thought he was just as an asshole. But you have to hand it to him, he made the ultimate sacrifice. Killed his own wife and there was nothing wrong with her. Just to make right what he had done wrong.'

'How do you know this for sure?' Dr Henry asked.

David was grim. 'Because ten minutes ago Spear went for Lucy, not the monster. He knew where the weak link was. Am I right about all this, Margaret?'

'Yes. You have insight.'

David gave a fey laugh. 'Oh, we all have insight. Panda has insight. Even Tom has insight. He doesn't want to get eaten. None of us want to get eaten or go through the black rite. Ned has the most insight but right now I bet he just wishes he could stop screaming. But it sounds like he's about to stop, and that's not cool either if you can believe the creature, which I'm inclined to do. I have to make a decision soon. I have to decide to set everything right.' David's voice cracked. 'Is it true? Do I have to kill her?'

Margaret looked at him. 'You know what's true. You don't need to ask me.'

'Damnit!' David cried, Lucy shaking in his arms. 'That's not good enough! You have to tell me why she has to die!'

'You just explained why,' Margaret said calmly.

'No! You have to tell me why *you* let it happen this way! Why the Big Mind has such a fucked sense of humour? Why God plays with our heads like we're fucking pawns in a fucking game? I tell you I am just sick and tired of having the people I love die on me. I am not going to kill her!'

'It's your choice,' Margaret said.

'You gave us no choice! You didn't even warn us!'

'But you were warned. All of you were.'

'Actually, the Big Mind says it's foolish. That we could be better not doing it.'

'But you were right there – *you knew* – and you just let us walk into this trap!'

'I watch. I witness. It was your choice. It still is.'

'Shit! That's no answer!' David screamed. 'I have gone through shit my entire life! I deserve an answer!'

Margaret sighed. 'David.' She picked up the sweater and smoothed it over her lap. 'I think it would look nice on either of them. The green brings out the green in their eyes, don't you think?'

David's fury, his pain, knew no bounds. 'You are a cold bitch.'

Margaret did not look up from her handiwork. 'Children don't often say that to their mothers. But I suppose they sometimes think it.'

David felt a hand on his arm, looked over. Dr Henry had tears on his face.

'If killing Lucy will stop it,' he said gently. 'Then maybe you'd better do it now. She's going to die anyway. Her EEG's flat. She's haemorrhaging in the neocortex.' He patted his arm. 'She won't last the day, David. No bullshit.'

David was having trouble breathing. 'Oh, I'm sure it's just her neocortex that it injured. The creature wouldn't have hurt the deeper layers of her brain. It needs those to keep working until it's through. It needs . . . I need . . .' He couldn't finish. Sobs racked his body and again Lucy shook in his arms. He ran his fingers through her hair but it only made his agony that much worse. How could he kill her when he wanted to kiss her and have her eyes open and have her mouth smile up at him? She could tell him that she had just being having an awful nightmare but now it was over and everything was wonderful because he was beside her. His hand fell limp by his side. 'I can't do it,' he moaned. 'Will somebody please do it for me?'

No one moved, and he understood their refusal to help him. He was the FBI agent, the stuff of legends, the man who had burned Failla, blown away Pokey, Dirty Dave. He had his own bad karma as well. He had killed before and he could kill again. He leaned over and kissed Lucy on the forehead. He could feel their eyes on him Just this one last female victim and they and the rest of humanity would be eternally grateful. He slipped his hands around her neck, feeling the base of her skull with the tips of his strong fingers. He had kissed her neck last night, many times. She had liked it. Now just this one last caress, he thought, and his career would finally be over. He could retire; he could even follow her and Sandy and Angela to the grave. But where was her tiny gold crucifix? Lucy always liked to wear it. He wished he could find it now, press it to her lips. He leaned over and kissed her again, on the lips.

'Jesus,' he whispered, getting a grip on her frail bones.

Then he heard a sound, they all heard it. Not Ned screaming, but heavy footsteps, rapidly approaching, pounding across the dining room floor above their heads. Of course, it could read their minds. It must have taken a peek over at his in the middle of its brain surgery and saw he was no wimp when it came to killing girlfriends. Almost caught me by surprise, human, but it was coming fast. Above them, up the steep stairway, they heard a pounding on the door. Then it just exploded open, as if touched by dynamite, sending splinters everywhere. David glanced up the stairs, saw the mass of red hair, felt the rake of poisonous green eyes. But he knew better than to look into those particular eyes.

David yanked Lucy's skull back as hard as he could.

Every bone in her neck popped. So loud. So sore, it must have hurt.

Then she went still. Just settled back in his arms and stopped breathing.

The creature stumbled down the stairs. It carried his gun in its left hand.

David quickly set aside Lucy and stood to greet it. The creature moved like a drunk. It brought up the weapon, took aim, and lost its grip and fired into the floor. Its head wobbled backwards as if its own spinal cord had been snapped. It managed a surprised grin.

'You are like us,' it said.

Then it collapsed. David caught it as it fell. The pistol bounced on the floor. A cold shudder went through its entire body. Its eyes opened briefly and looked up at him. No, Vera stared at him, her expression one of relief, puzzlement.

'David,' she whispered. 'I was having the worst nightmare.'

Then her eyes closed and she died. Yes, like her sister, she just stopped breathing. Her body sagged towards the floor, and it was there David let go of her. He glanced over at Margaret, who had worked so hard on her green and white sweater only to end up with no one to give it to. No one with green eyes, that is. David wanted to take the gun and shoot her in the head. He went so far as to pick up the pistol and point it in her direction. But you couldn't shoot the Goddess, that was not cool. It was much better to gouge out your own eyes than to do something foolish like that. He threw the gun against the far wall and fell to his knees beside Vera. Burying his face in his hands, his tears ran through his fingers as the blood must have run through the fingers of the Egyptian priestess, who so trusted in Isis that she offered her own mortal eyes in exchanged for freedom from the black rite and a promise of divine vision. But all he wanted was to know why he was crying again, when he had done everything he could to make things right.

A warm hand touched his arm.

'David?'

He opened his eyes. Margaret had wheeled herself over. 'Yes?' he said.

'When you came here, I asked what you wanted for dinner, more than anything else in the whole world. You said turkey and mashed potatoes, and I gave you that. Remember?'

'Yes.'

'David, David.' Brushing his hair from his eyes, she smiled at him with such love in her eyes, he honestly felt his mother had returned to life to comfort him. 'Now, tell me, what do you want more than anything else in the whole world?'

His throat was choked; he could hardly speak. 'Huh?'

'What do you want?'

His lips trembled. 'Lucy.'

Margaret nodded. 'All right.'

'What?'

Margaret smiled again but ignored him as well. She called for Tom to lift her out of her chair and set her on the floor beside Vera. Tom was happy to oblige, now that the screaming had stopped. He helped Margaret sit upright while she put one hand on Vera's head and the other over her heart. Closing her eyes, Margaret slowly inhaled a breath it seemed she never released. A moment of silence went by, or perhaps it was much longer than that, years, centuries, sixty millennium, or even as long as the eternity itself, that exists between each and every moment, and between each and every breath. David watched, fascinated, although he did not know what he was seeing.

'The purpose of life is unknown. It's a mystery, and you know mysteries can be lived, but never explained. Do you understand?'

He would never understand. Why Vera began to

breathe, to stir. Why Margaret opened her eyes, and smiled at him one last time, and told him not to worry, that Ned would be fine as well. Why she then left up the stairs, with Tom's help, without saying goodbye, and was never heard from again. David could not see the white light of Isis, which might have given him understanding. Probably no ordinary mortal ever would be able to. But Lucy had spoken highly of its power.

Vera opened her eyes and looked over at him.

'David,' she whispered.

He took her hand and kissed it. 'Vera.'

She frowned at him. Silly boy. 'No. It's me. It's Lucy.'

It took David several moments to realize that she was not kidding.

EPILOGUE

The cruise up the Nile was for romantic fools, the man thought as he stepped from the bar and plopped down on one of the many benches that ringed the large ship. He was not drunk but needed to clear his head, and the desert night air was best for that. The trip was no honeymoon for him. He was alone, trying to escape from business as well as personal pressures at home in England. They were three days out of Aswan, and would see the pyramids soon, if they hadn't already. Maybe he had drunk a little too much. The stars seemed to throb above the barren landscape, as close as his outstretched fingers. He had never seen so many in his life.

A couple stood nearby, leaning against the railing, looking at the stars, the desert. The woman's hair was a wonderful red, the man's face strong and grave. By the way they stood, their hands clasped, their bodies never far apart, the man from England could tell they were much in love, and the sight of such a couple brought an unexpected gladness to his cynical heart. The woman pointed to a bright blue star.

'There's Sirus,' she said. Her arm slowly lowered and pointed to the embankment, two hundred yards away. 'And there's where they caught the priestess.'

'You're sure that's the spot?'

'Yes. I still see the . . . red stains.'

The man shook his head in wonder. 'So long ago.'

The woman leaned over and kissed his cheek. 'It won't be so long for us.'

The man put his hand on her belly, above the sweater tied around her waist. 'What will we name her?'

'*Her*?'

He nodded. 'We both know it. What do you want? After your sister?'

'Would that be all right with you?'

'Yes, of course. I love the name.'

The woman laughed softly. 'I love you.' But she seemed to grow serious as her eyes returned to the embankment, and to the bright star. 'Let's call her Isis. My sister, the priestess – they both loved that name. And maybe it will bring her good luck.'